Count Lev Nikolayevich Tolstoy (9 September [O.S. 28 August] 1828 – 20 November [O.S. 7 November] 1910), usually referred to in English as Leo Tolstoy, was a Russian writer who is regarded as one of the greatest authors of all time. He received multiple nominations for Nobel Prize in Literature every year from 1902 to 1906, and nominations for Nobel Peace Prize in 1901, 1902 and 1910, and his miss of the prize is a major Nobel prize controversy. Born to an aristocratic Russian family in 1828, he is best known for the novels War and Peace (1869) and Anna Karenina (1877), often cited as pinnacles of realist fiction. He first achieved literary acclaim in his twenties with his semi-autobiographical trilogy, Childhood, Boyhood, and Youth (1852–1856), and Sevastopol Sketches (1855), based upon his experiences in the Crimean War. Tolstoy's fiction includes dozens of short stories and several novellas such as The Death of Ivan Ilyich (1886), Family Happiness (1859), and Hadji Murad (1912). He also wrote plays and numerous philosophical essays. (Source: Wikipedia)

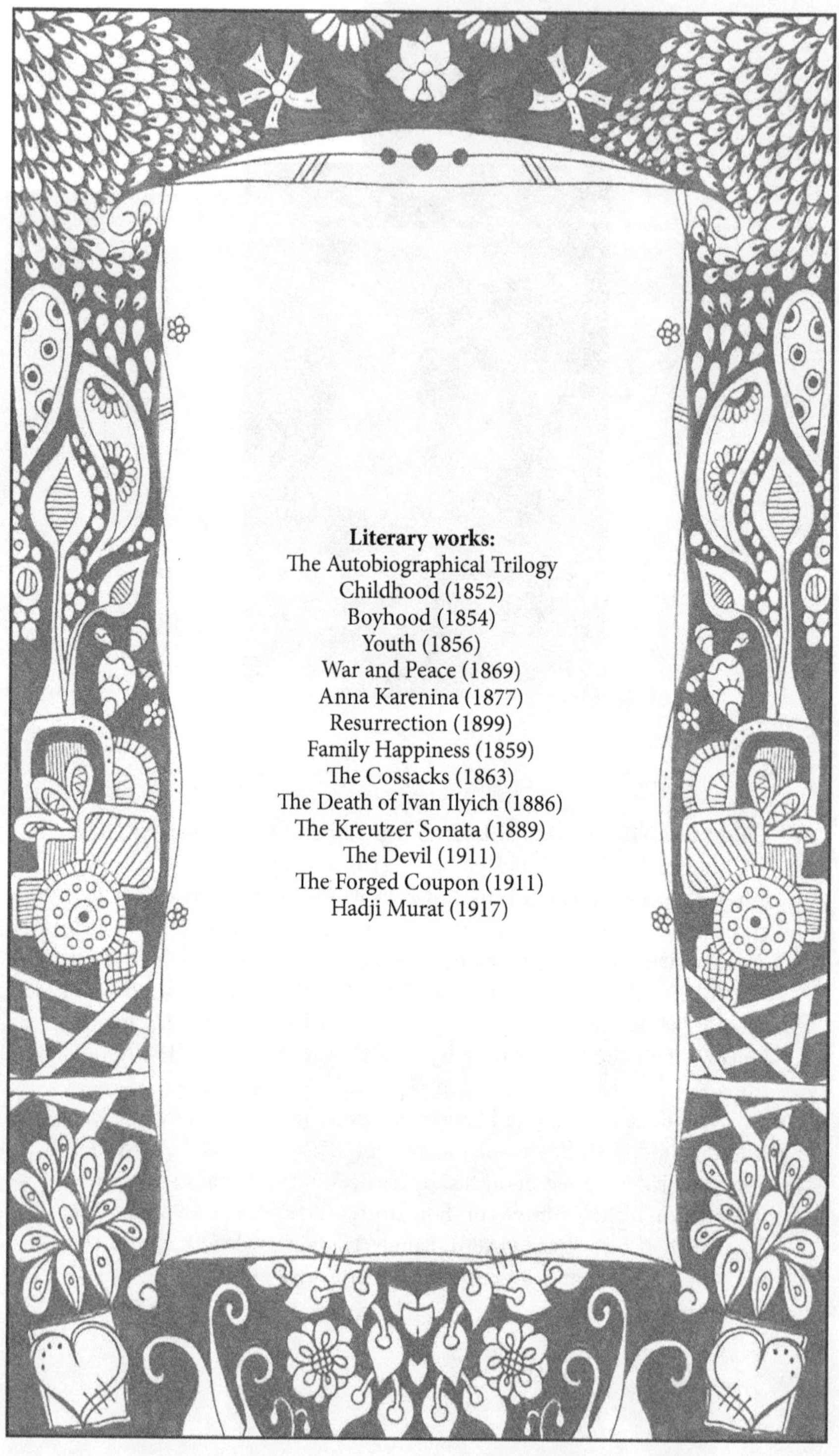

Literary works:

The Autobiographical Trilogy
Childhood (1852)
Boyhood (1854)
Youth (1856)
War and Peace (1869)
Anna Karenina (1877)
Resurrection (1899)
Family Happiness (1859)
The Cossacks (1863)
The Death of Ivan Ilyich (1886)
The Kreutzer Sonata (1889)
The Devil (1911)
The Forged Coupon (1911)
Hadji Murat (1917)

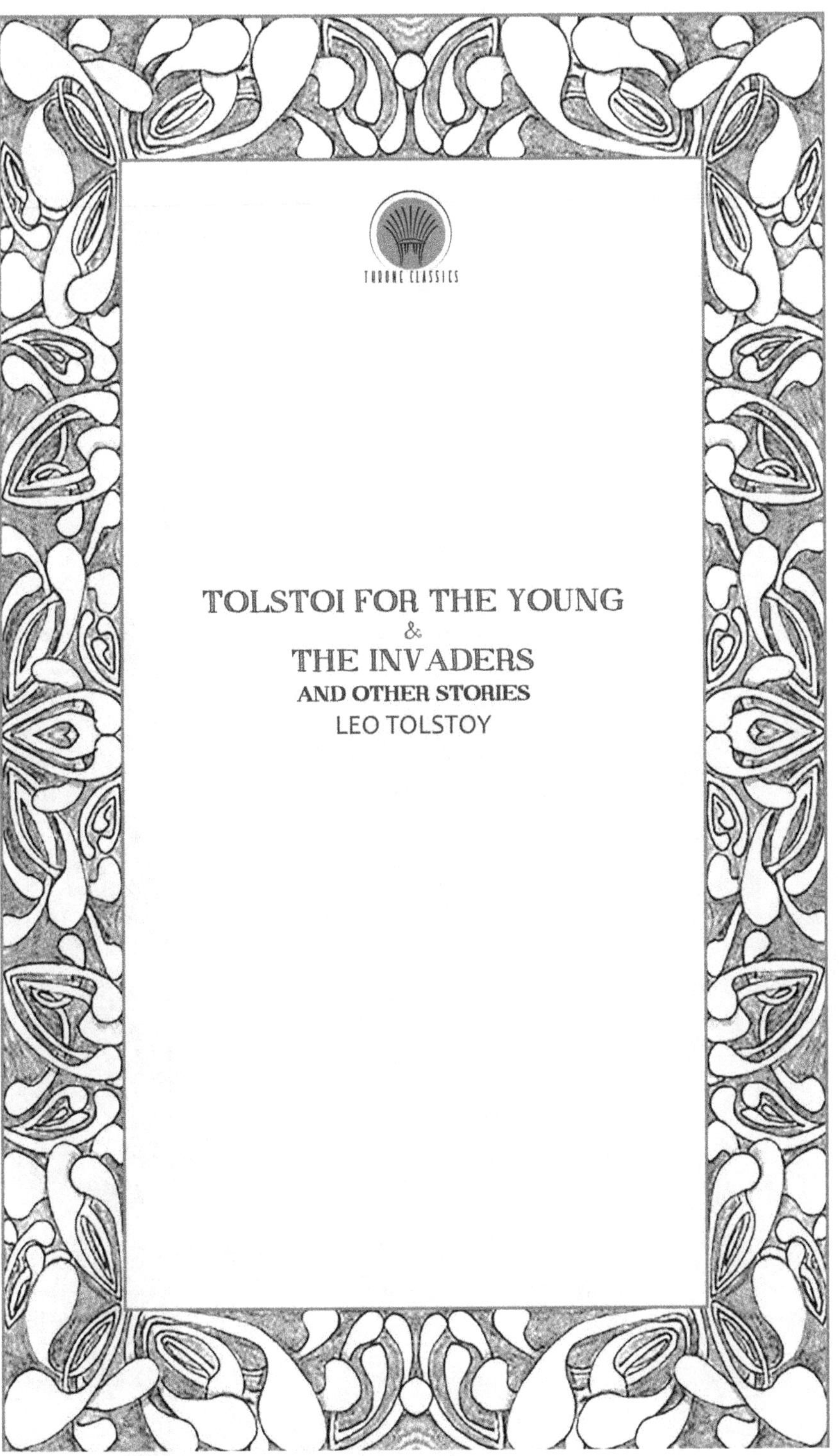

TOLSTOI FOR THE YOUNG
&
THE INVADERS
AND OTHER STORIES

LEO TOLSTOY

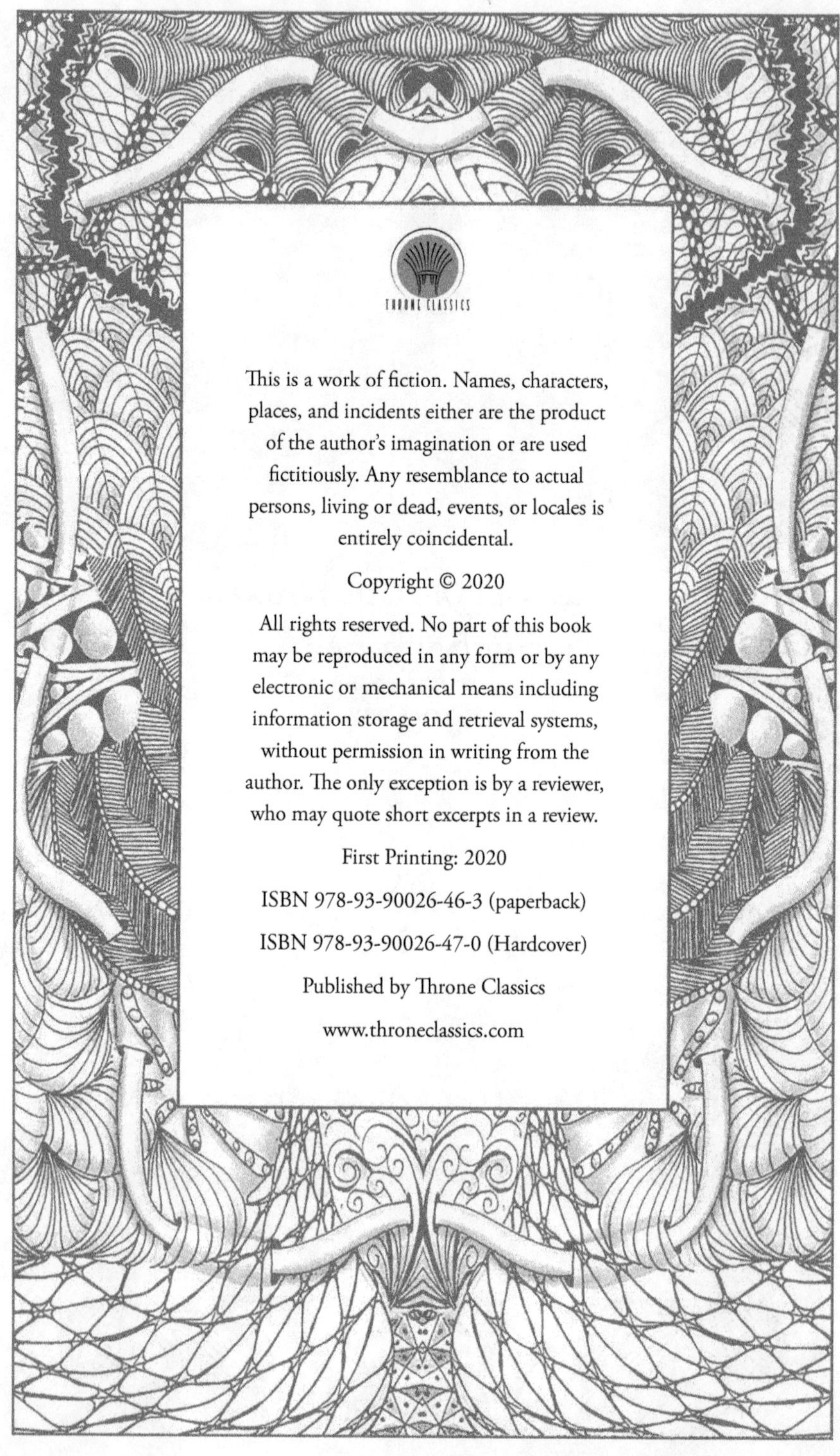

This is a work of fiction. Names, characters, places, and incidents either are the product of the author's imagination or are used fictitiously. Any resemblance to actual persons, living or dead, events, or locales is entirely coincidental.

First Printing: 2020

ISBN 978-93-90026-46-3 (paperback)

ISBN 978-93-90026-47-0 (Hardcover)

Published by Throne Classics

www.throneclassics.com

Contents

TOLSTOI FOR THE YOUNG

&

THE INVADERS

AND OTHER STORIES

TOLSTOI FOR THE YOUNG

IVAN THE FOOL

THE STORY OF IVAN THE FOOL AND HIS TWO BROTHERS SIMON THE WARRIOR AND TARAS THE POT-BELLIED, AND OF HIS DEAF AND DUMB SISTER, AND THE OLD DEVIL AND THREE LITTLE DEVILKINS.

Once upon a time there lived a rich peasant, who had three sons—Simon the Warrior, Taras the Pot-bellied, and Ivan the Fool, and a deaf and dumb daughter, Malania, an old maid.

Simon the Warrior went off to the wars to serve the King; Taras the Pot-bellied went to a merchant's to trade in the town, and Ivan the Fool and the old maid stayed at home to do the work of the house and the farm. Simon the Warrior earned a high rank for himself and an estate and married a nobleman's daughter. He had a large income and a large estate, but he could never make both ends meet, for, what he managed to gather in, his wife managed to squander; thus it was that he never had any money.

And Simon the Warrior went to his estate one day to collect his income, and his steward said to him, "There is nothing to squeeze money out of; we have neither cattle, nor implements, nor horses, nor cows, nor ploughs, nor harrows; we must get all these things first, then there will be an income."

Then Simon the Warrior went to his father and said, "You are rich, father; and have given me nothing, let me have a third of your possessions and I will set up my estate."

And the old man replied, "Why should I? You have brought nothing to the home. It would be unfair to Ivan and the girl."

And Simon said, "Ivan is a fool and Malania is deaf and dumb; they do not need much, surely."

"Ivan shall decide," the old man said.

And Ivan said, "I don't mind; let him take what he wants."

Simon took a portion of his father's goods and moved them to his estate, and once more he set out to serve the King.

Taras the Pot-bellied made a great deal of money and married a merchant's widow, but still, it seemed to him that he had not enough, so he too went to his father and said, "Give me my portion, father." And the old man was loath to give Taras his portion, and he said, "You have brought us nothing; everything in the home has been earned by Ivan; it would be unfair to him and the girl."

And Taras said, "Ivan is a fool, what does he need? He cannot marry, for no one would have him, and the girl is deaf and dumb and does not need much either." And turning to Ivan, he said, "Let me have half the corn, Ivan. I will not take any implements, and as for the cattle, I only want the grey cob; he is of no use to you for the plough."

Ivan laughed.

"Very well," he said, "you shall have what you want."

And Taras was given his portion, and he carted the corn off to the town and took away the grey cob, and Ivan was left with only the old mare to work the farm and support his father and mother.

II

The old Devil was annoyed that the three brothers had not quarrelled over the matter and had parted in peace. He summoned three little Devilkins.

"There are three brothers," he said, "Simon the Warrior, Taras the Pot-bellied, and Ivan the Fool. I want them all to quarrel and they live in peace and goodwill. It is the Fool's fault. Go to these three brothers, the three of you, and confound them so that they will scratch out each others' eyes. Do you think you can do it?"

"We can," they said.

"How will you do it?"

"We will ruin them first," they said, "so that they have nothing to eat, then we will put them all together and they will begin to fight."

"I see you know your work," the old Devil said. "Go then, and do not return to me until you have confounded the whole three, or else I will skin you alive."

And the Devilkins set out to a bog to confer on the matter, and they argued and argued, for each wanted the easiest work, and they decided to cast lots and each to take the brother that fell to him, and whichever finished his work first was to help the others. And the Devilkins cast lots and fixed a day when they should meet again in the bog, in order to find out who had finished his work and who was in need of help.

The day arrived and the Devilkins gathered together in the bog. They began to discuss their work. The first to give his account was the one who had undertaken Simon the Warrior. "My work is progressing well," he said. "To-morrow Simon will return to his father."

"How did you manage it?" the others asked him.

"First of all," he said, "I gave Simon so much courage that he promised the King to conquer the whole world. And the King made him the head of his army and sent him to make war on the King of India. That same night I damped the powder of Simon's troops and I went to the King of India and made him numberless soldiers out of straw. And when Simon saw himself surrounded by the straw soldiers, a fear came upon him and he ordered the guns to fire, but the guns and cannon would not go off. And Simon's troops were terrified and ran away like sheep, and the King of India defeated them. Simon was disgraced. He was deprived of his rank and estate and to-morrow he is to be executed. I have only one day left in which to get him out of the dungeon and help him to escape home. To-morrow I shall have finished with him, so I want you to tell me which of you two is in need of help."

Then the second Devilkin began to tell of his work with Taras. "I do not want help," he said; "my work is also going well. Taras will not live in the town another week. The first thing I did was to make his belly grow bigger and fill him with greed. He is now so greedy for other people's goods that whatever he sees he must buy. He has bought up everything he could lay his eyes on, and spent all his money, and is still buying with borrowed money. He has taken so much upon himself, and become so entangled that he will never pull himself out. In a week he will have to repay the borrowed money, and I will turn his wares into manure so that he cannot repay, then he will go to his father."

"And how is your work getting on?" they asked the third Devilkin about Ivan.

"My work is going badly," he said. "The first thing I did was to spit into Ivan's jug of kvas to give him a stomach-ache and then I went into his fields and made the soil as hard as stones so that he could not move it. I thought he would not plough it, but the fool came with his plough and began to pull. His stomach-ache made him groan, yet still he went on ploughing. I broke one plough for him and he went home and repaired another, and again persisted in his work. I crawled beneath the ground and clutched hold of his ploughshares, but I could not hold them—he pressed upon the plough so hard, and the shares were sharp and cut my hands. He has finished it all but one strip. You must come and help me, mates, for singly we shall never get the better of him, and all our labour will be wasted. If the fool keeps on tilling his land, the other two brothers will never know what need means, for he will feed them."

The first Devilkin offered to come and help to-morrow when he had disposed of Simon the Warrior, and with that the three Devilkins parted.

III

Ivan had ploughed all the fallow but one strip, and he went to finish that. His stomach ached, yet he had to plough. He undid the harness ropes, turned over the plough and set out to the fields. He drove one furrow, but coming back, the ploughshares caught on something that seemed like a root.

"What a strange thing!" Ivan thought. "There were no roots here, yet here's a root!"

He put his hand into the furrow and clutched hold of something soft. He pulled it out. It was a thing as black as a root and it moved. He looked closely and saw that it was a live Devilkin.

"You horrid little wretch, you!"

Ivan raised his hand to dash its head against the plough, but the Devilkin squealed, "Don't kill me, and I'll do whatever you want me to."

"What can you do?"

"Tell me what you want."

Ivan scratched his head.

"My stomach aches," he said; "can you make it well?"

"I can."

"Do it, then."

The Devilkin bent down, rummaged about with his nails in the furrow and pulled out three little roots, grown together.

"There," he said; "if any one swallows a single one of these roots all pain will pass away from him."

Ivan took the three roots, separated them and swallowed one. His stomach-ache instantly left him.

"Let me go now," the Devilkin begged once more. "I will dive through the earth and never bother you again."

"Very well," Ivan said; "go, in God's name."

At the mention of God the Devilkin plunged into the ground like a stone thrown into water, and there was nothing but the hole left. Ivan thrust the two remaining little roots into his cap and went on with his ploughing. He finished the strip, turned over his plough and set off home. He unharnessed and went into the house, and there was his brother, Simon the Warrior, sitting at table with his wife, having supper. His estate had been taken from him; he had escaped from prison and come back to live with his father.

As soon as Simon the Warrior saw Ivan, he said to him, "I have come with my wife to live with you; will you keep us both until I find another place?"

"Very well," Ivan said, "you can live here."

When Ivan sat down by the table, the smell of him was displeasing to the lady and she said to her husband, "I cannot sup together with a stinking peasant."

And Simon the Warrior said, "My lady says you do not smell sweet; you had better eat in the passage."

"Very well," Ivan said. "It is time for bed anyway, and I must feed the mare."

Ivan took some bread and his coat and went out for the night.

IV

That night, having freed himself of Simon the Warrior, the first little Devilkin set out to seek Ivan's Devilkin, to help him plague the Fool as they had agreed. He came to the fields, looked all round for his mate, but he was nowhere to be seen; he only found a hole. "I see some misfortune has happened to my mate; I must take his place. The ploughing is all finished; I must upset the Fool at the mowing."

And the Devilkin went to the meadow and flooded it and trampled the hay in the mud.

Ivan awoke at daybreak, put his scythe in order and set out to the meadow to mow the hay. Ivan swung the scythe once, he swung it twice, but the scythe grew blunt and would not cut; he had to sharpen it. Ivan struggled and struggled and struggled.

"This won't do," he said; "I must go home and bring a whetstone and a hunk of bread. If it takes me a week I'll not give up until I've mowed it every bit."

And the Devilkin grew pensive when he heard these words.

"The Fool has a temper," he said; "I can't catch him this way; I must think of something else."

Ivan returned, sharpened his scythe and began to mow. The Devilkin crept into the grass, caught hold of the scythe by the heel and pushed the point into the ground. It was hard for Ivan, but he mowed all the grass, except a little piece in the swamp.

The Devilkin crept into the swamp, thinking, "Even if I have to cut my hands I won't let him mow that!"

Ivan came to the swamp. The grass was not thick, but the scythe could not cut through it. Ivan grew angry and began to mow with all his might. The Devilkin began to lose hold, seeing that he was in a bad plight, but he had no time to get away and took refuge in a bush. Ivan swung the scythe near the bush and cut off half the Devilkin's tail. He finished mowing the grass, told the old maid to rake it up and went away to mow the rye.

He came to the field with his sickle, but the Devilkin with the clipped tail was there before him. He had entangled the rye, so that the sickle could not take it. Ivan went back for his reaping-hook and reaped the whole field of rye. "Now," he said, "I must tackle the oats."

At these words the Devilkin with the clipped tail thought, "I did not trip him up with the rye, but I'll do so with the oats. If only the morrow would come!"

In the morning the Devilkin hurried off to the field of oats, but the oats were all harvested. Ivan had reaped them overnight so that less of the grain should be wasted. The Devilkin lost his temper at that.

"He has mutilated and exhausted me, the fool! I've never had such trouble on the battlefield even. The wretch doesn't sleep and you can't get ahead of him. I'll creep into the stacks of sheaves and rot the grain."

And the Devilkin crept into a stack of sheaves, and began to rot them. He heated them, grew warm himself and fell asleep.

Ivan harnessed the mare and set out with his sister to gather in the sheaves. He stopped by the stack and began to throw the sheaves into the cart. He had thrown up two sheaves and was going to take up a third, when the fork dug into the Devilkin's back. He looked at the prongs and saw a live Devilkin with his tail clipped, wriggling and writhing and trying to get away.

"You horrid little wretch! You here again!"

"I'm not the same one," the Devilkin pleaded. "The other was my brother. I belong to your brother Simon."

"Whoever you are you shall share the same fate."

Ivan was about to dash it against the cart, when the Devilkin cried out, "Spare me! I'll not worry you again, and I'll do whatever you want me to."

"What can you do?"

"I can make soldiers out of anything you choose."

"What good are they?"

"You can make them do anything you like. Soldiers can do everything."

"Can they play songs?"

"They can."

"Very well; make some, then."

And the Devilkin said, "Take a sheaf of rye and bump it upright on the ground, saying,—

My slave bids you be a sheaf no more.

Every straw contained in you,

Must turn into a soldier true."

Ivan took the sheaf and banged it on the ground and repeated the Devilkin's words. And the sheaf burst asunder and every straw turned into a soldier and at their head the drummer and bugler were playing. Ivan laughed aloud.

"That was clever of you," he said. "It will amuse Malania."

"Let me go now," the Devilkin begged.

"Not yet," Ivan said. "I shall want to make the soldiers out of chaff so as not to waste the grain. Show me first how to turn the soldiers into a sheaf again, so that I can thrash it."

And the Devilkin said, "Repeat the words—

My slave bids every soldier be a straw

And turn into a sheaf once more."

Ivan repeated the Devilkin's words, and the soldiers turned into a sheaf again.

And again the Devilkin pleaded, "Let me go."

"Very well," Ivan said, taking him off the prongs. "Go, in God's name."

At the mention of God the Devilkin plunged into the ground like a stone thrown into water, and there was nothing but the hole left.

When Ivan reached home, his other brother, Taras, and his wife were sitting at table and having supper. Taras could not pay his debts; he fled from his creditors and came home to his father. As soon as he saw Ivan he said, "Until I can make some more money, will you keep me and my wife?"

"Very well," Ivan said. "You can live here."

Ivan took off his coat and sat down to table.

And Taras' wife said, "I cannot sup with a fool; he smells of sweat."

Taras the Pot-bellied said, "You do not smell sweet, Ivan; go and eat in the passage."

"Very well," Ivan said; "it's time for bed, anyhow, and I must feed the mare."

He took his coat and a piece of bread, and went out.

V

That night, having disposed of Taras, the third little Devilkin came to help his mates plague Ivan, as they had agreed. He came to the ploughed field and looked and looked, but could see no one; he only found the hole. Then he went to the meadow and found a piece of tail in the swamp, and in the rye-stubble field he found another hole.

"I see some misfortune has happened to my mates. I must take their places and tackle the Fool."

The Devilkin set out to find Ivan.

Ivan had finished his work in the fields and had gone into the copse to cut wood.

The brothers found it too crowded to live together in their father's house and they ordered Ivan to fell timber to build themselves new houses.

The Devilkin rushed into the wood and crept into the knots of the trees to prevent Ivan from felling them.

Ivan had cut a tree in the right way so that it should fall on to a clear space, but the tree seemed to be possessed, and fell over where it was not wanted, and got entangled among the branches. Ivan lopped them off with his bill-hook and at last, with great difficulty, brought down the tree. He began to fell another and the same thing was repeated. He struggled and struggled and succeeded only after great exertion. He began on a third and the same thing happened. Ivan had intended to fell fifty trees at least, and he had not managed more than ten, and night was coming on. Ivan was exhausted, and the steam rose from him and floated through the wood like a mist; yet still he would not give up. He felled another tree and his back began to ache so that he could not go on. He stuck his axe into the trunk of a tree and sat down to rest.

When the Devilkin realized that Ivan had ceased to work, he rejoiced. "He is worn out at last," he thought; "now I can rest too." And he sat himself astride on a branch, exulting.

Ivan rose, took out his axe, flourished it aloft, and brought it down so heavily that the tree came down with a crash. The Devilkin had no time to disentangle his legs; the branch broke and pinned down his paw.

Ivan began to clear the tree and behold! there was a live Devilkin. Ivan was amazed.

"You horrid little wretch! You here again!"

"I am not the same one," the Devilkin said. "I belong to your brother Taras."

"Whoever you may be, you shall share the same fate." And Ivan raised the axe to bring it down on its head, but the Devilkin began to plead.

"Don't kill me," he said, "and I'll do whatever you want me to."

"What can you do?"

"I can make as much money as you like."

"Very well," Ivan said; "make it, then."

And the Devilkin taught him what to do.

"Take some leaves from this oak and rub them in your hands and gold will fall to the ground."

Ivan took the leaves and rubbed them in his hand and gold rained down.

"This is well," he said; "on holidays it will amuse the children."

"Let me go," the Devilkin begged.

"I don't mind," Ivan said, and taking up his axe, he freed the Devilkin of the branch. "Go, in God's name."

At the mention of God the Devilkin plunged into the ground like a stone thrown into water and there was nothing but the hole left.

VI

The brothers built themselves houses and began to live apart. Ivan finished his work in the fields, brewed some beer and invited his brothers to a feast. The brothers did not accept his invitation.

"We do not go to feast with peasants," they said.

Ivan treated the peasants and the peasant-women and drank himself until he got tipsy, and he went into the street and joined the dancers and singers. He approached the women, and bade them sing his praises.

"I will give you something you have never seen in your lives," he said.

The women laughed and began to sing his praises, and when they had finished, they said, "Well, give us what you promised."

"I will bring it in a moment," Ivan said, and he took his seed-basket and ran into the wood.

The women laughed. "What a fool!" they said, and forgot all about him, when behold! Ivan returned, his basket full of something.

"Shall I share it out?"

"Do."

Ivan took up a handful of gold and threw it to the women. Heavens! The women rushed to pick it up, the peasants after them, snatching it out of each others' hands. One old woman was nearly killed in the fray.

Ivan laughed.

"You fools!" he said. "Why did you hurt Granny? If you are not so rough I'll give you some more."

He scattered more gold. The whole village came up. Ivan emptied his basket. The people asked for more, but he said, "Not now; another time I'll give you more. Now let us dance. You play some songs."

The women began to play.

"I don't like your songs," Ivan said.

"Do you know any better ones?"

"You shall see in a moment."

Ivan went into a barn, took up a sheaf, thrashed it, stood it up, and banged it on the floor, and said—

My slave bids you be a sheaf no more.

Every straw contained in you

Must turn into a soldier true.

And the sheaf burst asunder and turned into soldiers, and the drummers and buglers played at their head. Ivan asked the soldiers to play some songs, and led them into the street. The people were amazed.

When the soldiers had played their songs Ivan took them back into the barn, forbidding any one to follow. He turned the soldiers into a sheaf again and threw it on a pile of straw, then he went home and lay down to sleep in the stables.

VII

Simon the Warrior heard of these things next morning, and went to his brother.

"Tell me," he said, "where did you get the soldiers from, and where did you take them to?"

"What does it matter to you?"

"Matter, indeed! With soldiers one can do anything. One can conquer a kingdom."

Ivan wondered.

"Really! Then why didn't you tell me before?" he said. "I will make you as many soldiers as you like. It is well Malania and I have threshed so much straw."

Ivan took his brother to the barn and said, "Look here, if I make the soldiers you must take them away at once, for if we have to feed them they will eat up the whole village in a day."

Simon the Warrior promised to take the soldiers away, and Ivan began to make them. He banged a sheaf on the threshing-floor and a company appeared. He banged another sheaf and a second company appeared. He made so many soldiers that they filled the whole field.

"Are there enough now?" he asked.

Simon was overjoyed and said, "That will do, Ivan, thank you."

"Very well. If you want more, come back and I'll make them for you. There is plenty of straw this year."

Simon the Warrior soon put his troops in order, and went away to make war.

He had no sooner gone than Taras the Pot-bellied came along. He, too, had heard of yesterday's affair and he said to his brother, "Tell me where you get gold money from. If only I could get hold of some I could make it bring in money from the whole world."

Ivan wondered.

"Really? Then why didn't you tell me before? I'll make you as much as you like."

Taras was overjoyed.

"I shall be satisfied with three baskets full," he said.

"Very well; come into the wood," Ivan said; "but I had better harness the mare, for you won't be able to carry it away."

They rode into the wood. Ivan began to rub the oak leaves, and made a heap of gold.

"Is it enough?" he asked.

Taras was overjoyed.

"It will do for the present, thank you, Ivan," he said.

"Very well," Ivan said; "if you want more, come back and I'll make it for you. There are plenty of leaves left."

Taras the Pot-bellied gathered up a whole cartload of money, and went off to trade.

Both brothers had gone—Simon to make war and Taras to trade. And Simon the Warrior conquered a kingdom, and Taras the Pot-bellied made much money in trade.

When the two brothers met they told each other how they had come by their soldiers and money.

Simon the Warrior said to his brother, “I have conquered a kingdom for myself and live well, only I have not enough money to feed my soldiers.”

And Taras the Pot-bellied said, “I have made a heap of money, only unfortunately I have no one to guard it.”

And Simon the Warrior said, “Let us go to our brother Ivan. I will ask him to make more soldiers and give them to you to guard your money, and you must ask him to make more money and give it to me to feed my soldiers.”

And they came to Ivan.

And Simon said, “I haven’t enough soldiers, brother. Will you make another couple of sheaves for me?”

Ivan shook his head.

“No,” he said; “I won’t make you any more soldiers.”

“But you promised you would.”

“I know I promised, but I won’t make any more.”

“Why not, you fool?”

“Because your soldiers killed a man. I will not let you have any more.”

And he was obstinate, and would not make any more soldiers.

Then Taras the Pot-bellied asked Ivan the Fool to make him more golden money.

Ivan shook his head.

“No,” he said; “I won’t make any more money.”

“But you promised.”

“I know I promised, but I won’t make any more.”

"Why not, you fool?"

"Because your money took a cow away from a woman in the village."

"But how can that be?"

"The woman had a cow. The children used to drink the milk, but the other day they came to beg a little milk of me. 'But where's your cow?' I asked them, and they said, 'Taras' bailiff came and gave mother three golden coins and she gave him the cow; now we have no milk to drink.' I thought you only wanted to play with the golden coins, but you've taken away the cow from the children; I won't give you any more."

And the Fool was obstinate and kept to his word.

And the brothers went away and deliberated over their difficult situation in order to find a way out.

Simon said, "This is what we must do. You give me some of your money to feed my soldiers, and I'll give you half my kingdom and soldiers to guard your money."

Taras agreed. The brothers divided their possessions, and both became kings and both were rich.

VIII

And Ivan lived at home, supporting his father and mother and working in the fields with his deaf and dumb sister.

One day Ivan's yard-dog fell sick. He grew mangy, and was near dying. Ivan pitied it. He took a piece of bread from his sister, put it in his cap, carried it out and threw it to the dog. The creases in his cap parted and out rolled one of the little roots with the bread. The dog ate it up. As soon as it had swallowed the root it began to jump about and bark and play and wag its tail. It was quite well again.

The father and mother were amazed.

"How did you cure the dog?" they asked.

And Ivan said, "I had two little roots that could cure any pain, and the dog swallowed one."

It happened at the time that the King's daughter fell ill, and the King proclaimed to every town and village that he would reward any man who could cure her, and that if he were an unmarried man he should have her for his wife. The news came to Ivan's village.

And the father and mother summoned Ivan and said to him, "Have you heard of the King's promise? You told us you had a little root that could cure any sickness; go, cure the King's daughter, you will then be happy for life."

"Very well," Ivan said, "I will go."

And Ivan prepared himself for the journey, and they dressed him in his best clothes. When he came out on the doorstep he saw a beggar-woman with a crippled hand.

"I heard that you can cure the sick," she said. "Cure my hand, for I cannot even put on my own shoes."

"Very well," Ivan said. And he took the little root out of his cap, gave it to the beggar-woman and told her to swallow it. As soon as she swallowed it, she recovered, and began to wave her hand.

The father and mother came out to bid good-bye to Ivan, and they heard that he had given away his last root and had nothing left with which to cure the King's daughter, and they began to scold him.

"You pity a beggar-woman, yet have no pity for the King's daughter," they reproached him.

But Ivan was sorry for the King's daughter. He harnessed the mare, threw some straw into the cart and got in.

"Where are you going to, you fool?"

"To cure the King's daughter."

"But you have nothing to cure her with now."

"It doesn't matter," he said, and drove away.

He came to the King's palace, and as soon as he stepped over the threshold the King's daughter got well.

The King was overjoyed. He ordered Ivan to be brought to him, and dressed him in fine clothes.

"You must be my son-in-law," he said.

"Very well," Ivan said.

And Ivan married the princess. Her father died soon after, and Ivan became King.

All three brothers were now kings.

IX

The three brothers lived and reigned.

The elder brother Simon the Warrior lived well. With his straw soldiers he gathered together real soldiers. Throughout the whole of his kingdom he ordered a levy of one soldier for every ten houses, and each soldier had to be tall and whole of body and clean of face. In this way he gathered many soldiers and trained them. If any one opposed him he sent his soldiers off at once and imposed his will, and people began to fear him. His life was a very goodly one. Whatever he saw and wanted was his. He sent his soldiers and they brought him all he wanted.

Taras the Pot-bellied also lived well. He did not lose the money Ivan had given him, but increased it a hundredfold. He introduced law and order into his kingdom. He stowed his money away in coffers and levied taxes on the people. There was a poll-tax, and tolls for walking and driving, and a tax on shoes and stockings and frills. He got whatever he wanted. For money people brought him everything, and even worked for him, for every one wanted money.

Ivan the Fool, too, did not live badly. As soon as his father-in-law was dead he took off his royal robes and gave them to his wife to stow away in a chest. And he put on his coarse linen shirt and breeches and peasant shoes and began to work once more.

"It's so dull for me," he said. "I've got fat, lost my appetite and can't sleep."

He brought his father and mother and sister to live with him, and began to work as of old.

"But you are a king," people remonstrated.

"Even a king must eat," he said.

One of his ministers came to him and said, "We have no money to pay salaries."

"Don't pay them, then," he said.

"But no one will serve us."

"What does it matter? They needn't. They'll have more time for work. There's the manure to cart; heaps of it lying about."

When people came to Ivan for justice and said, "That man stole my money," Ivan said, "Never mind; he must have wanted it."

And all realized that Ivan was a fool. And his wife said to him, "People say you are a fool."

"What does it matter?" Ivan said.

His wife reflected awhile, but she was also a fool.

"Why should I go against my husband?" she said. "Where the needle goes, the thread follows."

So she took off her royal robes, put them away in a chest and went to Malania to learn to work. When she knew how, she began to help her husband.

All the wise left Ivan's kingdom, and only the fools remained.

Nobody had money. They lived and worked, fed themselves and others.

X

The old Devil waited and waited for news of the Devilkins. He was expecting to hear that they had ruined the three brothers, but no news came.

He set out himself to find them. He searched and searched, and found nothing but three holes.

"They've not been able to manage it, evidently," he thought. "I must tackle the job myself."

He went to look for the brothers, but they were no longer in their old places. He found them in their different kingdoms. All three lived and reigned. The old Devil was annoyed.

"Now we'll see what I can do!" he said.

First of all he went to King Simon.

He did not go in his own shape, but disguised himself as a general. In that guise he appeared before King Simon.

"I have heard that you are a great warrior, King Simon," he said. "I am well versed in these things and want to serve you."

And King Simon began to ask him all manner of questions, and seeing that he was a clever man, he took him into his service.

The new commander instructed King Simon how to collect a large army.

"First of all," he said, "we must get more soldiers. There are many idle people in your kingdom. We must conscript all the young men without exception, then you will have an army five times as large as the one you have now. Secondly, we must get new guns and cannons. I will get guns that will fire a hundred bullets at one shot; they will rain out like peas. And I will get cannons that will consume with fire either man or horse or wall; they will burn everything."

King Simon listened to the new commander, and enrolled all the young men as soldiers and built new factories where he manufactured new guns and cannons, then he made war on a neighbouring king. As soon as he was faced by the opposing army, King Simon ordered his soldiers to rain bullets against it and shoot fire from their cannons, in this way wiping out half the hostile troops. The neighbouring king was alarmed; he surrendered and gave up his kingdom. King Simon rejoiced.

"Now," he said, "I will make war on the King of India."

And the King of India heard of King Simon's doings. He adopted all his methods, and invented some improvements of his own. He not only enrolled all the young men as soldiers, but the unmarried women as well, and in consequence had a larger army than King Simon. And he made guns and cannons like King Simon's, and invented machines to fly in the air and drop explosive bombs from above.

And King Simon set out to make war on the King of India, thinking he would beat him as easily as he had beaten the other king, but the scythe that had cut so well had lost its edge. The King of India did not give Simon time to open fire, for he sent his women to fly in the air and drop explosive bombs on Simon's troops. And the women rained down bombs from above like borax upon cockroaches and Simon's troops scattered and fled, and Simon was left alone.

The King of India took possession of Simon's kingdom, and Simon the Warrior escaped as best he could.

Having disposed of this brother, the old Devil went to King Taras.

He changed himself into a merchant and settled in Taras' kingdom, where he opened establishments and began to circulate money freely. He paid high prices for everything, and the people flocked to him for the sake of the extra profit. And the people came to have so much money that they were able to settle all their arrears and to pay their taxes at the proper time. King Taras rejoiced.

"Thanks to the merchant," he thought, "I have more money than ever, and I'll be able to live better than I used to."

And he began making all sorts of new plans, and decided to have a new palace built for himself. He proclaimed to the people that he wanted timber and stone and labour, for which he was prepared to pay a high price. King Taras thought that for his money people would flock to work for him as of old. But lo! all the timber and stone was taken to the merchant, and all the labourers flocked to work for him. King Taras raised his price, and the merchant raised his. King Taras had much money, but the merchant had more and beat the King. The King's palace could not be built.

King Taras had arranged to make a new garden. When the autumn came he proclaimed that he wanted men to come and plant his garden, but no one came, for the people were all digging for the merchant.

Winter came. King Taras wanted to buy some sable skins for a new coat. He sent a messenger to buy it, but the messenger returned empty-handed, and said that there were no sable skins, for the merchant had bought them all at a higher price, and made himself a sable carpet.

King Taras wanted to buy some stallions. He sent a messenger, but the messenger returned and said that the merchant had all the good stallions; they were carting water for him to make a pond.

And the King's plans fell to pieces, for no one would work for him. All worked for the merchant, and only brought him the merchant's money to pay the taxes.

And the King came to have so much money that he did not know where to put it all, but he lived badly. The King gave up making plans; he would have been contented to live quietly somehow, but even that was difficult. He was hampered on all sides. His cook and coachman and servants left him to go to the merchant's. He even went short of food. When he sent to the market to buy some provisions there were none left, for the merchant had bought up everything, and the people only brought the King money for their taxes.

King Taras lost patience and banished the merchant from his kingdom. The merchant settled on the very border, and did exactly the same as before, and for his money the people dragged everything away from the King and brought it to the merchant. Life became very hard for the King. For whole days he did not eat, and to make matters worse a rumour went abroad that the merchant had boasted that he would buy the King himself. King Taras lost courage, and did not know what to do.

Simon the Warrior came to him and said, "Will you support me? I have been beaten by the King of India."

King Taras himself was in a sad plight.

"I haven't eaten anything myself for two days," he said.

XI

Having disposed of the two brothers, the old Devil went to Ivan. He changed himself into a general and came to Ivan, and began to persuade him to set up a large army.

"A king should not live without an army," he said. "Give me the power, and I'll collect soldiers from among your people and organize an army."

Ivan listened to all he had to say.

"Very well," he said, "organize one, then; only teach the soldiers to sing nice songs, for I like singing."

And the old Devil went through Ivan's kingdom to collect a voluntary army. To each recruit who should offer himself he promised a bottle of vodka and a red cap.

The fools laughed at him.

"We have plenty of drink," they said; "we brew it ourselves, and as for caps, our women can make us any kind we like—embroidered ones and even ones with fringes."

And no one offered himself.

The old Devil went back to Ivan and said, "Your fools won't enlist of their own accord; we'll have to force them."

"Very well; force them, then."

And the old Devil proclaimed throughout the kingdom that every man must enlist as a soldier, and if he fails to do so Ivan will have him put to death.

The fools came to the Devil and said, "You tell us that if we won't enlist as soldiers the King will have us put to death, but you don't say what will happen to us when we become soldiers. People say that soldiers are killed."

"You can't get over that."

When the fools heard this they kept to their decision.

"We won't go," they said. "We'd sooner die at home since we have to die in either case."

"What fools you are!" the old Devil said. "A soldier may or may not be killed, but if you don't go King Ivan will have you put to death for certain."

The fools reflected over this; then went to Ivan the Fool and said, "A general has appeared among us who orders us all to enlist as soldiers. 'If you go as a soldier,' he says, 'you may or you may not be killed, but if you don't go, King Ivan will have you put to death for certain.' Is it true?"

Ivan laughed.

"How can I alone have you all put to death? Had I not been a fool I would have explained it to you, but I don't understand it myself."

"Then we won't go," the fools said.

"Very well, don't."

The fools went to the general and refused to enlist as soldiers.

The old Devil saw that his plan would not work, so he went to the King of Tarakan and wormed himself into his favour.

"Come," he said, "let us go and make war on King Ivan. He has no money, but grain and cattle and all manner of good things he has in abundance."

The King of Tarakan prepared to make war. He gathered together a large army, repaired his guns and cannons and marched across the border on his way to Ivan's kingdom.

People came to Ivan and said, "The King of Tarakan is marching on us with his army."

"Very well; let him," Ivan said.

When the King of Tarakan crossed the border he sent his vanguard to find Ivan's troops. They searched and searched, but no troops were to be found anywhere. Should they wait and see if they showed themselves? But there was no sign of any troops and no one to fight with. The King of Tarakan sent men to seize the villages. The soldiers came to one village and the fools—men and women alike—rushed out and stood gaping at them in wonder. The soldiers began to take away their corn and cattle and the fools let them have what they wanted, making no resistance. The soldiers went to another village and the same thing was repeated. And they marched one day and another, and still the same thing happened. Everything was given up without any resistance and the fools even invited the soldiers to stay with them. "If you find it hard to live in your parts, good fellows, come and settle with us altogether." And the soldiers marched from village to village and no troops were to be found anywhere; the people lived, fed themselves and others; no one offered any resistance and every one invited them to settle there.

And the soldiers grew weary of the job and they went back to their King of Tarakan.

"We can't fight here," they said; "take us to another place. This is not war; this is child's-play. We can't fight here."

The King of Tarakan grew angry. He ordered his soldiers to go over the whole kingdom and lay waste the villages and burn the corn and kill the cattle.

"If you won't do what I tell you," he said, "I will punish you all."

The soldiers were frightened and began to carry out the King's commands. They burnt the houses and corn and killed the cattle. The fools made no resistance, they only wept. The old men wept and the old women and the little children.

"Why do you treat us like this?" they said. "Why do you waste the good things? If you want them, why not take them?"

And the soldiers grew to loathe their work. They refused to go further and the troops dispersed.

XII

And the old Devil went away, having failed to bring Ivan to reason by means of the soldiers.

The old Devil changed himself into a clean gentleman and came to live in Ivan's kingdom, hoping to ruin Ivan by money, as he had done Taras.

"I want to do you good and teach you common sense," he said. "I will build myself a house in your midst and open an establishment."

"Very well," the people said; "you can live here."

The clean gentleman spent the night and in the morning he went out to the square with a bag of gold and a bundle of papers and said, "You all live like swine. I want to teach you how you ought to live. Build me a house according to this plan. You will work for me and I will teach you and pay you in golden money." And he showed them the gold.

The fools marvelled. They had no money in circulation, but exchanged thing for thing, or paid by labour. And they began to exchange things with the gentleman and to work for his golden coins. And the old Devil, as in Taras' kingdom, began to circulate gold, and people brought him things and worked for him.

The old Devil rejoiced.

"At last my plan is beginning to work!" he thought. "I will ruin him as I ruined Taras, and will get him completely in my power."

The fools collected the golden coins and gave them to the women to make themselves necklaces and to the girls to plait into their hair; the children even played with the coins in the street. After a while every one had enough and refused to take more. And the clean gentleman's house was not half finished, and the corn and cattle had not yet been stored up for the year.

And the gentleman invited people to come and work for him to bring him corn and rear his cattle, offering to pay many golden coins for everything brought and every piece of work done.

But no one would come and work, and no one would bring him anything, unless a chance boy or girl brought him an egg in exchange for a golden coin; and no one else came and he was left without any food. And the clean gentleman was hungry and went through the village to buy himself something for dinner. He went into one house and offered a golden coin for a chicken, but the mistress would not take it.

"I have many such coins," she said.

He went into another place to buy a salt herring, offering a golden piece. "I don't want it, my good man," the mistress said. "I have no children to play with them, and have three of these pieces already as curiosities."

He went into a peasant's for some bread. The peasant too would not take the money.

"I don't want it," he said. "But if you want the bread in Christ's name, then wait, and I'll tell my old woman to cut you some."

The old Devil spat on the ground and fled from the peasant. To hear the word Christ was worse than a knife to him, let alone to take anything in His name.

And so he got no bread. All had gold; wherever the old Devil went no one would give him anything for money, and every one said, "Bring us something else instead, or come and work, or take it in Christ's name." And the Devil had nothing to offer but money and had no liking for work, and he could not take anything in Christ's name. He lost his temper.

"What more do you want when I offer you money?" he said. "You can buy anything you like for gold and employ any kind of labour."

But the fools did not heed him.

"We don't need money," they said. "We exchange everything in kind and have no taxes to pay; what good would it be to us?"

The old Devil went supperless to bed.

The story reached Ivan the Fool. People came to him and said, "What shall we do? A clean gentleman has appeared in our midst who likes to eat and drink well, and dress in fine clothes, but he won't work and won't take anything in Christ's name; he only offers us golden coins. People gave him what he wanted until they had enough of these coins, and now no one gives him anything. What are we to do with him? He may die of hunger."

Ivan listened to what they had to say.

"He must be fed, certainly. Let him act as a shepherd to you all in turn."

Since there was no way out, the old Devil had to go about shepherding. He went from house to house until it came to Ivan's turn. The old Devil came in to dinner and the deaf and dumb girl was getting it ready. She had often been deceived by lazy folk who came in early to dinner without having done their share of work and ate up all the porridge, so she invented a means of finding out the sluggards by their hands. Those who had horny hands were put at the table; the others were given the leavings. The old Devil sat down by the table, but the deaf and dumb girl seized him by the hands and looked at them to see if they had any blisters, but they were clean and smooth and the finger nails were long. The girl grunted and pulled the old Devil away from the table.

Ivan's wife said to him, "Don't be offended, fine gentleman. My sister-in-law never lets any one sit at the table who hasn't horny hands. In good time, when the others have finished, you shall get what is left."

And the old Devil was hurt that in the King's house they should want to feed him with the pigs. And he said to Ivan, "What a stupid custom there is in your kingdom that all people must work with their hands! I suppose you were too stupid to think of anything else. Do you think it's only with the hands people work? Do you know what wise men work with?"

And Ivan said, "How are we fools to know; we work only with our hands and backs."

"That is because you are fools. I will teach you how to work with the head, then you will know that it is more profitable than to work with the hands."

Ivan wondered.

"Really! No wonder people call us fools!"

And the old Devil said, "Only it's not easy to work with the head. You won't give me any dinner because my hands are smooth, but you don't know that it's a hundred times harder to work with the head. Sometimes one's head nearly splits."

Ivan grew thoughtful.

"Why should you torture yourself so, my good man? Wouldn't it be better to do the easier work with your hands and back?"

And the Devil said, "I torture myself because I pity you fools. If I were not to torture myself you would remain fools for ever. I have worked with the head and now I'm going to teach you."

Ivan wondered.

"Teach us, then," he said, "so that when our hands are tired we can work with the head."

The Devil promised to teach them.

And Ivan proclaimed throughout his kingdom that a clean gentleman had appeared among them who would teach every one to work with his head and that it was more profitable to work with the head than with the hands, and he bade every man come and hear him.

There was a high tower in Ivan's kingdom and a steep staircase leading up to it and there was a turret on the top. And Ivan took the gentleman up the tower, so that he might be seen by all.

And the gentleman took his place on the top of the tower and began to speak, and the fools flocked to look at him. They thought that the gentleman would really show them how to work with the head instead of the hands, but he merely told them in words how they could live without working at all. The fools did not understand him. They stared and stared, then went home to attend to their own affairs.

The old Devil stood on top of the tower one day and another, speaking all the time. He was hungry, but it never occurred to the fools to bring him some bread up the tower. They thought that if he could work with the head better than with the hands, he could easily make himself some bread. The old Devil stood on the tower for another day, still speaking. The people came and stared at him for a while; then went their ways.

"Well, has the gentleman begun to work with his head?" Ivan asked.

"Not yet; he is still jabbering."

The Devil stood on the tower for another day and began to grow faint. He swayed and knocked his head against a pillar. One of the fools saw him and told Ivan's wife, who hastened to Ivan at the ploughing.

"Come, come," she said. "They say the gentleman has begun to work with his head."

Ivan wondered.

"Really?" he said, and turning his horse round, he went to the tower. When he got there, the old Devil, who was quite faint with hunger by this time, was staggering and knocking his head against the pillars, and when Ivan came up he fell with a crash down the stairs, counting each step on the way with a knock of his head.

"Well," Ivan said, "the clean gentleman spoke truly when he said that the head splits sometimes. Blisters on the hands are nothing to this; after such work there will be bumps on the head."

The old Devil fell to the bottom of the stairs and thumped his head against the ground. Ivan was about to go up and see how much work he had done, when suddenly the earth opened and the old Devil fell through. Only a hole was left.

Ivan scratched his head.

"You horrid wretch! One of those devils again! The father of the others, no doubt. What a huge one too!"

Ivan is living to this day and people flock to his kingdom. His own brothers have come to him and he supports them. When any one comes and says, "Feed me," Ivan says, "Very well, you can live with us; we have plenty of everything." Only there is a special custom in his kingdom—whoever has horny hands comes to table; whoever has smooth ones eats the leavings.

WHERE THERE IS LOVE, THERE IS GOD ALSO

In the town there was a shoemaker by the name of Martin, who lived in a basement with a tiny little window looking out into the street. Martin could see the people pass, and though he only got a glimpse of their feet, he still knew every one, for Martin could recognize people by their boots. Martin had lived in that basement for many a long year and had numbers of acquaintances. There were not many pairs of boots in the neighbourhood that had not been through his hands at least once or twice—some for new soles, others for a patch or a stitch, or a second time for new tops, perhaps. Martin had plenty of work, for he always did it well; he gave good leather, did not overcharge, and kept true to his word. If he could do a piece of work for the time it was required, he took it; if not, he would not deceive his customers and told them so beforehand. And all knew Martin and he had no lack of work.

Martin had always been a good man, but as he grew older he began to think the more about his soul and to draw nearer to God. Martin's wife had died when he had still worked for a master, and he was left with a boy of three years old. Their children never survived; the eldest were all dead. At first Martin wanted to send his little son to a sister in the country, but he felt sorry for the child, thinking, "It will be hard for the poor boy to grow up in a strange family; I will keep him with me."

And Martin left his master and went into lodgings with his little son. But God had not ordained Martin to be happy in his children. The boy had no sooner grown up and become a help and a comfort to his father than he fell sick, tossed about with fever for a week and died. Martin buried his son and gave himself up to despair. His despair was so great that he even began to complain against God. Martin was so lonely that many were the times he prayed to God to let him die, reproaching Him for having spared an old man like himself and taken his only beloved son. Martin gave up going to church.

One day an old countryman came to visit him, who had been on a pilgrimage for eight years. Martin opened his heart to the old man and complained about his sorrow.

"I have no desire to live even," he said; "I only want to die. That is all I pray to God about. I am a desperate man now."

And the old man said to him, "It is not well what you say, Martin; we cannot judge the ways of God; they are beyond our understanding. He has judged it fitting to take away your son and to let you live, so it must be for the best. You despair because you want to live only for your own personal pleasure."

"And what else should I live for?" Martin asked.

And the old man said, "You must live for God, Martin. He gave you life and you must live for Him. When you begin to live for Him and cease to worry about anything, then all will become easy for you."

Martin was silent a while; then asked, "How can one live for God?"

And the old man said, "We must live for God as Christ taught us. You can read, can you not? Then buy the Gospels and read them and you will find out how to live for God. The Gospels tell us everything."

Martin took these words to heart. That very day he bought a copy of the New Testament, printed in large type, and began to read it.

Martin had intended to read only on holidays, but when he once began he grew so light-hearted that he read every day. Sometimes he got so absorbed in his reading that the oil in the lamp burnt low and still he could not tear himself away.

Martin read every evening, and the more he read the more clearly he understood what God required of him and how he was to live for God. And his heart grew lighter than ever. At one time when he went to bed he would sigh and moan and think of his boy; now he only said to himself, "Glory to Thee, glory to Thee, God! Thy will be done!"

And a change came into Martin's life. On holidays he used to hang about the public-houses to drink a cup of tea and did not refuse vodka even when it came his way. He would drink, as it happened, with some acquaintance, and though not exactly drunk, would come out of the public-house in an excited mood and speak vain words, giving back rough word for rough word.

But now this had all left him. His life became a peaceful and happy one.

In the morning he would sit down to his work and keep on for the necessary time, then he would take the lamp off the wall, put it on the table, fetch the Bible from a shelf, open it, and sit down to read. And the more he read, the more he understood, and the serener and lighter grew his heart.

One day Martin sat reading until late into the night. He was reading Luke's Gospel and had come to the sixth chapter and the verses, "And unto him that smiteth thee on the one cheek, offer also the other; and him that taketh away thy cloke forbid not to take thy coat also. Give to every man that asketh of thee; and of him that taketh away thy goods ask them not again. And as ye would that men should do to you, do ye also to them likewise."

And he also read the verses where our Lord says, "And why call ye me, Lord, Lord, and do not the things which I say? Whosoever cometh to me and heareth my sayings, and doeth them, I will show you to whom he is like. He is like a man which built an house, and digged deep, and laid the foundation on a rock; and when the flood arose, the stream beat vehemently upon that house, and could not shake it; for it was founded upon a rock. But he that heareth, and doeth not, is like a man that without a foundation built an house upon the earth; against which the stream did beat vehemently, and immediately it fell; and the ruin of that house was great."

When Martin read these words a feeling of joy entered his heart. He took off his spectacles, laid them on the Bible, then resting his elbows on the table, he began to ponder over what he had read. He compared his own life to the light of these words. "Is my house built on a rock or on sand?" he thought. "If on a rock it is well. It seems so easy when one sits alone here, and one thinks one has done all that God commands, but no sooner does one cease to be on one's guard than one falls into sin. I must persevere; it brings such happiness! Help me, oh God!"

With this thought in his mind, he was about to go to bed, but was loath to leave his Bible, and went on reading the seventh chapter. He read about the centurion, the widow's son, and the answer to John's disciples, and he came to the passage where a rich Pharisee invited the Lord to his house; and about the woman who was a sinner and anointed His feet and washed them with her tears, and how the Lord comforted her. And he came to the forty-fourth verse and began to read the words, "And he turned to the woman and said unto Simon, Seest thou this woman? I entered into thine house, thou gavest me no water for my feet; but she hath washed my feet with tears, and wiped them with the hairs of her head. Thou gavest me no kiss, but this woman since the time I came in, hath not ceased to kiss my feet; my head with oil thou didst not anoint, but this woman hath anointed my feet with ointment."

Martin read these verses and thought, "He gave no water for His feet, and no kiss, and he did not anoint His head with oil." Once more Martin took off his spectacles and laid them on the Bible.

"He must have been like me, that Pharisee. Like me he thought only of himself—how to get a cup of tea, how to live in warmth and comfort. He cared only for himself, with never a thought about his guest. And the Lord Himself was his guest! I wonder if I would act like that if He came to visit me?"

And Martin rested his elbows on the table and his head on his hands and fell into a doze.

"Martin!" Some one suddenly breathed into his ear.

Martin started. "Who is that?" he asked, half asleep.

He turned and looked at the door, but no one was there. He called again and this time he heard a voice say clearly, "Martin! Martin! Look out for me in the street to-morrow; I am coming to see you."

Martin roused himself, got up from the chair and began to rub his eyes. He did not know whether he had heard the words in a dream or when awake. He turned out the lamp and went to bed.

At daybreak next morning Martin arose, lit the stove, prepared some soup and porridge, got the samovar ready, put on his apron and sat down at the window to his work. As he worked he thought of what had happened yesterday. Now it seemed to him that he had heard the voice in his dreams, now that he had really heard it when awake.

"Things like that have happened before," he thought.

Martin sat at the window and did not work so much as peer out into the street, and when an unfamiliar pair of boots came along, he would stoop down and look up to catch a glimpse of the person to whom they belonged. A yard-porter passed in new felt boots and a water-carrier; then an old soldier of Nicholas' reign came alongside the window, spade in hand. Martin recognized him by his felt boots. The old man was called Stepan and a merchant who lived near by kept him out of charity. His duties were to help the yard-porter. He stopped opposite Martin's window to clear away the snow. Martin looked at him and again went on with his work.

"What a fool I am getting in my old age," Martin thought, amused at his own fancies. "Stepan is shovelling away the snow and I thought it was Christ come to visit me. Old dotard that I am!"

Yet after a dozen stitches or so Martin was again drawn to the window. He looked out and saw that Stepan had leaned his spade against the wall and was resting and trying to warm himself. The man was old and broken and had no strength even to clear away the snow. "Why not give him a cup of tea while the samovar is still on the boil?" Martin thought. And he put down his awl, rose, brought the samovar to the table, poured out a cup of tea and tapped on the window. Stepan turned and came up. Martin beckoned to him and went to open the door.

"Come in and get warm," he said; "you must be quite frozen."

"Christ save us! but my bones do ache," Stepan said. Stepan came in, shook the snow off himself and began to wipe his boots so as not to dirty the floor, reeling as he did so.

"Don't bother to wipe your feet," Martin said; "I will wipe the floor afterwards; I am used to that. Come in and sit down. Here is a cup of tea."

And Martin poured out two cups, gave one to his guest, poured some of his own into a saucer and began to blow on it in order to cool it.

Stepan finished his cup, turned it upside down in the saucer, put the remaining bit of sugar on top and began to thank Martin, who could see that the old man wanted some more.

"Have another cup," Martin said and poured out more tea for his guest and for himself, and as he drank, he kept peering out of the window.

"Are you expecting some one?" Stepan asked.

"I? I hardly like to tell you whom I expect. But I wait and wait. A certain word took possession of my heart. Was it a dream or not, I cannot tell. It was like this, brother; I was reading the Gospels last night about Christ our Father and how He suffered on earth. You have heard tell of it, I daresay."

"Yes," Stepan said, "but we are ignorant folk and cannot read."

"Well, I was reading how the Lord walked on earth, how He went to visit a Pharisee who did not receive Him well. And I wondered, as I read, how any man could receive the Lord without due honour. 'Supposing such a thing were to happen to me,' I thought, 'what would I not do to receive Him? And the Pharisee did nothing!' Thinking thus I fell asleep, and as I slept I heard a voice call to me. I rose; the voice seemed to whisper 'Expect me; I am coming to-morrow.' I heard it twice. Well, would you believe it? the idea took hold of my mind, and though I upbraid myself, I keep on expecting the Lord to come to me."

Stepan shook his head, but made no remark. He finished his cup of tea and laid it down on its side in the saucer, but Martin took it up and filled it again.

"Have some more, bless you! I was thinking, too, that our Lord despised no one when He walked on earth; He was mostly with common folk. He went about with plain people and chose His disciples from men of our kind—simple workmen and sinners like ourselves. 'He who raises himself,' He said, 'shall be humbled, and he who humbles himself shall be raised. You call Me Lord,' he said, 'and I will wash your feet. He who would be first,' He said, 'let him be the servant of all, because,' He said, 'blessed are the poor, the humble, the meek, the merciful.' "

Stepan forgot his tea. He was an old man and easily moved to tears; and as he listened the tears rolled down his cheeks.

"Have some more," Martin said, but Stepan crossed himself, thanked Martin, pushed away his cup and rose.

"Thank you Martin," he said; "you have nourished my body and my soul."

"You are welcome another time. I shall always be pleased to see you; come again."

Stepan went out; Martin poured himself out a last cup of tea, drank it, cleared away the dishes and sat down again by the window to work, stitching the back seam of a boot. As he stitched he peered out of the window to see if Christ was coming, and he kept on thinking of Him and His doings and recalling His words.

Two soldiers passed; one in Government boots, the other in boots of his own; then the owner of the next house went by in clean goloshes, and a baker with a basket. All these passed on; then a woman came up in woollen stockings and coarse country shoes. She went by the window and stopped by the wall. Martin looked up and saw that she was a stranger, poorly clad, with a baby in her arms. She was standing with her back to the wind, trying to wrap up the baby, but there was nothing to wrap it in. Her garments were summer ones and ragged, too. Through the window Martin heard the baby crying; the woman tried to comfort it but could not.

Martin rose and going out at the door and up the steps, he called to her.

"Come this way, my dear!"

The woman turned to him.

"Don't stand in the cold there with the baby; come inside in the warm;

you can make him more comfortable here. Come along!"

The woman was surprised to see an old man in an apron and spectacles on his nose inviting her to his room, but she followed him. They descended the stairs and entered the room. Martin led her to the bed.

"Come and sit here, my dear," he said. "It is nearer to the stove; you can warm yourself and feed the baby."

"I haven't any milk; I have eaten nothing myself since morning," the woman said, yet putting the child to the breast.

Martin shook his head. He got some bread and a cup, opened the oven door and filled the cup with soup. He then took the porridge-pot out of the oven, but the porridge was not quite done. He spread a cloth and put the soup and bread on the table.

"Sit down and have something to eat, my dear. I'll look after the baby. I have had children of my own and know how to nurse them."

The woman crossed herself, sat down by the table and began to eat, and Martin sat on the bed with the baby. He clucked and clucked, but having no teeth he could not do it well, and the baby would not stop its crying. And Martin tried to amuse him with his finger. He poked the finger straight at the baby's mouth, then drew it back again. He would not let the child take the finger in its mouth because it was black with cobbler's wax. The child looked at the finger, stopped crying and began to laugh. Martin was pleased.

As the woman ate she told him about herself, saying who she was and where she was going.

"I am a soldier's wife," she said. "It is now eight months that my husband has been taken away and I haven't heard a word from him. I had a place as a cook when the child was born, but they would not keep me after that. I've been without a place for three months now and eaten everything I possessed. I wanted to go as a wet-nurse, but no one would have me because they said I was too thin. I went to a merchant's wife with whom our grandmother is in service and she promised to take me. I thought she meant at once, but she told me to come next week, and she lives a long way. I'm quite worn out, and the baby is half-starved. If our landlady did not take pity on us, I don't know how we should live."

Martin sighed and said, "Have you no warm clothes?"

"How can I have warm clothes! I pawned my last shawl yesterday for sixpence!"

The woman went up to the bed and took the child. Martin rummaged about among the things hanging on the wall and brought out an old coat.

"Though it isn't much of a thing, it will do to wrap up in," he said.

The woman looked at the coat; then at the old man. She took the coat and burst into tears. Martin turned away, crawled under the bed and pulled out a box. He rummaged about in it and once more sat down facing the woman.

And the woman said, "Christ save you, Grandfather. It must have been He who sent me to your window, otherwise the child and I would have been starved to death. It was mild when I started, but it's very cold now. The dear Lord made you look out of the window and caused you to pity me."

Martin smiled and said, "He did make me, indeed! I was not gazing idly out of the window, my dear."

And Martin told the woman his dream and how he had heard a voice and how the voice had promised him that the Lord should come and visit him this day.

"All things are possible," the woman said, and she rose, put on the coat, wrapped the child in it and began to take her leave, thanking Martin.

"Take this in Christ's name," Martin said, thrusting a sixpence into her hand. "It will do to take out your shawl."

The woman crossed herself, Martin did likewise, then accompanied her to the door.

When she had gone Martin ate some soup, cleared the table, and again sat down to work. But he did not forget the window. As soon as a shadow fell across it, he looked up to see who it was. Acquaintances passed and strangers, and nothing particular happened. Suddenly Martin saw an old apple-woman stop by his window. She was carrying a basket of apples. She must have sold nearly all, for only a few remained. Over her shoulders was a bag of chips and shavings, she had collected no doubt in half-finished houses, and was taking home. The bag made her shoulder ache it seemed and she wanted to change it over to the other shoulder. She let it down on the pavement, placed her basket of apples on a post and shook the bag. As she was doing so a boy in a ragged cap appeared from somewhere, snatched an apple out of the basket and was about to slip away when the old woman saw him and caught him by the sleeve. The boy struggled to get away, but the old woman held him fast with both hands. She had knocked off his cap and clutched him by the hair. The boy screamed, the woman cursed. Martin did not wait to put the awl in its place, but dropped it on the floor and rushed out at the door and stumbled up the stairs, dropping his spectacles on the way. He ran out into the street. The old woman was pulling the boy by the hair, cursing and threatening to take him to the policeman; the boy struggled and resisted her. "Why do you strike me?" he was saying. "I didn't take anything!"

Martin tried to part them; he took the boy by the hand and said, "Let him go, Granny. Forgive him for Christ's sake."

"I'll forgive him so that he won't forget it for a long time! I'll take the rascal to the police-station!"

Martin began to plead with her.

"Let him go, Granny; he won't do it again. Let him go for Christ's sake!"

The old woman released the boy, who was about to run away when Martin stopped him.

"Ask Granny to forgive you and don't do it again in future; I saw you take the apple."

The boy burst into tears and begged the old woman to forgive him.

"There now, here's an apple for you," and Martin took an apple from the basket and gave it to the boy. "I'll pay for it, Granny," he said.

"You shouldn't spoil the rascal," the old woman said. "You ought to give him something he wouldn't forget in a week."

"Ah, Granny, Granny!" Martin said; "that is how we judge, but God does not judge like that. If the boy is to be whipped for an apple what do you suppose we deserve for our sins?"

The old woman was silent.

And Martin told her the parable of the Lord who forgave his servant a large debt and how the servant then seized his own debtor by the throat. The old woman listened; the boy, too, stood and listened.

"God bade us forgive," Martin said, "that we may be forgiven. Forgive every one, even a thoughtless boy."

The old woman shook her head with a sigh.

"It's true enough," she said, "but boys get very spoilt nowadays."

"Then we old folk must teach them better," Martin said.

"That's just what I said," the old woman replied. "I had seven of my own, but now I've only a daughter left." And the old woman began to tell him where and how she lived with her daughter and how many grandchildren she had. "You see," she said, "I'm old now, yet still I work, for the sake of the grandchildren. And nice children they are, too. No one is so kind to me as they. The youngest won't leave me for any one. It's nothing but Granny dear, Granny darling all the time."

The old woman had quite softened by now.

"Children will be children," she said to Martin in reference to the boy. "The Lord bless them."

She was about to raise her bag on to her shoulder when the boy rushed up and said, "Let me carry it, Granny; I'm going your way."

The old woman shook her head and put the bag on the boy's shoulder.

And they walked down the street side by side. The old woman had forgotten to ask Martin to pay for the apple. Martin stood and watched them, listening to their voices as they talked together.

When they were out of sight he turned in, found his spectacles on the stairs quite whole, took up his awl and sat down to his work once more. After a while he could not see to pass the thread through the holes and he noticed the lamplighter lighting the street lamps. "I must light up," he thought. And he trimmed the lamp, hung it up and went on with his work. He finished the boot he was doing and turned it over to examine it. He then put away his tools, cleared up the bits of leather and thread and awls, took down the lamp, put it on the table and took the Bible down from the shelf. He wanted to open it at the place he had marked with a piece of morocco, but it opened at another place. And as he opened the Gospels Martin recalled his dream of last night. And no sooner had he thought of it than he seemed to hear some one move behind him, as though some one were coming towards him. He turned, and it seemed to him that people were standing in the dark corner, but he could not make out who they were. And a voice whispered into his ear, "Martin, Martin, don't you know me?"

"Who is it?" Martin asked.

"It is I," the voice said.

And Stepan stepped out of the dark corner, smiling, and vanished like a cloud, and he was no more.

"It is I," the voice said again, and from out the dark corner stepped the woman with the baby, and she smiled and the child smiled, and they too vanished.

"It is I," said the voice once more, and out stepped the old woman and boy with an apple in his hand, and both smiled and also vanished.

And a feeling of gladness entered Martin's soul. He crossed himself, put on his spectacles and began to read the Gospel just where it had opened. At the top of the page were the words, "For I was an hungered, and ye gave me meat; I was thirsty and ye gave me drink; I was a stranger and ye took me in...."

And at the bottom of the page he read, "Inasmuch as ye have done it unto one of the least of these brethren, ye have done it unto me."

And Martin understood that his dream had come true and that his Saviour had really come to him that day, and that he had welcomed Him.

A PRISONER

An officer by the name of Jilin served in the army in the Caucasus.

One day he received a letter from home. It was from his mother, who wrote, "I am getting old now, and I want to see my beloved son before I die. Come and say good-bye to me, and when you have buried me, with God's grace, you can return to the Army. I have found a nice girl for you to marry; she is clever and pretty, and has some property of her own. If you like her perhaps you will marry and settle down for good."

Jilin pondered over the letter. It was true; his mother was really failing fast, and it might be his only chance of seeing her alive. He would go home, and if the girl was nice, he might even marry.

He went to his colonel and asked for leave, and bidding good-bye to his fellow-officers, gave his men four bucketfuls of vodka as a farewell treat, and got ready to go.

There was a war in the Caucasus at the time. The roads were not safe by day or by night. If a Russian ventured away from his fort, the Tartars either killed him or took him off to the hills. So it had been arranged that a body of soldiers should march from fortress to fortress to convoy any person who wanted to travel. The soldiers marched in front and behind; the travellers in between them.

It was summer. At daybreak the baggage-train was loaded behind the fort; the convoy came out and started along the road. Jilin was on horseback; his things were on a cart with the baggage-train.

They had about twenty miles to go. The baggage-train moved along slowly; now the soldiers would stop, now a wheel came off a cart, now a horse would refuse to go on, and then everybody had to wait.

It was already past noon and they had not covered half the distance. It was hot, dusty, the sun scorching and no shade at all—bare steppe, with not a tree or a bush the whole way.

Jilin rode on ahead and stopped to wait until the baggage-train should catch him up. He heard the signal-horn sounded; the company had stopped again. Jilin thought, "Why shouldn't I go on alone without the soldiers? I have a good horse, and if I come across any Tartars I can easily gallop away. I wonder if it would be safe?"

As he stood there thinking it over, another officer, by the name of Kostilin, rode up with a rifle and said, "Let us go on alone, Jilin. I'm dreadfully hungry, and the heat's unbearable. My shirt is wringing wet."

Kostilin was a big man and stout; his face was burning red, and the perspiration poured from his brow.

Jilin deliberated for a moment and said, "Is your rifle loaded?"

"It is."

"Very well; come along. Only the condition is to be that we don't part."

And they set off down the road alone. They were riding along the steppe talking together and keeping a sharp look-out from side to side. They could see a long way round them. When they left the steppe they came to a road running down a valley between two hills. And Jilin said, "Let's go up on that hill and look about; some Tartars might easily spring out from the hills and we shouldn't see them."

"What's the use?" Kostilin said. "We'd better go on."

Jilin paid no heed to him.

"You wait down here," he said, "and I'll just go up and have a look." And he turned his horse to the left up the hill. Jilin's horse was a hunter and carried him up the hill as though it had wings. He had bought it for a hundred roubles as a colt, and broken it in himself. When he reached the top of the hill he saw some thirty Tartars a few paces ahead of him. He turned hastily, but the Tartars had seen him and gave chase down the hill, getting their rifles out as they went. Jilin bounded down as fast as the horse's legs would carry him, crying out to Kostilin, "Get your rifle ready!" And in thought he said to his horse, "Get me out of this, my beauty; don't stumble, or I'm lost. Once I reach the rifle, they shan't take me alive!"

But Kostilin, instead of waiting when he saw the Tartars, set off full gallop in the direction of the fortress, lashing his horse now on one side, now on the other, and the horse's switching tail was all that could be seen of him in the clouds of dust.

Jilin saw that it was all up with him. The rifle was gone; with a sword alone he could do nothing. He turned his horse in the direction of the convoy, hoping to escape, but six Tartars rushed ahead to cut him off. His horse was a good one, but theirs were better, and they were trying to cross his path. He wanted to turn in another direction, but his horse could not pull up and dashed on straight towards the Tartars. A red-bearded Tartar on a grey horse caught Jilin's eyes. He was yelling and showing his teeth and pointing his rifle at him.

"I know what devils you are!" Jilin thought. "If you take me alive, you'll put me in a pit and have me flogged. I'll not be taken alive!"

Though Jilin was a little man, he was brave. He drew his sword and dashed at the red-bearded Tartar, thinking, "I'll either ride him down or kill him with my sword."

But he had no time to reach the Tartar; he was fired at from behind and his horse was hit. It fell to the ground full weight, pinning Jilin's leg. He attempted to rise, but two evil-smelling Tartars were already sitting on him, twisting his arms behind him. He struggled, flung the Tartars off, but three others leapt from their horses and fell on him, beating him on the head with the butt ends of their rifles. A mist rose before his eyes and he staggered. The Tartars seized him, and taking spare girths from their saddles twisted his hands behind him and tied them with a Tartar knot and dragged him to the saddle. They knocked off his cap, pulled off his boots, searched him all over, took his money and watch and tore his clothes. Jilin looked round at his horse. The poor creature lay on its side just as it had fallen, struggling with its legs in the air and unable to get them to the ground. There was a hole in its head from which the dark blood was oozing, laying the dust for a yard around.

One of the Tartars approached it and took off the saddle. As it was still struggling, he drew a dagger and cut its windpipe. A whistling sound came from its throat; the horse gave a shudder and died.

The Tartars took off the saddle and strappings. The red-bearded Tartar mounted his horse, the others lifted Jilin into the saddle behind him, and, to prevent his falling off, they strapped him to the Tartar's girdle, and took him off to the hills.

Jilin sat behind the Tartar, rocking from side to side, his face touching the evil-smelling Tartar's back. All he could see was the man's broad back and sinewy neck, the closely-shaven bluish nape peeping out from beneath his cap. Jilin had a wound in his head, from which the blood poured and congealed over his eyes, but he could not shift his position on the saddle, nor wipe off the blood. His arms were twisted so far behind his back that his collar-bones ached. They rode over the hills for some time, then they came to a river which they forded and got out on to a road running down a valley. Jilin wanted to see where they were going, but his eyes were matted with blood and he could not move.

It began to get dark; they forded another river and rode up a rocky hill; there was a smell of smoke and a barking of dogs. They had reached a Tartar village. The Tartars got off their horses; the Tartar children gathered round Jilin, yelling and throwing stones at him. A Tartar drove them away, took Jilin off the horse and called his servant. A man with high cheek-bones came up, clad in nothing but a shirt, and that so torn that his breast was bare. The Tartar gave him some order. The man brought some shackles, two blocks of oak with iron rings attached, and a clasp and lock was fixed to one of the rings.

They untied Jilin's arms, put on the shackles, took him to a shed, pushed him in and locked the door. Jilin fell on to a dung heap. He groped about in the darkness to find a softer place and lay down.

II

Jilin did not sleep the whole of that night. The nights were short. Through a chink he saw that it was getting light. He got up, made the chink a little bigger and peeped out.

He saw a road at the foot of a hill, to the right of which was a Tartar hut with two trees near it. A black dog lay on the threshold and a goat and kids were moving about and swishing their tails. Then he saw a young Tartar woman coming from the direction of the hill. She wore a coloured blouse and trousers with a girdle round her waist, high boots on her feet and a kerchief on her head, on which she was carrying a tin pitcher of water. Her back moved gracefully as she walked; she was leading a closely-shaven Tartar boy, who wore nothing but a shirt. The Tartar woman went into the hut with the water; the red-bearded Tartar of yesterday came out in a silken tunic, a silver-hilted knife stuck in his girdle and slippers on bare feet. A high, black sheepskin cap was pushed far back on his head. He stretched himself as he came out and stroked his red beard. He gave some order to his servant and went away.

Then two boys rode past. They had been to water their horses and the horses' noses were still wet. Some more closely-shaven boys came out, dressed only in shirts with no trousers. A whole group of them came up to the shed, and taking up a piece of stick, they thrust it through the chink. Jilin grunted at them and the boys ran off, yelling, their little white knees gleaming as they went.

Jilin was thirsty; his throat was parched. "If only some one would come," he thought. Soon the door of the shed opened and the red-bearded Tartar entered with another, shorter than he, and dark. He had bright black eyes, a ruddy complexion and a short beard. He had a jolly face, and was always laughing. This man was dressed better than the first, in a blue silken tunic, trimmed with braid. The knife in his broad girdle was of silver, the shoes on his feet were of red morocco, embroidered in silver thread, and over these he wore a thicker pair of shoes. His cap was high and of white sheepskin.

The red-bearded Tartar entered, muttering some angry words. He leant against the doorpost, playing with his dagger and looking askance at Jilin, like a wolf. The dark man, quick and lively and moving as if on springs, came up to Jilin and squatted down in front of him, showing his teeth. He clapped Jilin on the shoulder and began to jabber something in his own language, blinking his eyes and clacking his tongue. "Good Russ! Good Russ!" he said.

Jilin understood nothing. "I am thirsty; give me some water," he said.

The dark man laughed. "Good Russ!" he kept on saying.

Jilin made signs with his lips and hands that he wanted some water. The dark man laughed, and putting his head out at the door, he called to some one "Dina!"

A little girl came up. She was about thirteen, slight and thin, her face resembling the dark man's. She was obviously his daughter. She, too, had bright, black eyes and a rosy complexion. She was clad in a long blue blouse with broad sleeves, and loose at the waist—the hem and front and sleeves were embroidered in red. She wore trousers and slippers and shoes with high heels over them; she had a necklace round her throat made out of Russian coins. Her head was bare. Her black plait was tied with a ribbon, the ends of which were trimmed with silver roubles.

Her father said something to her. She ran away and came back again with a tin jug of water. She gave it to Jilin and also squatted down in front of him, huddled up, so that her shoulders came lower than her knees. She sat staring at Jilin as he drank, as at some strange animal.

Jilin handed her back the jug. She took it and bounded out like a wild goat. Even her father could not help laughing. He sent her off somewhere else. She ran away with the jug and brought back some unleavened bread on a round wooden platter, and huddling down in front of him once more, she again stared at him open-eyed.

The Tartars went out and locked the door.

After a while the red-bearded man's servant came up and called to Jilin. He too, did not know Russian, only Jilin understood that he wanted him to go somewhere.

Jilin followed him limping, for the shackles impeded his walking. He followed the servant. They came to a Tartar village, consisting of about ten houses, a Tartar church with a dome on top in the midst of them. In front of one house stood three saddled horses; some boys were holding them by their bridles. The dark little Tartar rushed out of this house and beckoned to Jilin to come to him. He laughed, jabbered something in his own tongue and went in again. Jilin came to the house. The room was large, the mud walls smoothly plastered. Near the front wall lay a pile of brightly coloured feather beds, on the side walls hung rich rugs with rifles and pistols and swords fastened to them, all inlaid in silver. At one wall was a small stove on a level with the earthen floor, which was beautifully clean. In the near corner a felt carpet was spread on which were rich rugs and down cushions. On these rugs, in slippers only, sat some Tartars—the dark one, the red-bearded one and three guests. All had down cushions at their backs. In front of them, on a wooden platter, were some millet pancakes, some melted butter in a cup and a jug of Tartar beer. They took the pancakes up with their fingers, and their hands were all greasy with the butter.

The dark Tartar jumped up and bade Jilin sit down, not on the rugs, but on the bare floor. Then he sat down on his rug again, and treated his guests to more pancakes and beer. The servant made Jilin sit down in the place assigned to him, took off his overshoes, which he placed by the door where the other shoes were standing, and sat down on the felt carpet, nearer to his master. He watched the others eating, his mouth watering. When the Tartars had finished, a woman came in dressed like the girl in trousers and a kerchief on her head. She cleared away the remains, and brought a basin and a narrow-necked jug of water. The Tartars washed their hands, laid them together, fell on their knees and said their prayers in their own tongue. When they had finished one of the guests turned to Jilin and addressed him in Russian.

"You were captured by Kasi-Mohammed," he said, indicating the red-bearded Tartar, "but he has given you to Abdul-Murat." And he indicated the dark Tartar. "Abdul-Murat is now your master."

Jilin was silent.

Abdul-Murat now began to speak, pointing at Jilin and laughing. "A soldier Russ, a good Russ," he said.

And the interpreter said, "He wants you to write home asking your people to send a ransom for you. When the money comes, he will let you go."

Jilin reflected and said, "How much does he want?"

The Tartars deliberated among themselves; the interpreter said, "Three thousand roubles."

"I can't pay as much as that," Jilin said.

Abdul leapt up and began to gesticulate violently. He was saying something to Jilin, thinking that he would understand.

"How much will you give?" the interpreter asked.

After reflection Jilin said, "Five hundred roubles."

At this the Tartars all began talking together. Abdul shouted at the red-bearded Tartar, jabbering away till he foamed at the mouth. The red-bearded Tartar merely frowned and clacked his tongue.

They grew silent and the interpreter said, "The master thinks a ransom of five hundred roubles is not enough. He himself paid two hundred roubles for you. Kasi-Mohammed was in his debt, and he took you in payment. He wants three thousand roubles and refuses to let you go for less. If you won't pay the money you'll be flung into a pit and flogged."

"The more you show you're afraid of them, the worse it is," Jilin thought. He leapt to his feet and said, "Tell the dog that if he begins to threaten me, he shan't have a farthing! I won't write home at all! I was never afraid of you, and I'm not going to be now, you dogs!"

The interpreter conveyed his words, and again the Tartars began to speak all at once.

They jabbered for a long time, then the dark one sprang up and came to Jilin.

"Russ," he said, "djigit, djigit Russ!" (Djigit in their tongue means brave.) He laughed and said a few words to the interpreter, who turned to Jilin.

"Will you give a thousand roubles?"

Jilin stuck to his own.

"I won't give more than five hundred, not if you kill me."

The Tartars conferred together, and sent the servant off somewhere, and when he was gone they stared now at Jilin, now at the door.

The servant returned, followed by a stout, bare-footed man, in torn clothes. On his feet were also shackles. Jilin gave an exclamation of surprise. It was Kostilin. He, too, had been captured then. The Tartars sat them down side by side, and they began to tell each other of their experiences, the Tartars looking on in silence. Jilin told Kostilin what had happened to him, and Kostilin told Jilin that his horse had got tired, his rifle missed fire, and that this same Abdul had caught him up and captured him.

Abdul jumped up and began to speak, pointing at Kostilin. The interpreter explained that they both belonged to the same master, and that the one who would produce the money first would be the first to be set free.

"See how quiet your comrade is," he said to Jilin. "You get angry and he has written home asking to have five thousand roubles sent him. He will be well fed, and no one will do him any harm."

And Jilin said, "My comrade can do what he likes. He may be rich, and I am not. I won't go back on my word. You can kill me if you like, but you get no advantage by that; I won't write for more than five hundred roubles."

The Tartars were silent. Suddenly Abdul sprang up, took out a pen, ink and a scrap of paper from a little box, put them in Jilin's hands and slapping him on the shoulder, said, "Write." He had agreed to the five hundred roubles.

"One moment," Jilin said to the interpreter; "tell him that he must feed and clothe us well, and that he must put us together so that we don't feel so lonely, and he must remove our shackles."

He looked at Abdul as he spoke and smiled. Abdul too smiled and said, "You shall have the best of clothes—coats and boots fit to be married in, and you shall be fed like princes, and you can be together in the shed if you like, but I can't take off the shackles because you might escape. You shall have them removed at night." He rushed up to Jilin and slapped him on the shoulder. "Fine fellow! fine fellow!" he said.

Jilin wrote the letter, but did not address it correctly, so that it should not reach home. "I will escape, somehow," he thought.

Jilin and Kostilin were taken back to the shed. They were given some straw, a jug of water and bread, two old coats and some worn boots, evidently taken from the bodies of dead soldiers. At night their shackles were removed and they were locked in the shed.

III

Thus Jilin and his comrade lived for a month. Their master was always cheerful. "You, good fellow, Ivan! I, Abdul, good fellow, too!" But he fed them badly. All the food they got was some unleavened bread of millet flour, or millet cakes, and sometimes nothing but raw dough.

Kostilin sent another letter home and did nothing but mope and wait for the money to arrive. He would sit in the barn day after day, either counting the days for the letter to come or sleeping. Jilin knew that his letter would not reach home, but he never wrote another.

"Where on earth could mother get so much money from?" he thought. "She lived mostly on what I used to send her, and if she has to procure five hundred roubles she'll be quite ruined. With God's help I'll get away myself."

So he kept his eyes open, planning how to run away.

He would walk about the village whistling, or doing something with his hands, such as modelling dolls out of clay, or plaiting baskets out of twigs. Jilin was very clever with his hands.

One day he modelled a doll with a nose, arms and legs and in a Tartar shirt, and he put this doll on the roof of the shed. The Tartar girls went to fetch water. The master's daughter Dina caught sight of the doll, and called to the others. They put down their pitchers and looked up laughing. Jilin took down the doll and held it out to them. They laughed, but dared not take it. He left the doll and went into the shed to see what would happen.

Dina ran up, looked about her, snatched up the doll and ran off with it.

The following morning, at daybreak, Dina came out on the threshold with the doll. She had bedecked it in bits of red stuff, and was rocking it to and fro like a baby and singing a lullaby. An old woman came out and began to scold her. She snatched the doll away from the child and broke it, and sent Dina off to her work.

Jilin made another doll—a better one this time—and gave it to Dina.

One day Dina brought Jilin a jug, and sitting down, she looked up at him, laughing and pointing to the jug.

"What is she so pleased about?" Jilin thought. He took up the jug to have a drink, thinking it was full of water, but it turned out to be milk. "How nice!" he said, and finished it. Dina was overjoyed.

"Nice, nice, Ivan!" She jumped up and clapped her hands in glee, then she seized the jug and ran away.

After that she brought Jilin milk in secret every day. When the Tartar women used to make cheese cakes out of goat's milk, which they baked on the roof, she would steal some and bring them to him. Once the master killed a sheep, and Dina brought Jilin a piece of the flesh hidden in her sleeve. She would throw the things down and run away.

One day there was a terrible storm; the rain poured down in torrents for a whole hour. The rivers became turbid. At the ford, the water rose till it was seven feet high and the current was so strong that it moved the stones along. Rivulets flowed everywhere and there was a roar in the hills. After the storm streams flowed down the village everywhere. Jilin asked his master for a knife, and with it he shaped a small cylinder and made a wheel out of a piece of board, to which he fixed two dolls, one on each side. The little girls brought him some bits of stuff with which he dressed the dolls—one as a peasant, the other as a peasant woman. He made them fast and set the wheel so that the stream should work it. When the wheel began to whirl the dolls danced.

The whole village gathered round—boys and girls and women and men came to look on, the latter clacking their tongues.

"Ah, Russ! Ah, Ivan!" they said.

Abdul had a Russian watch which was broken. He called Jilin and showed it to him. Jilin said, "Give it to me and I'll mend it."

He took it to pieces with the knife, sorted the pieces out, put them together again and the watch went quite well.

The master was pleased and presented him with one of his old tunics, all in holes. Jilin had to take it, besides, it would come in useful to cover up with at night.

From that day Jilin's fame as a man skilled in handiworks spread fast. People began to flock to him from distant villages, one bringing the lock of a rifle or a pistol that wanted mending; another a watch or a clock. The master gave him some tools—pincers, gimlets and a file.

One day a Tartar fell ill, and they came to Jilin, saying, "Come and heal him." Jilin did not know how to heal the sick, but he went just the same thinking, "The man will recover of his own accord." He disappeared into the shed and mixed up some sand and water. In the presence of the Tartars he mumbled some words over the mixture, and gave it to the sick man to drink. Fortunately the Tartar got well.

Jilin began to understand a little of their tongue. Some of the Tartars got quite used to him, and when they wanted him would call "Ivan, Ivan!" Others again looked at him askance as at some wild beast.

The red-bearded Tartar did not like Jilin. He frowned when he saw him, and either turned away or cursed. There was another old man, who did not live in the village, but somewhere at the foot of a hill. He came to the village only sometimes. Jilin saw him when the man went to the Mosque to say his prayers. He was short and had a white towel wound round his cap. His beard and moustaches were clipped and white as down; his face was wrinkled and brick-red. He had a hooked nose like a hawk's, and cruel grey eyes. He had no teeth, but two tusks in front. He would pass with his turban on his head, leaning on his staff, and peering round like a wolf. When he saw Jilin he snorted and turned away.

One day Jilin went to the hills to find out where the old man lived. He strolled down a path and saw a little garden and a stone wall; within the stone wall were wild cherry trees and peaches and a hut with a flat roof. He came a little closer and saw some hives made of plaited straw and humming bees flying hither and thither. The old man was on his knees, doing something to the hives. Jilin stood on tiptoe in order to get a better view; his shackles rattled. The old man turned and gave a yell and pulling a pistol out of his belt he aimed at Jilin, who just managed to shield himself behind the stone wall.

The old man came to the master to complain. The master summoned Jilin and laughing, asked him, "Why did you go to the old man's place?"

"I didn't mean to do him any harm," he said. "I only wanted to see how he lived."

The master conveyed his words to the old man.

But the old man was angry. He jabbered away, showing his tusks, and shook his fists menacingly at Jilin.

Jilin could not understand all he said, but he gathered that the old man was warning the master not to keep any Russians about the place, but to have them all killed.

The old man went away.

Jilin asked the master who the old man was, and the master said, "He is a great man! He was the bravest of us all, and killed many Russians, and he was rich, too. He had three wives and eight sons, who all lived in the same village. The Russians came, destroyed the village, and killed seven of his sons. One son only remained, and he surrendered to the Russians. The old man followed them, and also gave himself up. He lived with the Russians for three months, when he found his son. With his own hand he killed him and escaped. After that he gave up fighting. He went to Mecca to pray to God; that is why he wears a turban. Any man who has been to Mecca is called a Hadji and has to wear a turban. He does not like you Russians. He wanted me to kill you, but I can't kill you because I paid money for you. Besides, I have taken a fancy to you, Ivan; I would not let you go at all, if I had not given my word." He laughed and added in Russian, "You are a good fellow, Ivan, and I, Abdul, am a good fellow too."

IV

Jilin lived in this way for a month. During the day he wandered about the village or busied himself with some handicraft, and at night he dug in his shed. The digging was difficult because of the stones, but he worked away at them with his file and at last made a hole beneath the wall big enough to crawl through. "If only I knew the neighbourhood well and which way to turn," he thought; "the Tartars would not tell me."

He chose a day when the master was away, left the village after dinner and went up a hill, hoping to find out the lie of the land from there. But before the master departed he told one of his boys to look after Jilin and not let him out of his sight. The boy ran after Jilin, crying, "Don't go away! My father told you not to! I'll call for help!"

Jilin tried to soothe him.

"I'm not going far," he said. "I only want to go to the top of that hill to find a certain herb with which to cure your people when they are sick. Come with me; I can't run away with the shackles on my feet. I'll make you a bow and some arrows to-morrow."

After some persuasion the boy went with him. The hill did not seem very far off, but it was difficult to get there shackled as he was. He struggled and struggled until he got to the top. Jilin sat down and began to look about him. To the south, beyond the shed, a herd of horses could be seen in a valley, and at the bottom of the valley was another village. Beyond the village was a steep hill and another hill beyond that. Between the two hills was a dark patch that looked like a wood; hill upon hill rose beyond it, and higher than all rose the snow-capped mountains as white as sugar, the peak of one standing out above the rest. To the east and west were other such hills; here and there were villages in the valleys from which the smoke curled up. "This is all Tartar country," he thought. He looked in the direction of Russia—below was a river, and the village he lived in, surrounded by gardens. On the river bank, looking as tiny as dolls, sat Tartar women, washing clothes. Beyond the village was a hill, lower than the one to the south and beyond that two wooded hills. Between these two hills was a plain and away in the distance on this plain smoke seemed to rise. Jilin tried to recollect where the sun rose and set when he lived in the fort. He came to the conclusion that the fortress must lie in that very valley. Between these two hills would he have to make his way when he escaped.

The sun began to set. The snow-clad mountains turned from white to red; the dark mountains grew darker still; a vapour rose from the valley, and the plain where he supposed the fortress to be seemed on fire with the sunset's glow. Jilin gazed intently; something seemed to quiver in that plain, like smoke rising from a chimney, and Jilin felt sure that the Russian fortress was there.

It was getting late. The Mullah's cry was heard. The flocks and herds were driven home; the cows were lowing. The boy kept on begging "Come home," but Jilin had no desire to move.

They returned home. "Now that I know the place I must lose no time in running away," Jilin thought. He wanted to escape that very night, for the nights were dark then; the moon had waned, but as luck would have it, the Tartars returned that evening. Sometimes when they brought cattle home they would come back in a jolly mood, but this time there were no cattle, and on the saddle of his horse they brought back the red-bearded Tartar's brother who had been killed. They returned in a gloomy mood and gathered the village together for the burial. Jilin, too, came out to look on. They wrapped the body in a sheet and without a coffin carried it out and laid it on the grass beneath some plane-trees. The Mullah arrived and the old men; they wrapped towels around their caps, took off their shoes, and squatted down on their heels before the body. In front was the Mullah, behind him three old men in turbans, and behind them three other Tartars. They sat silent, eyes downcast, for a long time, then the Mullah raised his head and said, "Allah!" (meaning God). After this word he again bowed his head, and there was another long silence. They all sat motionless. Again the Mullah raised his head and said "Allah!" All repeated "Allah!" and again there was silence. The dead man lay on the grass motionless and the others, too, seemed dead. Not a single man moved. The only sound to be heard was the rustling of the leaves on the plane-trees. After a while the Mullah said a prayer; all rose, and raising the dead man with their hands they carried him away. They brought him to a pit. It was not an ordinary pit, but hollowed out under the ground like a vault. They lifted the dead man under the arms, bent him into a sitting posture and let him down into the pit, gently, his hands folded in front of him.

The master's servant brought some green rushes which they stuffed into the pit, then they hastily covered it with earth, levelled the ground properly and placed a stone, upright, at the head of the grave. They stamped down the soil and once more sat down round the grave side by side. For a long time they were silent.

"Allah! Allah!" they sighed and rose.

The red-bearded Tartar gave some money to the old men, then he took a whip, struck himself three times on the forehead and went home.

In the morning Jilin saw the red-bearded Tartar leading a mare out of the village, followed by three other Tartars. When they left the village behind them the red-bearded Tartar took off his coat, rolled up his sleeves—his arms were strong and muscular—and taking out a dagger, he sharpened it on a whetstone. The other Tartars raised the mare's head and he cut her throat. The mare dropped down and he began to skin her with his big hands. Women and girls came up and washed the entrails. The mare was cut up and the pieces carried to the red Tartar's hut, where the whole village gathered for a funeral feast.

For three days they ate the mare's flesh and drank beer in honour of the dead man. All the Tartars were at home. On the fourth day, about dinner time, Jilin saw that they were preparing to go away somewhere. The horses were brought out, they got ready, and about ten of the Tartars, the red one among them, went away, Abdul remaining at home. There was a new moon and the nights were still dark.

"To-night we must escape," Jilin thought, and he unfolded his plan to Kostilin. But Kostilin was afraid.

"How can we run away? We don't know the way even."

"I know the way."

"We couldn't get there in one night."

"If we can't, we can hide in the wood. I've got some cakes here for us to eat. What's the good of sitting here? If they send your ransom, well and good, but supposing they can't raise the money? The Tartars are getting vicious because our people have killed one of their men. They will probably kill us."

Kostilin reflected.

"Very well; let us go," he said.

V

Jilin went down the hole and made it a little bigger so that Kostilin could crawl through, then they sat down to wait till all grew quiet in the village.

When the Tartars had all retired to rest Jilin crawled under the wall and got outside. "Follow me," he whispered to Kostilin.

Kostilin crept into the hole, but his foot hit against a stone and made a clatter. The master had a speckled watch-dog—a vicious creature it was, called Ulashin. The dog growled and rushed forward, followed by other dogs. Jilin gave a low whistle and threw it a cake. Ulashin recognized him, wagged his tail and ceased his growling.

The master heard the dog and called from the hut, "Hait, hait, Ulashin!"

But Jilin stroked the dog by the ears and it did not move. It rubbed itself against Jilin's legs and wagged its tail.

They sat crouching round the corner. All grew quiet; only a sheep was heard to cough in a barn, and below, the water rippled over the stones. It was dark; the stars were high in the sky and the new moon looked red as it set behind the hill, horns upwards. A mist as white as milk lay over the valley.

Jilin got up and turning to Kostilin said, "Let us come, brother."

They set off, but they had no sooner done so than the Mullah intoned from the roof "Allah Besmilla! Ilrachman!" That meant that the people would be going to the Mosque. They sat down again, crouching behind the wall. For a long time they sat there waiting till the people went past. All grew quiet again.

"Now then; with God's help we must get away," Jilin said.

They crossed themselves and started. They went through the yard and downhill to the river which they forded and came out into the valley. The mist hung low and dense; above, the stars were visible. By the stars Jilin could tell the direction they had to take. It was cool in the mist and walking was easy, only their boots were uncomfortable, being old and worn out. Jilin cast his off and went bare-foot. He leapt over the stones, gazing up at the stars. Kostilin began to lag behind.

"Slower, please," he said, "these cursed boots hurt my feet."

"Take them off and you'll find it easier."

Kostilin too went barefoot, but that was still worse. The stones cut his feet and he lagged behind more than ever.

Jilin said to him, "The cuts on your feet will heal up soon enough, but if the Tartars catch us it will be much more serious; they will kill us."

Kostilin did not say anything, but walked along, groaning.

They walked along the valley for a long time, when suddenly they heard the barking of dogs. Jilin stopped and looked about him. He climbed up the hill on all fours.

"We mistook our way, and turned to the right. Another Tartar village lies here; I saw it from the hill the other day. We must turn back and go to the left up the hill. There must be a wood here."

And Kostilin said, "Let us rest a while; my feet are all bleeding."

"They'll get better in good time, brother. Walk more lightly—like this."

And Jilin turned back and went up the hill to the left into the wood. Kostilin kept on lagging behind and groaning. Jilin remonstrated with him and walked on ahead.

They reached the top of the hill, where they found a wood, as Jilin had surmised. They went into it. The brambles tore the last of their clothes. At last they found a path and followed it.

"Stop!" Jilin said. There was a trampling of hoofs on the path. They listened. It sounded like the trampling of horses' hoofs, but the sound ceased. They moved on and again they heard the trampling. They stopped again, and the sound ceased. Jilin crept nearer and in a patch of light on the path he saw something standing. It seemed like a horse, yet not like a horse, and it had something queer on its back that was not a man. The creature snorted. "What a strange thing!" Jilin thought, and gave a low whistle. The animal bounded off the path into the thicket and there was a sound of cracking branches as though a storm had swept through the wood.

Kostilin fell to the ground in terror; Jilin laughed, saying, "It's a stag. Can't you hear how it's breaking the branches with its antlers? We are afraid of him and he is afraid of us."

They went on further. The Great Bear was already setting and the dawn was not far off. They did not know whether they were going in the right direction. It seemed to Jilin that the Tartars had brought him along this path when they captured him and that it was still another seven miles to the fortress, but he had nothing certain to go by, and at night one could easily mistake the way.

Kostilin dropped to the ground and said, "Do what you like, but I can't go any further. My legs won't carry me."

Jilin attempted persuasion.

"It's no good," Kostilin said; "I can't go on."

Jilin grew angry and vented his disgust.

"Then I'm going alone—good-bye."

Kostilin jumped up and followed.

They walked another three miles. The mist grew denser; they could not see ahead of them and the stars were no longer visible.

They suddenly heard a trampling of horses coming from the direction in which they were going. They could hear the horse's hoofs hit against the stones. Jilin lay flat down and put his ear to the ground to listen.

"There is certainly a horseman coming towards us," he said. They ran off the path into the thicket and sat down to wait. After a while Jilin crept out into the path to look. A mounted Tartar was coming along, driving a cow and humming softly to himself. When he had passed Jilin turned to Kostilin, "Thank God the danger is over. Come, let us go."

Kostilin attempted to rise, but dropped down again.

"I can't, I can't! I've no more strength left."

The man was heavy and stout and had perspired freely. The heavy mist had chilled him, tired and bleeding as he was, and made him quite stiff. Jilin tried to lift him, but Kostilin cried out, "Oh, it hurts!"

Jilin turned to stone.

"Why did you shout? The Tartar is still near; he will have heard you," he remonstrated, while to himself he thought, "The man is evidently exhausted; what shall I do with him? I can't desert him." "Come," he said, "climb on to my back, then, and I'll carry you if you really can't walk."

He helped Kostilin up, put his arms under his thighs and carried him on to the path.

"For heaven's sake don't put your arms round my neck or you'll throttle me. Hold on to my shoulders."

It was hard work for Jilin; his feet, too, were bleeding and tired. He bent down now and then to get him in a more comfortable position, or jerked him up so that he sat higher up, and went on his weary way.

The Tartar had evidently heard Kostilin's cry. Jilin heard some one following behind, calling out in the Tartar tongue. Jilin rushed into the thicket. The Tartar seized his gun and aimed; the shot missed; the Tartar yelled and galloped down the path.

"I'm afraid we're lost," Jilin said. "He'll collect the Tartars to hunt us down. If we don't cover a couple of miles before they've time to set out, nothing will save us." To himself he thought, "Why the devil did I saddle myself with this block? I should have got there long ago had I been alone."

Kostilin said, "Why should you be caught because of me?"

"I can't go alone; it would be mean to desert a comrade."

Again he raised Kostilin on to his shoulders and went on. They walked along for another half-mile. They were still in the wood and could not see the end of it. The mist had dispersed; the clouds seemed to gather; the stars were no longer visible. Jilin was worn out. They came to a spring walled in by stones. He stopped and put Kostilin down.

"Let us rest a minute or two and have a drink and a bite of this cake. We can't be very far off now."

He had no sooner lain down to take a drink from the spring than he heard the stamping of horses behind him. Again they rushed into the thicket to the right and lay down on a slope.

They heard a sound of Tartar voices. The Tartars stopped at the very spot where they had turned off the path. They seemed to confer for a bit and then set a dog on the scent. There was a crackling among the bushes and a strange dog appeared. It stopped and began to bark. The Tartars followed it. They were also strangers. They bound Jilin and Kostilin and took them off on their horses.

When they had ridden for about two miles they were met by the master, Abdul, and two other Tartars. He exchanged some words with the strange Tartars, after which Jilin and Kostilin were removed to his horses and he took them back to the village.

Abdul was no longer laughing, and did not say a word to them.

They reached the village at daybreak and were placed in the street. The children gathered round them and threw stones at them and lashed them with whips, yelling all the time.

All the Tartars collected in a circle, the old man from the hills among them. They began to talk; Jilin gathered that they were considering what was to be done with him and Kostilin. Some said that they should be sent into the hills, and the old man persisted that they should be killed. Abdul would not agree to either plan, saying, "I paid money for them and must get their ransom."

The old man said, "They will not pay the ransom; they'll only do a great deal of harm. It is a sin to keep Russians. Kill them and have done with it."

The Tartars dispersed. The master came to Jilin and said to him, "If your ransom does not come in two weeks, I'll have you flogged, and if you attempt to run away again, I'll kill you like a dog. Write home, and write to the point!"

They brought them pen and paper and they wrote home. The shackles were put on them and they were taken behind the Mosque, where there was a pit of about twelve feet deep, into which they were flung.

VI

Life was very hard for them now. Their shackles were never removed, and they were never allowed out into the fresh air. Raw dough was thrown down to them, as one throws a scrap to a dog, and water was let down in a jug. The stench in the pit was awful and it was damp as well. Kostilin grew quite ill; he swelled very much and every bone in his body ached. He either groaned or slept all the time. Jilin, too, was depressed; he saw that their position was hopeless and did not know how to get out of it.

He tried to make a tunnel but there was nowhere to throw the earth, and when the master saw it, he threatened to kill him.

One day when he was most downcast, squatting in the pit and thinking of his freedom, a cake fell from above, then another, and some cherries rained down. Jilin looked up and saw Dina. She looked at him, laughed and ran away.

"I wonder if Dina would help us?" Jilin thought.

He cleared a space in the pit, dug a little clay and began to make some dolls. He moulded some men and horses and dogs, thinking, "When Dina comes, I will throw these up to her."

But Dina did not come the next day. Jilin heard a stamping of horses; some Tartars seemed to have come and all gathered at the Mosque, shouting and arguing. It was something about the Russians. The voice of the old man was heard, too. Jilin could not understand all they said, but he made out that the Russians were near, that the Tartars were afraid of them and did not know what to do with their prisoners.

After a while they dispersed. Suddenly Jilin heard a rustling overhead and saw Dina crouching at the edge of the pit, her knees higher than her head. She bent over so that the coins at the end of her plaits dangled over the pit. Her eyes were twinkling like two stars. From her sleeve she took two cakes made of cheese and threw them down to him. Jilin picked them up and said, "What a long time it is since you've been to see me! I've made you some toys. Look, here they are!" He threw them up to her one by one. She shook her head and averted her gaze. "I don't want them, Ivan," she said. "They want to kill you, Ivan," she added, pointing to her throat.

"Who wants to kill me?"

"My father. The old man told him to, but I'm sorry for you."

Jilin said, “If you are sorry for me, bring me a long pole.”

She shook her head, as much as to say that it was impossible.

He put up his hands and implored her, “Please, Dina! Be a dear and bring it!”

“I can’t,” she said; “they’ll catch me at home.” Then she went away.

In the evening Jilin sat in the pit wondering what would happen. He kept looking up; the stars were visible, but the moon had not yet risen. The Mullah’s call was heard, and all grew quiet. Jilin began to doze, thinking “The child is afraid.” Suddenly some clay dropped on to his head. He looked up, and saw a long pole poking into the opposite wall of the pit; it began to slide down. Jilin took hold of it and lowered it with a feeling of gladness at his heart. It was a stout, strong pole; he had noticed it many times on the roof of the master’s hut.

He looked up. The stars were shining high in the sky and above the pit Dina’s eyes gleamed in the darkness like a cat’s. She leant her head over the pit and whispered, “Ivan, Ivan!” making signs to him to speak low.

“What is it?” Jilin asked.

“They’ve all gone but two.”

“Come, Kostilin,” Jilin said; “let us try our luck for the last time; I’ll help you up.”

But Kostilin would not listen to him.

“No,” he said; “it seems that I can’t get away from here. How can I come when I’ve hardly strength enough to move?”

“Well, good-bye, then. Don’t think ill of me.”

He kissed Kostilin, and seizing the pole, he asked Dina to hold it at the top and swarmed up. Twice he fell back again; the shackles hindered him. But Jilin persevered and got to the top somehow. Dina clutched hold of his shirt and pulled at him with all her might, unable to control her laughter.

When he clambered out Jilin handed her the pole, saying, "Put it back in its place, Dina, for if they notice its absence they'll beat you."

Dina dragged the pole away, and Jilin went down the hill. When he got to the bottom he sat down under its shelter, took a sharp stone and tried to wrench the lock off the shackles. But the lock was a strong one and would not give way, and it was difficult to get at it. Suddenly he heard some one coming downhill, skipping lightly. "It must be Dina again," he thought.

She came up, took the stone and said, "Let me try."

She knelt down and tried to wrench the lock off, but her little hands were as slender as little twigs and there was no strength in them. She threw the stone down and burst into tears. Jilin made another attempt, while Dina squatted down beside him and put her hand on his shoulder.

Jilin looked round; to the left the sky was all red; the moon was beginning to rise. "I must cross the valley and be under shelter of the wood before the moon rises," he thought. He got up and threw away the stone. "I must go as I am in the shackles. Good-bye, Dina, dear; I shall always remember you."

Dina seized hold of him and groped about his coat with her hand to find a place to thrust some cakes into. Jilin took the cakes.

"Thank you, little one," he said. "There won't be any one to make you dolls when I am gone." He stroked her head.

Dina burst into tears and, covering her face with her hands, she fled up the hill, bounding along like a wild goat. The coins in her plait could be heard jingling in the darkness.

Jilin crossed himself, took the lock of his shackles in his hand to prevent a clatter and started on his way, dragging his shackled leg and gazing at the red in the sky where the moon was rising. This time he knew the way. He had to go straight on for six miles. If only he could reach the wood before the moon had quite risen! He forded the river. The red light over the hill had paled. He walked along the valley, looking back now and then; the moon was not yet visible. The light grew brighter and brighter; one side of the valley was quite light. The shadows crept along the foot of the hill, drawing nearer to him.

Jilin kept in the shadow. He hurried, but the moon moved faster than he; the hilltops on the right were already lit up. As he neared the wood, the moon rose over the hills, all white, and it grew as light as day. All the leaves on the trees could be seen distinctly. It was still and light on the hills; there was a dead silence, except for the murmur of the river below.

He reached the wood without meeting any one. He chose a dark spot and sat down to rest.

When he had rested a while and eaten a cake, he found a stone and once more tried to wrench the lock of the shackles. He cut his hands, but could not manage it. He rose and went on his way. After a mile he was quite worn out and his feet ached terribly. At every dozen steps or so he stopped. "It can't be helped," he thought. "I must drag myself on so long as my strength holds out, for if I once sit down I shan't be able to get up again. I can't reach the fortress to-night, that is obvious; as soon as it gets light I'll hide in the wood and go on again when it gets dark."

He walked the whole night, meeting only two Tartars, but Jilin heard them from a distance and took refuge behind a tree.

The moon began to pale; the dew fell; it was near dawn, but Jilin had not yet reached the end of the wood. "I'll walk another thirty steps or so then I'll creep into the thicket and sit down," he thought. He covered the thirty steps and saw that he had come to the edge of the wood. When he came out it was quite light. Before him stretched the steppe and to the left, near the foot of a hill, he saw a dying fire from which the smoke rose and men were sitting about it.

He looked intently; there was a flash of guns—they were soldiers, Cossacks!

Jilin was overjoyed. He summoned his remaining strength and began to descend the hill, thinking, "God forbid that any mounted Tartar should see me now in the open field; though near my own people, I could not escape."

The thought had no sooner crossed his mind than he saw three Tartars standing on a hill, not more than a few yards away. They had seen him and dashed down towards him. His heart gave a great bound. He waved his arms and shouted with all his might, "Help, help, brothers!"

The soldiers heard him; a few Cossacks sprang upon their horses and dashed forward to cut across the Tartars' path.

The Cossacks were far off and the Tartars were near, but Jilin made one last effort; lifting the shackles with his hand, he ran towards the Cossacks. He hardly knew what he was doing and crossed himself wildly, crying, "Help, brothers, help!"

The Cossacks numbered about fifteen.

The Tartars grew afraid and stopped in hesitation before they reached him. Jilin managed to get to the Cossacks. They surrounded him, asking who he was and where he came from, but Jilin was quite beside himself and could only repeat, through his tears, "Brothers, brothers!"

The soldiers came up and crowded round him, one giving him bread, another porridge, another some vodka to drink, another gave him his cloak to cover him, and another wrenched off the shackles.

The officers recognized him and took him to the fortress. His men were delighted to see him; his fellow-officers gathered about him.

Jilin told them all that had happened to him and ended by saying, "That's how I went home and got married. I wasn't meant to marry, evidently."

And Jilin remained in the army in the Caucasus. It was not until a month later that Kostilin was released, after paying a ransom of five thousand roubles. He was brought back in a half-dead condition.

EMELIAN AND THE EMPTY DRUM

Emelian was a labourer and worked for a master. He was walking through a field one day on his way to work, when a frog hopped in front of him and he just missed crushing it by stepping across. Suddenly some one called to him from behind. He turned, and there stood a beautiful maiden, who said to him, “Why don’t you marry, Emelian?”

“How can I, dear maiden? I possess nothing but the clothes I stand up in, and who would have a husband like that?”

“Marry me,” the maiden said.

Emelian looked at her in admiration.

“I would with pleasure,” he said, “but how should we live?”

“What a thing to trouble about,indeed!” the maiden said. “One has only to work the more and sleep the less and one can always be clothed and fed.”

“Very well; let us marry, then,” Emelian said. “Where shall we live?”

“In the town.”

Emelian and the maiden went to the town. She took him to a little house on the very edge and they married and set up housekeeping.

One day the King went for a drive beyond the town, and when passing Emelian’s gate, Emelian’s wife came out to look at him. When the King saw her he marvelled.

“What a beauty!” he thought. He stopped the carriage and called her to him.

“Who are you?” he asked.

“Emelian the peasant’s wife.”

“How came a beauty like you to marry a peasant?” he asked. “You should have been a queen."

"Thank you for your kind words," she said; "a peasant husband is good enough for me."

The King talked to her a while and went on his way. When he returned to the palace Emelian's wife did not go out of his head for a moment. The whole night he could not sleep and kept on thinking how he could take her away from Emelian, but no possible way occurred to him. He summoned his servants and asked them to think of a way.

And the servants said to him, "Get Emelian to come and be a labourer in the palace. We will wear him out with work, then his wife will become a widow and you can have her."

The King followed their advice. He sent a messenger to tell Emelian that he was to come and be a yard-porter in the palace and bring his wife to live with him there.

The messenger came to Emelian and repeated the King's words. And Emelian's wife said to her husband, "It can't be helped; you must go. You can work there in the day and return to me at night."

Emelian went away. When he came to the palace the King's steward said to him, "Why have you come without your wife?"

"Why should I drag her about with me? She has a home of her own."

In the King's yard Emelian was given enough work for two men. Emelian set about it, not expecting to get it all finished, but behold! before evening came it was all done. The steward, seeing that he had got through the work, gave him four times as much for the morrow.

Emelian went home. The house was scrubbed and cleaned, the fire lighted, the bread baked, the supper cooked. His wife was sitting at the table sewing, waiting for him. She flew to the door to meet him, then laid the supper and fed him well; afterwards she began to ask him about his work.

"It's rather bad," he said; "they set me tasks beyond my strength; they wear me out with too much work."

"Don't you think about the work," she said, "don't look back to see how much you have done, nor look ahead to see how much there is left. Just keep straight on and all will be done in time."

Emelian went to bed. In the morning he again set out to the palace. He began his work and did not look round once, and behold! by evening it was all finished; he went home when it was still light.

Again they increased Emelian's work, but Emelian finished it all in time and went home for the night as usual. A week passed. The King's servants saw that they could not get the better of Emelian by giving him rough work so they gave him difficult work instead, but even that did not help. No matter what they set him to do—carpentering, stone-cutting, thatching—he got everything done in time and went home for the night to his wife. Another week passed.

The King summoned his servants and said, "Is it for nothing that I keep you? Two weeks have passed and still I do not see the fruits of your work. You promised to wear Emelian out with work and each night from my window I see him going home singing to himself. Are you making sport of me, eh?"

The King's servants began to excuse themselves. "We are doing the best we can. We thought at first to wear him out with rough work, but you can't get him anyhow. We set him all kinds of tasks, such as sweeping, but he doesn't know what it means to be tired. Then we gave him difficult work, thinking that he wouldn't have brains enough to do it, yet still, we couldn't get the better of him. No matter what the work, he tackles it and gets it all done in time. He must either be extraordinarily strong or his wife must be a witch. We are sick of him ourselves. We want to set him such a task that he cannot possibly do. We thought of asking him to build a temple in a single day. You must send for him and command him to build a temple opposite the palace in a single day, and if he fails to do it, we can cut off his head for disobedience."

The King sent for Emelian.

"Build me a new temple in the square opposite the palace; by to-morrow evening it must all be finished. If you do it, I will reward you; if not, I will cut off your head."

Emelian listened to the King's words; then turned and went his way home. When he got there he said to his wife, "Make yourself ready, wife; we must run away or else we are both lost."

"Why," she said, "have you grown so faint-hearted that you want to run away?"

"How can I help it when the King commanded me to build a temple to-morrow before nightfall? If I fail to do it, he will have my head cut off. There is only one way out. We must run away while there is yet time."

The wife did not approve of his words.

"The King has many soldiers; we shall not be able to escape them. And while you have strength enough you must obey the King's command."

"But how can I obey if it's beyond my strength?"

"My dear, don't get excited. Have your supper and go to bed; get up early in the morning and you'll manage in good time."

Emelian went to bed. His wife woke him in the morning.

"Go," she said; "make haste and finish the temple. Here are nails and a hammer. There is still a day's work for you left to do."

Emelian set out. When he came to the square, there in the middle stood a new temple not quite finished. Emelian set to work to finish it and by the evening it was all done.

The King awoke and looking out of the palace window he saw a new temple in the square. Emelian was busy around, knocking a nail in here and there. The King was not pleased with the temple; he was annoyed that he had no pretext for cutting off Emelian's head and taking his wife for himself.

Again the King summoned his servants.

"Emelian has done this task too," he said, "and I have no reason for cutting off his head. This was not difficult enough; we must give him something more difficult still. You decide what it shall be, or else I'll have your heads cut off first."

And the servants bethought them to set Emelian to make a river that was to wind round the palace and have ships sailing on it.

The King summoned Emelian and set him the new task.

"If you could make a temple in a single night," he said, "you can do this too. See that it is all finished by to-morrow, or else I shall cut off your head."

Emelian's spirits fell lower than ever and he went home to his wife in a sad mood.

"Why so sad?" asked his wife. "Has the King set you a new task?"

Emelian told her what it was.

"We must run away," he concluded.

And the wife said, "We cannot escape the soldiers. You must obey."

"But how can I?"

"My dear, don't worry. Have your supper and go to bed. Get up early in the morning and all will be ready in time."

Emelian went to bed. In the morning his wife woke him.

"Go to the palace," she said; "everything is finished. Only by the harbour, opposite the palace, there is a little mound that wants levelling; take the spade and level it."

Emelian set out. He came to the town and there around the palace a river flowed with ships sailing on it. Emelian went up to the harbour opposite the palace and he saw an uneven place and began to level it.

The King awoke and looking out of his palace window he saw a river where there was not one before and ships were sailing on it and Emelian was levelling a little mound with his spade. And the King was alarmed. He took no pleasure in the river or the ships, he was only annoyed that he could not cut off Emelian's head. "There is no task he cannot do," he thought. "What shall we do now?"

And the King summoned his servants and conferred with them.

"Think of a task," he said, "that will be beyond Emelian's strength, for so far he has done everything we have thought of and I cannot take away his wife."

And the courtiers thought for a long time, then came to the King and said, "You must summon Emelian and say to him, 'Go to—I don't know where, and bring me—I don't know what.' He won't be able to escape you then, for wherever he goes you can say it was not the right place and whatever he brings was not the right thing. Then you can cut off his head and take away his wife."

The King was pleased with the idea. He sent for Emelian and said to him, "Go to—I don't know where, and bring me—I don't know what. And if you don't, I'll cut off your head."

Emelian went back to his wife and told her what the King had said. The wife reflected.

"Well," she said. "Be it on the King's own head what his courtiers have taught him. We must act with cunning now."

She sat and thought it over for a while; then said to her husband, "You must go a long way to our old grandmother, a peasant soldier's mother, and ask her to help you. She will give you something which you must take straight to the palace and I will be there already. I cannot escape them now; they will take me by force, but only for a short while. If you do what grandmother tells you, you will soon set me free."

And the wife prepared Emelian for the journey and gave him a bundle and a spindle.

"Give grandmother this spindle," she said; "by this she will know that you are my husband."

And the wife showed him the way. Emelian left the town and saw some soldiers drilling. He stopped and watched them. The soldiers finished their drill and sat down to rest. Emelian approached them and asked, "Can you tell me, mates, how to get to—I don't know where and bring back—I don't know what."

The soldiers were perplexed at his words.

"Who sent you?" they asked.

"The King," he said.

"We too," they said, "since the day we became soldiers want to go to—we don't know where and find—we don't know what, but we've never been able to find it and so cannot help you."

Emelian sat with the soldiers awhile then went on his way. He wandered and wandered till he came to a wood. In the wood was a cottage and in the cottage sat an old woman, a peasant soldier's mother, spinning at her wheel, and she wept as she spun and moistened her fingers with the tears that flowed from her eyes.

"Who are you?" she cried in anger when she saw Emelian.

Emelian gave her the spindle and said that his wife had sent him. The old woman instantly softened and began to ask him questions. And Emelian told her his whole story of how he had married the maiden and gone to live in the town, and how he had been taken to the King's as a yard-porter, and of the work he had done in the palace, and the temple he had built in a night, and the river and ships he had made, and that now the King had sent him to—I don't know where to bring back—I don't know what.

The old woman listened to what he had to say and ceased her weeping. She began to mutter to herself, "The time has come, I see. Very well," she said aloud; "sit down, my son, and have something to eat."

Emelian had something to eat and the old woman said to him, "Here is a ball of thread; roll it before you and follow wherever it leads. You will have to go a long way, to the very sea. When you come to the sea you will see a large town. Ask to be allowed to stay the night in the outermost house and look for what you want there."

"But by what signs shall I know it, grandmother?"

"When you see that which men listen to more than to father or mother, that will be the thing you want. Seize it and take it to the King. He will tell you-you haven't brought the right thing, and you must say to him, 'If it is not the right thing then I must break it.' Then strike this thing; carry it out to the river; break it and throw it into the water. Then you will get back your wife and dry up my tears."

Emelian took leave of the grandmother and went where the ball of thread took him to. The ball rolled and rolled till it brought him to the sea, where there was a large town. Emelian knocked at a house and asked to be allowed to stay the night. The people let him in. He went to bed. In the morning he woke early and heard the father of the house trying to wake his son to chop some wood. The son would not listen to him. "It is early yet," he said, "there's plenty of time."

And he heard the mother near the stove say, "Do go, my son. Your father's bones ache; surely you wouldn't let him go? Get up."

The son only smacked his lips and went to sleep again. He had no sooner fallen asleep than there was a banging and a rumbling in the street. The son jumped up, dressed and ran out. Emelian ran out after him to see what it was that a son obeyed more than father or mother.

When Emelian got outside he saw a man coming up the street carrying some round object on his belly that he was beating with sticks. It was this thing that had made the noise and that the son had obeyed. Emelian approached and examined it. The thing was round like a small tub with skin drawn tightly on either side of it.

"What is this thing called?" he asked.

"A drum," they said.

"Is it empty?"

"Yes," they said.

Emelian wondered and asked the people to give him the thing, but they would not. Emelian gave up asking and followed the drummer. He walked about the whole day and when the drummer went to bed at night, Emelian seized the drum and ran away with it. He ran and ran until he came to his own town. He wanted to give his wife a surprise, but she was not at home. She had been taken to the King the day after Emelian had left.

Emelian went to the palace and asked to be announced as the man who had gone to—I don't know where and brought back—I don't know what. The King was informed of his return and he ordered Emelian to come to him on the morrow. Emelian again demanded to see the King, saying, "I have brought back what I was ordered to; let the King come out to me, or I will go in to him myself."

The King came out.

"Where have you been?" he asked.

Emelian told him.

"That was not the place," he said. "And what have you brought?"

Emelian wanted to show him, but the King would not even look.

"That was not the thing," he said.

"If it is not the thing," Emelian said, "I must break it and let it go to the devil."

Emelian came out of the palace and struck the drum. He had no sooner done so than all the King's troops gathered around him. They saluted Emelian and waited for his commands. From the window of his palace the King called to the troops, forbidding them to follow Emelian, but the troops would not listen to the King and followed Emelian. When the King saw this he ordered Emelian's wife to be given back to him and he begged Emelian to give him the drum.

"I can't," Emelian said. "I was told to break it and throw the bits into the river."

Emelian took the drum to the river and the soldiers followed him. Emelian struck the drum and broke it into little bits which he threw into the water and the troops all scattered and dispersed. And Emelian took his wife back home.

From that day the King left off worrying him and Emelian and his wife lived happily ever after.

THE GREAT BEAR

A long, long time ago there was a big drought on the earth. All the rivers dried up and the streams and wells, and the trees withered and the bushes and grass, and men and beasts died of thirst.

One night a little girl went out with a pitcher to find some water for her sick mother. She wandered and wandered everywhere, but could find no water, and she grew so tired that she lay down on the grass and fell asleep. When she awoke and took up the pitcher she nearly upset the water it contained. The pitcher was full of clear, fresh water. The little girl was glad and was about to put it to her lips, but she remembered her mother and ran home with the pitcher as fast as she could. She hurried so much that she did not notice a little dog in her path; she stumbled over it and dropped the pitcher. The dog whined pitifully; the little girl seized the pitcher.

She thought the water would have been upset, but the pitcher stood upright and the water was there as before. She poured a little into the palm of her hand and the dog lapped it and was comforted. When the little girl again took up the pitcher, it had turned from common wood to silver. She took the pitcher home and gave it to her mother.

The mother said, "I shall die just the same; you had better drink it," and she handed the pitcher to the child. In that moment the pitcher turned from silver to gold. The little girl could no longer contain herself and was about to put the pitcher to her lips, when the door opened and a stranger entered who begged for a drink. The little girl swallowed her saliva and gave the pitcher to him. And suddenly seven large diamonds sprang out of the pitcher and a stream of clear, fresh water flowed from it. And the seven diamonds began to rise, and they rose higher and higher till they reached the sky and became the Great Bear.

THREE QUESTIONS

It once occurred to a King that if he knew the right moment when to begin on any work and the right kind of people to have or not to have dealings with and the thing to do that was more important than any other thing, he would always be successful.

And he proclaimed throughout his kingdom that he would give a great reward to any one who could tell him what was the right moment for any action, and who were the most essential of all people, and what was the most essential thing of all to do.

Many learned men came to the King and answered his questions in different ways.

In answer to the first question some said that to know the right time for any action, one must draw up a time-table of all the days, months and years and observe it strictly, then one could do everything at the proper time. Others said that it was impossible to decide beforehand the proper time for any action; the only thing one could do was to waste no time in vain amusements, but to pay attention to what was going on around one, and to do the thing that came to hand. A third said that however attentive the King might be to what went on around him, one man alone could not decide the proper time for every action and that he needed a council of wise men to advise him. Still a fourth maintained that as certain action had to be decided at once and could not wait a council the proper thing to do was to find out beforehand what was going to happen so as to be always prepared. But as only magicians knew what was going to happen, then it followed that in order to find out the proper time for any action one must consult the magicians.

The second question, too, was answered in various ways. Some said that the most essential people to the King were his helpers and ministers; others said priests; still others that the most essential people to the King were doctors; a fourth party said that the most essential people to the King were soldiers.

To the third question about the most important occupation, some declared it was science, others, the art of war, and others, divine worship.

The answers being different, the King agreed with none of them and gave no man the promised reward. But still wishing to find out the answers to his questions, he resolved to consult a hermit who was famous throughout the land for his wisdom.

The hermit lived in a wood which he never left, and received none but common folk. For this reason the King put on simple garments, and, dismissing his body-guard before he reached the hermit's cell, he climbed down from his horse and went the rest of the way alone and on foot.

He found the hermit digging a bed in front of the hermitage. When the hermit saw the King, he greeted him and went on with his digging. He was frail and thin and each time he dug his spade into the ground and turned over a little soil, he gasped for breath.

The King approached him and said, "I have come, oh, wise hermit, to ask you to give me the answers to these three questions—what hour must one remember and not allow to slip by, so as not to regret it afterwards? What people are the most essential and with whom should one or should one not have dealings? What things are the most essential to do and which of those things must one do first of all?"

The hermit heard what the King had to say, but made no reply. He spat on his hand and went on with his digging.

"You are tired," the King said; "give me the spade and I will do the digging for you."

The King took the spade and began to dig, but after a while he stopped and repeated his question. The hermit made no reply, but stretched out his hand for the spade.

"You rest now," he said, "and I will work."

But the King would not give up the spade and went on with the digging. One hour passed and another; the sun began to set behind the trees when the

King stuck his spade into the ground and said, "I came to you, wise man, to find the answers to my three questions. If you cannot answer them, then tell me and I will go my way home."

"Some one is running hither," the hermit said. "Let us see who it is."

The King turned and saw a bearded man running towards them. The man's hands were clasped over his stomach and the blood flowed from beneath them. He fell at the King's feet and lay motionless, rolling his eyes and moaning faintly.

The King and the hermit unfastened the man's clothes. He had a large wound in his stomach. The King bathed it as well as he could with his handkerchief and bandaged it with the hermit's towel. The blood did not cease to flow, and several times the King had to remove the bandages, soaked with warm blood, and rebathe and rebandage the wound.

When the blood ceased to flow, the wounded man came to himself and asked for some water. The King brought some fresh water and raised it to the wounded man's lips.

The sun had quite set meanwhile and it began to get cold. The King, with the hermit's help, carried the wounded man into the cell and put him on the bed. The wounded man shut his eyes and went to sleep. The King was so tired with the walk and the work that he curled up by the door and fell into a sound sleep. He slept through the whole mild summer night, and when he awoke in the morning he could not make out where he was and who was the strange bearded man staring at him from the bed with glistening eyes.

"Forgive me," the bearded man said in a faint voice, when he saw that the King was awake and observing him.

"I don't know you and have nothing to forgive you for," the King said.

"You don't know me, but I know you. I am your enemy who vowed to be revenged on you for having executed my brother and taken away my property: I knew that you went alone to the hermit and resolved to kill you on your way back. But the day passed and you did not come. I lost patience and came out to find you, when I stumbled upon your body-guard. They recognized me and wounded me. I escaped from them, but would have died from loss of blood had you not bound my wound. I wanted to kill you and you saved my life. If I continue to live I will serve you as your most faithful slave should you desire it, and I will order my sons to do likewise. Forgive me."

The King was very glad that he had been able to make peace with his enemy so easily, and not only forgave him but promised to return his property and to send him his own servants and physician.

Taking leave of the wounded man the King came out of the cell and sought for the hermit with his eyes. Before going away he wanted to ask him for the last time to answer his three questions. The hermit was on his knees by the beds they had dug yesterday, sowing vegetable seeds.

The King approached him and said, "For the last time, wise man, I ask you to answer my questions."

"But they are answered already," the hermit said, squatting on his emaciated legs and looking at up the King, who stood before him.

"How?" the King asked.

"Don't you see?" the hermit began; "had you not pitied my weakness yesterday and dug these beds for me and gone back alone, the man would have attacked you and you would have regretted that you had not stayed with me. The important hour at the time was when you dug these beds, and I was the most essential person to you, and the most essential act was to do me a kindness. And later, when the man ran up, the most important hour was when you looked after him, for, had you not bandaged his wound, he would have died without making his peace with you. He was the most essential man to you at that time, and what you did for him was the most essential thing to be done. Always bear in mind that the most important time is now, for it is the only time we have any power over ourselves; the most essential man is the one with whom you happen to be at the moment, because you can never be sure whether you will ever have relations with any one else, and the most essential thing to do is a kindness to that man, for it was for this purpose we were sent into the world."

THE GODSON

I

A son was born to a poor peasant. He rejoiced and went to a neighbour to ask him to stand as godfather to the boy. The neighbour refused. He did not want to be godfather to a poor man's son. So the peasant went to another neighbour and he, too, refused. He walked from house to house, but could find no one who would be godfather to his son, so he set out to another village. On his way he met a stranger, who stopped him and said, "Good day, peasant; where are you going to?"

"God has given me a child," the peasant said, "to gladden my sight in my youth, to comfort me in my old age and to pray for my soul when I die. No one in our village will be godfather to him, so I am going to seek one elsewhere."

"Let me be his godfather," the stranger said.

The peasant rejoiced. He thanked the stranger and said, "But whom shall I ask to be his godmother?"

"Go into the town," the stranger said; "in the square you will see a stone house with shop windows; go in and ask the merchant to let his daughter stand as godmother to your son."

The peasant was doubtful.

"But how can I ask a rich merchant? He will be too proud to let his daughter come to a poor man like me."

"That won't be your fault; go and ask him. Have everything ready by the morning and I'll come to the christening."

The peasant went home, then drove into the town to the merchant. He had no sooner stopped in the yard than the merchant came out.

"What do you want?" he asked.

"God has given me a child," the peasant said, "to gladden my sight in my youth, to comfort me in my old age and to pray for my soul when I die. Will you be kind enough to let your daughter come and be godmother to the child?"

"When is the christening?"

"To-morrow morning."

"Very well; go, in God's name. To-morrow my daughter will be at the church."

The next day the godmother and godfather came; the child was christened, but directly after the christening the godfather disappeared. No one knew who he was and no one saw him from that day.

II

The child grew up to the parents' great joy; and he was strong and industrious and clever and humble. When he was ten years old the parents sent him to school, and what it took others five years to learn the boy learnt in one. And there was no one in the village who could teach him more.

Easter came round and the boy went to his godmother to give her the Easter greeting. When he returned home he said, "Father and mother, where does my godfather live? I should like to give him the Easter greeting, too."

And the father said, "We don't know where your godfather lives, dear son. We, too, have worried over that. We have not seen him since you were christened. We have not heard of him and don't know where he lives, nor whether he is alive at all."

The boy bowed to his father and mother.

"Let me go," he said, "to seek my godfather. I want to find him and give him the Easter greeting."

The father and mother gave their consent and the boy set out to find his godfather.

III

The boy left the house and set out on his way. About midday he met a stranger and the stranger stopped and said, "Good day to you, boy. Where are you going?"

And the boy said, "I went to my godmother to give her the Easter greeting and when I returned home I asked my parents where my godfather lived, because I wanted to give him the greeting too, but my parents said, 'We don't know where your godfather lives, dear son. We have not heard of him since you were christened and we don't know anything about him, or whether he is alive at all.' And I wanted to see my godfather, so I am going to find him."

"I am your godfather," the stranger said.

The boy rejoiced and gave him the Easter greeting.

"Where are you going to, godfather? If you are going in our direction come in to us, or if you are going home, may I come with you?"

And the stranger said, "I have no time to come to you now, because I have some business in the villages. I shall not be home until to-morrow, then you can come to me if you like."

"But how shall I find you, godfather?"

"Walk straight towards the east until you come to a wood in the midst of which you will find a clearing. Sit down to rest in that clearing and look about you to see what is happening. When you come out of the wood you will see a garden and in the garden is a house with a golden roof. That is my house. Go in at the gate; I will meet you there myself."

Saying these words the godfather vanished from the godson's sight.

IV

The boy followed the godfather's directions. He wandered and wandered till he came to a wood and found the clearing, and in the midst of the clearing stood a pine tree to a branch of which a heavy block of oak was attached with string, and beneath the block was a trough of honey. As the boy was wondering why the honey and the block were there, a crackling was heard among the trees and out came a family of bears. The mother came in front and a yearling and some cubs followed behind. The mother, sniffing the air, went straight to the trough, the cubs following. She thrust her muzzle into the honey and called to the cubs to do the same. They scampered up and thrust in their muzzles. The block swung back a little and returning, hit against the cubs. When the mother saw this, she shoved the block away with her paw. The block swung back further, and returning more forcibly struck one cub on the back, another on the head. The cubs jumped away, howling with pain. The mother bear growled, and seizing the block in her fore-paws, flung it away from her violently. The block flew up high. The yearling ran up to the trough, thrust his muzzle into the honey, the other cubs followed him, but no sooner had they got there than the block swung back, struck the yearling on the head and killed him. The mother-bear growled more angrily as she seized the block and flung it away with all her might. The block flew higher than the branch, the string it was tied to even slackened; the mother-bear and the cubs came up to the trough; the block flew higher and higher, then stopped and began to descend; the lower it got the swifter became its course. It crashed down on the mother-bear's head. She fell over; her legs twitched and she died. The cubs ran away into the wood.

V

The boy wondered and went on further. He came to a large garden and in the garden was a high house with a golden roof. At the gate stood his godfather, smiling. He greeted his godson, made him come inside the gate and took him round the garden. He had never even dreamt of such beauty and joy as there was in that garden.

The godfather took the boy into the house and he found that more wonderful still. The godfather showed him all the rooms—one more beautiful than the other—then he brought him to a sealed door. "Do you see this door?" he asked. "It is not locked, only sealed. It can be opened, but I forbid you to do it. You can live here and go where you like and do what you like; taste of every pleasure; I forbid you only one thing—to pass that door. But if it should happen that you do go in, remember what you saw in the wood." With these words the godfather went away, and the godson was left alone. His life was so full of pleasure and such a happy one that when he had been there thirty years it seemed to him no more than three hours. Thus the thirty years passed and the godson came to the sealed door, thinking, "I wonder why my godfather forbade me to go into this room? I will go in and see what is there."

He pushed the door; the seal gave way and the door opened. The godson went in and saw that the room was large and more beautiful than all the others, and in the middle of it stood a golden throne. The godson wandered and wandered over the room; then he stopped by the throne, mounted the steps and sat down. He saw a sceptre by the throne and he took it up in his hand. He had no sooner touched the sceptre than the walls of the room rolled asunder. The godson looked about and saw the whole world and everything people were doing in it. Straight before him was the sea and ships sailing on it. To the right were foreign lands, where heathens lived. To the left were Christians, but not Russians. On the fourth side were our own Russian people.

"I will look and see what is happening at home," he said. "I wonder if the corn is good this year?"

He looked at his father's fields and saw the sheaves standing in them. He began to count the sheaves to see if the harvest had been good, when he saw a cart coming over the field with a peasant sitting in it. He looked closer and saw that it was Vasily, a thief. Vasily stopped by the sheaves and began putting them into the cart. The godson could not endure this and cried aloud, "Father, they are stealing your sheaves!"

The father awoke in the night. "I dreamt that some one was stealing my sheaves," he said; "I will go and see." He got upon his horse and rode out.

When he got to the fields he saw Vasily and called aloud for help. Some peasants came up. Vasily was beaten, bound and taken to prison.

The godson then looked towards the town where his godmother lived and saw that she had married a merchant. She was lying in bed and her husband got up to leave her to go to another woman. And the godson cried aloud to his godmother, "Get up! Your husband is going to do something wicked!"

The godmother jumped up, dressed and set out to find her husband. She brought him to shame, beat the other woman and would not take her husband back again.

The godson looked again towards his home and saw his mother lying in the house and that a robber had stolen in and was breaking open a trunk. The mother awoke and cried out in terror. The robber raised his axe, and was about to kill her, but the godson could endure no more; he thrust the sceptre straight into the robber's temple and killed him on the spot.

VI

He had no sooner slain the robber than the walls rose up again and the room became as before.

The door opened and the godfather entered. He approached the godson, took him by the hand, led him from the throne and said, "You did not obey my commands. You did one wrong thing in opening the forbidden door, another when you mounted the throne and took my sceptre into your hand, and a third wrong, which has added to the evil in the world. Had you sat on the throne an hour longer, you would have ruined half mankind."

And the godfather once more led the godson up to the throne and he took the sceptre in his hand and the walls rolled asunder.

And the godfather said, "See what you have done to your father. Vasily sat in prison for a year and learnt every kind of wickedness and came out completely corrupted. See, he has driven off two of your father's horses and is now setting fire to his barns. This is what you have done to your father."

As soon as the godson saw his father's barns burst into flame the godfather hid the view from his sight and bade him look in another direction.

"See," he said; "it is now a year since your godmother's husband left her, and he goes after other women and his wife has taken to drink and his former mistress has fallen to still lower depths. This is what you have done to your godmother."

This sight, too, he hid from the godson's gaze and bade him look towards his own home. His mother was weeping and saying, "It would have been better if the robber had killed me than that I should have so many sins on my soul."

"This is what you have done to your mother."

This sight, too, the godfather shut out and bade the godson look below. And he saw two keepers guarding the robber in a dungeon.

And the godfather said, "This man has killed nine people. He should have atoned for his sins himself, but in killing him you have taken them upon your own soul. Now you must answer for all his sins. This is what you have done to yourself. When the mother-bear first pushed the block aside she merely disturbed her cubs; when she pushed it a second time, she killed her yearling; when she pushed it a third time, she was killed herself. You have done exactly the same. I give you a term of thirty years. Go into the world and atone for the robber's sins; if you fail to do so, you will have to take his place."

"But how shall I atone for his sins?" the godson asked.

And the godfather said, "When you have rid the world of as much evil as you brought into it, then you will have atoned for your own and the robber's sins."

And the godson asked, "How can I rid the world of evil?"

And the godfather said, "Walk straight towards the east until you come to some fields on which you will find some people. Take note of what they are doing and teach them what you know, then go on further, observing everything on the way. On the fourth day you will come to a wood in which you will find a cell, and in this cell a hermit lives. Tell this hermit all that has happened and he will instruct you in what you are to do. When you have done all that the hermit has told you, you will have atoned for your own and the robber's sins."

With these words the godfather put the godson out at the gate.

VII

And the godson set out, thinking as he walked, "How can I rid the world of evil? People rid the world of evil by banishing evil men or putting them in prison or executing them. But how can I rid the world of evil without taking other men's sins upon myself?" And the godson wondered and wondered, but could come to no decision.

He wandered and wandered till he came to a field on which tall rich corn was growing, ready to be harvested. And the godson saw a calf that had strayed in among the corn and he saw men on horseback chasing the calf this way and that and trampling down the corn. Each time the calf was about to come out of the corn some one rode up and the calf got frightened and ran back again, the men after it. In the road stood a woman, crying, "They will chase my calf to death!"

And the godson said to the men, "What are you doing? Come out of the corn and let the woman call to her calf."

The men did so. The woman came up to the edge of the field and called to the calf, who pricked up its ears, listening awhile, then it ran towards her and buried its nose in her skirts, nearly knocking her down. The men were glad, and the woman was glad, and the calf, too, was glad.

The godson went on his way thinking, "I see that evil breeds evil. The more people try to drive away evil, the more the evil grows, which shows that it is impossible to drive out evil by evil. But how can one drive it out? I don't know. It is well that the calf obeyed its mistress; if it had not done so, how should we have got it out of the corn?"

And the godson wondered and wondered, but could come to no decision and went on further.

VIII

He wandered and wandered till he came to a village where he asked to be allowed to stay the night at the first house. The mistress let him in. Besides herself no one was in the house. The mistress was busy cleaning.

When the godson came in he climbed on to the stove and began watching to see what the mistress was doing. She had finished cleaning the floor and was scrubbing the table. She scrubbed it and wiped it with a dirty cloth. She rubbed the cloth one way, but the table would not come clean. The cloth left streaks of dirt. She rubbed it the other way—the first streaks came out, new ones were made. She rubbed it lengthwise again and the same thing happened. The dirty cloth rubbed out one streak of dirt and left another. The godson watched for some time and then said, "What are you doing, mistress?"

"Don't you see that I'm cleaning the house for the festival? I can't get the table clean, anyhow. The dirt will not come off and I'm quite worn out."

"You should rinse out the cloth, then wipe the table."

The mistress did as he told her and the table came clean. "Thank you," she said, "for your lesson."

In the morning the godson took leave of the mistress and went on further. He wandered and wandered till he came to a wood where he saw some peasants making hoops. He approached them and saw them struggling and struggling, but they could not bend the wood. He looked closer and saw that the block on which they were working was not firmly fixed. And the godson said, "What are you doing, brothers?"

"Making hoops, as you see. We have steamed the wood twice, yet cannot bend it. We are quite worn out."

"You should fix the block more firmly, mates. It moves round with you as it is."

The peasants did so and their work went smoothly afterwards.

The godson stayed the night with them, then went on his way. He walked the whole of that day and the night and just before daybreak he came upon some shepherds encamped for the night, and joined them. They had settled their cattle and were trying to light a fire. They took some dry twigs and lighted them, and not giving them time to burn up, they put some damp brushwood on top and smothered the fire. The shepherds took some more dry twigs and lighted them, and again they smothered the fire with damp brushwood. For a long time they struggled, but could get no fire.

And the godson said, "Don't be in such a hurry to put on the brushwood, but wait until the twigs have caught well. When the fire gets hot then you can put on the brushwood."

The shepherds did as he told them. When the twigs had caught well, they put on the brushwood, and in a few minutes they had a blazing fire.

The godson stayed with them for a while then went on further. He wondered what these three things he had seen might mean, but could not understand, nor see the reason of them.

IX

The godson wandered and wandered until nightfall, when he came to a wood, and in the wood was a cell. He went up to the cell and knocked at the door.

A voice from within asked, "Who is that?"

"A great sinner. I have come to atone for the sins of another."

And the hermit asked, "What are these sins you have taken upon yourself?"

And the godson told him everything about his godfather and the mother-bear and the cubs and about the throne in the sealed room, and about his godfather's commands, and about the peasants who had trampled the corn in the field, and the calf that had come to its mistress at her call.

"I know now," he said, "that you cannot drive out evil by evil, but I don't know how it can be driven out and I want you to tell me."

And the hermit said, "Tell me what else you have seen on the way?"

The godson told him about the woman and how she had tried to clean the table, and of the peasants who had tried to make the hoops, and the shepherds who had tried to light a fire.

The hermit waited until he had finished, then he went into his cell and brought out a jagged axe.

"Come," he said.

The hermit walked away from the cell and pointed to a tree. "Cut it down," he said.

The godson felled it.

"Chop it into three parts."

The godson chopped it into three parts. The hermit again went into his cell and brought out a light.

"Set fire to those three logs," he said.

The godson made a fire and burnt the three logs till only three pieces of charcoal were left.

"Now plant them half into the ground, like this."

The godson planted them.

"Do you see a river there by that hill? Fetch some water in your mouth and water them. Water this one in the way you taught the woman to clean, this one in the way you taught the hoopers, and this one in the way you taught the shepherds. When the three pieces of charcoal grow into apple-trees you will know how to rid the world of evil, and will then have atoned for your sins."

With these words the hermit went into his cell. The godson pondered and pondered and could not understand what the hermit had said, but he did what the hermit had told him.

X

The godson went to the river, filled his mouth with water and watered one piece of charcoal; then he went again and again, until he had watered the other two. The godson was tired and hungry. He went to the hermit's cell to ask for some food. When he opened the door there was the hermit lying dead on a bench. The godson looked about the cell and found some rusks, which he ate; then he discovered a spade and went out to dig a grave for the old man. By night he carried water to water the pieces of charcoal, and by day he dug the grave. He had no sooner finished it and was about to bury the hermit, when some people came from the village to bring the hermit food.

When the people heard that the hermit was dead they asked the godson to take his place. They buried the hermit, left the bread with the godson and went away, promising to bring him more food later on.

And the godson fell into the hermit's place and he lived and nourished himself with the food people brought him, and went on watering the pieces of charcoal as the hermit had bidden him do.

The godson lived thus for a year and many people began to visit him. He grew famous throughout the country as a saint who saved his soul by carrying water in his mouth from beneath a hill, and watering stumps of charcoal. People flocked to him. Rich merchants brought him gifts, but the godson used nothing but what he needed, giving the rest to the poor.

And the godson began to live thus—for half the day he carried water in his mouth to water the pieces of charcoal, for the other half he rested and received people.

And the godson came to think that he had been told to live thus and that in this way he would atone for his sins.

The godson lived thus for another year, not missing a single day for watering the charcoal, yet not a single piece had begun to sprout.

One day when he was sitting in his cell he heard a horseman gallop past, singing to himself. The hermit came out to see what manner of man he was. And he saw that the man was young and strong and was dressed in fine clothes and seated on a spirited horse.

The godson stopped him and asked him who he was and where he was going. The man pulled up.

"I am a robber," he said; "I roam the highway and kill whomever I have a mind to. The more men I kill the merrier are my songs."

The godson was horrified and thought, "How can one destroy evil in such a man? It is well to talk to the people who come to me; they repent of their own accord, but this man glories in the evil he does." The godson said nothing to him and turned away, thinking, "What shall I do? If this robber makes up his mind to stay here, he will scare away my people and no one will come to see me. They will lose some good thereby, and I shall have nothing to live on."

And the godson stopped and said to the robber, "People come to me not to boast of the evil they do, but to repent and pray for their sins to be forgiven them. You repent likewise, if you have the fear of God in your heart, and if you do not seek repentance, go away from this place and do not come back again, so as not to hinder me or scare away my people. If you fail to listen to my words God will punish you."

The robber laughed.

"I am not afraid of your God and I won't listen to you. You are not my master to order me about. You live by your piety, I by my robbery. We must all live. Teach the women who come to you, but let me alone. Since you have dared to mention the name of God to me I will kill two extra people to-morrow. I would kill you now, only I don't want to soil my hands, but take care never to cross my path again."

The robber threatened him thus and rode away. He did not come again and the godson lived in the hermitage as before for another eight years.

XI

One night the godson set out to water his pieces of charcoal and when he had finished he sat down in his cell to rest. He peered along the path now and again to see if any visitor was coming, but no one came that day. The godson sat alone until evening and he grew lonesome and weary and began to think about his life. He recollected how the robber had reproached him for living by his piety. He began to look back upon his life. "I am not living as the hermit told me," he thought. "The hermit imposed a penance on me and I have used it as a means of earning my bread and even gaining fame thereby. I have been so led astray over it that I am even dull when people do not come to see me, and when they do come, I rejoice when they praise my saintliness. This is not the way one must live. I have been blinded by fame. Not only have I not atoned for past sins but have taken new ones upon myself. I will go away to another place far into the wood, where the people will not find me, and I will live alone there and atone for my past sins, taking care not to commit new ones."

Thinking thus the godson took a bag of rusks and a spade, and he left the cell and set out down a ravine to build himself a mud hut in the thicket and disappear from people's sight.

The godson was walking along with his bag and spade when the robber jumped out upon him. The godson was afraid and would have run away, but the robber stopped him.

"Where are you going?" he asked.

The godson told him that he wanted to go away from people and bury himself in a wild part of the wood where no one would come to him.

The robber wondered.

"But what will you live on if no one comes to see you?"

The godson had not thought of that, but now the robber had mentioned it he remembered that he had to eat.

"On what God gives," he said.

The robber made no reply and went his way.

"Why didn't I say anything to him about his life?" the godson thought. "He may be repentant now. He seemed softer of manner and did not threaten to kill me to-day." And he called to the robber saying, "It is time you repented. You cannot get away from God."

The robber turned his horse round, seized a knife from his girdle and brandished it aloft. The godson took fright and ran away into the wood.

The robber did not trouble to go after him, he merely said, "I have let you off twice, old man; take care not to come my way a third time, or I'll kill you."

With these words the robber rode away.

That evening the godson went to water his pieces of charcoal and behold! one of the pieces had sprouted! A young apple-tree had shot forth.

XII

The godson hid himself from the eyes of men and began to live alone. His rusks were all gone. "I must hunt for some roots," he thought, but he had no sooner gone out than he saw a bag of rusks hanging on the branch of a tree. He took the bag and began to eat.

When that was all gone he found another bag in the very same place. Thus the godson lived. He had only one care—his fear of the robber. When he heard him coming he hid himself, thinking, "If he kills me I shall not be able to atone for my sins."

Another ten years passed. One apple-tree grew up, the other pieces of charcoal remained as they were before.

One day the godson went out early to do his watering. He moistened the soil around the stumps until he was tired and sat down to rest. As he rested he thought, "I have sinned greatly in fearing death. If it be God's will I will atone for my sins by death even."

The thought had no sooner occurred to him than he heard the robber come along cursing at some one. And the godson thought, "Besides God no one can do me either good or evil." And he went to meet the robber. He saw that the robber was not alone. On the saddle, behind him, was another man, and this man's hands were bound and his mouth was gagged. The man made no sound and the robber kept on abusing him. The godson approached the robber and stopped before his horse.

"Where are you taking this man to?" he asked.

"Into the wood. He is a merchant's son and won't tell me where his father's money is hidden. I will keep him prisoner until he tells me."

The robber was about to go on, but the godson would not let him, seizing the horse by the bridle.

"Let the man go," he said.

The robber grew angry and raised his arm to strike him.

"Do you want to share his fate? I told you I would kill you. Let go!"

The godson was not afraid.

"I won't let go," he said. "I'm not afraid of you; I only fear God. He tells me not to let go. Set the man free."

The robber frowned; he seized the knife from his girdle, cut the cords and released the merchant's son.

"Be gone, the two of you!" he said, "and don't come across my path a second time!"

The merchant's son fled. The robber was about to go, but the godson stopped him and once more beseeched him to abandon his wicked life. The robber stood and listened without saying a word, then turned and rode away.

In the morning the godson went to water his pieces of charcoal. Behold! another one had burst forth, another apple-tree had grown!

XIII

Ten more years passed. The godson lived desiring nothing, afraid of nothing, and a feeling of gladness always at his heart. And he thought one day, "What blessings the good Lord gives us! And we torment ourselves for nothing. People should live in joy and happiness." And he remembered the evil men suffered and how they tormented themselves and he grew to pity them. "It is in vain that I live as I do," he thought; "I must go among people and tell them what I know."

The thought had no sooner occurred to him than he heard the robber come along, but he took no notice of him, thinking, "What is the use of talking to that man? He will not understand."

This was his first thought, but in a little while he repented of it and went out in the road. The robber sat on his horse, frowning and looking at the ground. When the godson saw him, a feeling of pity came over him; he rushed up and seized the robber's knee.

"My dear brother," he said, "take pity on your soul! Don't you know that the spirit of God is in you? You torment yourself and others, and as time goes on your torments will grow worse, and God loves you and wants to heap His blessings upon you. Don't destroy yourself, brother; change your way of life."

The robber frowned and turned away. "Leave me alone," he said.

The godson clutched the robber's knee still firmer and the tears stood in his eyes. The robber raised his eyes to his, gazed into them for a long time, then climbed down from his horse and fell on his knees before the godson.

"You have subdued me, old man," he said. "For twenty years I struggled against you, but you have won. I am powerless before you. Do what you want with me. When you spoke to me the first time, I grew more hardened still. I only began to take your words to heart when you went away from people and I knew that you needed nothing from them. It was then I began to supply you with rusks."

And the godson recollected that the woman had only managed to clean the table after she had washed the cloth. When he ceased to care for himself and cleansed his heart, he was able to cleanse the hearts of others.

And the robber continued, "And my heart turned when I saw that you had no fear of death."

And the godson remembered that the hoopers began to bend the hoops only when they had made the block firm. When he ceased to fear death and established his life firmly in God he had been able to subdue this man's wild heart.

And the robber said, "And the heart in me melted altogether when I saw that you pitied me and wept before me."

The godson rejoiced. He led the robber to the place where his pieces of charcoal were planted and behold! a third apple-tree had grown. And the godson remembered that when the shepherds had allowed their dry twigs to catch well, a big fire blazed up. It was only when his heart grew warm that he had been able to kindle the heart of another.

And the godson rejoiced that he had now atoned for all his sins.

He told the robber everything and died. The robber buried him and began to live as the godson had told him, and to teach other men what he knew.

THE INVADERS, AND OTHER STORIES

THE INVADERS.[1]

A VOLUNTEER'S NARRATIVE.

I.

On the 24th of July, Captain Khlopof in epaulets and cap—a style of dress in which I had not seen him since my arrival in the Caucasus—entered the low door of my earth-hut.

"I'm just from the colonel's," he said in reply to my questioning look; "to-morrow our battalion is to move."

"Where?" I asked.

"To N——. The troops have been ordered to muster at that place."

"And probably some expedition will be made from there?"

"Of course."

"In what direction, think you?"

"I don't think. I tell you all I know. Last night a Tatar from the general came galloping up,—brought orders for the battalion to march, taking two days' rations. But whither, why, how long, isn't for them to ask. Orders are to go—that's enough."

"Still, if they are going to take only two days' rations, it's likely the army will not stay longer."

"That's no argument at all."

"And how is that?" I asked with astonishment.

"This is the way of it: When they went against Dargi they took a week's rations, but they spent almost a month."

"And can I go with you?" I asked, after a short silence.

"Yes, you can go; but my advice is—better not. Why run the risk?"

"No, allow me to disregard your advice. I have been spending a whole month here for this very purpose,—of having a chance to see action,—and you want me to let it have the go-by!"

"All right, come with us; only isn't it true that it would be better for you to stay behind? You could wait for us here, you could go hunting. But as to us,—God knows what will become of us!... And that would be first-rate," he said in such a convincing tone that it seemed to me at the first moment that it would actually be first-rate. Nevertheless, I said resolutely that I wouldn't stay behind for any thing.

"And what have you to see there?" said the captain, still trying to dissuade me. "If you want to learn how battles are fought, read Mikhaïlovski Danilevski's 'Description of War,' a charming book; there it's all admirably described,—where every corps stands, and how battles are fought."

"On the contrary, that does not interest me," I replied.

"Well, now, how is this? It simply means that you want to see how men kill each other, doesn't it?... Here in 1832 there was a man like yourself, not in the regular service,—a Spaniard, I think he was. He went on two expeditions with us,... in a blue mantle or something of the sort, and so the young fellow was killed. Here, bátiushka, one is not surprised at any thing."

Ashamed as I was at the captain's manifest disapprobation of my project, I did not attempt to argue him down.

"Well, he was brave, wasn't he?"

"God knows as to that. He always used to ride at the front. Wherever there was firing, there he was."

"So he must have been brave, then," said I.

"No, that doesn't signify bravery,—his putting himself where he wasn't called."

"What do you call bravery, then?"

"Bravery, bravery?" repeated the captain with the expression of a man to whom such a question presents itself for the first time. "A brave man is one who conducts himself as he ought," said he after a brief consideration.

I remembered that Plato defined bravery as the knowledge of what one ought and what one ought not to fear; and in spite of the triteness and obscurity in the terminology of the captain's definition, I thought that the fundamental conception of both was not so unlike as might at first sight appear, and that the captain's definition was even more correct than the Greek philosopher's, for the reason, that, if he could have expressed himself as Plato did, he would in all probability have said that that man is brave who fears only what he ought to fear and not what there is no need of fearing.

I was anxious to explain my thought to the captain.

"Yes," I said, "it seems to me that in every peril there is an alternative, and the alternative adopted under the influence of, say, the sentiment of duty, is bravery, but the alternative adopted under the influence of a lower sentiment is cowardice; therefore it is impossible to call a man brave who risks his life out of vanity or curiosity or greediness, and, vice versa, the man who under the influence of the virtuous sentiment of family obligation, or simply from conviction, avoids peril, cannot be called a coward."

The captain looked at me with a queer sort of expression while I was talking.

"Well, now, I don't know how to reason this out with you," said he, filling his pipe, "but we have with us a junker, and he likes to philosophize. You talk with him. He also writes poetry."

I had only become intimate with the captain in the Caucasus, but I had known him before in Russia. His mother, Marya Ivanovna Khlopova, the owner of a small landed estate, lives about two versts[2] from my home. Before I went to the Caucasus I visited her. The old lady was greatly delighted that I was going to see her Páshenka[3] (thus she called the old gray-haired captain), and, like a living letter, could tell him about her circumstances and give him a little message. Having made me eat my fill of a glorious pie and roast chicken, Marya Ivanovna went to her sleeping-room and came back with a rather large black relic-bag,[4] to which was attached some kind of silken ribbon.

"Here is this image of our Mother-Intercessor from the September festival," she said, kissing the picture of the divine Mother attached to the cross, and putting it into my hand. "Please give it to him, bátiushka. You see, when he went to the Kaikaz, I had a Te Deum sung, and made a vow, that if he should be safe and sound, I would order this image of the divine Mother. And here it is seventeen years that the Mátushka and the saints have had him in their keeping; not once has he been wounded, and what battles he has been in, as it seems!... When Mikhailo, who was with him, told me about it, my hair actually stood on end. You see, all that I know about him I have to hear from others; he never writes me any thing about his doings, my dove,[5]—he is afraid of frightening me."

(I had already heard in the Caucasus, but not from the captain himself, that he had been severely wounded four times; and, as was to be expected, he had not written his mother about his wounds any more than about his campaigns.)

"Now let him wear this holy image," she continued. "I bless him with it. The most holy Intercessor protect him, especially in battle may she always look after him! And so tell him, my dear, friend,[6] that thy mother gave thee this message."

I promised faithfully to fulfil her commission.

"I know you will be fond of him, of my Páshenka," the old lady continued,—"he is such a splendid fellow! Would you believe me, not a year goes by without his sending me money, and he also helps Annushka my daughter, and all from his wages alone. Truly I shall always thank God," she concluded with tears in her eyes, "that he has given me such a child."

"Does he write you often?" I asked.

"Rarely, bátiushka,—not more than once a year; and sometimes when he sends money he writes a little word, and sometimes he doesn't. 'If I don't write you, mámenka,' he says, 'it means that I'm alive and well; but if any thing should happen,—which God forbid,—then they will write you for me.'"

When I gave the captain his mother's gift (it was in my room), he asked me for some wrapping-paper, carefully tied it up, and put it away. I gave him many details of his mother's life: the captain was silent. When I had finished, he went into a corner, and took a very long time in filling his pipe.

"Yes, she's a fine old lady," said he from the corner, in a rather choked voice: "God grant that we may meet again!"

Great love and grief were expressed in these simple words.

"Why do you serve here?" I asked.

"Have to serve," he replied with decision. "And double pay means a good deal for our brother, who is a poor man."

The captain lived economically; he did not play cards, he rarely drank to excess, and he smoked ordinary tobacco, which from some inexplicable reason he did not call by its usual name,[7] but sambrotalicheski tabák. The captain had pleased me even before this. He had one of those simple, calm Russian faces, and looked you straight in the eye agreeably and easily. But after this conversation I felt a genuine respect for him.

[1] Nabég (pronounced Na-be-ukh), the Invasion or Raid.

[2] One and a third miles.

[3] An affectionate diminished diminutive: Pavel (Paul), Pasha, Pashenka.

[4] ládanka, the bag containing sacred things worn by the pious, together with the baptismal cross.

[5] golubchik.

[6] moï bátiushka.

[7] tiutiún.

II.

At four o'clock on the morning of the next day, the captain came riding up to my door. He had on an old well-worn coat without epaulets, wide Lesghian trousers, a round white Circassian cap, with drooping lambskin dyed yellow, and an ugly-looking Asiatic sabre across his shoulder. The little white horse[8] on which he rode came with head down, and mincing gait, and kept switching his slender tail. In spite of the fact that the good captain's figure was neither very warlike nor very handsome, yet there was in it such an expression of good-will toward every one around him, that it inspired involuntary respect.

I did not keep him waiting a minute, but immediately mounted, and we rode off together from the gate of the fortress.

The battalion was already two hundred sazhens[9] ahead of us, and had the appearance of some black, solid body in motion. It was possible to make out that it was infantry, only from the circumstance that while the bayonets appeared like long, dense needles, occasionally there came to the ear the sounds of a soldier's song, the drum, and a charming tenor, the leader of the sixth company,—a song which I had more than once enjoyed at the fort.

The road ran through the midst of a deep, wide ravine, or balka as it is called in the Caucasian dialect, along the banks of a small river, which at this time was playing, that is, was having a freshet. Flocks of wild pigeons hovered around it, now settling on the rocky shore, now wheeling about in mid-air in swift circles and disappearing from sight.

The sun was not yet visible, but the summit of the balka on the right began to grow luminous. The gray and white colored crags, the greenish-yellow moss wet with dew, the clumps of different kinds of wild thorn,[10] stood out extraordinarily distinct and rotund in the pellucid golden light of the sunrise.

On the other hand, the ravine, hidden in thick mist which rolled up like smoke in varying volumes, was damp, and dark, and gave the impression of an indistinguishable mixture of colors—pale lilac, almost purple, dark green, and white.

Directly in front of us, against the dark blue of the horizon, with startling distinctness appeared the dazzling white, silent masses of the snow-capped mountains with their marvellous shadows and outlines exquisite even in the smallest details. Crickets, grasshoppers, and a thousand other insects, were awake in the tall grass, and filled the air with their sharp, incessant clatter: it seemed as though a numberless multitude of tiny bells were jingling in our very ears. The atmosphere was alive with waters, with foliage, with mist; in a word, had all the life of a beautiful early summer morning.

The captain struck a light, and began to puff at his pipe; the fragrance of sambrotalicheski tabák and of the punk struck me as extremely pleasant.

We rode along the side of the road so as to overtake the infantry as quickly as possible. The captain seemed more serious than usual; he did not take his Daghestan pipe from his mouth, and at every step he dug his heels into his horse's legs as the little beast, capering from one side to the other, laid out a scarcely noticeable dark green track through the damp, tall grass. Up from under his very feet, with its shrill cry,[11] and that drumming of the wings that is so sure to startle the huntsman in spite of himself, flew the pheasant, and slowly winged its flight on high. The captain paid him not the slightest attention.

"We had almost overtaken the battalion, when behind us was heard the sound of a galloping horse, and in an instant there rode by us a very handsome young fellow in an officer's coat, and a tall white Circassian cap.[12] As he caught up with us he smiled, bowed to the captain, and waved his whip.... I only had time to notice that he sat in the saddle and held the bridle with peculiar grace, and that he had beautiful dark eyes, a finely cut nose, and a mustache just beginning to grow. I was particularly attracted by the way in which he could not help smiling, as if to impress it upon us that we were friends of his. If by nothing else than his smile, one would have known that he was still very young.

"And now where is he going?" grumbled the captain with a look of dissatisfaction, not taking his pipe from his mouth.

"Who is that?" I asked.

"Ensign Alánin, a subaltern officer of my company.... Only last month he came from the School of Cadets."

"This is the first time that he is going into action, I suppose?" said I.

"And so he is overjoyed," replied the captain thoughtfully, shaking his head; "it's youth."

"And why shouldn't he be glad? I can see that for a young officer this must be very interesting."

The captain said nothing for two minutes.

"And that's why I say 'it's youth,'" he continued in a deep tone. "What is there to rejoice in, when there's nothing to see? Here when one goes often, one doesn't find any pleasure in it. Here, let us suppose there are twenty of us officers going: some of us will be either killed or wounded; that's likely. To-day my turn, to-morrow his, the next day somebody else's. So what is there to rejoice in?"

[8] mashtak in the Caucasian dialect.

[9] Fourteen hundred feet.

[10] Paliurus, box-thorn, and karachag.

[11] tordoka'yé.

[12] papákha.

III.

Scarcely had the bright sun risen above the mountains, and begun to shine into the valley where we were riding, when the undulating clouds of mist scattered, and it grew warm. The soldiers with guns and knapsacks on their backs marched slowly along the dusty road. In the ranks were frequently heard Malo-Russian dialogues and laughter. A few old soldiers in white linen coats—for the most part non-commissioned officers—marched along the roadside with their pipes, engaged in earnest conversation. The triple rows of heavily laden wagons advanced step by step, and raised a thick dust, which hung motionless.

The mounted officers rode in advance; a few jiggited, as they say in the Caucasus;[13] that is, applying the whip to their horses, they spurred them on to make four or five leaps, and then reined them in suddenly, pulling the head back. Others listened to the song-singers, who notwithstanding the heat and the oppressive air indefatigably tuned up one song after another.

A hundred sazhens in advance of the infantry, on a great white horse, surrounded by mounted Tatars, rode a tall, handsome officer in Asiatic costume, known to the regiment as a man of reckless valor, one who cuts any one straight in the eyes![14] He wore a black Tatar half-coat or beshmét trimmed with silver braid, similar trousers, new leggings[15] closely laced with chirazui as they call galloons in the Caucasus, and a tall, yellow Cherkessian cap worn jauntily on the back of his head. On his breast and back were silver lacings. His powder-flask and pistol were hung at his back; another pistol, and a dagger in a silver sheath, depended from his belt. Besides all this was buckled on a sabre in a red morocco sheath adorned with silver; and over the shoulder hung his musket in a black case.

By his garb, his carriage, his manner, and indeed by every motion, it was manifest that his ambition was to ape the Tatars. He was just saying something, in a language that I did not understand, to the Tatars who rode with him; but from the doubtful, mocking glances which these latter gave each other, I came to the conclusion that they did not understand him either.

This was one of our young officers of the dare-devil, jigit order, who get themselves up à la Marlinski and Lermontof. These men look upon the Caucasus, as it were, through the prism of the "Heroes of our Time," Mulla-Nurof[16] and others, and in all their activities are I directed not by their own inclinations but by the example of these models.

This lieutenant, for instance, was very likely fond of the society of well-bred women and men of importance, generals, colonels, adjutants,—I may even go so far as to believe that he was very fond of this society, because he was in the highest degree vainglorious,—but he considered it his unfailing duty to show his rough side to all important people, although he offended them always more or less; and when any lady made her appearance at the fortress, then he considered it his duty to ride by her windows with his cronies, or kunaki as they are called in the dialect of the Caucasus, dressed in a red shirt and nothing but chuviaki on his bare legs, and shouting and swearing at the top of his voice—but all this not only with the desire to insult her, but also to show her what handsome white legs he had, and how easy it would be to fall in love with him if only he himself were willing. Or he often went by at night with two or three friendly Tatars to the mountains into ambush by the road so as to take by surprise and kill hostile Tatars coming along; and though more than once his heart told him that there was nothing brave in such a deed, yet he felt himself under obligations to inflict suffering upon people in whom he thought that he was disappointed, and whom he affected to hate and despise. He always carried two things,—an immense holy image around his neck, and a dagger above his shirt. He never took them off, but even went to bed with them. He firmly believed that enemies surrounded him. It was his greatest delight to argue that he was under obligations to wreak vengeance on some one and wash out insults in blood. He was persuaded that spite, vengeance, and hatred of the human race were the highest and most poetical of feelings. But his mistress,—a Circassian girl course,—whom I happened afterwards to meet, said that he was the mildest and gentlest of men, and that every evening he wrote in his gloomy diary, cast up his accounts on ruled paper, and got on his knees to say his prayers. And how much suffering he endured, to seem to himself only what he desired to be, because his comrades and the soldiers could not comprehend him as he desired!

Once, in one of his nocturnal expeditions with his Tatar friends, it happened that he put a bullet into the leg of a hostile Tchetchenets, and took him prisoner. This Tchetchenets for seven weeks thereafter lived with the lieutenant; the lieutenant dressed his wound, waited on him as though he were his nearest friend, and when he was cured sent him home with gifts. Afterwards, during an expedition when the lieutenant was retreating from the post, having been repulsed by the enemy, he heard some one call him by name, and his wounded kunák strode out from among the hostile Tatars, and by signs asked him to do the same. The lieutenant went to meet his kunák, and shook hands with him. The mountaineers stood at some little distance, and refrained from firing; but, as soon as the lieutenant turned his horse to go back, several shot at him, and one bullet grazed the small of his back.

Another time I myself saw a fire break out by night in the fortress, and two companies of soldiers were detailed to put it out. Amid the crowd, lighted up by the ruddy glare of the fire, suddenly appeared the tall form of the man on a coal-black horse. He forced his way through the crowd, and rode straight to the fire. As soon as he came near, the lieutenant leaped from his horse, and hastened into the house, which was all in flames on one side. At the end of five minutes he emerged with singed hair and burned sleeves, carrying in his arms two doves which he had rescued from the flames.

His name was Rosenkranz; but he often spoke of his ancestry, traced it back to the Varangians, and clearly showed that he and his forefathers were genuine Russians.

[13] jigit or djigit in the Kumuits dialect signifies valiant. The Russians make from it the verb jigitovat.

[14] That is, known for telling the plain truth.

[15] chuviaki.

[16] The name of a character In one of Marlinski's novels.

IV.

The sun had travelled half its course, and was pouring down through the glowing atmosphere its fierce rays upon the parched earth. The dark blue sky was absolutely clear; only the bases of the snow-capped mountains began to clothe themselves in pale lilac clouds. The motionless atmosphere seemed to be full of some impalpable dust; it became intolerably hot.

When the army came to a small brook that had overflowed half the road, a halt was called. The soldiers, stacking their arms, plunged into the stream. The commander of the battalion sat down in the shade, on a drum, and, showing by his broad countenance the degree of his rank, made ready, in company with a few officers, to take lunch. The captain lay on the grass under the company's transport-wagon; the gallant lieutenant Rosenkranz and some other young officers, spreading out their Caucasian mantles, or burki, threw themselves down, and began to carouse as was manifest by the flasks and bottles scattered around them and by the extraordinary liveliness of their singers, who, standing in a half-circle behind them, gave an accompaniment to the Caucasian dance-song sung by a Lesghian girl:—

Shamyl resolved to make a league

In the years gone by,

Traï-raï, rattat-taï,

In the years gone by.

Among these officers was also the young ensign who had passed us in the morning. He was very entertaining: his eyes gleamed, his tongue never grew weary. He wanted to greet every one, and show his good-will to them all. Poor lad! he did not know that in acting this way he might be ridiculous, that his frankness and the gentleness which he showed to every one might win for him, not the love which he so much desired, but ridicule; he did not know this either, that when at last, thoroughly heated, he threw himself down on his burka, and leaned his head on his hand, letting his thick black curls fall over, he was a very picture of beauty.

Two officers crouched under a wagon, and were playing cards on a hamper.

I listened with curiosity to the talk of the soldiers and officers, and attentively watched the expression of their faces; but, to tell the truth, in not one could I discover a shadow of that anxiety which I myself felt; jokes, laughter, anecdotes, expressed the universal carelessness, and indifference to the coming peril. How impossible to suppose that it was not fated for some never again to pass that road!

V.

At seven o'clock in the evening, dusty and weary, we entered the wide, fortified gate of Fort N——. The sun was setting, and shed oblique rosy rays over the picturesque batteries and lofty-walled gardens that surrounded the fortress, over the fields yellow for the harvest, and over the white clouds which, gathering around the snow-capped mountains, simulated their shapes, and formed a chain no less wonderful and beauteous. A young half moon, like a translucent cloud, shone above the horizon. In the native village or aul, situated near the gate, a Tatar on the roof of a hut was calling the faithful to prayer. The singers broke out with new zeal and energy.

After resting and making my toilet I set out to call upon an adjutant who was an acquaintance of mine, to ask him to make my intention known to the general. On the way from the suburb where I was quartered, I chanced to see a most unexpected spectacle in the fortress of N——. I was overtaken by a handsome two-seated vehicle in which I saw a stylish bonnet, and heard French spoken. From the open window of the commandant's house came floating the sounds of some "Lízanka" or "Kátenka" polka played upon a wretched piano, out of tune. In the tavern which I was passing were sitting a number of clerks over their glasses of wine, with cigarettes in their hands, and I overheard one saying to another,—

"Excuse me, but taking politics into consideration, Márya Grigór'yevna is our first lady."

A humpbacked Jew of sickly countenance, dressed in a dilapidated coat, was creeping along with a shrill, broken-down hand-organ; and over the whole suburb echoed the sounds of the finale of "Lucia."

Two women in rustling dresses, with silk kerchiefs around their necks and bright-colored sun-shades in their hands, hastened past me on the plank sidewalk. Two girls, one in pink, the other in a blue dress, with uncovered heads, were standing on the terrace of a small house, and affectedly laughing with the obvious intention of attracting the notice of some passing officers. Officers in new coats, white gloves, and glistening epaulets, were parading up and down the streets and boulevards.

I found my acquaintance on the lower floor of the general's house. I had scarcely had time to explain to him my desire, and have his assurance that it could most likely be gratified, when the handsome carriage, which I had before seen, rattled past the window where I was sitting. From the carriage descended a tall, slender man, in uniform of the infantry service and major's epaulets, and came up to the general's rooms.

"Akh! pardon me, I beg of you," said the adjutant, rising from his place: "it's absolutely necessary that I tell the general."

"Who is it that just came?" I asked.

"The countess," he replied, and donning his uniform coat hastened upstairs.

In the course of a few minutes there appeared on the steps a short but very handsome man in a coat without epaulets, and a white cross in his button-hole. Behind him came the major, the adjutant, and two other officers.

In his carriage, his voice, in all his motions, the general showed that he had a very keen appreciation of his high importance.

"Bon soir, Madame la Comtesse," he said, extending his hand through the carriage window.

A dainty little hand in dog-skin glove took his hand, and a pretty, smiling little visage under a yellow bonnet appeared in the window.

From the conversation which lasted several minutes, I only heard, as I went by, the general saying in French with a smile,—

"You know that I have vowed to fight the infidels; beware of becoming one!"

A laugh rang from the carriage.

"Adieu donc, cher général."

"Non, au revoir," said the general, returning to the steps of the staircase; "don't forget that I have invited myself for to-morrow evening.".

The carriage drove away.

"Here is a man," said I to myself as I went home, "who has every thing that Russians strive after,—rank, wealth, society,—and this man, before a battle the outcome of which God only knows, jests with a pretty little woman, and promises to drink tea with her on the next day, just as though he had met her at a ball!"

There at that adjutant's I became acquainted with a man who still more surprised me; it was the young lieutenant of the K. regiment, who was distinguished for his almost feminine mildness and cowardice. He came to the adjutant to pour out his peevishness and ill humor against those men who, he thought, were intriguing against him to keep him from taking part in the matter in hand.

He declared that it was hateful to be treated so, that it was not doing as comrades ought, that he would remember him, and so forth.

As soon as I saw the expression of his face, as soon as I heard the sound of his voice, I could not escape the conviction that he was not only not putting it on, but was deeply stirred and hurt because he was not allowed to go against the Cherkess, and expose himself to their fire: he was as much hurt as a child is hurt who is unjustly punished. I could not understand it at all.

VI.

At ten o'clock in the evening the troops were ordered to march. At half-past nine I mounted my horse, and started off to find the general; but on reflecting that he and his adjutant must be busy, I remained in the street, and, tying my horse to a fence, sat down on the terrace to wait until the general should come.

The heat and glare of the day had already vanished in the fresh night air; and the obscure light of the young moon, which, infolding around itself a pale gleaming halo against the dark blue of the starry sky, was beginning to decline. Lights shone in the windows of the houses and in the chinks of the earth huts. The gracefully proportioned poplars in the gardens, standing out against the horizon from behind the earth huts, whose reed-thatched roofs gleamed pale in the moonlight, seemed still taller and blacker.

The long shadows of the houses, of the trees, of the fences, lay beautifully across the white dusty road. In the river rang incessantly the voice of the frogs;[17] in the streets were heard hurrying steps, and sounds of voices, and the galloping of horses. From the suburb came floating, now and again, the strains of the hand-organ; now the popular Russian air, "The winds are blowing," now one of the Aurora waltzes.

I will not tell what my thoughts were: in the first place, because I should be ashamed to confess to the melancholy ideas which without cessation arose in my mind, while all around me I perceived only gayety and mirth; and, in the second place, because they have nothing to do with my story.

I was so deeply engrossed in thought, that I did not notice that the bell was ringing for eleven o'clock, and the general was riding past me with his suite.

The rearguard was just at the fortress gate. I galloped at full speed across the bridge, amid a crush of cannon, caissons, military wagons, and commanding officers shouting at the top of their voices. After reaching the gate, I rode at a brisk trot for almost a verst, past the army stretched out and silently moving through the darkness, and overtook the general. As I made my way past the mounted artillery dragging their ordnance, amid the cannon and officers, a German voice, like a disagreeable dissonance interrupting soft and majestic harmony, struck my ear. It screamed, "Agkhtingkhist,[18] bring a linstock."

And a soldier's voice replied, quick as a flash, "Chevchenko! the lieutenant asks for a light!"

The greater part of the sky had become enveloped in long steel-gray clouds: here and there gleamed from between them the lustreless stars. The moon was now sinking behind the near horizon of dark mountains which were on the right; and it shed on their summits a feeble, waning, half light, which contrasted sharply with the impenetrable darkness that marked their bases.

The air was mild, and so still, that not a single grass-blade, not a single mist-wreath, moved. It became so dark, that it was impossible to distinguish objects, even though very near at hand. On the side of the road, there seemed to me sometimes to be rocks, sometimes animals, sometimes strange men; and I knew that they were bushes only when I heard them rustle, and felt the coolness of the dew with which they were covered. In front of me I saw a dense, waving black shadow, behind which followed a few moving spots; this was the van-guard of cavalry, and the general with his suite. Between us moved another similar black mass, but this was not as high as the first; this was the infantry.

Such silence reigned in the whole detachment, that there could be plainly distinguished all the harmonious voices of the night, full of mysterious charm. The distant melancholy howls of jackals, sometimes like the wails of despair, sometimes like laughter; the monotonous ringing song of the cricket, the frog, the quail; a gradually approaching murmur, the cause of which I could not make clear to my own mind; and all those nocturnal, almost audible motions of nature, which it is so impossible either to comprehend or define,—unite into one complete, beautiful harmony which we call silent night.

This silence was broken, or rather was unified, by the dull thud of the hoofs, and the rustling of the tall grass through which the division was slowly moving.

Occasionally, however, was heard in the ranks the ring of a heavy cannon, the sound of clashing bayonets, stifled conversation, and the snorting of a horse.

Nature breathed peacefully in beauty and power.

Is it possible that people find no room to live together in this beautiful world, under this boundless starry heaven? Is it possible that amid this bewitching nature, the soul of man can harbor the sentiments of hatred and revenge, or the passion for inflicting destruction upon his kind? All ugly feelings in the heart of man ought, it would seem, to vanish away in this intercourse with nature,—with this immediate expression of beauty and goodness!

[17] The frogs in the Caucasus make a sound entirely different from the

Kvakan'yé of the Russian frogs.

[18] German mispronunciation for Antichrist, the accent of which in Russian falls on the penult.

VII.

We had now been marching more than two hours. I began to feel chilly, and to be overcome with drowsiness. In the darkness the same indistinct objects dimly appeared: at a little distance, the same black shadow, the same moving spots. Beside me was the crupper of a white horse, which switched his tail and swung his hind-legs in wide curves. I could see a back in a white Circassian shirt, against which was outlined a carbine in its black case, and the handle of a pistol in an embroidered holster: the glow of a cigarette casting a gleam on a reddish mustache, a fur collar, and a hand in a chamois-skin glove.

I leaned over my horse's neck, closed my eyes, and lost myself for a few minutes: then suddenly the regular hoof-beat[19] and rustling came into my consciousness again. I looked around, and it seemed to me as though I were standing still in one spot, and that the black shadow in front of me was moving down upon me; or else that the shadow stood still, and I was rapidly riding down upon it.

At one such moment I was more strongly than ever impressed by that incessantly approaching sound, the cause of which I could not fathom: it was the roar of water. We were passing though a deep gulch, and coming close to a mountain river, which at that season was in full flood.[20] The roaring became louder, the damp grass grew taller and thicker, bushes were encountered in denser clumps, and the horizon narrowed itself down to closer limits. Now and then, in different places in the dark hollows of the mountains, bright fires flashed out and were immediately extinguished.

"Tell me, please, what are those fires," I asked in a whisper of the Tatar riding at my side.

"Don't you really know?" was his reply.

"No," said I.

"That is mountain straw tied to a pole,[21] and the light is waved."

"What for?"

"So that every man may know the Russian is coming. Now in the Auls," he added with a smile, "aï, aï the tomásha[22] are flying about; every sort of khurda-murda[23] will be hurried into the ravines."

"How do they know so soon in the mountains that the expedition is coming?" I asked.

"Eï! How can they help knowing? It's known everywhere: that's the kind of people we are."

"And so Shamyl is now getting ready to march out?" I asked.

"Yok (no)," he replied, shaking his head as a sign of negation, "Shamyl will not march out. Shamyl will send his naïbs[24] and he himself will look down from up yonder through his glass."

"But doesn't he live a long way off?"

"Not a long way off. Here, at your left, about ten versts he will be."

"How do you know that?" I inquired. "Have you been there?"

"I've been there. All of us in the mountains have."

"And you have seen Shamyl?"

"Pikh! Shamyl is not to be seen by us. A hundred, three hundred, a thousand murids[25] surround him. Shamyl will be in the midst of them," he said with an expression of fawning servility.

Looking up in the air, it was possible to make out that the sky which had become clear again was lighter in the east, and the Pleiades were sinking down into the horizon. But in the gulch through which we were passing, it was humid and dark.

Suddenly, a little in advance of us, from out the darkness flashed a number of lights; at the same instant, with a ping some bullets whizzed by, and from out the silence that surrounded us from afar arose the heavy, overmastering roar of the guns. This was the vanguard of the enemy's pickets.

The Tatars, of which it was composed, set up their war-cry, shot at random, and fled in all directions.

Every thing became silent again. The general summoned his interpreter. The Tatar in a white Circassian dress hastened up to him, and the two held a rather long conversation in a sort of whisper and with many gestures.

"Colonel Khasánof! give orders to scatter the enemy," said the general in a low, deliberate, but distinct tone of voice.

The division went down to the river. The black mountains stood back from the pass; it was beginning to grow light. The arch of heaven, in which the pale, lustreless stars were barely visible, seemed to come closer; the dawn began to glow brightly in the east; a cool, penetrating breeze sprang up from the west, and a bright mist like steam arose from the foaming river.

[19] topot.

[20] In the Caucasus the freshets take place in the mouth of July.

[21] tayak in the Caucasian dialect.

[22] tomásha means slaves in the ordinary dialect invented for intercourse between Russians and Tatars. There are many words in this strange dialect, the roots of which are not to be found either in Russian or Tatar.—AUTHOR'S NOTE.

[23] Goods and chattels in the same dialect.

[24] naïb ordinarily means a Mohammedan judge or high religious officer, in Turkey and the Caucasus; hero it means an officer whom the great Circassian chieftain Shamyl endowed with special authority.

[25] The word murid has many significations, but in the sense here employed it means something between adjutant and body-guard.—AUTHOR'S NOTE.

VIII.

The guide pointed out the ford; and the vanguard of cavalry, with the general and his suite immediately in its rear, began to cross the river.

The water, which reached the horses' breasts, rushed with extraordinary violence among the white bowlders which in some places came to the top, and formed foaming, gurgling whirlpools around the horses' legs. The horses were frightened at the roar of the water, lifted their heads, pricked up their ears, but slowly and carefully picked their way against the stream along the uneven bottom. The riders held up their legs and fire-arms. The foot-soldiers, literally in their shirts alone, lifting above the water their muskets to which were fastened their bundles of clothing, struggled against the force of the stream by clinging together, a score of men at a time, showing noticeable determination on their excited faces. The artillery-men on horseback, with a loud shout, put their horses into the water at full trot. The cannon and green-painted caissons, over which now and then, the water came pouring, plunged with a clang over the rocky bottom; but the noble Cossack horses pulled with united effort, made the water foam, and with dripping tails and manes emerged on the farther shore.

As soon as the crossing was effected, the general's face suddenly took on an expression of deliberation and seriousness; he wheeled his horse around, and at full gallop rode across the wide forest-surrounded field which spread before us. The Cossack horses were scattered along the edge of the forest.

In the forest appeal's a man in Circassian dress and round cap; then a second and a third ... one of the officers shouts, "Those are Tatars!" At this instant a puff of smoke came from behind a tree ... a report—another. The quick volleys of our men drown out those of the enemy. Only occasionally a bullet, with long-drawn ping like the hum of a bee, flies by, and is the only proof that not all the shots are ours.

Here the infantry at double quick, and with fixed bayonets, dash against the chain; one can hear the heavy reports of the guns, the metallic clash of grape-shot, the whiz of rockets, the crackling of musketry. The cavalry, the infantry, converge from all sides on the wide field. The smoke from the guns, rockets, and fire-arms, unites with the early mist arising from the dew-covered grass.

Colonel Khasánof gallops up to the general, and reins in his horse while at full tilt.

"Your Excellency," says he, lifting his hand to his cap, "give orders for the cavalry to advance. The standards are coming,"[26] and he points with his whip to mounted Tatars, at the head of whom rode two men on white horses with red and blue streamers on their lances.

"All right,[27] Iván Mikháïlovitch," says the general. The colonel wheels his horse round on the spot, draws his sabre, and shouts "Hurrah!"

"Hurrah! hurrah! hurrah!" echoes from the ranks, and the cavalry dash after him.

All look on with excitement: there is a standard;[28] another; a third; a fourth!...

The enemy, not waiting the assault, fly into the forest, and open a musket fire from behind the trees. The bullets fly more and more thickly.

"Quel charmant coup d'œil!" exclaimed the general as he easily rose in English fashion on his coal-black, slender-limbed little steed.

"Charmant," replies the major, who rolls his r's like a Frenchman, and whipping up his horse dashes after the general. "It's a genuine pleasure to carry on war in such a fine country," says he.[29]

"And above all in good company," adds the general still in French, with a pleasant smile.

The major bowed.

At this time a cannon-ball from the enemy comes flying by with a swift, disagreeable whiz, and strikes something; immediately is heard the groan of a wounded man. This groan impresses me so painfully that the martial picture instantly loses for me all its fascination: but no one beside myself seems to be affected in the same way; the major smiles apparently with the greatest satisfaction; another officer with perfect equanimity repeats the opening words of a speech; the general looks in the opposite direction, and with the most tranquil smile says something in French.

"Will you give orders to reply to their heavy guns?" asks the commander of the artillery, galloping up. "Yes, scare them a little," says the general carelessly, lighting a cigar.

The battery is unlimbered, and the cannonade begins. The ground shakes under the report; the firing continues without cessation; and the smoke in which it is scarcely possible to distinguish those attending the guns, blinds the eyes.

The aul is battered down. Again Colonel Khasánof dashes up, and at the general's command darts off to the aul. The war-cry is heard again, and the cavalry disappears in the cloud of its own dust.

The spectacle was truly grandiose. One thing only spoiled the general impression for me as a man who had no part in the affair, and was wholly unwonted to it; and this was that there was too much of it,—the motion and the animation and the shouts. Involuntarily the comparison occurred to me of a man who in his haste would cut the air with a hatchet.

[26] znatchki. This word among the mountaineers has almost the signification of banner, with this single distinction, that each jigit can make a standard for himself and carry it.—AUTHOR'S NOTE.

[27] S Bógom, literally "with God," but a mere phrase.

[28] znatchók.

[29] C'est un vrai plaisir, que la guerre dans un aussi beau pays.

IX.

The aul was already in the possession of our men, and not a soul of the enemy remained in it when the general with his suite, to which I had joined myself, entered it.

The long neat huts or saklí, with their flat earthen roofs and red chimneys, were situated on rough, rocky hills, between which ran a small river. On one side were seen the green gardens, shining in the clear sun-light, with monstrous pear-trees, and the plum-trees, called luitcha. The other side bristled with strange shadows, where stood the high perpendicular stones of a cemetery, and the tall wooden poles adorned at the ends with balls and variegated banners. These were the tombs of jigits.

The army stood drawn up within the gates.

After a moment the dragoons, the Cossacks, the infantry, with evident joy were let loose through the crooked streets, and the empty aul suddenly teemed with life. Here a roof is crushed in; the axe rings on the tough trees, and the plank door is broken down; there hay-ricks, fences, and huts are burning, and the dense smoke arises like a tower in the clear air. Here a Cossack is carrying off sacks of flour, and carpets; a soldier with a gay face lugs from a hut a tin basin and a dish-clout; another with outstretched arms is trying to catch a couple of hens, which cackling furiously fly about the yard; a third is going somewhere with a monstrous kumgan or pitcher of milk, and drinking as he goes, and when he has had his fill smashes it on the ground with a loud laugh.

The battalion which I had accompanied from Fort N—— was also in the aul. The captain was sitting on the roof of a hut, and was puffing from his short little pipe clouds of smoke of sambrotalicheski tabák with such an indifferent expression of countenance that when I saw him I forgot that I was in a hostile aul, and it seemed to me that I was actually at home with him.

"Ah! and here you are?" he said as he caught sight of me.

The tall form of Lieutenant Rosenkranz flashed here and there through the aul. Without a moment's pause he was engaged in carrying out orders, and he had the appearance of a man who had all he could do. I saw him coming out of a hut, his face full of triumph; behind him two soldiers were dragging an old Tatar with his arms tied. The old man, whose garb consisted merely of a many-colored beshmét torn in tatters, and ragged drawers, was so feeble that it seemed as if his bony arms, tightly tied behind his misshapen back, were almost falling from his shoulders; and his crooked bare legs moved with difficulty. His face, and even a part of his shaven head, were covered with deep wrinkles; his distorted toothless mouth, encircled by gray clipped mustache and beard, incessantly mumbled as though whispering something; but his handsome eyes, from which the lashes were gone, still gleamed with fire, and clearly expressed an old man's indifference to life.

Rosenkranz through an interpreter asked him why he had not gone with the others.

"Where should I go?" he replied, calmly looking away.

"Where the rest have gone," suggested some one.

"The jigits have gone to fight with the Russians, and I am an old man."

"Aren't you afraid of the Russians?"

"What will the Russians do to me? I am an old man," he repeated, carelessly glancing at the circle surrounding him.

On the way back, I saw this old man without a hat, with his hands still tied, jolting behind a mounted Cossack, and he was looking about him with the same expression of unconcern. He was necessary in an exchange of prisoners.

I went to the staircase, and crept up to where the captain was.

"Not many of the enemy, it seems," I said to him, wishing to obtain his opinion about the affair.

"The enemy," he repeated with surprise, "there weren't any at all. Do you call these enemies?... Here when evening comes, you will see how we shall retreat; you will see how they will go with us! Won't they show themselves there?" he added, pointing with his pipe to the forest which we had passed in the morning.

"What is that?" I asked anxiously, interrupting the captain, and drawing his attention to some Don Cossacks who were grouped around some one not far from us.

Among them was heard something like the weeping of a child, and the words,—

"Eh! don't cut—hold on—you will be seen—here's a knife—give him the knife."

"They are up to some mischief, the brutes," said the captain indifferently.

But at this very instant, suddenly from around the corner came the handsome ensign with burning, horror-stricken face, and waving his hands rushed among the Cossacks.

"Don't you move! don't kill him!" he cried in his boyish treble.

When the Cossacks saw the officer they started back, and allowed a little white goat to escape from their hands. The young ensign was wholly taken aback, began to mutter something, and stood before them full of confusion. When he caught sight of the captain and me on the roof, he grew still redder in the face, and springing up the steps joined us.

"I thought they were going to kill a child," he said with a timid smile.

X.

The general had gone on ahead with the cavalry.

The battalion with which I had come from Fort N—— remained in the rear-guard. The companies under command of Captain Khlopof and Lieutenant Rosenkranz were retreating together.

The captain's prediction was fully justified: as soon as we had reached the narrow forest of which he had spoken, from both sides the mountaineers, mounted and on foot, began to show themselves incessantly, and so near that I could very distinctly see many crouching down, with muskets in their hands, and running from tree to tree.

The captain took off his hat, and piously made the sign of the cross; a few old soldiers did the same. In the forest were heard shouts, the words, "iáï! Giaur! Urús! iáï!"

Dry, short musket reports followed in quick succession, and bullets whizzed from both sides. Our men silently replied with rapid fire; only occasionally in the ranks were heard exclamations in the guise of directions: "He[30] has stopped shooting there;" "He has a good chance behind the trees;" "We ought to have cannon," and such expressions.

The cannon were brought to bear on the range, and after a few discharges of grape the enemy apparently gave way; but after a little their fire became more and more violent with each step that the army took, and the shouts and war-cries increased.

We were scarcely three hundred sazhens[31] from the aul when the enemy's shot began to hail down upon us. I saw a ball with a thud strike one soldier dead ... but why relate details of this terrible spectacle, when I myself would give much to forget it?

Lieutenant Rosenkranz was firing his musket without a moment's cessation; with animating voice he was shouting to the soldiers, and galloping at full speed from one end of the line to the other. He was slightly pale, and this was decidedly becoming to his martial countenance.

The handsome ensign was in his element: his beautiful eyes gleamed with resolution, his mouth was slightly parted with a smile; he was constantly riding up to the captain, and asking permission to charge.[32]

"We'll drive them back," he said impulsively,—"we'll drive them back surely."

"No need of it," replied the captain gently: "we must get out of here."

The captain's company occupied the edge of the forest, and was fully exposed to the enemy's fire. The captain in his well-worn coat and tattered cap, slackening the reins for his white trotter and clinging by his short stirrups, silently staid in one place. (The soldiers were so well trained, and did their work so accurately, that there was no need of giving commands to them.) Only now and then he raised his voice, and shouted to those who exposed their heads. The captain's face was very far from martial; but such truth and simplicity were manifest in it, that it impressed me profoundly.

"There is some one who is truly brave," I said to myself involuntarily.

He was almost exactly the same as I had always seen him; the same tranquil motions, the same even voice, the same expression of frankness on his homely but honest face; but by his more than ordinarily keen glance it was possible to recognize him as a man who infallibly knew his business. It is easy to say the same as always; but how different were the traits brought out in others! one tried to seem calmer, another rougher, a third gayer, than usual; but by the captain's face it was manifest that he did not even understand how to seem.

The Frenchman who at Waterloo said, La garde meurt, mais ne se rend pas, and other heroes, especially among the French, who have uttered notable sayings, were brave, and really uttered notable sayings; but between their bravery, and the bravery of the captain, is this difference, that if a great saying in regard to any subject came into my hero's mind, I believe that he would not have uttered it; in the first place, because he would have feared that in saying something great he might spoil a great deed, and, secondly, because when a man is conscious within himself of the power to do a great deed, there is no need of saying any thing at all. This, in my opinion, is the especial and lofty character of Russian bravery; and how, henceforth, can it fail to wound the Russian heart when among our young warriors one hears French platitudes which have their vogue because they were the stock phrases of the old French nobility?...

Suddenly, from the direction in which the handsome ensign with his division was stationed, was heard a faint hurrah from the enemy. Turning round at this shouting I saw thirty soldiers who with muskets in their hands and knapsacks on their shoulders were going at double-quick across the ploughed field. They stumbled, but still pushed ahead and shouted. Leading them galloped the young ensign, waving his sabre.

All were lost to sight in the forest.

At the end of a few moments of shouting and clash of arms, a frightened horse came dashing out of the woods, and just at the edge soldiers were seen bearing the killed and wounded. Among the latter was the young ensign. Two soldiers carried him in their arms. He was pale as a sheet, and his graceful head, where could be now detected only the shadow of that martial enthusiasm which inspired him but a moment before, was strangely drawn down between his shoulders and rested on his breast. On his white shirt under his coat, which was torn open, could be seen a small blood-stain.

"Akh! what a pity!" I said in spite of myself, as I turned away from this heart-rending spectacle.

"Indeed it's too bad," said an old soldier who with gloomy face stood beside me leaning on his musket. "He wasn't afraid of any thing! How is this possible?" he added, looking steadily at the wounded lad. "Always foolish! and now he has to pay for it!"

"And aren't you afraid?" I asked.

"No, indeed!"

[30] On—he—the collective expression by which the soldiers in the Caucasus indicate the enemy.—AUTHOR'S NOTE.

[31] 2,100 feet.

[32] brosítsa na urá— to rush with a hurrah!

XI.

Four soldiers bore the ensign on a litter; behind them followed a soldier from the suburb, leading a lean, foundered horse laden with two green chests in which were the surgeon's implements. They were expecting the doctor. The officers hurried up to the litter, and tried to encourage and comfort the wounded lad.

"Well, brother Alánin, it'll be some time before you dance and make merry again," said Lieutenant Rosenkranz coming up with a smile.

He probably intended these words to sustain the handsome ensign's courage; but as could be easily seen from the coldly mournful expression in the eyes of the latter, these words did not produce the wished-for effect.

The captain also came up. He gazed earnestly at the wounded young fellow, and his always cold, calm face expressed heartfelt pity.

"How is it, my dear Anatoli Ivánuitch?" said he in a tone which rang with a deeper sympathy than I had expected from him: "we see it's as God wills."

The wounded lad looked up; his pale face was lighted with a mournful smile.

"Yes, I disobeyed you."

"Say rather, it was God's will," replied the captain.

The doctor, who had now arrived, took from his chest, bandages, probes, and other instruments, and, rolling up his sleeves with a re-assuring smile, approached the sufferer.

"So it seems they have been making a little hole through you," he said in a tone of jesting unconcern. "Let us have a look at the place."

The ensign listened, but in the gaze which he fixed on the jolly doctor were expressed surprise and reproachfulness which the latter did not expect. He began to probe the wound and examine it from all sides; but at last the sufferer, losing his patience, pushed away his hand with a heavy groan.

"Let me be," he said in an almost inaudible voice: "it makes no difference; I am dying." With these words he fell on his back; and five minutes later when I joined the group gathered about him, and asked a soldier, "How is the ensign?" I was told, "He has gone."

XII.

It was late when the expedition, deploying in a broad column, entered the fortress with songs. The sun had set behind the snow-covered mountain crest, and was throwing its last rosy rays on the long delicate clouds which stretched across the bright pellucid western sky. The snow-capped mountains began to clothe themselves in purple mist; only their upper outlines were marked with extraordinary distinctness against the violet light of the sunset. The clear moon, which had long been up, began to shed its light through the dark blue sky. The green of the grass and of the trees changed to black, and grew wet with dew. The dark masses of the army, with gradually increasing tumult, advanced across the field; from different sides were heard the sounds of cymbals, drums, and merry songs. The leader of the sixth company sang out with full strength, and full of feeling and power the clear chest-notes of the tenor were borne afar through the translucent evening air.

THE WOOD-CUTTING EXPEDITION.

(Rúbka L'ýesa.)

THE STORY OF A YUNKER'S[1] ADVENTURE.

I.

In midwinter, in the year 185-, a division of our batteries was engaged in an expedition on the Great Chetchen River. On the evening of Feb. 26, having been informed that the platoon which I commanded in the absence of its regular officer was detailed for the following day to help cut down the forest, and having that evening obtained and given the necessary directions, I betook myself to my tent earlier than usual; and as I had not got into the bad habit of warming it with burning coals, I threw myself, without undressing, down on my bed made of sticks, and, drawing my Circassian cap over my eyes, I rolled myself up in my shuba, and fell into that peculiarly deep and heavy sleep which one obtains at the moment of tumult and disquietude on the eve of a great peril. The anticipation of the morrow's action brought me to such a state.

At three o'clock in the morning, while it was still perfectly dark, my warm sheep-skin was pulled off from me, and the red light of a candle was unpleasantly flashed upon my sleepy eyes.

"It's time to get up," said some one's voice. I shut my eyes involuntarily, wrapped my sheep-skin around me again, and dropped off into slumber.

"It's time to get up," repeated Dmitri relentlessly, shaking me by the shoulder. "The infantry are starting." I suddenly came to a sense of the reality of things, started up, and sprang to my feet.

Hastily swallowing a glass of tea, and taking a bath in ice-water, I crept out from my tent, and went to the park (where the guns were placed). It was dark, misty, and cold. The night fires, lighted here and there throughout the camp, lighted up the forms of drowsy soldiers scattered around them, and seemed to make the darkness deeper by their ruddy flickering flames. Near at hand one could hear monotonous, tranquil snoring; in the distance, movement, the babble of voices, and the jangle of arms, as the foot-soldiers got in readiness for the expedition. There was an odor of smoke, manure, wicks, and fog. The morning frost crept down my back, and my teeth chattered in spite of all my efforts to prevent it.

Only by the snorting and occasional stamping of horses could one make out in the impenetrable darkness where the harnessed limbers and caissons were drawn up, and, by the flashing points of the lintstocks, where the cannon were. With the words s Bógom,— God speed it,—the first gun moved off with a clang, followed by the rumbling caisson, and the platoon got under way.

We all took off our caps, and made the sign of the cross. Taking its place in the interval between the infantry, our platoon halted, and waited from four o'clock until the muster of the whole force was made, and the commander came.

"There's one of our men missing, Nikolaï Petróvitch," said a black form coming to me. I recognized him by his voice only as the platoon-artillerist Maksímof.

"Who?"

"Velenchúk is missing. When we hitched up he was here, I saw him; but now he's gone."

As it was entirely unlikely that the column would move immediately, we resolved to send Corporal Antónof to find Velenchúk. Shortly after this, the sound of several horses riding by us in the darkness was heard; this was the commander and his suite. In a few moments the head of the column started and turned,—finally we also moved,—but Antónof and Velenchúk had not appeared. However, we had not gone a hundred paces when the two soldiers overtook us.

"Where was he?" I asked of Antónof.

"He was asleep in the park."

"What! he was drunk, wasn't he?"

"No, not at all."

"What made him go to sleep, then?"

"I don't know."

During three hours of darkness we slowly defiled in monotonous silence across uncultivated, snowless fields and low bushes which crackled under the wheels of the ordnance.

At last, after we had crossed a shallow but phenomenally rapid brook, a halt was called, and from the vanguard were heard desultory musket-shots. These sounds, as always, created the most extraordinary excitement in us all. The division had been almost asleep; now the ranks became alive with conversation, repartees, and laughter. Some of the soldiers wrestled with their mates; others played hop, skip and jump; others chewed on their hard-tack, or, to pass away the time, engaged in drumming the different roll-calls. Meantime the fog slowly began to lift in the east, the dampness became more palpable, and the surrounding objects gradually made themselves manifest emerging from the darkness.

I already began to make out the green caissons and gun-carriages, the brass cannon wet with mist, the familiar forms of my soldiers whom I knew even to the least details, the sorrel horses, and the files of infantry, with their bright bayonets, their knapsacks, ramrods, and canteens on their backs.

We were quickly in motion again, and, after going a few hundred paces where there was no road, were shown the appointed place. On the right were seen the steep banks of a winding river and the high posts of a Tatar burying-ground. At the left and in front of us, through the fog, appeared the black belt. The platoon got under way with the limbers. The eighth company, which was protecting us, stacked their arms, and a battalion of soldiers with muskets and axes started for the forest.

Not five minutes had elapsed when on all sides piles of wood began to crackle and smoke; the soldiers swarmed about, fanning the fires with their hands and feet, lugging brush-wood and logs; and in the forest were heard the incessant strokes of a hundred axes and the crash of falling trees.

The artillery, with not a little spirit of rivalry with the infantry, heaped up their piles; and soon the fire was already so well under way that it was impossible to get within a couple of paces of it. The dense black smoke arose through the icy branches, from which the water dropped hissing into the flames, as the soldiers heaped them upon the fire; and the glowing coals dropped down upon the dead white grass exposed by the heat. It was all mere boy's play to the soldiers; they dragged great logs, threw on the tall steppe grass, and fanned the fire more and more.

As I came near a bonfire to light a cigarette, Velenchúk, always officious, but, now that he had been found napping, showing himself more actively engaged about the fire than any one else, in an excess of zeal seized a coal with his naked hand from the very middle of the fire, tossed it from one palm to the other, two or three times, and flung it on the ground. "Light a match and give it to him," said another. "Bring a lintstock, fellows," said still a third.

When I at last lighted my cigarette without the aid of Velenchúk, who tried to bring another coal from the fire, he rubbed his burnt fingers on the back of his sheepskin coat, and, doubtless for the sake of exercising himself, seized a great plane-tree stump, and with a mighty swing flung it on the fire. When at last it seemed to him that he might rest, he went close to the fire, spread out his cloak, which he wore like a mantle fastened at the back by a single button, stretched his legs, folded his great black hands in his lap, and opening his mouth a little, closed his eyes.

"Alas![2] I forgot my pipe! What a shame, fellows!" he said after a short silence, and not addressing anybody in particular.

[1] Yunker (German Junker) is a non-commissioned officer belonging to the nobility. Count Tolstoi himself began his military service in the Caucasus as a Yunker.

[2] Ekh-ma.

II.

In Russia there are three predominating types of soldiers, which embrace the soldiers of all arms,—those of the Caucasus, of the line, the guards, the infantry, the cavalry, the artillery, and the others.

These three types, with many subdivisions and combinations, are as follows:—

(1) The obedient,

(2) The domineering or dictatorial, and

(3) The desperate.

The obedient are subdivided into the apathetic obedient and the energetic obedient.

The domineering are subdivided into the gruffly domineering and the diplomatically domineering.

The desperate are subdivided into the desperate jesters and the simply desperate.

The type more frequently encountered than the rest—the type most gentle, most sympathetic, and for the most part endowed with the Christian virtues of meekness, devotion, patience, and submission to the will of God—is that of the obedient.

The distinctive character of the apathetic obedient is a certain invincible indifference and disdain of all the turns of fortune which may overtake him.

The characteristic trait of the drunken obedient is a mild poetical tendency and sensitiveness.

The characteristic trait of the energetic obedient is his limitation in intellectual faculties, united with an endless assiduity and fervor.

The type of the domineering is to be found more especially in the higher spheres of the army: corporals, non-commissioned officers, sergeants and others. In the first division of the gruffly domineering are the high-born, the energetic, and especially the martial type, not excepting those who are stern in a lofty poetic way (to this category belonged Corporal Antónof, with whom I intend to make the reader acquainted).

The second division is composed of the diplomatically domineering, and this class has for some time been making rapid advances. The diplomatically domineering is always eloquent, knows how to read, goes about in a pink shirt, does not eat from the common kettle, often smokes cheap Muscat tobacco, considers himself immeasurably higher than the simple soldier, and is himself rarely as good a soldier as the gruffly domineering of the first class.

The type of the desperate is almost the same as that of the domineering, that is, it is good in the first division,—the desperate jesters, the characteristic features of whom are invariably jollity, a huge unconcern in regard to every thing, a wealth of nature and boldness.

The second division is in the same way detestable: the criminally desperate, who, however, it must be said for the honor of the Russian soldier, are very rarely met with, and, if they are met with, then they are quickly drummed out of comradeship with the true soldier. Atheism, and a certain audacity in crime, are the chief traits of this character.

Velenchúk came under the head of the energetically obedient. He was a Little Russian by birth, had been fifteen years in the service; and while he was not a fine-looking nor a very skilful soldier, still he was simple-hearted, kind, and extraordinarily full of zeal, though for the most part misdirected zeal, and he was extraordinarily honest. I say extraordinarily honest, because the year before there had been an occurrence in which he had given a remarkable exhibition of this characteristic. You must know that almost every soldier has his own trade. The greater number are tailors and shoemakers. Velenchúk himself practised the trade of tailoring; and, judging from the fact that Sergeant Mikháil Doroféïtch gave him his custom, it is safe to say that he had reached a famous degree of accomplishment. The year before, it happened that while in camp, Velenchúk took a fine cloak to make for Mikháil Doroféïtch. But that very night, after he had cut the cloth, and stitched on the trimmings, and put it under his pillow in his tent, a misfortune befell him: the cloth, which was worth seven rubles, disappeared during the night. Velenchúk with tears in his eyes, with pale quivering lips and with stifled lamentations, confessed the circumstance to the sergeant.

Mikháil Doroféïtch fell into a passion. In the first moment of his indignation he threatened the tailor; but afterwards, like a kindly man with plenty of means, he waved his hand, and did not exact from Velenchúk the value of the cloak. In spite of the fussy tailor's endeavors, and the tears that he shed while telling about his misfortune, the thief was not detected. Although strong suspicions were attached to a corruptly desperate soldier named Chernof, who slept in the same tent with him, still there was no decisive proof. The diplomatically dictatorial Mikháil Doroféïtch, as a man of means, having various arrangements with the inspector of arms and steward of the mess, the aristocrats of the battery, quickly forgot all about the loss of this particular cloak. Velenchúk, on the contrary, did not forget his unhappiness. The soldiers declared that at this time they were apprehensive about him, lest he should make way with himself, or flee to the mountains, so heavily did his misfortune weigh upon him. He did not eat, he did not drink, was not able to work, and wept all the time. At the end of three days he appeared before Mikháil Doroféïtch, and without any color in his face, and with a trembling hand, drew out of his sleeve a piece of gold, and gave it to him.

"Faith,[3] and here's all that I have, Mikháil Doroféïtch; and this I got from Zhdánof," he said, beginning to sob again. "I will give you two more rubles, truly I will, when I have earned them. He (who the he was, Velenchúk himself did not know) made me seem like a rascal in your eyes. He, the beastly viper, stole from a brother soldier his hard earnings; and here I have been in the service fifteen years." ...

To the honor of Mikháil Doroféïtch, it must be said that he did not require of Velenchúk the last two rubles, though Velenchúk brought them to him at the end of two months.

[3] yéï Bogu.

III.

Five other soldiers of my platoon besides Velenchúk were warming themselves around the bonfire.

In the best place, away from the wind, on a cask, sat the platoon artillerist[4] Maksímof, smoking his pipe. In the posture, the gaze, and all the motions of this man it could be seen that he was accustomed to command,

and was conscious of his own worth, even if nothing were said about the cask whereon he sat, which during the halt seemed to become the emblem of power, or the nankeen short-coat which he wore.

When I approached, he turned his head round toward me; but his eyes remained fixed upon the fire, and only after some time did they follow the direction of his face, and rest upon me. Maksímof came from a semi-noble family.[5] He had property, and in the school brigade he obtained rank, and acquired some learning. According to the reports of the soldiers, he was fearfully rich and fearfully learned.

I remember how one time, when they were making practical experiments with the quadrant, he explained, to the soldiers gathered around him, that the motions of the spirit level arise from the same causes as those of the atmospheric quicksilver. At bottom Maksímof was far from stupid, and knew his business admirably; but he had the bad habit of speaking, sometimes on purpose, in such a way that it was impossible to understand him, and I think he did not understand his own words. He had an especial fondness for the words "arises" and "to proceed;" and whenever he said "it arises," or "now let us proceed," then I knew in advance that I should not understand what would follow. The soldiers, on the contrary, as I had a chance to observe, enjoyed hearing his "arises," and suspected it of containing deep meaning, though, like myself, they could not understand his words. But this incomprehensibility they ascribed to his depth, and they worshipped Feódor Maksímuitch accordingly. In a word, Maksímof was diplomatically dictatorial.

The second soldier near the fire, engaged in drawing on his sinewy red legs a fresh pair of stockings, was Antónof, the same bombardier Antónof who as early as 1837, together with two others stationed by one gun without shelter, was returning the shot of the enemy, and with two bullets in his thigh continued still to serve his gun and load it.

"He would have been artillerist long before, had it not been for his character," said the soldiers; and it was true that his character was odd. When he was sober, there was no man more calm, more peaceful, more correct in his deportment; when he was drunk he became an entirely different man.

Not recognizing authority, he became quarrelsome and turbulent, and was wholly valueless as a soldier. Not more than a week before this time he got drunk at Shrovetide; and in spite of all threats and exhortations, and his attachment to his cannon, he got tipsy and quarrelsome on the first Monday in Lent. Throughout the fast, notwithstanding the order for all in the division to eat meat, he lived on hard-tack alone, and in the first week he did not even take the prescribed allowance of vodka. However, it was necessary to see this short figure, tough as iron, with his stumpy, crooked legs, his shiny face with its mustache, when he, for example, under the influence of liquor, took the balaláïka, or three-stringed guitar of the Ukraïna, into his strong hands, and, carelessly glancing to this side and that, played some love-song, or with his cloak thrown over his shoulders, and the orders dangling from it, and his hands thrust into the pockets of his blue nankeen trousers, he rolled along the street; it was necessary to see his expression of martial pride, and his scorn for all that did not pertain to the military,—to comprehend how absolutely impossible it was for him to compare himself at such moments with the rude or the simply insinuating servant, the Cossack, the foot-soldier, or the volunteer, especially those who did not belong to the artillery. He quarrelled and was turbulent, not so much for his own pleasure as for the sake of upholding the spirit of all soldierhood, of which he felt himself to be the protector.

The third soldier, with ear-rings in his ears, with bristling mustaches, goose-flesh, and a porcelain pipe in his lips, crouching on his heels in front of the bonfire, was the artillery-rider Chikin. The dear man Chikin, as the soldiers called him, was a jester. In bitter cold, up to his knees in the mud, going without food two days at a time, on the march, on parade, undergoing instruction, the dear man always and everywhere screwed his face into grimaces, executed flourishes with his legs, and poured out such a flood of nonsense that the whole platoon would go into fits of laughter. During a halt or in camp Chikin had always around him a group of young soldiers, whom he either played cards with, or amused with tales about some sly soldier or English milord, or by imitating the Tatar and the German, or simply by making his jokes, at which everybody nearly died with laughter. It was a fact, that his reputation as a joker was so widespread in the battery, that he had only to open his mouth and wink, and he would be rewarded with a universal burst of guffaws; but he really had a great gift for the comic and unexpected. In every thing he had the wit to see something remarkable, such as never came into anybody else's head; and, what is more important, this talent for seeing something ridiculous never failed under any trial.

The fourth soldier was an awkward young fellow, a recruit of the last year's draft, and he was now serving in an expedition for the first time. He was standing in the very smoke, and so close to the fire that it seemed as if his well-worn short-coat[6] would catch on fire; but, notwithstanding this, by the way in which he had flung open his coat, by his calm, self-satisfied pose, with his calves arched out, it was evident that he was enjoying perfect happiness.

And finally, the fifth soldier, sitting some little distance from the fire, and whittling a stick, was Uncle Zhdánof. Zhdánof had been in service the longest of all the soldiers in the battery,—knew all the recruits; and everybody, from force of habit, called him dy'á-denka, or little uncle. It was said that he never drank, never smoked, never played cards (not even the soldier's pet game of noski), and never indulged in bad talk. All the time when military duties did not engross him he worked at his trade of shoemaking; on holidays he went to church wherever it was possible, or placed a farthing candle before the image, and read the psalter, the only book in which he cared to read. He had little to do with the other soldiers,—with those higher in rank,—though to the younger officers he was coldly respectful. With his equals, since he did not drink, he had little reason for social intercourse; but he was extremely fond of recruits and young soldiers: he always protected them, read them their lessons, and often helped them. All in the battery considered him a capitalist, because he had twenty-five rubles, which he willingly loaned to any soldier who really needed it. That same Maksímof who was now artillerist used to tell me that when, ten years before, he had come as a recruit, and the old drunken soldiers helped him to drink up the money that he had, Zhdánof, pitying his unhappy situation, took him home with him, severely upbraided him for his behavior, even administered a castigation, read him the lesson about the duties of a soldier's life, and sent him away after presenting him with a shirt (for Maksímof hadn't one to his back) and a half-ruble piece.

"He made a man of me," Maksímof used to say, always with respect and gratitude in his tone. He had also taken Velenchúk's part always, ever since he came as a recruit, and had helped him at the time of his misfortune about the lost cloak, and had helped many, many others during the course of his twenty-five years' service.

In the service it was impossible to find a soldier who knew his business better, who was braver or more obedient; but he was too meek and homely to be chosen as an artillerist,[7] though he had been bombardier fifteen years. Zhdánof's one pleasure, and even passion, was music. He was exceedingly fond of some songs, and he always gathered round him a circle of singers from among the young soldiers; and though he himself could not sing, he stood with them, and putting his hands into the pockets of his short-coat,[8] and shutting his eyes, expressed his contentment by the motions of his head and cheeks. I know not why it was, that in that regular motion of the cheeks under the mustache, a peculiarity which I never saw in any one else, I found unusual expression. His head white as snow, his mustache dyed black, and his brown, wrinkled face, gave him at first sight a stern and gloomy appearance; but as you looked more closely into his great round eyes, especially when they smiled (he never smiled with his lips), something extraordinarily sweet and almost childlike suddenly struck you.

[4] feierverker; German, Feuerwerker.

[5] odnodvortsui, of one estate; freemen, who in the seventeenth century were settled in the Ukrafoa with special privileges.

[6] polushubochek, little half shuba.

[7] feierverker.

[8] polushubka.

IV.

"Alas! I have forgotten my pipe; that's a misfortune, fellows," repeated Velenchúk.

"But you should smoke cikarettes,[9] dear man," urged Chikin, screwing up his mouth, and winking. "I always smoke cikarettes at home: it's sweeter."

Of course, all joined in the laugh.

"So you forgot your pipe?" interrupted Maksímof, proudly knocking out the ashes from his pipe into the palm of his left hand, and not paying any attention to the universal laughter, in which even the officers joined. "You lost it somewhere here, didn't you, Velenchúk?"

Velenchúk wheeled to right face at him, started to lift his hand to his cap, and then dropped it again.

"You see, you haven't woke up from your last evening's spree, so that you didn't get your sleep out. For such work you deserve a good raking."

"May I drop dead on this very spot, Feódor Maksímovitch, if a single drop passed my lips. I myself don't know what got into me," replied Velenchúk. "How glad I should have been to get drunk!" he muttered to himself.

"All right. But one is responsible to the chief for his brother's conduct, and when you behave this way it's perfectly abominable," said the eloquent Maksímof savagely, but still in a more gentle tone.

"Well, here is something strange, fellows," continued Velenchúk after a moment's silence, scratching the back of his head, and not addressing any one in particular; "fact, it's strange, fellows. I have been sixteen years in the service, and have not had such a thing happen to me. As we were told to get ready for a march, I got up, as my duty behooved. There was nothing at all, when suddenly in the park it came over me—came over me more and more; laid me out—laid me out on the ground—and everything.... And when I got asleep, I did not hear a sound, fellows. It must have been that I fainted away," he said in conclusion.

"At all events, it took all my strength to wake you up," said Antónof, as he pulled on his boot. "I pushed you, and pushed you. You slept like a log."

"See here," remarked Velenchúk, "if I had been drunk" ...

"Like a peasant-woman we had at home," interrupted Chikin. "For almost two years running she did not get down from the big oven. They tried to wake her up one time, for they thought she was asleep; but there she was, lying just as though she was dead: the same kind of sleep you had—isn't that so, clear man?"

"Just tell us, Chikin, how you led the fashion the time when you had leave of absence," said Maksímof, smiling, and winking at me as much as to say, "Don't you like to hear what the foolish fellow has to say?"

"How led the fashion, Feódor Maksímuitch?" asked Chikin, casting a quick side glance at me. "Of course, I merely told what kind of people we are here in the Kapkas."[10]

"Well, then, that's so, that's so. You are not a fashion leader ... but just tell us how you made them think you were commander."

"You know how I became commander for them. I was asked how we live," began Chikin, speaking rapidly, like a man who has often told the same story. "I said, 'We live well, dear man: we have plenty of victuals. At morning and night, to our delight all we soldiers get our chocolet;[11] and then at dinner every sinner has his imperial soup of barley groats, and instead of vodka, Modeira at each plate, genuine old Modeira in the cask, forty-second degree!'".

"Fine Modeira!" replied Velenchúk louder than the others, and with a burst of laughter. "Let's have some of it."

"Well, then, what did you have to tell them about the Esiatics?" said Maksímof, carrying his inquiries still further, as the general merriment subsided.

Chikin bent down to the fire, picked up a coal with his stick, put it on his pipe, and, as though not noticing the discreet curiosity aroused in his hearers, puffed for a long time in silence.

When at last he had raised a sufficient cloud of smoke, he threw away the coal, pushed his cap still farther on the back of his head, and making a grimace, and with an almost imperceptible smile, he continued: "They asked," said he, "'What kind of a person is the little Cherkés yonder? or is it the Turk that you are fighting with in the Kapkas country?' I tell 'em, 'The Cherkés here with us is not of one sort, but of different sorts. Some are like the mountaineers who live on the rocky mountain-tops, and eat stones instead of bread. The biggest of them,' I say, 'are exactly like big logs, with one eye in the middle of the forehead, and they wear red caps;' they glow like fire, just as you do, my dear fellow," he added, addressing a young recruit, who, in fact, wore an odd little cap with a red crown.

The recruit, at this unexpected sally, suddenly sat down on the ground, slapped his knees, and burst out laughing and coughing so that he could hardly command his voice to say, "That's the kind of mountaineers we have here."

"'And,' says I, 'besides, there are the mumri,'" continued Chikin, jerking his head so that his hat fell forward on his forehead; "'they go out in pairs, like little twins,—these others. Every thing comes double with them,' says I,' and they cling hold of each other's hands, and run so queek that I tell you-you couldn't catch up with them on horseback.'—'Well,' says he, 'these mumri who are so small as you say, I suppose they are born hand in hand?'" said Chikin, endeavoring to imitate the deep throaty voice of the peasant. "'Yes,' says I, 'my dear man, they are so by nature. You try to pull their hands apart, and it makes 'em bleed, just as with the Chinese: when you pull their caps off, the blood comes.'—'But tell us,' says he, 'how they kill any one.'—'Well, this is the way,' says I: 'they take you, and they rip you all up, and they reel out your bowels in their hands. They reel 'em out, and you defy them and defy them—till your soul'" ...

"Well, now, did they believe any thing you said, Chikin?" asked Maksímof with a slight smile, when those standing round had stopped laughing.

"And indeed it is a strange people, Feódor Maksímuitch: they believe every one; before God, they do. But still, when I began to tell them about Mount Kazbek, and how the snow does not melt all summer there, they all burst out laughing at the absurdity of it. 'What a story!' they said. 'Could such a thing be possible,—a mountain so big that the snow does not melt on it?' And I say, 'With us, when the thaw comes, there is such a heap; and even after it begins to melt, the snow lies in the hollows.'—'Go away,'" said Chikin, with a concluding wink.

[9] sikhárki.

[10] Kaphas for Kavkas, Caucasus.

[11] shchikuláta id'yót na soldátá.

V.

The bright disk of the sun, gleaming through the milk-white mist, had now got well up; the purple-gray horizon gradually widened: but, though the view became more extended, still it was sharply defined by the delusive white wall of the fog.

In front of us, on the other side of the forest, could be seen a good-sized field. Over the field there spread from all sides the smoke, here black, here milk-white, here purple; and strange forms swept through the white folds of the mist. Far in the distance, from time to time, groups of mounted Tatars showed themselves; and the occasional reports from our rifles, guns, and cannon were heard.

"This isn't any thing at all of an action—mere boys' play," said the good Captain Khlopof.

The commander of the ninth company of cavalry,[12] who was with us as escort, rode up to our cannon, and pointing to three mounted Tatars who were just then riding under cover of the forest, more than six hundred sazhens from us, asked me to give them a shot or a shell. His request was an illustration of the love universal among all infantry officers for artillery practice.

"You see," said he, with a kindly and convincing smile, laying his hand on my shoulder, "where those two big trees are, right in front of us: one is on a white horse, and dressed in a black Circassian coat; and directly behind him are two more. Do you see? If you please, we must" ...

"And there are three others riding along under the lee of the forest," interrupted Antónof, who was distinguished for his sharp eyes, and had now joined us with the pipe that he had been smoking concealed behind his back. "The front one has just taken his carbine from its case. It's easy to see, your Excellency."

"Ha! he fired then, fellows. See the white puff of smoke," said Velenchúk to a group of soldiers a little back of us.

"He must be aiming at us, the blackguard!" replied some one else.

"See, those fellows only come out a little way from the forest. We see the place: we want to aim a cannon at it," suggested a third. "If we could only blant a krenade into the midst of 'em, it would scatter 'em." ...

"And what makes you think you could shoot to such a tistance, dear man?" asked Chikin.

"Only five hundred or five hundred and twenty sazhens——it can't be less than that," said Maksímof coolly, as though he were speaking to himself; but it was evident that he, like the others, was terribly anxious to bring the guns into play. "If the howitzer is aimed up at an angle of forty-five degrees, then it will be possible to reach that spot; that is perfectly possible."

"You know, now, that if you aim at that group, it would infallibly hit some one. There, there! as they are riding along now, please hurry up and order the gun to be fired," continued the cavalry commander, beseeching me.

"Will you give the order to limber the gun?" asked Antónof suddenly, in a jerky base voice, with a slight touch of surliness in his manner.

I confess that I myself felt a strong desire for this, and I commanded the second cannon to be unlimbered.

The words had hardly left my mouth ere the bomb was powdered and rammed home; and Antónof, clinging to the gun-cheek, and leaning his two fat fingers on the carriage, was already getting the gun into position.

"Little ... little more to the left—now a little to the right—now, now the least bit more—there, that's right," said he with a proud face, turning from the gun.

The infantry officer, myself, and Maksímof, in turn sighted along the gun, and all gave expression to various opinions.

"By God! it will miss," said Velenchúk, clicking with his tongue, although he could only see over Antónof's shoulder, and therefore had no basis for such a surmise.

"By-y-y God! it will miss: it will hit that tree right in front, fellows."

"Two!" I commanded.

The men about the gun scattered. Antónof ran to one side, so as to follow the flight of the ball. There was a flash and a ring of brass. At the same instant we were enveloped in gunpowder smoke; and after the startling report, was heard the metallic, whizzing sound of the ball rushing off quicker than lightning, amid the universal silence and dying away in the distance.

Just a little behind the group of horsemen a white puff of smoke appeared; the Tatars scattered in all directions, and then the sound of a crash came to us.

"Capitally done!" "Ah! they take to their heels;" "See! the devils don't like it," were types of the exclamations and jests heard among the ranks of the artillery and infantry.

"If you had aimed a trifle lower, you'd have hit right in the midst of him," remarked Velenchúk. "I said it would strike the tree: it did; it took the one at the right."

[12] jägers.

VI.

Leaving the soldiers to argue about the Tatars taking to flight when they saw the shell, and why it was that they came there, and whether there were many in the forest, I went with the cavalry commander a few steps aside, and sat down under a tree, expecting to have some warmed chops which he had offered me. The cavalry commander, Bolkhof, was one of the officers who are called in the regiment bonjour-oli. He had property, had served before in the guards, and spoke French. But, in spite of this, his comrades liked him. He was rather intellectual, had tact enough to wear his Petersburg overcoat, to eat a good dinner, and to speak French without too much offending the sensibilities of his brother officers. As we talked about the weather, about the events of the war, about the officers known to us both, and as we became convinced, by our questions and answers, by our views of things in general, that we were mutually sympathetic, we involuntarily fell into more intimate conversation. Moreover, in the Caucasus, among men who meet in one circle, the question invariably arises, though it is not always expressed, "Why are you here?" and it seemed to me that my companion was desirous of satisfying this inarticulate question.

"When will this expedition end?" he asked lazily: "it's tiresome."

"It isn't to me," I said: "it's much more so serving on the staff."

"Oh, on the staff it's ten thousand times worse!" said he fiercely. "No, I mean when will this sort of thing end altogether?"

"What! do you wish that it would end?" I asked.

"Yes, all of it, altogether!... Well, are the chops ready, Nikoláief?" he inquired of his servant.

"Why do you serve in the Caucasus, then," I asked, "if the Caucasus does not please you?"

"You know wiry," he replied with an outburst of frankness: "on account of tradition. In Russia, you see, there exists a strange tradition about the Caucasus, as though it were the promised land for all sorts of unhappy people."

"Well," said I, "it's almost true: the majority of us here "...

"But what is better than all," said he, interrupting me, "is, that all of us who come to the Kavkas are fearfully deceived in our calculations; and really, I don't see why, in consequence of disappointment in love or disorder in one's affairs, one should come to serve in the Caucasus rather than in Kazan or

Kaluga. You see, in Russia they imagine the Kavkas as something immense,—everlasting virgin ice-fields, with impetuous streams, with daggers, cloaks, Circassian girls,—all that is strange and wonderful; but in reality there is nothing gay in it at all. If they only knew, for example, that we have never been on the virgin ice-fields, and that there was nothing gay in it at all, and that the Caucasus was divided into the districts of Stavropol, Tiflis, and so forth" ...

"Yes," said I, laughing, "when we are in Russia we look upon the Caucasus in an absolutely different way from what we do here. Haven't you ever noticed it: when you read poetry in a language that you don't know very well, you imagine it much better than it really is, don't you?"

"I don't know how that is, but this Caucasus doesn't please me," he said, interrupting me.

"It isn't so with me," I said: "the Caucasus is delightful to me now, but only" ...

"Maybe it is delightful," he continued with a touch of asperity, "but I know that it is not delightful to me."

"Why not?" I asked, with a view of saying something.

"In the first place, it has deceived me—all that which I expected, from tradition, to be delivered of in the Caucasus, I find in me just the same here, only with this distinction, that before, it was all on a larger scale, but now on a small and nasty scale, at each round of which I find a million petty annoyances, worriments, and miseries; in the second place, because I find that each day I am falling morally lower and lower; and principally because I feel myself incapable of service here—I cannot endure to face the danger ... simply, I am a coward." ...

He got up and looked at me earnestly.

Though this unbecoming confession completely took, me by surprise, I did not contradict him, as my messmate evidently expected me to do; but I awaited from the man himself the refutation of his words, which is always ready in such circumstances.

"You know to-day's expedition is the first time that I have taken part in action," he continued, "and you can imagine what my evening was. When the sergeant brought the order for my company to join the column, I became as pale as a sheet, and could not utter a word from emotion; and if you knew how I spent the night! If it is true that people turn gray from fright, then I ought to be perfectly white-headed to-day, because no man condemned to death ever suffered so much from terror in a single night as I did: even now, though I feel a little more at my ease than I did last night, still it goes here in me," he added, pressing his hand to his heart. "And what is absurd," he went on to say, "while this fearful drama is playing here, I myself am eating chops and onions, and trying to persuade myself that I am very gay.... Is there any wine, Nikoláief?" he added with a yawn.

"There he is, fellows!" shouted one of the soldiers at this moment in a tone of alarm, and all eyes were fixed upon the edge of the far-off forest.

In the distance a puff of bluish smoke took shape, and, rising up, drifted away on the wind. When I realized that the enemy were firing at us, every thing that was in the range of my eyes at that moment, every thing suddenly assumed a new and majestic character. The stacked muskets, and the smoke of the bonfires, and the blue sky, and the green gun-carriages, and Nikoláief's sunburned, mustachioed face,—all this seemed to tell me that the shot which at that instant emerged from the smoke, and was flying through space, might be directed straight at my breast.

"Where did you get the wine?" I meanwhile asked Bolkhof carelessly, while in the depths of my soul two voices were speaking with equal distinctness; one said, "Lord, take my soul in peace;" the other, "I hope I shall not duck my head, but smile while the ball is coming." And at that instant something horribly unpleasant whistled above our heads, and the shot came crashing to the ground not two paces away from us.

"Now, if I were Napoleon or Frederick the Great," said Bolkhof at this time, with perfect composure, turning to me, "I should certainly have said something graceful."

"But that you have just done," I replied, hiding with some difficulty the panic which I felt at being exposed to such a danger.

"Why, what did I say? No one will put it on record."

"I'll put it on record."

"Yes: if you put it on record, it will be in the way of criticism, as Mishchenkof says," he replied with a smile.

"Tfu! you devils!" exclaimed Antónof in vexation just behind us, and spitting to one side; "it just missed my leg."

All my solicitude to appear cool, and all our refined phrases, suddenly seemed to me unendurably stupid after this artless exclamation.

VII.

The enemy, in fact, had posted two cannon on the spot where the Tatars had been scattered, and every twenty or thirty minutes sent a shot at our wood-choppers. My division was sent out into the field, and ordered to reply to him. At the skirt of the forest a puff of smoke would show itself, the report would be heard, then the whiz of the ball, and the shot would bury itself behind us or in front of us. The enemy's shots were placed fortunately for us, and no loss was sustained.

The artillerists, as always, behaved admirably, loaded rapidly, aimed carefully wherever the smoke appeared, and jested unconcernedly with each other. The infantry escort, in silent inactivity, were lying around us, awaiting their turn. The wood-cutters were busy at their work; their axes resounded through the forest more and more rapidly, more and more eagerly, save when the svist of a cannon-shot was heard, then suddenly the sounds ceased, and amid the deathlike stillness a voice, not altogether calm, would exclaim, "Stand aside, boys!" and all eyes would be fastened upon the shot ricocheting upon the wood-piles and the brush.

The fog was now completely lifted, and, taking the form of clouds, was disappearing slowly in the dark-blue vault of heaven. The unclouded orb of the sun shone bright, and threw its cheerful rays on the steel of the bayonets, the brass of the cannon, on the thawing ground, and the glittering points of the icicles. The atmosphere was brisk with the morning frost and the warmth of the spring sun. Thousands of different shades and tints mingled in the dry leaves of the forest; and on the hard, shining level of the road could be seen the regular tracks of wheel-tires and horse-shoes.

The action between the armies grew more and more violent and more striking. In all directions the bluish puffs of smoke from the firing became more and more frequent. The dragoons, with bannerets waving from their lances, kept riding to the front. In the infantry companies songs resounded, and the train loaded with wood began to form itself as the rearguard. The general rode up to our division, and ordered us to be ready for the return. The enemy got into the bushes over against our left flank, and began to pour a heavy musketry-fire into us. From the left-hand side a ball came whizzing from the forest, and buried itself in a gun-carriage; then—a second, a third.... The infantry guard, scattered around us, jumped up with a shout, seized their muskets, and took aim. The cracking of the musketry was redoubled, and the bullets began to fly thicker and faster. The retreat had begun, and the present attack was the result, as is always the case in the Caucasus.

It became perfectly manifest that the artillerists did not like the bullets as well as the infantry had liked the solid shot. Antónof put on a deep frown. Chikin imitated the sound of the bullets, and fired his jokes at them; but it was evident that he did not like them. In regard to one he said, "What a hurry it's in!" another he called a "honey-bee;" a third, which flew over us with a sort of slow and lugubrious drone, he called an "orphan,"—a term which raised general amusement.

The recruit, who had the habit of bending his head to one side, and stretching out his neck, every time he heard a bullet, was also a source of amusement to the soldiers, who said, "Who is it? some acquaintance that you are bowing to?" And Velenchúk, who always showed perfect equanimity in time of danger, was now in an alarming state of mind; he was manifestly vexed because we did not send some canister in the direction from which the bullets came. He more than once exclaimed in a discontented tone, "What is he allowed to shoot at us with impunity for? If we could only answer with some grape, that would silence him, take my word for it."

In fact, it was time to do this. I ordered the last shell to be fired, and to load with grape.

"Grape!" shouted Antónof bravely in the midst of the smoke, coming up to the gun with his sponge as soon as the discharge was made.

At this moment, not far-behind us, I heard the quick whiz of a bullet suddenly striking something with a dry thud. My heart sank within me. "Some one of our men must have been struck," I said to myself; but at the same time I did not dare to turn round, under the influence of this powerful presentiment. True enough, immediately after this sound the heavy fall of a body was heard, and the "o-o-o-oï,"—the heart-rending groan of the wounded man. "I'm hit, fellows," remarked a voice which I knew. It was Velenchúk. He was lying on his back between the limbers and the gun. The cartridge-box which he carried was flung to one side. His forehead was all bloody, and over his right eye and his nose flowed a thick red stream. The wound was in his body, but it bled very little; he had hit his forehead on something when he fell.

All this I perceived after some little time. At the first instant I saw only a sort of obscure mass, and a terrible quantity of blood as it seemed to me.

None of the soldiers who were loading the gun said a word,—only the recruit muttered between his teeth, "See, how bloody!" and Antónof, frowning still blacker, snorted angrily; but all the time it was evident that the thought of death presented itself to the mind of each. All took hold of their work with great activity. The gun was discharged every instant; and the gun-captain, in getting the canister, went two steps around the place where lay the wounded man, now groaning constantly.

VIII.

Evert one who has been in action has doubtless experienced the strange although illogical but still powerful feeling of repulsion for the place in which any one has been killed or wounded. My soldiers were noticeably affected by this feeling at the first moment when it became necessary to lift Velenchúk and carry him to the wagon which had driven up. Zhdánof angrily went to the sufferer, and, notwithstanding his cry of anguish, took him under his arms and lifted him. "What are you standing there for? Help lug him!" he shouted; and instantly the men sprang to his assistance, some of whom could not do any good at all. But they had scarcely started to move him from the place when Velenchúk began to scream fearfully and to struggle.

"What are you screeching for, like a rabbit?" said Antónof, holding him roughly by the leg. "If you don't stop we'll drop you."

And the sufferer really calmed down, and only occasionally cried out, "Okh! I'm dead! o-okh, fellows![13] I'm dead!"

As soon as they laid him in the wagon, he ceased to groan, and I heard that he said something to his comrades—it must have been a farewell—in a weak but audible voice.

Indeed, no one likes to look at a wounded man; and I, instinctively hastening to get away from this spectacle, ordered the men to take him as soon as possible to a suitable place, and then return to the guns. But in a few minutes I was told that Velenchúk was asking for me, and I returned to the ambulance.

The wounded man lay on the wagon bottom, holding the sides with both hands. His healthy, broad face had in a few seconds entirely changed; he had, as it were, grown gaunt, and older by several years. His lips were pinched and white, and tightly compressed, with evident effort at self-control; his glance had a quick and feeble expression; but in his eyes was a peculiarly clear and tranquil gleam, and on his blood-stained forehead and nose already lay the seal of death.

In spite of the fact that the least motion caused him unendurable anguish, he was trying to take from his left leg his purse,[14] which contained money.

A fearfully burdensome thought came into my mind when I saw his bare, white, and healthy-looking leg as he was taking off his boot and untying his purse.

"There are three silver rubles and a fifty-kopek piece," he said when I took the girdle-purse. "You keep them."

The ambulance had started to move, but he stopped it.

"I was working on a cloak for Lieutenant Sulimovsky. He had paid me two-o-o silver rubles. I spent one and a half on buttons, but half a ruble lies with the buttons in my bag. Give them to him."

"Very good, I will," said I. "Keep up good hopes, brother."

He did not answer me; the wagon moved away, and he began once more to groan, and to exclaim "Okh!" in the same terribly heart-rending tone. As though he had done with earthly things, he felt that he had no longer any pretext for self-restraint, and he now considered this alleviation permissible.

[13] bratsuí moï.

[14] chéres; diminutive, chéresok,—a leather purse in the form of a girdle, which soldiers wear usually under the knee.—AUTHOR'S NOTE.

IX.

"Where are you off to? Come back! Where are you going?" I shouted to the recruit, who, carrying in his arms his reserve linstock, and a sort of cane in his hand, was calmly marching off toward the ambulance in which the wounded man was carried.

But the recruit lazily looked up at me, and kept on his way, and I was obliged to send a soldier to bring him back. He took off his red cap, and looked at me with a stupid smile.

"Where were you going?" I asked.

"To camp."

"Why?"

"Because—they have wounded Velenchúk," he replied, still smiling.

"What has that to do with you? It's your business to stay here."

He looked at me in amazement, then coolly turned round, put on his cap, and went to his place.

The result of the action had been fortunate. The Cossacks, it was reported, had made a brilliant attack, and had captured three bodies of the Tatars; the infantry had laid in a store of firewood, and had suffered in all a loss of six men wounded. In the artillery, from the whole array only Velenchúk and two horses were put hors du combat. Moreover, they had cut the forest for three versts, and cleared a place, so that it was impossible to recognize it; now, instead of a seemingly impenetrable forest girdle, a great field was opened up, covered with heaps of smoking bonfires, and lines of infantry and cavalry on their way to camp. Notwithstanding the fact that the enemy incessantly harassed us with cannonade and musketry, and followed us down to the very river where the cemetery was, that we had crossed in the morning, the retreat was successfully managed.

I was already beginning to dream of the cabbage-soup and rib of mutton with kasha gruel that were awaiting me at the camp, when the word came, that the general had commanded a redoubt to be thrown up on the river-bank, and that the third battalion of regiment K, and a division of the fourth battery, should stay behind till the next day for that purpose. The wagons with the firewood and the wounded, the Cossacks, the artillery, the infantry with muskets and fagots on their shoulders,—all with noise and songs passed by us. On the faces of all shone enthusiasm and content, caused by the return from peril, and hope of rest; only we and the men of the third battalion were obliged to postpone these joyful feelings till the morrow.

X.

While we of the artillery were busy about the guns, disposing the limbers and caissons, and picketing the horses, the foot-soldiers had stacked their arms, piled up bonfires, made shelters of boughs and cornstalks, and were cooking their grits.

It began to grow dark. Across the sky swept bluish-white clouds. The mist, changing into fine drizzling fog, began to wet the ground and the soldiers' cloaks. The horizon became contracted, and all our surroundings took on gloomy shadows. The dampness which I felt through my boots and on my neck, the incessant motion and chatter in which I took no part, the sticky mud with which my legs were covered, and my empty stomach, all combined to arouse in me a most uncomfortable and disagreeable frame of mind after a day of physical and moral fatigue. Velenchúk did not go out of my mind. The whole simple story of his soldier's life kept repeating itself before my imagination.

His last moments were as unclouded and peaceful as all the rest of his life. He had lived too honestly and simply for his artless faith in the heavenly life to come, to be shaken at the decisive moment.

"Your health," said Nikoláïef, coming to me. "The captain begs you to be so kind as to come and drink tea with him."

Somehow making my way between stacks of arms and the camp-fires, I followed Nikoláïef to where Captain Bolkhof was, and felt a glow of satisfaction in dreaming about the glass of hot tea and the gay converse which should drive away my gloomy thoughts.

"Well, has he come?" said Bolkhof's voice from his cornstalk wigwam, in which the light was gleaming.

"He is here, your honor,"[15] replied Nikoláïef in his deep bass.

In the hut, on a dry burka, or Cossack mantle, sat the captain in négligé, and without his cap. Near him the samovar was singing, and a drum was standing, loaded with lunch. A bayonet stuck into the ground held a candle.

"How is this?" he said with some pride, glancing around his comfortable habitation. In fact, it was so pleasant in his wigwam, that, while we were at tea I absolutely forgot about the dampness, the gloom, and Velenchúk's wound. We talked about Moscow and subjects that had no relation to the war or the Caucasus.

After one of the moments of silence which sometimes interrupt the most lively conversations, Bolkhof looked at me with a smile.

"Well, I suppose our talk this morning must have seemed very strange to you?" said he.

"No. Why should it? It only seemed to me that you were very frank;

but there are things which we all know, but which it is not necessary to speak about."

"Oh, you are mistaken! If there were only some possibility of exchanging this life for any sort of life, no matter how tame and mean, but free from danger and service, I would not hesitate a minute."

"Why, then, don't you go back to Russia?" I asked.

"Why?" he repeated. "Oh, I have been thinking about that for a long time. I can't return to Russia until I have won the Anna and Vladímir, wear the Anna ribbon around my neck, and am major, as I expected when I came here."

"Why not, pray, if you feel that you are so unfitted as you say for service here?"

"Simply because I feel still more unfitted to return to Russia the same as I came. That also is one of the traditions existing in Russia which were handed down by Passek, Sleptsof, and others,—that you must go to the Caucasus, so as to come home loaded with rewards. And all of us are expecting and working for this; but I have been here two years, have taken part in two expeditions, and haven't won any thing. But still, I have so much vanity that I shall not go away from here until I am, major, and have the Vladímir and Anna around my neck. I am already accustomed to having every thing avoid me, when even Gnilokishkin gets promoted, and I don't. And so how could I show myself in Russia before the eyes of my elder, the merchant Kotelnikof, to whom I sell wheat, or to my aunty in Moscow, and all those people, if I had served two years in the Caucasus without getting promoted? It is true that I don't wish to know these people, and, of course, they don't care very much about me; but a man is so constituted, that though I don't wish to know them, yet on account of them I am wasting my best years, and destroying all the happiness of my life, and all my future."

[15] váshie blagoródié.

XI.

At this moment the voice of the battalion commander was heard on the outside, saying, "Who is it with you, Nikoláï Feódorovitch?" Bolkhof mentioned my name, and in a moment three officers came into the wigwam,—Major Kirsánof, the adjutant of his battalion, and company commander Trosenko.

Kirsánof was a short, thick-set fellow, with black mustaches, ruddy cheeks, and little oily eyes. His little eyes were the most noticeable features of his physiognomy. When he laughed, there remained of them only two moist little stars; and these little stars, together with his pursed-up lips and long neck, sometimes gave him a peculiar expression of insipidity. Kirsánof considered himself better than any one else in the regiment. The under officers did not dispute this; and the chiefs esteemed him, although the general impression about him was, that he was very dull-witted. He knew his duties, was accurate and zealous, kept a carriage and a cook, and, naturally enough, managed to pass himself off as arrogant.

"What are you gossiping about, captain?" he asked as he came in.

"Oh, about the delights of the service here."

But at this instant Kirsánof caught sight of me, a mere yunker; and in order to make me gather a high impression of his knowledge, as though he had not heard Bolkhof's answer, and glancing at the drum, he asked,—

"What, were you tired, captain?"

"No. You see, we" ... began Bolkhof.

But once more, and it must have been the battalion commander's dignity that caused him to interrupt the answer, he put a new question:—

"Well, we had a splendid action to-day, didn't we?"

The adjutant of the battalion was a young fellow who belonged to the fourteenth army-rank, and had only lately been promoted from the yunker service. He was a modest and gentle young fellow, with a sensitive and good-natured face. I had met him before at Bolkhof's. The young man would come to see him often, make him a bow, sit down in a corner, and for hours at a time say nothing, and only make cigarettes and smoke them; and then he would get up, make another bow, and go away. He was the type of the poor son of the Russian noble family, who has chosen the profession of arms as the only one open to him in his circumstances, and who values above every thing else in the world his official calling,—an ingenuous and lovable type, notwithstanding his absurd, indefeasible peculiarities: his tobacco-pouch, his dressing-gown, his guitar, and his mustache brush, with which we used to picture him to ourselves. In the regiment they used to say of him that he boasted of being just but stern with his servant, and quoted him as saying, "I rarely punish; but when I am driven to it, then let 'em beware:" and once, when his servant got drunk, and plundered him, and began to rail at his master, they say he took him to the guard-house, and commanded them to have every thing ready for the chastisement; but when he saw the preparations, he was so confused, that he could only stammer a few meaningless words: "Well, now you see—I might," ... and, thoroughly upset, he set off home, and from that time never dared to look into the eyes of his man. His comrades gave him no peace, but were always nagging him about this; and I often heard how the ingenuous lad tried to defend himself, and, blushing to the roots of his hair, avowed that it was not true, but absolutely false.

The third character, Captain Trosenko, was an old Caucasian[16] in the full acceptation of the word: that is, he was a man for whom the company under his command stood for his family; the fortress where the staff was, his home; and the song-singers his only pleasure in life,—a man for whom every thing that was not Kavkas was worthy of scorn, yes, was almost unworthy of belief; every thing that was Kavkas was divided into two halves, ours and not ours. He loved the first, the second he hated with all the strength of his soul. And, above all, he was a man of iron nerve, of serene bravery, of rare goodness and devotion to his comrades and subordinates, and of desperate frankness, and even insolence in his bearing, toward those who did not please him; that is, adjutants and bon jourists. As he came into the wigwam, he almost bumped his head on the roof, then suddenly sank down and sat on the ground.

"Well, how is it?"[17] said he; and suddenly becoming cognizant of my presence, and recognizing me, he got up, turning upon me a troubled, serious gaze.

"Well, why were you talking about that?" asked the major, taking out his watch and consulting it, though I verily believe there was not the slightest necessity of his doing so.

"Well,[18] he asked me why I served here."

"Of course, Nikoláï Feódorovitch wants to win distinction here, and then go home."

"Well, now, you tell us, Abram Ilyitch, why you serve in the Caucasus."

"I? Because, as you know, in the first place we are all in duty bound to serve. What?" he added, though no one spoke. "Yesterday evening I received a letter from Russia, Nikoláï Feódorovitch," he continued, eager to change the conversation. "They write me that ... what strange questions are asked!"

"What sort of questions?" asked Bolkhof.

He blushed.

"Really, now, strange questions ... they write me, asking, 'Can there be jealousy without love?' ... What?" he asked, looking at us all.

"How so?" said Bolkhof, smiling.

"Well, you know, in Russia it's a good thing," he continued, as though his phrases followed each other in perfectly logical sequence. "When I was at Tambof in '52 I was invited everywhere, as though I were on the emperor's suite. Would you believe me, at a ball at the governor's, when I got there ... well, don't you know, I was received very cordially. The governor's wife[19] herself, you know, talked with me, and asked me about the Caucasus; and so did all the rest ... why, I don't know ... they looked at my gold cap as though it were some sort of curiosity, and they asked me how I had won it, and how about the Anna and the Vladímir; and I told them all about it.... What? That's why the Caucasus is good, Nikoláï Feódorovitch," he continued, not waiting for a response. "There they look on us Caucasians very kindly. A young man, you know, a staff-officer with the Anna and Vladímir,—that means a great deal in Russia. What?"

"You boasted a little, I imagine, Abram Ilyitch," said Bolkhof.

"He-he," came his silly little laugh in reply. "You know, you have to. Yes, and didn't I feed royally those two months!"

"So it is fine in Russia, is it?" asked Trosenko, asking about Russia as though it were China or Japan.

"Yes, indeed![20] We drank so much champagne there in those two months, that it was a terror!"

"The idea! you?[21] You drank lemonade probably. I should have died to show them how the Kavkázets drinks. The glory has not been won for nothing. I would show them how we drink.... Hey, Bolkhof?" he added.

"Yes, you see, you have been already ten years in the Caucasus, uncle," said Bolkhof, "and you remember what Yermolof said; but Abram Ilyitch has been here only six." ...

"Ten years, indeed! almost sixteen."

"Let us have some salvia, Bolkhof: it's raw, b-rr! What?" he added, smiling, "shall we drink, major?"

But the major was out of sorts, on account of the old captain's behavior to him at first; and now he evidently retired into himself, and took refuge in his own greatness. He began to hum some song, and again looked at his watch.

"Well, I shall never go there again," continued Trosenko, paying no heed to the peevish major. "I have got out of the habit of going about and speaking Russian. They'd ask, 'What is this wonderful creature?' and the answer'd be, 'Asia.' Isn't that so, Nikoláï Feódoruitch? And so what is there for me in Russia? It's all the same, you'll get shot here sooner or later. They ask, 'Where is Trosenko?' And down you go! What will you do then in the eighth company—heh?" he added, continuing to address the major.

"Send the officer of the day to the battalion," shouted Kirsánof, not answering the captain, though I was again compelled to believe that there was no necessity upon him of giving any orders.

"But, young man, I think that you are glad now that you are having double pay?" said the major after a few moments' silence, addressing the adjutant of the battalion.

"Why, yes, very."

"I think that our salary is now very large, Nikoláï Feódoruitch," he went on to say. "A young man can live very comfortably, and even allow himself some little luxury."

"No, truly, Abram Ilyitch," said the adjutant timidly: "even though we get double pay, it's only so much; and you see, one must keep a horse." ...

"What is that you say, young man? I myself have been an ensign, and I know. Believe me, with care, one can live very well. But you must calculate," he added, tapping his left palm with his little finger.

"We pledge all our salary before it's due: this is the way you economize," said Trosenko, drinking down a glass of vodka.

"Well, now, you see that's the very thing.... What?"

At this instant at the door of the wigwam appeared a white head with a flattened nose; and a sharp voice with a German accent said,—

"You there, Abram Ilyitch? The officer of the day is hunting for you."

"Come in, Kraft," said Bolkhof.

A tall form in the coat of the general's staff entered the door, and with remarkable zeal endeavored to shake hands with every one.

"Ah, my dear captain, you here too?" said he, addressing Trosenko.

The new guest, notwithstanding the darkness, rushed up to the captain and kissed him on the lips, to his extreme astonishment, and displeasure as it seemed to me.

"This is a German who wishes to be a hail fellow well met," I said to myself.

[16] Kavkázets.

[17] nu chto?

[18] da voi.

[19] gubernátorsha.

[20] da s.

[21] da chto vui.

XII.

My presumption was immediately confirmed. Captain Kraft called for some vodka, which he called corn-brandy,[22] and threw back his head, and made a terrible noise like a duck, in draining the glass.

"Well, gentlemen, we rolled about well to-day on the plains of the Chetchen," he began; but, catching sight of the officer of the day, he immediately stopped, to allow the major to give his directions.

"Well, you have made the tour of the lines?"

"I have."

"Are the pickets posted?"

"They are."

"Then you may order the captain of the guard to be as alert as possible."

"I will."

The major blinked his eyes, and went into a brown study.

"Well, tell the boys to get their supper."

"That's what they're doing now."

"Good! then you may go. Well,"[23] continued the major with a conciliating smile, and taking up the thread of the conversation that we had dropped, "we were reckoning what an officer needed: let us finish the calculation."

"We need one uniform and trousers, don't we?"[24]

"Yes. That, let us suppose would amount to fifty rubles every two years; say, twenty-five rubles a year for dress. Then for eating we need every day at least forty kopeks, don't we?[25]"

"Yes, certainly as much as that."

"Well, I'll call it so. Now, for a horse and saddle for remount, thirty rubles; that's all. Twenty-five and a hundred and twenty and thirty make a hundred and seventy-five rubles. All the rest stands for luxuries,—for tea and for sugar and for tobacco,—twenty rubles. Will you look it over?... It's right, isn't it, Nikoláï Feódoruitch?"

"Not quite. Excuse me, Abram Ilyitch," said the adjutant timidly, "nothing is left for tea and sugar. You reckon one suit for every two years, but here in field-service you can't get along with one pair of pantaloons and boots. Why, I wear out a new pair almost every month. And then linen, shirts, handkerchiefs, and leg-wrappers: all that sort of thing one has to buy. And when you have accounted for it, there isn't any thing left at all. That's true, by God![26] Abram Ilyitch."

"Yes, it's splendid to wear leg-wrappers," said Kraft suddenly, after a moment's silence, with a loving emphasis on the word "leg-wrappers;"[27] "you know it's simply Russian fashion."

"I will tell you," remarked Trosenko, "it all amounts to this, that our brother imagines that we have nothing to eat; but the fact is, that we all live, and have tea to drink, and tobacco to smoke, and our vodka to drink. If you served with me," he added, turning to the ensign, "you would soon learn how to live. I suppose you gentlemen know how he treated his denshchik."

And Trosenko, dying with laughter, told us the whole story of the ensign and his man, though we had all heard it a thousand times.

"What makes you look so rosy, brother?" he continued, pointing to the ensign, who turned red, broke into a perspiration, and smiled with such constraint that it was painful to look at him.

"It's all right, brother. I used to be just like you; but now, you see, I have become hardened. Just let any young fellow come here from Russia,—we have seen 'em,—and here they would get all sorts of rheumatism and spasms; but look at me sitting here: it's my home, and bed, and all. You see" ... Here he drank still another glass of vodka. "Hah?" he continued, looking straight into Kraft's eyes.

"That's what I like in you. He's a genuine old Kavkázets. Kive us your hant."

And Kraft pushed through our midst, rushed up to Trosenko, and, grasping his hand, shook it with remarkable feeling.

"Yes, we can say that we have had all sorts of experiences here," he continued. "In '45 you must have been there, captain? Do you remember the night of the 24th and 25th, when we camped in mud up to our knees, and the next day went against the intrenchments? I was then with the commander-in-chief, and in one day we captured fifteen intrenchments. Do you remember, captain?"

Trosenko nodded assent, and, pushing out his lower lip, closed his eyes.

"You ought to have seen," Kraft began with extraordinary animation, making awkward gestures with his arms, and addressing the major.

But the major, who must have more than once heard this tale, suddenly threw such an expression of muddy stupidity into his eyes, as he looked at his comrade, that Kraft turned from him, and addressed Bolkhof and me, alternately looking at each of us. But he did not once look at Trosenko, from one end of his story to the other.

"You ought to have seen how in the morning the commander-in-chief came to me, and says, 'Kraft, take those intrenchments.' You know our military duty,—no arguing, hand to visor. 'It shall be done, your Excellency,'[28] and I started. As soon as we came to the first intrenchment, I turn round, and shout to the soldiers, 'Poys, show your mettle! Pe on your guard. The one who stops I shall cut down with my own hand.' With Russian soldiers you know you have to be plain-spoken. Then suddenly comes a shell—I look—one soldier, two soldiers, three soldiers, then the bullets—vz-zhin! vz-zhin! vz-zhin! I shout, 'Forward, boys; follow me!' As soon as we reach it, you know, I look and see—how it—you know: what do you call it?" and the narrator waved his hands in his search for the word.

"Rampart," suggested Bolkhof.

"No.... Ach! what is it? My God, now, what is it?... Yes, rampart," said he quickly. "Then clubbing their guns!... hurrah! ta-ra-ta-ta-ta! The enemy—not a soul was left. Do you know, they were amazed. All right. We rush on—the second intrenchment. This was quite a different affair. Our hearts poiled within us, you know. As soon as we got there, I look and I see the second intrenchment—impossible to mount it. There—what was it—what was it we just called it? Ach! what was it?" ...

"Rampart," again I suggested.

"Not at all," said he with some heat. "Not rampart. Ah, now, what is it called?" and he made a sort of despairing gesture with his hand. "Ach! my God! what is it?" ...

He was evidently so cut up, that one could not help offering suggestions.

"Moat, perhaps," said Bolkhof.

"No; simply rampart. As soon as we reached it, if you will believe me, there was a fire poured in upon us—it was hell." ...

At the crisis, some one behind the wigwam inquired for me. It was Maksímof. As there still remained thirteen of the intrenchments to be taken in the same monotonous detail, I was glad to have an excuse to go to my division. Trosenko went with me.

"It's all a pack of lies," he said to me when we had gone a few steps from the wigwam. "He wasn't at the intrenchments at all;" and Trosenko laughed so good-naturedly, that I could not help joining him.

[22] gorílka in the Malo-Russian dialect.

[23] nu-s.

[24] tak-s.

[25] tak-s.

[26] Yĕï Bogu.

[27] podviortki.

[28] slusháïu, váshe Siyátelstvo.

XIII.

It was already dark night, and the camp was lighted only by the flickering bonfires, when I rejoined my soldiers, after giving my orders. A great smouldering log was lying on the coals. Around it were sitting only three of the men,—Antónof, who had set his kettle on the fire to boil his ryábko, or hard-tack and tallow; Zhdánof, thoughtfully poking the ashes with a stick; and Chikin, with his pipe, which was forever in his mouth. The rest had already turned in, some under gun carriages, others in the hay, some around the fires. By the faint light of the coals I recognized the backs, the legs, and the heads of those whom I knew. Among the latter was the recruit, who, curling up close to the fire, was already fast asleep. Antónof made room for me. I sat down by him, and began to smoke a cigarette. The odor of the mist and of the smoke from the wet branches spreading through the air made one's eyes smart, and the same penetrating drizzle fell from the gloomy sky.

Behind us could be heard regular snoring, the crackling of wood in the fire, muffled conversation, and occasionally the clank of muskets among the infantry. Everywhere about us the watch-fires were glowing, throwing their red reflections within narrow circles on the dark forms of the soldiers. Around the nearer fires I distinguished, in places where it was light, the figures of naked soldiers waving their shirts in the very flames. Many of the men had not yet gone to bed, but were wandering round, and talking over a space of fifteen square sazhens; but the thick, gloomy night imparted a peculiarly mysterious tone to all this movement, as though each felt this gloomy silence, and feared to disturb its peaceful harmony. When I spoke, it seemed to me that my voice sounded strange. On the faces of all the soldiers sitting by the fire I read the same mood. I thought, that, when I joined them, they were talking about their wounded comrade; but it was nothing of the sort. Chikin was telling about the condition of things at Tiflis, and about school-children there.

Always and everywhere, especially in the Caucasus, I have remarked in our soldiery at the time of danger peculiar tact in ignoring or avoiding those things that might have a depressing effect upon their comrades' spirits. The spirit of the Russian soldier is not constituted, like the courage of the Southern nations, for quickly kindled and quickly cooling enthusiasm; it is as hard to set him on fire as it is to cause him to lose courage. For him it is not necessary to have accessories, speeches, martial shouts, songs, and drums; on the contrary, he wants calmness, order, and avoidance of every thing unnatural. In the Russian, the genuine Russian soldier, you never find braggadocio, bravado, or the tendency to get demoralized or excited in time of danger; on the contrary, discretion, simplicity, and the faculty of seeing in peril something quite distinct from the peril, constitute the chief traits of his character. I have seen a soldier wounded in the leg, at the first moment mourning only over the hole in his new jacket; a messenger thrown from his horse, which was killed under him, unbuckling the girth so as to save the saddle. Who does not recollect the incident at the siege of Hergebel when the fuse of a loaded bomb was on fire in the powder-room, and the artillerist ordered two soldiers to take the bomb and fling it over the wall, and how the soldiers did not take it to the most convenient place, which was near the colonel's tent on the rampart, but carried it farther, lest it should wake the gentlemen who were asleep in the tent, and both of them were blown to pieces?

I remember, that, during this same expedition of 1852, one of the young soldiers, during action, said to some one that it was not proper for the division to go into danger, and how the whole division in scorn went for him for saying such shameful words that they would not even repeat them. And here now the thought of Velenchúk must have been in the mind of each; and when any second might bring upon us the broadside of the stealthy Tatars, all were listening to Chikin's lively story, and no one mentioned the events of the day, nor the present danger, nor their wounded friend, as though it had happened God knows how long ago, or had never been at all. But still, it seemed to me that their faces were more serious than usual; they listened with too little attention to Chikin's tale, and even Chikin himself felt that they were not listening to him, but let him talk to himself.

Maksímof came to the bonfire, and sat down by me. Chikin made room for him, stopped talking, and again began to suck at his pipe.

"The infantry have sent to camp for some vodka," said Maksímof after a considerably long silence. "They'll be back with it very soon." He spat into the fire. "A subaltern was saying that he had seen our comrade."

"Was he still alive?" asked Antónof, turning his kettle round.

"No, he is dead."

The recruit suddenly raised above the fire his graceful head within his red cap, for an instant gazed intently at Maksímof and me, then quickly dropped it, and rolled himself up in his cloak.

"You see, it was death that was coming upon him this morning when I woke him in the gun-park," said Antónof.

"Nonsense!" said Zhdánof, turning over the smouldering log; and all were silent.

Amid the general silence a shot was heard behind us in the camp. Our drummers took it up immediately, and beat the tattoo. When the last roll had ceased, Zhdánof was already up, and the first to take off his cap. The rest of us followed his example.

Amid the deep silence of the night a choir of harmonious male voices resounded:—

"Our Father who art in heaven, hallowed be thy name. Thy kingdom come; thy will be done, as on earth, so in heaven. Give us this day our daily bread, and forgive us our debts as we forgive our debtors. And lead us not into temptation, but deliver us from the evil one."

"It was just so with us in '45: one man was contused in this place," said Antónof when we had put on our hats and were sitting around the fire, "and so we carried him two days on the gun. Do you remember Shevchenko,

Zhdánof?... We left him there under a tree."

At this time a foot-soldier with tremendous whiskers and mustaches, carrying a gun and a knapsack, came to our fire.

"Please give a fellow-countryman a coal for his pipe," said he.

"Of course,[29] smoke away; there is plenty of fire," remarked Chikin.

"You were talking about Dargi, weren't you, friend?" asked the soldier, addressing Antónof.

The soldier shook his head, frowned, and squatted down near us on his heels.

"There were all sorts of things there," he remarked.

"Why did you leave him?" I asked of Antónof.

"He had awful cramps in his belly. When we stood still, he did not feel it; but when we moved, he screeched and screeched. He besought us by all that was holy to leave him: it was pitiful. Well, and when he began to vex us solely, and had killed three of our men at the guns and one officer, then our batteries opened on him, and did some execution too. We weren't able to drag out the guns, there was such mud."

"It was muddier under the Indian mountains than anywhere else," remarked the strange soldier.

"Well, but indeed it kept growing worse and worse for him; and we decided, Anóshenka—he was an old artillerist—and the rest of us, that indeed there was no chance for him but to say a prayer, and so we left him there. And so we decided. A tree grew there, welcome enough. We left some hard-tack for him,—Zhdánof had some,—we put him against the tree, put a clean shirt on him, said good-by to him, and so we left him."

"Was he a man of importance?"

"Not at all: he was a soldier," remarked Zhdánof.

"And what became of him, God knows," added Antónof. "Many of our brothers were left there."

"At Dargi?" asked the infantry man, standing up and picking up his pipe, and again frowning and shaking his head.... "There were all sorts of things there."

And he left us.

"Say, are there many of the soldiers in our battery who were at Dargi?" I asked.

"Let us see;[30] here is Zhdánof, myself, Patsan,—who is now on furlough,—and some six men more. There wouldn't be any others."

"Why has our Patsan gone off on leave of absence?" asked Chikin, shaking out his legs, and laying his head on a log. "It's almost a year since he went."

"Well, are you going to take your furlough?" I asked of Zhdánof.

"No, I'm not," he replied reluctantly.

"I tell you it's a good thing to go," said Antónof, "when you come from a rich home, or when you are able to work; and it's rather flattering to go and have the folks glad to see you."

"But how about going when you have a brother,", asked Zhdánof, "and would have to be supported by him? They have enough for themselves, but there's nothing for a brother who's a soldier. Poor kind of help after serving twenty-five years. Besides, whether they are alive or no, who knows?"

"But why haven't you written?" I asked.

"Written? I did send two letters, but they don't reply. Either they are dead, or they don't reply because, of course, they are poor. It's so everywhere."

"Have you written lately?"

"When we left Dargi I wrote my last letter."

"You had better sing that song about the birch," said Zhdánof to

Antónof, who at this moment was on his knees, and was purring some song.

Antónof sang his "Song of the White Birch."

"That's Uncle Zhdánof's very most favorite song," said Chikin to me in a whisper, as he helped me on with my cloak. "The other day, as Filipp Antónuitch was singing it, he actually cried."

Zhdánof at first sat absolutely motionless, with his eyes fastened on the smouldering embers, and his face, shining in the ruddy glow, seemed extraordinarily gloomy; then his cheek under his mustaches began to move quicker and quicker; and at last he got up, and, spreading out his cloak, he lay down in the shadow behind the fire. Either he tossed about and groaned as he got ready for bed, or the death of Velenchúk and this wretched weather had completely upset me; but it certainly seemed to me that he was weeping.

The bottom of the log which had been rolled on the fire, occasionally blazing up, threw its light on Antónof's form, with his gray moustache, his red face, and the ribbons on the cloak flung over his shoulders, and brought into relief the boots, heads, or backs of other sleeping soldiers.

From above the same wretched drizzle was falling; in the atmosphere was the same odor of dampness and smoke; around us could be seen the same bright dots of the dying fires, and amid the general silence the melancholy notes of Antónof's song rang out. And when this ceased for a moment, the faint nocturnal sounds of the camp, the snoring, the clank of a sentinel's musket, and quiet conversation, chimed in with it.

"Second watch! Makatiuk and Zhdánof," shouted Maksímof.

Antónof ceased to sing; Zhdánof arose, drew a deep sigh, stepped across the log, and went off quietly to the guns.

[29] chïo-sh.

[30] da chïo.

JULY 27, 1855.

AN OLD ACQUAINTANCE.

PRINCE NEKHILUDOF RELATES HOW, DURING AN EXPEDITION IN THE CAUCASUS, HE MET AN ACQUAINTANCE FROM MOSCOW.

Our division had been out in the field.

The work in hand was accomplished: we had cut a way through the forest, and each day we were expecting from headquarters orders for our return to the fort. Our division of field-pieces was stationed at the top of a steep mountain-crest which was terminated by the swift mountain river Mechik, and had to command the plain that stretched before us. Here and there on this picturesque plain, out of the reach of gunshot, now and then, especially at evening, groups of mounted mountaineers showed themselves, attracted by curiosity to ride up and view the Russian camp.

The evening was clear, mild, and fresh, as it is apt to be in December in the Caucasus; the sun was setting behind the steep chain of the mountains at the left, and threw rosy rays upon the tents scattered over the slope, upon the soldiers moving about, and upon our two guns, which seemed to crane their necks as they rested motionless on the earthwork two paces from us. The infantry picket, stationed on the knoll at the left, stood in perfect silhouette against the light of the sunset; no less distinct were the stacks of muskets, the form of the sentry, the groups of soldiers, and the smoke of the smouldering camp-fire.

At the right and left of the slope, on the black, sodden earth, the tents gleamed white; and behind the tents, black stood the bare trunks of the platane forest, which rang with the incessant sound of axes, the crackling of the bonfires, and the crashing of the trees as they fell under the axes. The bluish smoke arose from tobacco-pipes on all sides, and vanished in the transparent blue of the frosty sky. By the tents and on the lower ground around the arms rushed the Cossacks, dragoons, and artillerists, with great galloping and snorting of horses as they returned from getting water. It began to freeze; all sounds were heard with extraordinary distinctness, and one could see an immense distance across the plain through the clear, rare atmosphere. The groups of the enemy, their curiosity at seeing the soldiers satisfied, quietly galloped off across the fields, still yellow with the golden coru-stubble, toward their auls or villages, which were visible, beyond the forest, with the tall posts of the cemeteries and the smoke rising in the air.

Our tent was pitched not far from the guns on a place high and dry, from which we had a remarkably extended view. Near the tent, on a cleared space, around the battery itself, we had our games of skittles, or chushki. The obliging soldiers had made for us rustic benches and tables. On account of all these amusements, the artillery officers, our comrades, and a few infantry men liked to gather of an evening around our battery, and the place came to be called the club.

As the evening was fine, the best players had come, and we were amusing ourselves with skittles.[1] Ensign D., Lieutenant O., and myself had played two games in succession; and to the common satisfaction and amusement of all the spectators, officers, soldiers, and servants[2] who were watching us from their tents, we had twice carried the winning party on our backs from one end of the ground to the other. Especially droll was the situation of the huge fat Captain S., who, puffing and smiling good-naturedly, with legs dragging on the ground, rode pickapack on the feeble little Lieutenant O.

When it grew somewhat later, the servants brought three glasses of tea for the six men of us, and not a spoon; and we who had finished our game came to the plaited settees.

There was standing near them a small bow-legged man, a stranger to us, in a sheepskin jacket, and a papákha, or Circassian cap, with long overhanging white crown. As soon as we came near where he stood, he took a few irresolute steps, and put on his cap; and several times he seemed to make up his mind to come to meet us, and then stopped again. But after deciding, probably, that it was impossible to remain irresolute, the stranger took off his cap, and, going in a circuit around us, approached Captain S.

"Ah, Guskantini, how is it, old man?"[3] said S., still smiling good-naturedly, under the influence of his ride.

Guskantini, as S. called him, instantly replaced his cap, and made a motion as though to thrust his hands into the pockets of his jacket;[4] but on the side toward me there was no pocket in the jacket, and his small red hand fell into an awkward position. I felt a strong desire to make out who this man was (was he a yunker, or a degraded officer?) and, not realizing that my gaze (that is, the gaze of a strange officer) disconcerted him, I continued to stare at his dress and appearance.

I judged that he was about thirty. His small, round, gray eyes had a sleepy expression, and at the same time gazed calmly out from under the dirty white lambskin of his cap, which hung down over his face. His thick, irregular nose, standing out between his sunken cheeks, gave evidence of emaciation that was the result of illness, and not natural. His restless lips, barely covered by a sparse, soft, whitish mustache, were constantly changing their shape, as though they were trying to assume now one expression, now another. But all these expressions seemed to be endless, and his face retained one predominating expression of timidity and fright. Around his thin neck, where, the veins stood out, was tied a green woollen scarf tucked into his jacket. His fur jacket, or polushúbok, was worn bare, short, and had dog-fur sewed on the collar and on the false pockets. The trousers were checkered, of ash-gray color, and his sapogi had short, unblacked military bootlegs.

"I beg of you, do not disturb yourself," said I when he for the second time, timidly glancing at me, had taken off his cap.

He bowed to me with an expression of gratitude, replaced his hat, and, drawing from his pocket a dirty chintz tobacco-pouch with lacings, began to roll a cigarette.

I myself had not been long a yunker, an elderly yunker; and as I was incapable, as yet, of being good-naturedly serviceable to my younger comrades, and without means, I well knew all the moral difficulties of this situation for a proud man no longer young, and I sympathized with all men who found themselves in such a situation, and I endeavored to make clear to myself their character and rank, and the tendencies of their intellectual peculiarities, in order to judge of the degree of their moral sufferings. This yunker or degraded officer, judging by his restless eyes and that intentionally constant variation of expression which I noticed in him, was a man very far from stupid, and extremely egotistical, and therefore much to be pitied.

Captain S. invited us to play another game of skittles, with the stakes to consist, not only of the usual pickapack ride of the winning party, but also of a few bottles of red wine, rum, sugar, cinnamon, and cloves for the mulled wine which that winter, on account of the cold, was greatly popular in our division.

Guskantini, as S. again called him, was also invited to take part; but before the game began, the man, struggling between gratification because he had been invited and a certain timidity, drew Captain S. aside, and began to say something in a whisper. The good-natured captain punched him in the ribs with his big, fat hand, and replied, loud enough to be heard,—

"Not at all, old fellow,[5] I assure you."

When the game was over, and that side in which the stranger whose rank was so low had taken part, had come out winners, and it fell to his lot to ride on one of our officers, Ensign D., the ensign grew red in the face: he went to the little divan and offered the stranger a cigarette by way of a compromise.

While they were ordering the mulled wine, and in the steward's tent were heard assiduous preparations on the part of Nikíta, who had sent an orderly for cinnamon and cloves, and the shadow of his back was alternately lengthening and shortening on the dingy sides of the tent, we men, seven in all, sat around on the benches; and while we took turns in drinking tea from the three glasses, and gazed out over the plain, which was now beginning to glow in the twilight, we talked and laughed over the various incidents of the game.

The stranger in the fur jacket took no share in the conversation, obstinately refused to drink the tea which I several times offered him, and as he sat there on the ground in Tatar fashion, occupied himself in making cigarettes of fine-cut tobacco, and smoking them one after another, evidently not so much for his own satisfaction as to give himself the appearance of a man with something to do. When it was remarked that the summons to return was expected on the morrow, and that there might be an engagement, he lifted himself on his knees, and, addressing Captain B. only, said that he had been at the adjutant's, and had himself written the order for the return on the next day. We all said nothing while he was speaking; and notwithstanding the fact that he was so bashful, we begged him to repeat this most interesting piece of news. He repeated what he had said, adding only that he had been staying at the adjutant's (since he made it his home there) when the order came.

"Look here, old fellow, if you are not telling us false, I shall have to go to my company and give some orders for to-morrow," said Captain S.

"No ... why ... it may be, I am sure" ... stammered the stranger, but suddenly stopped, and, apparently feeling himself affronted, contracted Ins brows, and, muttering something between his teeth, again began to roll a cigarette. But the fine-cut tobacco in his chintz pouch began to show signs of giving out, and he asked S. to lend him a little cigarette.[6]

We kept on for a considerable time with that monotonous military chatter which every one who has ever been on an expedition will appreciate; all of us, with one and the same expression, complaining of the dulness and length of the expedition, in one and the same fashion sitting in judgment on our superiors, and all of us likewise, as we had done many times before, praising one comrade, pitying another, wondering how much this one had gained, how much that one had lost, and so on, and so on.

"Here, fellows, this adjutant of ours is completely broken up," said Captain S. "At headquarters he was everlastingly on the winning side; no matter whom he sat down with, he'd rake in every thing: but now for two months past he has been losing all the time. The present expedition hasn't been lucky for him. I think he has got away with two thousand silver rubles and five hundred rubles' worth of articles,—the carpet that he won at Mukhin's, Nikitin's pistols, Sada's gold watch which Vorontsof gave him. He has lost it all."

"The truth of the matter in his case," said Lieutenant O., "was that he used to cheat everybody; it was impossible to play with him."

"He cheated every one, but now it's all gone up in his pipe;" and here Captain S. laughed good-naturedly. "Our friend Guskof here lives with him. He hasn't quite lost him yet: that's so, isn't it, old fellow?"[7] he asked, addressing Guskof.

Guskof tried to laugh. It was a melancholy, sickly laugh, which completely changed the expression of his countenance. Till this moment it had seemed to me that I had seen and known this man before; and, besides, the name Guskof, by which Captain S. called him, was familiar to me; but how and when I had seen and known him, I actually could not remember.

"Yes," said Guskof, incessantly putting his hand to his mustaches, but instantly dropping it again without touching them. "Pavel Dmitriévitch's luck has been against him in this expedition, such a veine de malheur," he added in a careful but pure French pronunciation, again giving me to think that I had seen him, and seen him often, somewhere. "I know Pavel Dmitriévitch very well. He has great confidence in me," he proceeded to say; "he and I are old friends; that is, he is fond of me," he explained, evidently fearing that it might be taken as presumption for him to claim old friendship with the adjutant. "Pavel Dmitriévitch plays admirably; but now, strange as it may seem, it's all up with him, he is just, about perfectly ruined; la chance a tourné," he added, addressing himself particularly to me.

At first we had listened to Guskof with condescending attention; but as soon as he made use of that second French phrase, we all involuntarily turned from him.

"I have played with him a thousand times, and we agreed then that it was strange," said Lieutenant O., with peculiar emphasis on the word strange. [8] "I never once won a ruble from him. Why was it, when I used to win of others?"

"Pavel Dmitriévitch plays admirably: I have known him for a long time," said I. In fact, I had known the adjutant for several years; more than once I had seen him in the full swing of a game, surrounded by officers, and

I had remarked his handsome, rather gloomy and always passionless calm face, his deliberate Malo-Russian pronunciation, his handsome belongings and horses, his bold, manly figure, and above all his skill and self-restraint in carrying on the game accurately and agreeably. More than once, I am sorry to say, as I looked at his plump white hands with a diamond ring—on the index-finger, passing out one card after another, I grew angry with that ring, with his white hands, with the whole of the adjutant's person, and evil thoughts on his account arose in my mind. But as I afterwards reconsidered the matter coolly, I persuaded myself that he played more skilfully than all with whom he happened to play: the more so, because as I heard his general observations concerning the game,—how one ought not to back out when one had laid the smallest stake, how one ought not to leave off in certain cases as the first rule for honest men, and so forth, and so forth,—it was evident that he was always on the winning side merely from the fact that he played more sagaciously and coolly than the rest of us. And now it seemed that this self-reliant, careful player had been stripped not only of his money but of his effects, which marks the lowest depths of loss for an officer.

"He always had devilish good luck with me," said Lieutenant O. "I made a vow never to play with him again."

"What a marvel you are, old fellow!" said S., nodding at me, and addressing O. "You lost three hundred silver rubles, that's what you lost to him."

"More than that," said the lieutenant savagely. "And now you have come to your senses; it is rather late in the day, old man, for the rest of us have known for a long time that he was the cheat of the regiment," said S., with difficulty restraining his laughter, and feeling very well satisfied with his fabrication. 'Here is Guskof right here,—he fixes his cards for him. That's the reason of the friendship between them, old man"[9] ... and Captain S., shaking all over, burst out into such a hearty "ha, ha, ha!" that he spilt the glass of mulled wine which he was holding in his hand. On Guskof's pale emaciated face there showed something like a color; he opened his mouth several times, raised his hands to his mustaches and once more dropped them to his side where the pockets should have been, stood up, and then sat down again, and finally in an unnatural voice said to S.,—

"It's no joke, Nikolai Ivánovitch, for you to say such things before people who don't know me and who see me in this unlined jacket ... because"—His voice failed him, and again his small red hands with their dirty nails went from his jacket to his face, touching his mustache, his hair, his nose, rubbing his eyes, or needlessly scratching his cheek.

"As to saying that, everybody knows it, old fellow," continued S., thoroughly satisfied with his jest, and not heeding Guskof's complaint. Guskof was still trying to say something; and placing the palm of his right hand on his left knee in a most unnatural position, and gazing at S., he had an appearance of smiling contemptuously.

"No," said I to myself, as I noticed that smile of his, "I have not only seen him, but have spoken with him somewhere."

"You and I have met somewhere," said I to him when, under the influence of the common silence, S.'s laughter began to calm down. Guskof's mobile face suddenly lighted up, and his eyes, for the first time with a truly joyous expression, rested upon me.

"Why, I recognized you immediately," he replied in French. "In '48 I had the pleasure of meeting you quite frequently in Moscow at my sister's."

I had to apologize for not recognizing him at first iii that costume and in that new garb. He arose, came to me, and with his moist hand irresolutely and weakly seized my hand, and sat down by me. Instead of looking at me, though he apparently seemed so glad to see me, he gazed with an expression of unfriendly bravado at the officers.

Either because I recognized in him a man whom I had met a few years before in a dress-coat in a parlor, or because he was suddenly raised in his own opinion by the fact of being recognized,—at all events it seemed to me that his face and even his motions completely changed: they now expressed lively intelligence, a childish self-satisfaction in the consciousness of such intelligence, and a certain contemptuous indifference; so that I confess, notwithstanding the pitiable position in which he found himself, my old acquaintance did not so much excite sympathy in me as it did a sort of unfavorable sentiment.

I now vividly remembered our first meeting. In 1848, while I was staying at Moscow, I frequently went to the house of Iváshin, who from childhood had been an old friend of mine. His wife was an agreeable hostess, a charming woman, as everybody said; but she never pleased me.... The winter that I knew her, she often spoke with hardly concealed pride of her brother, who had shortly before completed his course, and promised to be one of the most fashionable and popular young men in the best society of Petersburg. As I knew by reputation the father of the Guskofs, who was very rich and had a distinguished position, and as I knew also the sister's ways, I felt some prejudice against meeting the young man. One evening when I was at Iváshin's, I saw a short, thoroughly pleasant-looking young man, in a black coat, white vest and necktie. My host hastened to make me acquainted with him. The young man, evidently dressed for a bail, with his cap in his hand, was standing before Iváshin, and was eagerly but politely arguing with him about a common friend of ours, who had distinguished himself at the time of the Hungarian campaign. He said that this acquaintance was not at all a hero or a man born for war, as was said of him, but was simply a clever and cultivated man. I recollect, I took part in the argument against Guskof, and went to the extreme of declaring also that intellect and cultivation always bore an inverse relation to bravery; and I recollect how Guskof pleasantly and cleverly pointed out to me that bravery was necessarily the result of intellect and a decided degree of development,—a statement which I, who considered myself an intellectual and cultivated man, could not in my heart of hearts agree with.

I recollect that towards the close of our conversation Madame Iváshina introduced me to her brother; and he, with a condescending smile, offered me his little hand on which he had not yet had time to draw his kid gloves, and weakly and irresolutely pressed my hand as he did now. Though I had been prejudiced against Guskof, I could not help granting that he was in the right, and agreeing with his sister that he was really a clever and agreeable young man, who ought to have great success in society. He was extraordinarily neat, beautifully dressed, and fresh, and had affectedly modest manners, and a thoroughly youthful, almost childish appearance, on account of which, you could not help excusing his expression of self-sufficiency, though it modified the impression of his high-mightiness caused by his intellectual face and especially his smile. It was said that he had great success that winter with the high-born ladies of Moscow. As I saw him at his sister's I could only infer how far this was true by the feeling of pleasure and contentment constantly excited in me by his youthful appearance and by his sometimes indiscreet anecdotes. He and I met half a dozen times, and talked a good deal; or, rather, he talked a good deal, and I listened. He spoke for the most part in French, always with a good accent, very fluently and ornately; and he had the skill of drawing others gently and politely into the conversation. As a general thing, he behaved toward all, and toward me, in a somewhat supercilious manner, and I felt that he was perfectly right in this way of treating people. I always feel that way in regard to men who are firmly convinced that they ought to treat me superciliously, and who are comparative strangers to me.

Now, as he sat with me, and gave me his hand, I keenly recalled in him that same old haughtiness of expression; and it seemed to me that he did not properly appreciate his position of official inferiority, as, in the presence of the officers, he asked me what I had been doing in all that time, and how I happened to be there. In spite of the fact that I invariably made my replies in Russian, he kept putting his questions in French, expressing himself as before in remarkably correct language. About himself he said fluently that after his unhappy, wretched story (what the story was, I did not know, and he had not yet told me), he had been three months under arrest, and then had been sent to the Caucasus to the N. regiment, and now had been serving three years as a soldier in that regiment.

"You would not believe," said he to me in French, "how much I have to suffer in these regiments from the society of the officers. Still it is a pleasure to me, that I used to know the adjutant of whom we were just speaking: he is a good man—it's a fact," he remarked condescendingly. "I live with him, and that's something of a relief for me. Yes, my dear, the days fly by, but they aren't all alike,"[10] he added; and suddenly hesitated, reddened, and stood up, as he caught sight of the adjutant himself coming toward us.

"It is such a pleasure to meet such a man as you," said Guskof to me in a whisper as he turned from me. "I should like very, very much, to have a long talk with you.".

I said that I should be very happy to talk with him, but in reality I confess that Guskof excited in me a sort of dull pity that was not akin to sympathy.

I had a presentiment that I should feel a constraint in a private conversation with him; but still I was anxious to learn from him several things, and, above all, why it was, when his father had been so rich, that he was in poverty, as was evident by his dress and appearance.

The adjutant greeted us all, including Guskof, and sat down by me in the seat which the cashiered officer had just vacated. Pavel Dmitriévitch, who had always been calm and leisurely, a genuine gambler, and a man of means, was now very different from what he had been in the flowery days of his success; he seemed to be in haste to go somewhere, kept constantly glancing at everybody, and it was not five minutes before he proposed to Lieutenant O., who had sworn off from playing, to set up a small faro-bank. Lieutenant O. refused, under the pretext of having to attend to his duties, but in reality because, as he knew that the adjutant had few possessions and little money left, he did not feel himself justified in risking his three hundred rubles against a hundred or even less which the adjutant might stake.

"Well, Pavel Dmitriévitch," said the lieutenant, anxious to avoid a repetition of the invitation, "is it true, what they tell us, that we return to-morrow?"

"I don't know," replied the adjutant. "Orders came, to be in readiness; but if it's true, then you'd better play a game. I would wager my Kabarda cloak."

"No, to-day already" ...

"It's a gray one, never been worn; but if you prefer, play for money. How is that?"

"Yes, but ... I should be willing—pray don't think that" ... said Lieutenant O., answering the implied suspicion; "but as there may be a raid or some movement, I must go to bed early."

The adjutant stood up, and, thrusting his hands into his pockets, started to go across the grounds. His face assumed its ordinary expression of coldness and pride, which I admired in him.

"Won't you have a glass of mulled wine?" I asked him.

"That might be acceptable," and he came back to me; but Guskof politely took the glass from me, and handed it to the adjutant, striving at the same time not to look at him. But as he did not notice the tent-rope, he stumbled over it, and fell on his hand, dropping the glass.

"What a bungler!" exclaimed the adjutant, still holding out his hand for the glass. Everybody burst out laughing, not excepting Guskof, who was rubbing his hand on his sore knee, which he had somehow struck as he fell. "That's the way the bear waited on the hermit," continued the adjutant. "It's the way he waits on me every day. He has pulled up all the tent-pins; he's always tripping up."

Guskof, not hearing him, apologized to us, and glanced toward me with a smile of almost noticeable melancholy as though saying that I alone could understand him. He was pitiable to see; but the adjutant, his protector, seemed, on that very account, to be severe on his messmate, and did not try to put him at his ease.

"Well, you're a graceful lad! Where did you think you were going?"

"Well, who can help tripping over these pins, Pavel Dmitriévitch?" said Guskof. "You tripped over them yourself the other day."

"I, old man,[11]—I am not of the rank and file, and such gracefulness is not expected of me."

"He can be lazy," said Captain S., keeping the ball rolling, "but low-rank men have to make their legs fly."

"Ill-timed jest," said Guskof almost in a whisper, and casting down his eyes. The adjutant was evidently vexed with his messmate; he listened with inquisitive attention to every word that he said.

"He'll have to be sent out into ambuscade again," said he, addressing S., and pointing to the cashiered officer.

"Well, there'll be some more tears," said S., laughing. Guskof no longer looked at me, but acted as though he were going to take some tobacco from his pouch, though there had been none there for some time.

"Get ready for the ambuscade, old man," said S., addressing him with shouts of laughter. "To-day the scouts have brought the news, there'll be an attack on the camp to-night, so it's necessary to designate the trusty lads." Guskof's face showed a fleeting smile as though he were preparing to make some reply, but several times he cast a supplicating look at S.

"Well, you know I have been, and I'm ready to go again if I am sent," he said hastily.

"Then you'll be sent."

"Well, I'll go. Isn't that all right?"

"Yes, as at Arguna, you deserted the ambuscade and threw away your gun," said the adjutant; and turning from him he began to tell us the orders for the next day.

As a matter of fact, we expected from the enemy a Cannonade of the camp that night, and the next day some sort of diversion. While we were still chatting about various subjects of general interest, the adjutant, as though from a sudden and unexpected impulse, proposed to Lieutenant O. to have a little game. The lieutenant most unexpectedly consented; and, together with S. and the ensign, they went off to the adjutant's tent, where there was a folding green table with cards on it. The captain, the commander of our division, went to our tent to sleep; the other gentlemen also separated, and Guskof and I were left alone. I was not mistaken, it was really very uncomfortable for me to have a tête-à-tête with him; I arose involuntarily, and began to promenade up and down on the battery. Guskof walked in silence by my side, hastily and awkwardly wheeling around so as not to delay or incommode me.

"I do not annoy you?" he asked in a soft, mournful voice. So far as I could see his face in the dim light, it seemed to me deeply thoughtful and melancholy.

"Not at all," I replied; but as he did not immediately begin to speak, and as I did not know what to say to him, we walked in silence a considerably long time.

The twilight had now absolutely changed into dark night; over the black profile of the mountains gleamed the bright evening heat-lightning; over our heads in the light-blue frosty sky twinkled the little stars; on all sides gleamed the ruddy flames of the smoking watch-fires; near us, the white tents stood out in contrast to the frowning blackness of our earth-works. The light from the nearest watch-fire, around which our servants, engaged in quiet conversation, were warming themselves, occasionally flashed on the brass of our heavy guns, and fell on the form of the sentry, who, wrapped in his cloak, paced with measured tread along the battery.

"You cannot imagine what a delight it is for me to talk with such a man as you are," said Guskof, although as yet he had not spoken a word to me. "Only one who had been in my position could appreciate it."

I did not know how to reply to him, and we again relapsed into silence, although it was evident that he was anxious to talk, and have me listen to him.

"Why were you ... why did you suffer this?" I inquired at last, not being able to invent any better way of breaking the ice.

"Why, didn't you hear about this wretched business from Metenin?"

"Yes, a duel, I believe; I did not hear much about it," I replied. "You see, I have been for some time in the Caucasus."

"No, it wasn't a duel, but it was a stupid and horrid story. I will tell you all about it, if you don't know. It happened, that the same year that I met you at my sister's, I was living at Petersburg. I must tell you I had then what they call une position dans le monde,— a position good enough if it was not brilliant. Mon père me donnait ten thousand par an. In '49 I was promised a place in the embassy at Turin; my uncle on? my mother's side had influence, and was always ready to do a great deal for me. That sort of thing is all past now. J'étais reçu dans la meilleure société de Petersburg; I might have aspired to any girl in the city. I was well educated, as we all are who come from the school, but was not especially cultivated; to be sure, I read a good deal afterwards, mais j'avais surtout, you know, ce jargon du monde, and, however it came about, I was looked upon as a leading light among the young men of Petersburg. What raised me more than all in common estimation, c'est cette liaison avec Madame D., about which a great deal was said in Petersburg; but I was frightfully young at that time, and did not prize these advantages very highly. I was simply young and stupid. What more did I need? Just then that Metenin had some notoriety"—

And Guskof went on in the same fashion to relate to me the history of his misfortunes, which I will omit, as it would not be at all interesting.

"Two months I remained under arrest," he continued, "absolutely alone; and what thoughts did I not have during that time? But, you know, when it was all over, as though every tie had been broken with the past, then it became easier for me. Mon père,—you have heard tell of him, of course, a man of iron will and strong convictions,—il m'a désherité, and broken off all intercourse with me. According to his convictions he had to do as he did, and I don't blame him at all. He was consistent. Consequently I have not taken a step to induce him to change his mind. My sister was abroad. Madame D. is the only one who wrote to me when I was released, and she sent me assistance; but you understand that I could not accept it, so that I had none of those little things which make one's position a little easier, you know,—books, linen, food, nothing at all. At this time I thought things over and over, and began to look at life with different eyes. For instance, this noise, this society gossip about me in Petersburg, did not interest me, did not flatter me: it all seemed to me ridiculous. I felt that I myself had been to blame; I was young and indiscreet; I had spoiled my career, and I only thought how I might get into the right track again. And I felt that I had strength and energy enough for it. After my arrest, as I told you, I was sent here to the Caucasus to the N. regiment.

"I thought," he went on to say, all the time becoming more and more animated,—"I thought that here in the Caucasus, la vie de camp, the simple, honest men with whom I should associate, and war and danger, would all admirably agree with my mental state, so that I might begin a new life. They will see me under fire.[12] I shall make myself liked; I shall be respected for my real self,—the cross—non-commissioned officer; they will relieve me of my fine; and I shall get up again, et vous savez avec ce prestige du malheur! But, quel désenchantement! You can't imagine how I have been deceived! You know what sort of men the officers of our regiment are."

He did not speak for some little time, waiting, as it appeared, for me to tell him that I knew the society of our officers here was bad; but I made him no reply. It went against my grain that he should expect me, because I knew French, forsooth, to be obliged to take issue with the society of the officers, which, during my long residence in the Caucasus, I had had time enough to appreciate fully, and for which I had far higher respect than for the society from which Mr. Guskof had sprung. I wanted to tell him so, but his position constrained me.

"In the N. regiment the society of the officers is a thousand times worse than it is here," he continued. "I hope that it is saying a good deal; j'espère que c'est beaucoup dire; that is, you cannot imagine what it is. I am not speaking of the yunkers and the soldiers, That is horrible, it is so bad. At first they received me very kindly, that is absolutely the truth; but when they saw that I could not help despising them, you know, in these inconceivably small circumstances, they saw that I was a man absolutely different, standing far above them, they got angry with me, and began to put various little humiliations on me. You haven't an idea what I had to suffer.[13] Then this forced relationship with the yunkers, and especially with the small means that I had—I lacked every thing;[14] I had only what my sister used to send me. And here's a proof for you! As much as it made me suffer, I with my character, avec ma fierté, j'ai écris à mon père, begged him to send me something. I understand how living four years of such a life may make a man like our cashiered Dromof who drinks with soldiers, and writes notes to all the officers asking them to loan him three rubles, and signing it, tout à vous, Dromof. One must have such a character as I have, not to be mired in the least by such a horrible position."

For some time he walked in silence by my side.

"Have you a cigarette?"[15] he asked me.

"And so I staid right where I was? Yes. I could not endure it physically, because, though we were wretched, cold, and ill-fed, I lived like a common soldier, but still the officers had some sort of consideration for me. I had still some prestige that they regarded. I wasn't sent out on guard nor for drill. I could not have stood that. But morally my sufferings were frightful; and especially because I didn't see any escape from my position. I wrote my uncle, begged him to get me transferred to my present regiment, which, at least, sees some service; and I thought that here Pavel Dmitriévitch, qui est le fils de l'intendant de mon père, might be of some use to me. My uncle did this for me; I was transferred. After that regiment this one seemed to me a collection of chamberlains. Then Pavel Dmitriévitch was here; he knew who I was, and I was splendidly received. At my uncle's request—a Guskof, vous savez; but I forgot that with these men without cultivation and undeveloped,—they can't appreciate a man, and show him marks of esteem, unless he has that aureole of wealth, of friends; and I noticed how, little by little, when they saw that I was poor, their behavior to me showed more and more indifference until they have come almost to dispise me. It is horrible, but it is absolutely the truth.

"Here I have been in action, I have fought, they have seen me under fire,"[16] he continued; "but when will it all end? I think, never. And my strength and energy have already begun to flag. Then I had imagined la guerre, la vie de camp; but it isn't at all what I see, in a sheepskin jacket, dirty linen, soldier's boots, and you go out in ambuscade, and the whole night long lie in the ditch with some Antónof reduced to the ranks for drunkenness, and any minute from behind the bush may come a rifle-shot and hit you or Antónof,—it's all the same which. That is not bravery: it's horrible, c'est affreux, it's killing!"[17]

"Well, you can be promoted a non-commissioned officer for this campaign, and next year an ensign," said I.

"Yes, it may be: they promised me that in two years, and it's not up yet. What would those two years amount to, if I knew any one! You can imagine this life with Pavel Dmitriévitch; cards, low jokes, drinking all the time; if you wish to tell any thing that is weighing on your mind, you would not be understood, or you would be laughed at; they talk with you, not for the sake of sharing a thought, but to get something funny out of you. Yes, and so it has gone—in a brutal, beastly way, and you are always conscious that you belong to the rank and file; they always make you feel that. Hence you can't realize what an enjoyment it is to talk à cœur ouvert to such a man as you are."

I had never imagined what kind of a man I was, and consequently I did not know what answer to make him.

"Will you have your lunch now?" asked Nikíta at this juncture, approaching me unseen in the darkness, and, as I could perceive, vexed at the presence of a guest. "Nothing but curd dumplings, there's none of the roast beef left."

"Has the captain had his lunch yet?"

"He went to bed long ago," replied Nikíta gruffly. "According to my directions, I was to bring you lunch here and your brandy." He muttered something else discontentedly, and sauntered off to his tent. After loitering a while longer, he brought us, nevertheless, a lunch-case; he placed a candle on the lunch-case, and shielded it from the wind with a sheet of paper. He brought a saucepan, some mustard in a jar, a tin dipper with a handle, and a bottle of absinthe. After arranging these things, Nikíta lingered around us for some moments, and looked on as Guskof and I were drinking the liquor, and it was evidently very distasteful to him. By the feeble light shed by the candle through the paper, amid the encircling darkness, could be seen the seal-skin cover of the lunch-case, the supper arranged upon it, Guskof's sheepskin jacket, his face, and his small red hands which he used in lifting the patties from the pan. Every thing around us was black; and only by straining the sight could be seen the dark battery, the dark form of the sentry moving along the breastwork, on all sides the watch-fires, and on high the ruddy stars.

Guskof wore a melancholy, almost guilty smile, as though it were awkward for him to look into my face after his confession. He drank still another glass of liquor, and ate ravenously, emptying the saucepan.

"Yes; for you it must be a relief all the same," said I, for the sake of saying something,—"your acquaintance with the adjutant. He is a very good man, I have heard."

"Yes," replied the cashiered officer, "he is a kind man; but he can't help being what he is, with his education, and it is useless to expect it."

A flush seemed suddenly to cross his face. "You remarked his coarse jest this evening about the ambuscade;" and Guskof, though I tried several times to interrupt him, began to justify himself before me, and to show that he had not run away from the ambuscade, and that he was not a coward as the adjutant and Capt. S. tried to make him out.

"As I was telling you," he went on to say, wiping his hands on his jacket, "such people can't show any delicacy toward a man, a common soldier, who hasn't much money either. That's beyond their strength. And here recently, while I haven't received any thing at all from my sister, I have been conscious that they have changed toward me. This sheepskin jacket, which I bought of a soldier, and which hasn't any warmth in it, because it's all worn off" (and here he showed me where the wool was gone from the inside), "it doesn't arouse in him any sympathy or consideration for my unhappiness, but scorn, which he does not take pains to hide. Whatever my necessities may be, as now when I have nothing to eat except soldiers' gruel, and nothing to wear," he continued, casting down his eyes, and pouring out for himself still another glass of liquor, "he does not even offer to lend me some money, though he knows perfectly well that I would give it back to him; but he waits till I am obliged to ask him for it. But you appreciate how it is for me to go to him. In your case I should say, square and fair, Vous êtes au dessus de cela, mon cher, je n'ai pas le sou. And you know," said he, looking straight into my eyes with an expression of desperation, "I am going to tell you, square and fair, I am in a terrible situation: pouvez-vous me prêter dix rubles argent? My sister ought to send me some by the next mail, et mon père"—

"Why, most willingly," said I, although, on the contrary, it was trying and unpleasant, especially because the evening before, having lost at cards, I had left only about five rubles in Nikíta's care. "In a moment," said I, arising, "I will go and get it at the tent."

"No, by and by: ne vous dérangez pas."

Nevertheless, not heeding him, I hastened to the closed tent, where stood my bed, and where the captain was sleeping.

"Alekséi Ivánuitch, let me have ten rubles, please, for rations," said I to the captain, shaking him.

"What! have you been losing again? But this very evening, you were not going to play any more," murmured the captain, still half asleep.

"No, I have not been playing; but I want the money; let me have it, please."

"Makatiuk!" shouted the captain to his servant,[18] "hand me my bag with the money."

"Hush, hush!" said I, hearing Guskof's measured steps near the tent.

"What? Why hush?"

"Because that cashiered fellow has asked to borrow it of me. He's right there."

"Well, if you knew him, you wouldn't let him have it," remarked the captain. "I have heard about him. He's a dirty, low-lived fellow."

Nevertheless, the captain gave me the money, ordered his man to put away the bag, pulled the flap of the tent neatly to, and, again saying, "If you only knew him, you wouldn't let him have it," drew his head down under the coverlet. "Now you owe me thirty-two, remember," he shouted after me.

When I came out of the tent, Guskof was walking near the settees; and his slight figure, with his crooked legs, his shapeless cap, his long white hair, kept appearing and disappearing in the darkness, as he passed in and out of the light of the candles. He made believe not to see me.

I handed him the money. He said "Merci" and, crumpling the bank-bill, thrust it into his trousers pocket.

"Now I suppose the game is in full swing at the adjutant's," he began immediately after this.

"Yes, I suppose so."

"He's a wonderful player, always bold, and never backs out. When he's in luck, it's fine; but when it does not go well with him, he can lose frightfully. He has given proof of that. During this expedition, if you reckon his valuables, he has lost more than fifteen hundred rubles. But, as he played discreetly before, that officer of yours seemed to have some doubts about his honor."

"Well, that's because he ... Nikíta, haven't we any of that red Kavkas wine[19] left?" I asked, very much enlivened by Guskof's conversational talent. Nikíta still kept muttering; but he brought us the red wine, and again looked on angrily as Guskof drained his glass. In Guskof's behavior was noticeable his old freedom from constraint. I wished that he would go as soon as possible; it seemed as if his only reason for not going was because he did not wish to go immediately after receiving the money. I said nothing.

"How could you, who have means, and were under no necessity, simply de gaieté de cœur, make up your mind to come and serve in the Caucasus? That's what I don't understand," said he to me.

I endeavored to explain this act of renunciation, which seemed so strange to him.

"I can imagine how disagreeable the society of these officers—men without any comprehension of culture—must be for you. You could not understand each other. You see, you might live ten years, and not see any thing, and not hear about anything, except cards, wine, and gossip about rewards and campaigns."

It was unpleasant for me, that he wished me to put myself on a par with him in his position; and, with absolute honesty I assured him that I was very fond of cards and wine, and gossip about campaigns, and that I did not care to have any better comrades than those with whom I was associated. But he would not believe me.

"Well, you may say so," he continued; "but the lack of women's society,—I mean, of course, femmes comme il faut,—is that not a terrible deprivation? I don't know what I would give now to go into a parlor, if only for a moment, and to have a look at a pretty woman, even though it were through a crack."

He said nothing for a little, and drank still another glass of the red wine.

"Oh, my God, my God![20] If it only might be our fate to meet again, somewhere in Petersburg, to live and move among men, among ladies!"

He drank up the dregs of the wine still left in the bottle, and when he had finished it he said, "Akh! pardon, maybe you wanted some more. It was horribly careless of me. However, I suppose I must have taken too much, and my head isn't very strong.[21] There was a time when I lived on Morskaia Street, au rez-de-chaussée, and had marvellous apartments, furniture, you know, and I was able to arrange it all beautifully, not so very expensively though; my father, to be sure, gave me porcelains, flowers, and silver,—a wonderful lot. Le matin je sortais, visits, à 5 heures régulièrement. I used to go and dine with her; often she was alone. Il faut avouer que c'était une femme ravissante! You didn't know her at all, did you?"

"No."

"You see, there was such a high degree of womanliness in her, and such tenderness, and what love! Lord! I did not know how to appreciate my happiness then. We would return after the theatre, and have a little supper together. It was never dull where she was, toujours gaie, toujours aimante.

Yes, and I had never imagined what rare happiness it was. Et j'ai beaucoup à me reprocher in regard to her. Je l'ai fait souffrir et souvent. I was outrageous. Akh! What a marvellous time that was! Do I bore you?"

"No, not at all."

"Then I will tell you about our evenings. I used to go—that stairway, every flower-pot I knew,—the door-handle, all was so lovely, so familiar; then the vestibule, her room ... No, it will never, never come back to me again! Even now she writes to me: if you will let me, I will show you her letters. But I am not what I was; I am ruined; I am no longer worthy of her.... Yes, I am ruined forever. Je suis cassé. There's no energy in me, no pride, nothing—nor even any rank.[22] ... Yes, I am ruined; and no one will ever appreciate my sufferings. Every one is indifferent. I am a lost man. Never any chance for me to rise, because I have fallen morally ... into the mire—I have fallen." ...

At this moment there was evident in his words a genuine, deep despair: he did not look at me, but sat motionless.

"Why are you in such despair?" I asked.

"Because I am abominable. This life has degraded me, all that was in me, all is crushed out. It is not by pride that I hold out, but by abjectness: there's no dignité dans le malheur. I am humiliated every moment; I endure it all; I got myself into this abasement. This mire has soiled me. I myself have become coarse; I have forgotten what I used to know; I can't speak French any more; I am conscious that I am base and low. I cannot tear myself away from these surroundings, indeed I cannot. I might have been a hero: give me a regiment, gold epaulets, a trumpeter, but to march in the ranks with some wild Anton Bondarenko or the like, and feel that between me and him there was no difference at all—that he might be killed or I might be killed—all the same, that thought is maddening. You understand how horrible it is to think that some ragamuffin may kill me, a man who has thoughts and feelings, and that it would make no difference if alongside of me some Antónof were killed,—a being not different from an animal—and that it might easily happen that I and not this Antónof were killed, which is always une fatalité for every lofty and good man. I know that they call me a coward: grant that I am a coward, I certainly am a coward, and can't be any thing else. Not only am I a coward, but I am in my way a low and despicable man. Here I have just been borrowing money of you, and you have the right to despise me. No, take back your money." And he held out to me the crumpled bank-bill. "I want you to have a good opinion of me." He covered his face with his hands, and burst into tears. I really did not know what to say or do.

"Calm yourself," I said to him. "You are too sensitive; don't take every thing so to heart; don't indulge in self-analysis, look at things more simply. You yourself say that you have character. Keep up good heart, you won't have long to wait," I said to him, but not very consistently, because I was much stirred both by a feeling of sympathy and a feeling of repentance, because I had allowed myself mentally to sin in my judgment of a man truly and deeply unhappy.

"Yes," he began, "if I had heard even once, at the time when I was in that hell, one single word of sympathy, of advice, of friendship—one humane word such as you have just spoken, perhaps I might have calmly endured all; perhaps I might have struggled, and been a soldier. But now this is horrible.... When I think soberly, I long for death. Why should I love my despicable life and my own self, now that I am ruined for all that is worth while in the world? And at the least danger, I suddenly, in spite of myself, begin to pray for my miserable life, and to watch over it as though it were precious, and I cannot, je ne puis pas, control myself.—That is, I could," he continued again after a minute's silence, "but this is too hard work for me, a monstrous work, when I am alone. With others, under special circumstances, when you are going into action, I am brave, j'ai fait mes épreuves, because I am vain and proud: that is my fading, and in presence of others.... Do you know, let me spend the night with you: with us, they will play all night long; it makes no difference, anywhere, on the ground."

While Nikíta was making the bed, we got up, and once more began to walk up and down in the darkness on the battery. Certainly Guskof's head must have been very weak, because two glasses of liquor and two of wine made him dizzy. As we got up and moved away from the candles, I noticed that he again thrust the ten-ruble bill into his pocket, trying to do so without my seeing it. During all the foregoing conversation, he had held it in his hand. He continued to reiterate how he felt that he might regain his old station if he had a man such as I were to take some interest in him.

We were just going into the tent to go to bed when suddenly a cannon-ball whistled over us, and buried itself in the ground not far from us. So strange it was,—that peacefully sleeping camp, our conversation, and suddenly the hostile cannon-ball which flew from God knows where, into the midst of our tents,—so strange that it was some time before I could realize what it was. Our sentinel, Andréief, walking up and down on the battery, moved toward me.

"Ha! he's crept up to us. It was the fire here that he aimed at," said he.

"We must rouse the captain," said I, and gazed at Guskof.

He stood cowering close to the ground, and stammered, trying to say, "Th-that's th-the ene-my's ... f-f-fire—th-that's—hidi—." Further he could not say a word, and I did not see how and where he disappeared so instantaneously.

In the captain's tent a candle gleamed; his cough, which always troubled him when he was awake, was heard; and he himself soon appeared, asking for a linstock to light his little pipe.

"What does this mean, old man?"[23] he asked with a smile. "Aren't they willing to give me a little sleep to-night? First it's you with your cashiered friend, and then it's Shamyl. What shall we do, answer him or not? There was nothing about this in the instructions, was there?"

"Nothing at all. There he goes again," said I. "Two of them!"

Indeed, in the darkness, directly in front of us, flashed two fires, like two eyes; and quickly over our heads flew one cannon-ball and one heavy shell. It must have been meant for us, coming with a loud and penetrating hum. From the neighboring tents the soldiers hastened. You could hear them hawking and talking and stretching themselves.

"Hist! the fuse sings like a nightingale," was the remark of the artillerist.

"Send for Nikíta," said the captain with his perpetually benevolent smile. "Nikíta, don't hide yourself, but listen to the mountain nightingales."

"Well, your honor,"[24] said Nikíta, who was standing near the captain, "I have seen them—these nightingales. I am not afraid of 'em; but here was that stranger who was here, he was drinking up your red wine. When he heard how that shot dashed by our tents, and the shell rolled by, he cowered down like some wild beast."

"However, we must send to the commander of the artillery," said the captain to me in a serious tone of authority, "and ask whether we shall reply to the fire or not. It will probably be nothing at all, but still it may. Have the goodness to go and ask him. Have a horse saddled. Do it as quickly as possible, even if you take my Polkan."

In five minutes they brought me a horse, and I galloped off to the commander of the artillery. "Look you, return on foot," whispered the punctilious captain, "else they won't let you through the lines."

It was half a verst to the artillery commander's, the whole road ran between the tents. As soon as I rode away from our fire, it became so black that I could not see even the horse's ears, but only the watch-fires, now seeming very near, now very far off, as they gleamed into my eyes. After I had ridden some distance, trusting to the intelligence of the horse whom I allowed free rein, I began to distinguish the white four-cornered tents and then the black tracks of the road. After a half-hour, having asked my way three times, and twice stumbled over the tent-stakes, causing each time a volley of curses from the tents, and twice been detained by the sentinels, I reached the artillery commander's. While I was on the way, I heard two more cannon shot in the direction of our camp; but the projectiles did not reach to the place where the headquarters were. The artillery commander ordered not to reply to the firing, the more as the enemy did not remain in the same place; and I went back, leading the horse by the bridle, making my way on foot between the infantry tents. More than once I delayed my steps, as I went by some soldier's tent where a light was shining, and some merry-andrew was telling a story; or I listened to some educated soldier reading from some book while the whole division overflowed the tent, or hung around it, sometimes interrupting the reading with various remarks; or I simply listened to the talk about the expedition, about the fatherland, or about their chiefs.

As I came around one of the tents of the third battalion, I heard Guskof's rough voice: he was speaking hilariously and rapidly. Young voices replied to him, not those of soldiers, but of gay gentlemen. It was evidently the tent of some yunker or sergeant-major. I stopped short.

"I've known him a long time," Guskof was saying. "When I lived in Petersburg, he used to come to my house often; and I went to his. He moved in the best society."

"Whom are you talking about?" asked a drunken voice.

"About the prince," said Guskof. "We were relatives, you see, but, more than all, we were old friends. It's a mighty good thing, you know, gentlemen, to have such an acquaintance. You see, he's fearfully rich. To him a hundred silver rubles is a mere bagatelle. Here, I just got a little money out of him, enough to last me till my sister sends."

"Let's have some."

"Right away.—Savelitch, my dear," said Guskof, coming to the door of the tent, "here's ten rubles for you: go to the sutler, get two bottles of Kakhetinski. Any thing else, gentlemen? What do you say?" and Guskof, with unsteady gait, with dishevelled hair, without his hat, came out of the tent. Throwing open his jacket, and thrusting his hands into the pockets of his trousers, he stood at the door of the tent. Though he was in the light, and I in darkness, I trembled with fear lest he should see me, and I went on, trying to make no noise.

"Who goes there?" shouted Guskof after me in a thoroughly drunken voice. Apparently, the cold took hold of him. "Who the devil is going off with that horse?"

I made no answer, and silently went on my way.

[1] gorodki.

[2] denshchiki.

[3] nu chto, bátenka.

[4] polushúbok, little half shuba, or fur cloak.

[5] bátenka, Malo-Russian diminutive, little father.

[6] papírósotchka, diminished diminutive of papiróska, from papiros.

[7] bátenka.

[8] stranno.

[9] bátenka moï.

[10] Oui, mon cher, lea jours se suivent, mais ne se ressemblent pas: in French in the original.

[11] bátiushka.

[12] On me verra au feu.

[13] Ce que j'ai eu à souffrir vous ne vous faites pas une idée.

[14] Avec les petits moyens que j'avais, je manquais de tout.

[15] "Avez-vous un papiros?"

[16] On m'a vu au feu.

[17] Ça tue.

[18] denshchik.

[19] chikír.

[20] Akh, Bozhe moï, Bozhe moï!

[21] Et je n'ai pas la tête forte.

[22] blagorodstva, noble birth, nobility.

[23] bátiushka.

[24] váshe vuisokoblagorodïe. German, hochwohlgeborener, high-well born; regulation title of officers from major to general.

LOST ON THE STEPPE; OR, THE SNOWSTORM.

A TALE.

I.

At seven o'clock in the evening, having taken my tea, I started from a station, the name of which I have quite forgotten, though I remember that it was somewhere in the region of the Don Cossacks, not far from Novocherkask. It was already dark when I took my seat in the sledge next to Alyoshka, and wrapped myself in my fur coat and the robes. Back of the station-house it seemed warm and calm. Though it was not snowing, not a single star was to be seen overhead, and the sky it seemed remarkably low and black, in contrast with the clear snowy expanse stretching out before us.

We had scarcely passed by the black forms of the windmills, one of which was awkwardly waving its huge wings, and had left the station behind us, when I perceived that the road was growing rougher and more drifted; the wind began to blow more fiercely on the left, and to toss the horses' manes and tails to one side, and obstinately to lift and carry away the snow stirred up by the runners and hoofs. The little bell rang with a muffled sound; a draught of cold air forced its way through the opening in my sleeves, to my very back; and the inspector's advice came into my head, that I had better not go farther, lest I wander all night, and freeze to death on the road.

"Won't you get us lost?" said I to the driver,[1] but, as I got no answer, I put the question more explicitly: "Say, shall we reach the station, driver? We sha'n't lose our way?"

"God knows," was his reply; but he did not turn his head. "You see what kind of going we have. No road to be seen. Great heavens!"[2]

"Be good enough to tell me, do you hope to reach the station, or not?" I insisted. "Shall we get there?"

"Must get there," said the driver; and he muttered something else, which

I could not hear for the wind.

I did not wish to turn about, but the idea of wandering all night in the cold and snow over the perfectly shelterless steppe, which made up this part of the Don Cossack land, was very unpleasant. Moreover, notwithstanding the fact that I could not, by reason of the darkness, see him very well, my driver, somehow, did not please me, "nor inspire any confidence. He sat exactly in the middle, with his legs in, and not on one, side; his stature was too great; his voice expressed indolence; his cap, not like those usually worn by his class, was large and loose on all sides. Besides, he did not manage his horses in the proper way, but held the reins in both hands, just like the lackey who sat on the box behind the coachman; and, chiefly, I did not believe in him, because he had his ears wrapped up in a handkerchief. In a word, he did not please me; and it seemed as if that crooked, sinister back looming before me boded nothing good.

"In my opinion, it would be better to turn about," said Alyoshka to me: "fine thing it would be to be lost!"

"Great heavens! see what a snowstorm's coming! No road in sight. It blinds one's eyes. Great heavens!" repeated the driver.

We had not been gone a quarter of an hour when the driver stopped the horses, handed the reins to Alyoshka, awkwardly liberated his legs from the seat, and went to search for the road, crunching over the snow in his great boots.

"What is it? Where are you going? Are we lost?" I asked, but the driver made no reply, but, turning his face away from the wind, which cut his eyes, marched off from the sledge.

"Well, how is it?" I repeated, when he returned.

"Nothing at all," said he to me impatiently and with vexation, as though I were to blame for his missing the road; and again slowly wrapping up his big legs in the robe, he gathered the reins in his stiffened mittens.

"What's to be done?" I asked as we started off again.

"What's to be done? We shall go as God leads."

And we drove along in the same dog-trot over what was evidently an untrodden waste, sometimes sinking in deep, mealy snow, sometimes gliding over crisp, unbroken crust.

Although it was cold, the snow kept melting quickly on my collar. The low-flying snow-clouds increased, and occasionally the dry snowflakes began to fall.

It was clear that we were going out of our way, because, after keeping on for a quarter of an hour more, we saw no sign of a verst-post.

"Well, what do you think about it now?" I asked of the driver once more. "Shall we get to the station?"

"Which one? We should go back if we let the horses have their way: they will take us. But, as for the next one, that's a problem.... Only we might perish."

"Well, then, let us go back," said I. "And indeed"—

"How is it? Shall we turn about?" repeated the driver.

"Yes, yes: turn back."

The driver shook the reins. The horses started off more rapidly; and, though I did not notice that we had turned around, the wind changed, and soon through the snow appeared the windmills. The driver's good spirits returned, and he began to be communicative.

"Lately," said he, "in just such a snowstorm some people coming from that same station lost their way. Yes: they spent the night in the hayricks, and barely managed to get here in the morning. Thanks to the hayricks, they were rescued. If it had not been for them, they would have frozen to death, it was so cold. And one froze his foot, and died three weeks afterwards."

"But now, you see, it's not cold; and it's growing less windy," I said. "Couldn't we go on?"

"It's warm enough, but it's snowing. Now going back, it seems easier.

But it's snowing hard. Might go on, if you were a courier or something; but this is for your own sake. What kind of a joke would that be if a passenger froze to death? How, then, could I be answerable to your grace?"

[1] yamshchík.

[2] gospodi-bátiushka! Literally, Lord, little father.

II.

At this moment we heard behind us the bells of a troïka which was rapidly overtaking us.

"A courier's bell," said my driver. "There's one such for every station."

And, in fact, the bell of the courier's troïka, the sound of which now came clearly to me on the wind, was peculiarly beautiful,—clear, sonorous, deep, and jangling a little. As I then knew, this was a huntsman's team; three bells,—one large one in the centre, with the crimson tone, as it is called, and two small ones tuned in thirds. The sound of this triad and the tinkling fifth, ringing through the air, was extraordinarily effective and strangely pleasant in this dark desert steppe.

"The posht is coming," said my driver when the foremost of the three troikas drew up in line with ours. "Well, how is the road? is it possible to go on?" he cried to the last of the drivers. But the yamshchík only shouted to his horses, and made no reply.

The sound of the bells quickly died away on the wind, almost as soon as the post-team passed us.

Of course my driver felt ashamed.

"Well, you shall go, bárin," he said to me. "People have made their way through, now their tracks will be fresh."

I agreed; and once more we faced the wind, and began to crawl along on the deep snow. I kept my eyes on one side on the road, so that we should not get off the track that had been made by the other sledges. For two versts the tracks were clearly visible, then there began to be only a slight irregularity where the runners had gone; and soon I really could no longer distinguish whether it was the track, or merely a layer of snow heaped up. My eyes grew weary of gazing at the monotonous stretch of snow under the runners, and I began to look ahead. The third verst-post we had already seen, but the fourth we could not find at all. As before, we went in the teeth of the wind, and with the wind, and to the right and to the left; and finally we reached such a state that the driver declared that we must have turned off to the right. I declared that we must have turned off to the left, and Alyoshka was sure that we ought to go back. Again we stopped a number of times, the driver uncoiled his long legs, and crawled along trying to find the road. But all in vain. I also got out once to see whether it were the road or something else that attracted my attention. But I had scarcely taken six steps with difficulty against the wind, and convinced myself that we were surrounded by the same monotonous white heaps of snow, and that the road existed only in my imagination, when I lost sight of the sledge. I shouted, "Yamshchík! Alyoshka!" but my voice,—I felt how the wind tore it right out of my mouth, and carried it in a twinkling far from me. I went in the direction where the sledge had been—the sledge was not there. I went to the right—not there either. I am ashamed to recollect what a loud, penetrating, and even rather despairing voice, I summoned to shout once more, "Yamshchík!" and there he was two steps away. His black figure, with his whip, and his huge cap hanging down on one side, suddenly loomed up before me. He led me to the sledge.

"Thank the Lord, it's still warm!" said he. "To perish with the cold—awful! Great heavens!"[3]

"Let the horses find their own way, let us turn back," said I, as I took my place in the sledge. "Won't they take us back? hey, driver?"

"They ought to."

He gave the horses the reins, cracked his whip three times over the saddle of the shaft-horse, and again we started off at hap-hazard. We went for half an hour. Suddenly before us again I heard the well-known bell of the hunting establishment, and the other two. But now they were coming toward us. It was the same three troikas, which had already deposited the mail, and, with a change of horses attached behind, were returning to the station. The courier's troïka, with powerful horses with the hunting-bell, quickly dashed ahead. A single driver sat in it on the driver's seat, and was shouting vigorously. Behind him, in the middle one of the empty troikas, were two other drivers; and their loud and hilarious talk could be heard. One of them was smoking a pipe; and the spark, brightened by the wind, lighted up a part of his face.

As I looked at them, I felt ashamed that I was afraid to go on; and my driver doubtless had the same feeling, because we both said with one voice, "Let us follow them."

[3] gospodi-bátiushka.

III.

My driver, without waiting for the last troïka to pass, began awkwardly to turn around; and the thills hit the horses attached behind. One of the troïka teams shied, tore away the reins, and galloped off.

"Hey there, you squint-eyed devil! Don't you see where you are turning? Running people down, you devil!" in a hoarse, discordant voice scolded one of the drivers, a short, little old man, as I judged by his voice and expression. He sprang hastily out of the hindmost sledge where he had been sitting, and started to run after the horses, still continuing roughly and violently to vilify my yamshchík.

But the horses did not come back. The driver ran after them, and in one instant both horses and driver were lost from sight in the white mist of the storm.

"Vasi-i-i-li! bring the bay horse here. Can't ketch him, so-o-o," echoed his voice in the distance.

One of the drivers, a very tall fellow, got out of his sledge, silently unhitched his troïka, mounted one of the horses by the breeching, and crunching over the snow in a clumsy gallop, disappeared in the same direction.

Our own troïka, with the two others, followed on over the steppe, behind the courier's which dashed ahead in full trot, jingling its bell.

"How is it? He'll get 'em?" said my driver, referring to the one who had gone to catch the horses. "If that mare didn't find the horses she wouldn't be good for much, you know: she'd wander off, so that—she'd get lost."

From the moment that my driver had the company of other teams he became more hilarious and talkative; and, as I had no desire to sleep, I did not fail, as a matter of course, to make the most of it. I took pains to ask him about his home and his family, and soon learned that he was a fellow-countryman of mine from Tula,—a peasant, belonging to a noble family from the village of Kirpitchnoé; that they had very little land, and the grain had entirely ceased to grow, owing to the cholera; that he and one of his brothers had staid at home, and a third had gone as a soldier; that since Christmas they had lacked bread, and had been obliged to work out; that his younger brother had kept the farm because he was married, but that he himself was a widower; that his villagers every year came here to exercise the trade of yamshchík, or driver; that, though he had not come as a regular driver, yet he was in the postal-service, so as to help his brother; that he earned there, thanks to God, a hundred and twenty paper rubles a year, of which he sent a hundred to his family; and that it would be good living, "but the couliers were very wild beasts, and the people here were impudent."

"Now, what was that driver scolding about? Great heavens![4] did I mean to lose his horses for him? Did I treat him in a mean way? And why did he go galloping off after 'em? They'd have come in of their own accord. Anyway, 'twould be better for the horses to freeze to death than for him to get lost," said the pious muzhík.

"What is that black thing I see coming?" I asked, pointing to some dark object in front of us.

"That's a baggage-train. Splendid wheeling!" he added, as he came up with the huge mat-covered vans on wheels, following one after the other. "See, not a soul to be seen—all asleep. The wise horse knows: you won't drive her from the road, never.... We've driven in that same way—so we know," he added.

It was indeed strange to see the huge vans covered with snow from the matted tops to the wheels, moving along, absolutely alone. Only the front corner of the snow-covered mat would be lifted by two fingers; and, for a moment, a cap would peer out as our bells jingled past the train. A great piebald horse, stretching out his neck, and straining his back, walked with measured pace over the drifted road, monotonously shaking his shaggy head under the whitened bell-bow,[5] and pricking up one snow-covered ear as we went by.

After we had gone still another, half-hour, the driver once more turned to me,—

"Well, what do you think, bárin? Are we getting along well?"

"I don't know," I said.

"Before, the wind blew in our faces, but now we go right along with it. No, we sha'n't get there: we are off the track," he said in conclusion, with perfect equanimity.

It was evident, that, though he was very timid, yet, as "death in company with others is pleasant," he was perfectly content to die now that there were a number of us, and he was not obliged to take the lead, and be responsible. He coolly made observations on the mistakes of the head driver, as though it were not of the least consequence to himself. In fact, I had noticed that sometimes the front troïka appeared on my right, and again on my left. It seemed to me, too, that we were making a circle in very small space. However, it might be that it was an ocular deception, just as sometimes it seemed as if the front troïka were climbing up a mountain or were going along a slope or down a mountain, even when the steppe was everywhere perfectly level.

After we had gone on a little while longer, I saw, as it seemed to me, at a distance, on the very horizon, a long black, moving line; but it quickly became plain to me that it was the same baggage-train which we had passed. In exactly the same way, the snow covered the creaking wheels, several of which did not turn; in exactly the same way, the men were sleeping under the matted tops; and likewise the piebald leader, swelling out his nostrils, snuffed out the road, and pricked back his ears.

"See, we've gone round in a circle; we've gone round in a circle! Here's the same baggage-train again!" exclaimed my driver in a discontented tone. "The coulier's horses are good ones, so it makes no difference to him, even if he does go on a wild-goose chase. But ours will get tired out if we have to spend the whole night here."

He had an attack of coughing.

"Should we go back, bárin, owing to the mistake?"

"No! Why? We shall come out somewhere."

"Come out where? We shall have to spend the night in the steppe. How it's snowing!... Great heavens!"[6]

Although it was clear to me that the head driver had lost both the road and the direction, and yet was not hunting for the road, but was singing at the top of his voice, and letting his horses take their own speed; and so I did not like to part company from them.

"Follow them," said I.

The yamshchík drove on, but followed them less willingly than before, and no longer had any thing to say to me.

[4] gospodi-bátiushka.

[5] dugá, the distinctive part of the Russian harness, rising high above the horse, and carrying the bells.

[6] gospodi-bátiushka.

IV.

The storm became more and more violent, and the snow fell dry and fine; it seemed as if we were in danger of freezing. My nose and cheeks began to tingle; more frequently the draught of cold air insinuated itself under my furs, and it became necessary to bundle up warmer. Sometimes the sledges bumped on the bare, icy crust from which the snow had been blown away. As I had already gone six hundred versts without sleeping under roof, and though I felt great interest in the outcome of our wanderings, my eyes closed in spite of me, and I drowsed. Once when I opened my eyes, I was struck, as it seemed to me at the first moment, by a bright light, gleaming over the white plain: the horizon widened considerably, the lowering black sky suddenly lifted up on all sides, the white slanting lines of the falling snow became visible, the shapes of the head troikas stood out clearly; and when I looked up, it seemed to me at the first moment that the clouds had scattered, and that only the falling snow veiled the stars. At the moment that I awoke from my drowse, the moon came out, and cast through the tenuous clouds and the falling snow her cold bright beams. I saw clearly my sledge, horses, driver, and the three troikas, ploughing on in front: the first, the courier's, in which still sat on the box the one yamshchík driving at a hard trot; the second, in which rode the two drivers, who let the horses go at their own pace, and had made a shelter out of a camel's-hair coat[7] behind which they still smoked their pipes as could be seen by the sparks glowing in their direction; and the third, in which no one was visible, for the yamshchík was comfortably sleeping in the middle. The leading driver, however, while I was napping had several times halted his horses, and attempted to find the road. Then while we stopped the howling of the wind became more audible, and the monstrous heaps of snow piling through the atmosphere seemed more tremendous. By the aid of the moonlight which made its way through the storm, I could see the driver's short figure, whip in hand, examining the snow before him, moving back and forth in the misty light, again coming back to the sledge, and springing sidewise on the seat; and then again I heard above the monotonous whistling of the wind, the comfortable, clear jingling and melody of the bells. When the head driver crept out to find the marks of the road or the hayricks, each time was heard the lively, self-confident voice of one of the yamshchíks in the second sledge shouting, "Hey, Ignashka![8] you turned off too much to the left. Strike off to the right into the storm." Or, "Why are you going round in a circle? keep straight ahead as the snow flies. Follow the snow, then you'll hit it." Or, "Take the right, take the right, old man.[9] There's something black, it must be a post." Or, "What are you getting lost for? why are you getting lost? Unhitch the piebald horse, and let him find the road for you. He'll do it every time. That would be the best way."

The man who was so free with his advice not only did not offer to unhitch his off-horse, or go himself across the snow to hunt for the road, but did not even put his nose outside of his shelter-coat; and when Ignashka the leader, in reply to one of his proffers of advice, shouted to him to come and take the forward place since he knew the road so well, the mentor replied that when he came to drive a courier's sledge, then he would take the lead, and never once miss the road. "But our horses wouldn't go straight through a snowdrift," he shouted: "they ain't the right kind."

"Then don't you worry yourselves," replied Ignashka, gayly whistling to his horses.

The yamshchík who sat in the same sledge with the mentor said nothing at all to Ignashka, and paid no attention to the difficulty, though he was not yet asleep, as I concluded by his pipe which still glowed, and because, when we halted, I heard his measured voice in uninterrupted flow. He was telling a story. Once only, when Ignashka for the sixth or seventh time came to a stop, it seemed to vex him because his comfort in travelling was disturbed, and he shouted,—

"Stopping again? He's missing the road on purpose. Call this a snowstorm! The surveyor himself could not find the road! he would let the horses find it. We shall freeze to death here; just let him go on regardless!"

"What! Don't you know a poshtellion froze to death last winter?" shouted my driver.

All this time the driver of the third troïka had not been heard from. But once while we were stopping, the mentor shouted, "Filipp! ha! Filipp!" and not getting any response remarked,—

"Can he have frozen to death? Ignashka, you go and look."

Ignashka, who was responsible for all, went to his sledge, and began to shake the sleeper.

"See what drink has done for him! Tell us if you are frozen to death!" said he, shaking him.

The sleeper grunted a little, and then began to scold.

"Live enough, fellows!" said Ignashka, and again started ahead, and once more we drove on; and with such rapidity that the little brown off-horse, in my three-span, which was constantly whipping himself with his tail, did not once interrupt his awkward gallop.

[7] armyák.

[8] diminished diminutive of Ignat.

[9] bratets tui moï; literally, "thou brother mine."

V.

It was already about midnight, I judge, when the little old man and Vasíli, who had gone in search of the runaway horses, rejoined us. They had caught the horses, and had now overtaken us; but how in the world they had accomplished this in the thick, blinding snowstorm, in the midst of the bare steppe, was more than I could comprehend. The little old man, with his elbows and legs flying, came trotting up on the shaft-horse (the two other horses he had caught by the collars; it was impossible to lead them in the snowstorm). When they had caught up with me, he began to scold at my driver.

"You see, you cross-eyed devil! you"—

"O Uncle Mitritch,"[10] cried the talkative fellow in the second sledge, "you alive? Come along where we are!"

The old man did not answer him, but continued to scold. When he had satisfied himself, he rejoined the second sledge.

"Get em all?" was asked him.

"Why, of course we did."

And his small figure leaped up and down on the horse's back as he went off at full trot; then he sprang down into the snow, and without stopping caught up with the sledge, and sat in it with his legs hanging over the side. The tall Vasíli, just as before, took his place in perfect silence in the front sledge with Ignashka; and then the two began to look for the road together.

"What a spitfire! Great heavens!" muttered my driver.

For a long time after this we drove on without stopping, over the white waste, in the cold, pellucid, and wavering light of the snowstorm. When I opened my eyes, there before me rose the same clumsy, snow-covered cap; the same low dugá or bell-bow, under which, between the leathern reins tightly stretched, there moved always at the same distance the head of the shaft-horse with the black mane blown to one side by the wind. And I could see, above his back, the brown off-horse on the right, with his short braided tail, and the whiffletree sometimes knocking against the dasher of the sleigh. If I looked below, then I saw the scurrying snow stirred up by the runners, and constantly tossed and borne by the wind to one side. In front of me, always at the same distance, glided the other troïkas. To left and right, all was white and bewildering. Vainly the eye sought for any new object: neither verst-post, nor hayrick, nor fence was to be seen; nothing at all. Everywhere, all was white, white and fluctuating. Now the horizon seems to be indistinguishably distant, then it comes down within two steps on every side; now suddenly a high white wall grows up on the right, and accompanies the course of the sledges, then it suddenly vanishes, and grows up in front, only to glide on in advance, farther and farther away, and disappear again.

As I look up, it seems light. At the first moment, I imagine that through the mist I see the stars; but the stars, as I gaze, flee into deeper and deeper depths, and I see only the snow falling into face and eyes, and the collar of my fur coat;[11] the sky has everywhere one tone of light, one tone of white,—colorless, monotonous, and constantly shifting. The wind seems to vary: at one moment it blows into my face, and flings the snow into my eyes; the next it goes to one side, and peevishly tosses the collar of my shuba over my head, and insultingly slaps me in the face with it; then it finds some crevice behind, and plays a tune upon it. I hear the soft, unceasing crunching of the hoofs and the runners on the snow, and the muffled tinkling of the bells, as we speed over the deep snow. Only occasionally when we drive against the wind, and glide over the bare frozen crust, I can clearly distinguish Ignat's energetic whistling, and the full chords of the chime, with the resounding jarring fifth; and these sounds break suddenly and comfortingly upon the melancholy character of the desert; and then again rings monotonously, with unendurable fidelity of execution, the whole of that motive which involuntarily coincides with my thoughts.

One of my feet began to feel cold, and when I turned round so as to protect it better, the snow which covered my collar and my cap sifted down my neck, and made me shiver; but still I was, for the most, comfortable in my warm shuba, and drowsiness overcame me.

[10] Condensed form for Dmitriyévitch, "son of Dmitri." The peasants often call each other by the patronymic.

[11] shuba.

VI.

Things remembered and things conceived mixed and mingled with wonderful quickness in my imagination.

"The mentor who is always shouting from the second sledge, what kind of a man must he be? Probably red-haired, thick-set, with short legs, a man somewhat like Feódor Filíppuitch our old butler," is what I say to myself.

And here I see the staircase of our great house, and five of the house-servants who with towels, with heavy steps, carry the pianoforte from the L; I see Feódor Filíppuitch with the sleeves of his nankeen coat tucked up, carrying one of the pedals, and going in advance, unbolting the door, taking hold of the door-knob here, there pushing a little, now crawling under the legs; he is here, there, and everywhere, crying with an anxious voice continually, "Look out, take more weight, you there in front! Be careful, you there at the tail-end! Up—up—up—don't hit the door. There, there!"

"Excuse me, Feódor Filíppuitch! There ain't enough of us," says the gardener timidly, crushed up against the balustrade, and all red with exertion, lifting one end of the grand with all his remaining strength. But Feódor Filíppuitch does not hold his peace.

"And what does it mean?" I ask myself. "Does he think that he is of any use, that he is indispensable for the work in hand? or is he simply glad that God has given him this self-confident persuasive eloquence, and takes enjoyment in squandering it?"

And I somehow see the pond, the weary servants, who, up to their knees in the water, drag the heavy net; and again Feódor Filíppuitch, shouting to everybody, walking up and down on the bank, and only now and then venturing to the brink, taking with his hand the golden carp, and letting the dirty water run out from his watering-pot, so as to fill it up with fresh.

But here it is midday, in the month of July. Across the newly mown turf of the lawn, under the burning perpendicular rays of the sun, I seem to be going somewhere. I am still very young; I am free from yearnings, free from desires. I am going to the pond, to my own favorite spot between the rose-bushes and the birch-tree alley; and I shall lie down and nap. Keen is the sensation that I have, as I lie down, and look across the red thorny stems of the rose-bushes upon the dark ground with its dry grass and on the gleaming bright-blue mirror of the pond. It is a sensation of a peculiarly simple self-contentment and melancholy. All around me is so lovely, and this loveliness has such a powerful effect upon me, that it seems to me as if I myself were good; and the one thing that vexes me is, that no one is there to admire me.

It is hot. I try to go to sleep for comfort's sake; but the flies, the unendurable flies, even here, give me no rest. They begin to swarm around me, and obstinately, insolently as it were, heavy as cherry-stones, jump from my forehead to my hands. A bee buzzes near me in the sunbeam. Yellow-winged butterflies fly wearily from flower to flower.

I gaze up. It pains my eyes. The sun shines too bright through the light foliage of the bushy birch-tree, gracefully waving its branches high above my head, and it grows hotter still. I cover my face with my handkerchief. It becomes stifling; and the flies seem to stick to my hands, on which the perspiration stands. In the rose-bush the sparrows twitter under the thick leaves. One hops to the ground almost within my reach, makes two or three feints to peck energetically at the ground, and after making the little twigs crackle, and chirping gayly, flies away from the bushes; another also hops to the ground, wags his little tail, looks around, and, like an arrow, flies off twittering after the first. At the pond are heard the blows of the pounder on the wet clothes; and the noise re-echoes, and is carried far away, down along the shore. I hear laughter and talking, and the splashing of bathers. The breath of the wind sweeps the tops of the birches far above my head, and bends them down again. I hear it moving the grass, and now the leaves of the rose-bushes toss and rustle on their stems. And now, lifting the corner of my handkerchief, it tickles my sweaty face, and pours in upon me in a cooling current. Through the opening where the handkerchief is lifted a fly finds his way, and timidly buzzes around my moist mouth. A dry twig begins to make itself felt under my back. No: it becomes unendurable; I must get it out. But now, around the clump of bushes, I hear the sound of footsteps, and the frightened voice of a woman:—

"Mercy on me![12] what's to be done? And no man anywhere!"

"What's the matter?" I ask, running out into the sun, as a serving-woman, screaming, hurries past me. She merely glances at me, wrings her hands, and hurries along faster. And here comes also the seventy-year-old Matryóna, holding her handkerchief to her head, with her hair all in disorder, and hopping along with her lame leg in woollen stockings. Two girls come running, hand in hand; and a ten-year-old boy in his father's jacket runs behind, clinging to the linen petticoat of one of them.

"What has happened?" I ask of them.

"A muzhík drowned!"

"Where?"

"In the pond."

"Who is he? one of ours?"

"No, a tramp."

The coachman Iván, bustling about in his big boots over the mown grass, and the fat overseer[13] Yakof, all out of breath, come hurrying to the pond; and I follow after them.

I experience the feeling which says to me, "Now jump in, and pull the muzhík out, and save him; and all will admire you," which was exactly what I wanted.

"Where is he? where?" I asked of the throng of domestics gathered on the shore.

"Over there in the deepest part, on the other shore, almost at the baths," says the laundress, stowing away the wet linen on her yoke.... "I see him dive; there he comes up again, then he sinks a second time, and comes up again, and then he cries, 'I'm drowning, help!' And then he goes down again—and then a lot of bubbles. And while I am looking on, the muzhík gets drowned. And so I give the alarm: 'Help! a muzhík is drowning!'"

And the laundress, lifting the yoke upon her shoulder, turning to one side, goes along the narrow footpath away from the pond.

"See! what a shame," says Yakof Ivánof the overseer, in a despairing voice; "now there'll be a rumpus with the police court[14]—we'll have enough of it."

One muzhík with a scythe makes his way through the throng of peasant women, children, and old men gathered round the shore, and, hanging the scythe on the limb of a willow, leisurely takes off his clothes.

"Where was it? where was he drowned?" I keep asking, having still the desire to jump in, and do something extraordinary.

They point out to me the smooth surface of the pond, which is now and then just ruffled by the puffs of the breeze. It is incomprehensible how he came to drown; for the water lies so smooth, beautiful and calm above him, shining golden in the midday sun, and it seems to me that I could not do any thing or surprise any one, the more as I am a very poor swimmer; but the muzhík is now pulling his shirt over his head, and instantly throws himself into the water. All look at him with hope and anxiety. After going into the water up to his neck, the muzhík turns back, and puts on his shirt again: he knows not how to swim.

People keep coming down to the shore; the throng grows larger and larger; the women cling to each other: but no one brings any help. Those who have just come, offer advice, and groan; fear and despair are stamped on all faces. Of those who had come first, some have sat down, or stand wearily on the grass, others have gone back to their work. The old Matryóna asks her daughter whether she shut the oven-door. The small boy in his father's jacket industriously flings stones into the water.

And now from the house down the hill comes Trezorka, the butler's dog, barking, and looking at the stupid people. And lo! there is Feódor's tall figure hurrying from the hill-top, and shouting something as he comes out from behind the rose-bushes.

"What are you standing there for?" he shouts, taking off his coat as he runs. "A man drowning, and there you are standing around! Give us a rope."

All look at Feódor with hope and fear while he, leaning his hand on the shoulder of one of the men-servants, pries off his left boot with the toe of the right.

"There it was, where the people are standing, there at the right of the willows, Feódor Filíppuitch, right there," says some one to him.

"I know it," he replies; and knitting his brows; probably as a rebuke to the manifestations of modesty visible among the women, he takes off his shirt and baptismal cross, handing them to the gardener-boy who stands officiously near him, and then stepping energetically across the mown grass comes to the pond.

Trezorka, unable to explain the reason for his master's rapid motions, stands irresolute near the crowd, and noisily eats a few grass-blades on the shore, then looks questioningly at his master, and suddenly with a joyous bark plunges after him into the water. At first nothing can be seen except foam, and splashing water, which reached even to us. But soon the butler, gracefully spreading his arms in long strokes, and with regular motion lifting and sinking his back, swims across to the other shore. Trezorka, however, gurgling in the water, hastily returns, shakes himself near the crowd, and rolls over on his back upon the shore.

While the butler is swimming to the other side, two coachmen hasten to the willows with a net fastened to a stake. The butler for some reason lifts up his hands, dives once, twice, three times, each time spewing from his mouth a stream of water, gracefully shaking his long hair, and paying no heed to the questions which are showered upon him from all sides. At last he comes to the shore, and, so far as I can see, arranges for the disposition of the net.

They haul out the net, but it contains nothing except slime and a few small carp flopping in it. They have just cast the net once more as I reach that side.

The voice of the butler giving directions, the water dripping from the wet rope, and the sighs of dismay, alone break the silence. The wet rope stretches to the right wing, covers up more and more of the grass, slowly emerges farther and farther out of the water.

"Now pull all together, friends, once more!" cries the butler's voice. The net appears, dripping with water.

"There's something! it comes heavy, fellows," says some one's voice.

And here the wings with two or three carp flapping in them, wetting and crushing down the grass, are drawn to shore. And through the delicate strata of the agitated depths of the waters, something white gleams in the tightly stretched net. Not loud, but plainly audible amid the dead silence, a sigh of horror passes over the throng.

"Pull it up on the dry land! pull it up, friends!" says the butler's resolute voice; and the drowned man is pulled up across the mown burdocks and other weeds, to the shelter of the willows.

And here I see my good old auntie in her silk dress. I see her lilac sunshade with its fringe,—which somehow is incongruous with this picture of death terrible in its very simplicity,—and her face ready this moment to be convulsed with sobs. I realize the disappointment expressed on her face, because it is impossible to use the arnica; and I recall the sickening melancholy feeling that I have when she says with the simple egoism of love, "Come, my dear. Ah! how terrible this is! And here you always go in swimming by yourself."

I remember how bright and hot the sun shines on the dry ground, crumpling under the feet; how it gleams on the mirror of the pond; how the plump carp flap on the bank; how the schools of fish stir the smooth surface in the middle of the pond; how high in the air a hawk hangs, watching the ducklings which, quacking and spattering, swim through the reeds toward the centre; how the white tumulous thunder-clouds gather on the horizon; how the mud, brought up by the net, is scattered over the bank; and how, as I come to the dike, I again hear the blows of the clothes-pounders at work along the pond.

But the clothes-pounder has a ringing sound; two clothes-pounders, as it were, ring together, making a chord; and this sound torments, pains me, the more as I know that this clothes-pounder is a bell, and Feódor Filíppuitch does not cease to ring it. And this clothes-pounder, like an instrument of torture, squeezes my leg, which is freezing.—I fall into deep sleep.

I was waked by what seemed to me our very rapid progress, and by two voices speaking close to me.

"Say, Ignat, Ignat," says the voice of my driver. "You take my passenger; you've got to go anyway; it's only wasted labor for me: you take him."

Ignat's voice near me replies, "What fun would it be for me to answer for a passenger?... Will you treat me to a half-pint of brandy?"

"Now! a half-pint! Call it a glass."

"The idea, a glass!" cries the other voice; "bother my horses for a glass of vodka!"

I open my eyes. Still the same unendurable whirling snowflakes dazzling me, the same drivers and horses, but next me I see some sledge or other. My driver has caught up with Ignat, and for some time we have been going side by side.

Notwithstanding the fact that the voice from the other sledge advises not to take less than the half-pint, Ignat suddenly reins, up his troïka.

"Change the things; just your good luck! You'll give me the brandy when we meet to-morrow. Have you got much luggage?"

My driver, with unwonted liveliness, leaps into the snow, makes me a bow, and begs me to change into Ignat's sledge. I am perfectly willing. But evidently the pious little muzhík is so delighted that he must needs express to every one his gratefulness and pleasure. He bows to me, to Alyoshka, to Ignashka, and thanks us.

"Well, now, thank the Lord! What a scheme this is! Heavens and earth![15] we have been going half the night. Don't know ourselves where we are. He will take you, sir;[16] but my horses are all beat out."

And he transfers the luggage with vigorous activity.

When it was moved, I got into the other sledge in spite of the wind which almost carried me away. The sledge, especially on that side toward which was spread the coat as a protection against the wind, for the two yamshchíks, was quarter buried in the snow; but behind the coat, it was warm and cosey. The little old man was lying with his legs hanging over, and the story-teller was still spinning his yarn: "At that very same time when the general in the king's name, you know, comes to Marya, you know, in the darkness, at this same time, Marya says to him, 'General, I do not need you, and I cannot love you; and, you know, you are not my lover, but my lover is the prince himself'—At this very time," he was going on to say; but, catching sight of me, he kept silence for a time, and began to puff at his pipe.

"Well, bárin, you missed the story, didn't you?" said the other, whom I have called the mentor.

"Yes; but you are finely provided for behind here," said I.

"Out of sheer dulness,—have to keep ourselves from thinking."'

"But, say, don't you know where we are now?"

This question, as it seemed to me, did not please the yamshchíks.

"Who can tell where we are? Maybe we are going to the Kalmucks," replied the mentor.

"But what are we going to do?" I asked.

"What are we going to do? Well, we are going, and will keep on going," he said in a fretful tone.

"Well, what will keep us from getting lost? Besides, the horses will get tired in the snow. What then?"

"Well, nothing."

"But we may freeze to death."

"Of course we may, because we don't see any hayricks just now; but we may come, you know, to the Kalmucks. First thing, we must look at the snow."

"But you aren't afraid of freezing to death, are you, bárin?" asked the little old man with quavering voice.

Notwithstanding that he was making sport of me, as it were, it was plain that he was trembling all over.

"Yes: it is growing very cold," I replied.

"Ekh! bárin! You ought to do like me. No, no: stamp up and down,—that will warm you up."

"Do it the first thing when you get to the sledge," said the mentor.

[12] akh, bátiushki!

[13] prikáshchik.

[14] zemski sūt.

[15] gospodi-bátiushka..

[16] bátiushka-bárin.

VII.

"If you please: all ready!" shouted Alyoshka from the front sledge.

The storm was so violent that only by violent exertion, leaning far forward and holding down the folds of my cloak with both hands, was I able to make my way through the whirling snow, drifting before the wind under my very feet, over the short distance between me and the sledge. My former driver was still on his knees in the middle of the empty sledge; but when he saw me going he took off his big cap, the wind angrily tossing up his hair, and asked me for a fee. Apparently he did not expect me to give it to him, because my refusal did not affront him in the least. He even thanked me, waved his cap, and said, "Well, good luck to you, sir!"[17] and picking up the reins, and clucking to the horses, turned from us.

Immediately Ignashka straightened his back, and shouted to his horses. Again the sound of crunching hoofs, voices, bells, took the place of the howling wind which was chiefly audible when we stood still. For a quarter of an hour after my transfer I did not sleep, and I diverted my mind by contemplating the form of my new driver and horses. Ignashka was youthful in appearance, was constantly jumping up, cracking his whip over the horses, shouting out, changing from one leg to the other, and leaning forward to fix the breeching for the shaft-horse, which was always slipping to one side. The man was not tall in stature, but well built as it seemed. Over his unlined sheepskin coat[18] he wore an ungirdled cloak, the collar of which was turned back, leaving his neck perfectly bare; his boots were of leather, not felt; and he wore a small cap which he constantly took off and straightened. In all his motions was manifest not only energy, but much more, as it seemed to me, the desire to keep his energy alive. Moreover, the farther we went, the more frequently he settled himself on his seat, changed the position of his legs, and addressed himself to Alyoshka and me: it seemed to me that he was afraid of losing his spirits. And there was good reason: though the horses were excellent, the road at each step grew heavier and heavier, and it was noticeable that the horses' strength was flagging. It was already necessary to use the whip; and the shaft-horse, a good big, shaggy animal, stumbled once or twice, though immediately, as if frightened, it sprang forward and tossed up its shaggy head almost to the bell itself. The right off-horse, which I could not help watching, had a long leather breeching adorned with tassels, slipping and sliding to the left, and kept dropping the traces, and required the whip; but, being naturally a good and even zealous horse, seemed to be vexed at his own weakness, and angrily tossed his head, as if asking to be driven. Indeed, it was terrible to see how, as the storm and cold increased, the horses grew weak, the road became worse; and we really did not know where we were, or where we were going, whether to a station or to any shelter whatsoever. And strange and ridiculous it was to hear the bells jingling so merrily and carelessly, and Ignatka shouting so energetically and delightfully as though it were a sunny Christmas noon, and we were hurrying to a festival along the village street; and stranger than all it was to think that we were always riding and riding rapidly away from the place where we had been.

Ignat began to sing some song in a horrible falsetto, but so loud and with such stops, during which he whistled, that it was weird to listen to, and made one melancholy.

"Hey-y-y! Why are you splitting your throat, Ignat? Hold on a bit!" said the voice of the mentor.

"What?"

"Hold o-o-o-o-n!"

Ignat reined up. Again silence only broken by the wailing and whistling of the wind, while the snow began to pile up, rustling on the sledge. The mentor drove up to us.

"Well, what is it?"

"Say![19] where are you going?"

"Who knows?"

"Are your feet frozen, that you stamp so?"

"They're frozen off."

"Well, you ought to go this way. The way you were going means starvation,—not even a Kalmuck there. Get out, and it will warm your legs."

"All right. Hold the horses—there."

And Ignat stumped off in the direction indicated.

"Have to keep looking all the time, have to get out and hunt; then you find the way. But this way's a crazy way to go," said the mentor. "See how tired the horses are."

All the time that Ignat was gone, and it was so long that I actually began to be afraid that he had lost his way, the mentor kept talking to me in a self-confident, easy tone, telling me how it was necessary to behave in a snowstorm; how much better it was to unhitch one of the horses, and let her go as God Almighty should direct; how sometimes you can see the stars occasionally; and how, if he had taken the front place, we should have been at the station long before.

"Well, how is it?" he asked, as Ignat came back, ploughing with difficulty knee-deep in snow.

"Not so bad. I found a Kalmuck camp," replied the driver, out of breath. "Still I don't know where we are. It must be that we have been going toward Prolgovsky forest. We must turn to the left."

"Why worry? It must be the camp just behind our station," replied the mentor.

"I tell you it isn't."

"Well, I've seen it, and so I know. If it isn't that, then it's Tamuishevskoé. You must turn to the right; and soon we'll be on the big bridge,—eight versts."

"Say what you will, 'tain't so. I have seen it," said Ignat angrily.

"Eh! what's that? I am a yamshchík as much as you are."

"Fine yamshchík! you go ahead, then."

"Why should I go ahead? But I know."

Ignat was evidently angry. Without replying, he climbed to his seat, and drove on.

"You see how cold one's feet get. No way to warm them," said he to Alyoshka, pounding his feet more and more frequently, and brushing and shaking off the snow which had got into his boot-legs.

I felt an uncontrollable desire to sleep.

[17] Nu, daï Bog vam, bárin.

[18] polushubka; a garment of tanned sheepskin, the wool inwards, and reaching to the knees or even the ankles.

[19] da chïo!

VIII.

"Can it be that I am going to freeze to death?" I asked myself, as I dropped off. "Death, they say, always begins with drowsiness. It's much better to drown than freeze to death, then they would pull me out of the net. However, it makes no difference whether one drowns or freezes to death. If only this stake did not stick into my back so, I might forget myself."

For a second I lost consciousness.

"How will all this end?" I suddenly ask myself in thought, for a moment opening my eyes, and gazing at the white expanse,—"how will it end? If we don't find some hayricks, and the horses get winded, as it seems likely they will be very soon, we shall all freeze to death."

I confess, that, though I was afraid, I had a desire for something extraordinarily tragic to happen to us; and this was stronger than the small fear. It seemed to me that it would not be unpleasant if at morning the horses themselves should bring us, half-frozen, to some far-off, unknown village, where some of us might even perish of the cold.

And while I have this thought, my imagination works with extraordinary clearness and rapidity. The horses become weary, the snow grows deeper and deeper, and now only the ears and the bell-bow are visible; but suddenly Ignashka appears on horseback, driving his troïka past us. We beseech him, we shout to him to take us: but the wind carries away our voices; we have no voices left. Ignashka laughs at us, shouts to his horses, whistles, and passes out of our sight in some deep snow-covered ravine. A little old man climbs upon a horse, flaps his elbows, and tries to gallop after him; but he cannot stir from the place. My old driver, with his great cap, throws himself upon him, drags him to the ground, and tramples him into the snow. "You're a wizard!" he cries. "You're a spitfire. We are all lost on your account." But the little old man flings a snowball at his head. He is no longer a little old man, but only a hare, and bounds away from us. All the dogs bound after him. The mentor, who is now the butler, tells us to sit around in a circle, that nothing will happen to us if we protect ourselves with snow: it will be warm.

In fact, it is warm and cosey: our only trouble is thirst. I get out my travelling-case; I offer every one rum and sugar, and drink myself with great satisfaction. The story-teller spins some yarn about the rainbow, and over our heads is a roof of snow and a rainbow.

"Now each of you," I say, "make a chamber in the snow, and go to sleep." The snow is soft and warm like wool. I make myself a room, and am just going into it; but Feódor Filíppuitch, who has caught a glimpse of my money in my travelling-case, says, "Hold! give me your money, you won't need it when you're dead," and seizes me by the leg. I hand him the money, asking him only to let me go; but they will not believe that it is all my money, and they are going to kill me. I seize the old man's hand, and with indescribable pleasure kiss it: the old man's hand is tender and soft. At first he takes it away from me, but afterwards he lets me have it, and even caresses me with his other hand. Nevertheless, Feódor Filíppuitch comes near and threatens me. I hasten to my chamber; it is not a chamber, but a long white corridor, and some one pulls back on my leg. I tear myself away. In the hand of the man who holds me back, remain my trousers and a part of my skin; but I feel only cold and ashamed,—all the more ashamed because my auntie with her sunshade, and homœopathic pellets, comes arm in arm with the drowned man to meet me. They smile, but do not understand the signs that I make to them. I fling myself after the sledge; my feet glide over the snow, but the little old man follows after me, flapping his elbows. He comes close to me. But I hear just in front of me two church-bells, and I know that I shall be safe when I reach them. The church-bells ring nearer and nearer; but the little old man has caught up with me, and falls with his body across my face, so that I can scarcely hear the bells. Once more I seize his hand, and begin to kiss it; but the little old man is no longer the little old man, but the drowned man, and he cries,—

"Ignashka, hold on! here are Akhmet's hayricks! just look!"

That is strange to hear! no, I would rather wake up.

I open my eyes. The wind is flapping the tails of Alyoshka's cloak into my face; my knees are uncovered. We are going over the bare crust, and the triad of the bells rings pleasantly through the air with its dominant fifth.

I look, expecting to see the hayricks; but instead of hayricks, now that my eyes are wide open, I see something like a house with a balcony, and the crenellated walls of a fortress. I feel very little interest in seeing this house and fortress; my desire is much stronger to see the white corridor where I had been walking, to hear the sound of the church-bells, and to kiss the little old man's hand. Again I close my eyes and sleep.

IX.

I sleep sound. But all the time I can hear the chords of the bells, and in my dream I can see a dog barking and jumping after me; then the organ, one stop of which I seem to draw out; then the French poem which I am composing. Then it seems to me that this triad is some instrument of torture with which my right foot is constantly compressed. This was so severe that I woke up, and opening my eyes I rubbed my leg. It was beginning to grow numb with cold.

The night was, as before, light, melancholy, white. The sledge and its passengers were still shaken by the same motion; there was Ignashka sitting on one side and stamping his feet. There was the off-horse as before, straining her neck, lifting her feet, as she trotted over the deep snow; the tassel slipping along the reins, and whipping against the horse's belly; the head of the shaft-horse, with the waving mane, alternately pulling and loosening the reins attached to the bell-bow as it nodded up and down. But all this was covered and hidden with snow far more than before. The snow was whirled about in front of us, and covered up our runners, and reached above the horses' knees, and fell thick and fast on our collars and caps. The wind blew now from the right, now from the left, and played with the collar and tails of Ignashka's cloak, the mane of the horses, and howled above the bell-bow and the shafts.

It had become fearfully cold; and I had scarcely lifted my head out of my collar ere the frosty dry snow made its way, rustling, into my eyelids, nose, and mouth, and ran down my neck. Looking around, all was white, light, and snowy; nothing anywhere except a melancholy light and the snow. I felt a sensation of real terror. Alyoshka was sitting cross-legged in the very depths of the sledge; his whole back was covered with a thick deposit of snow.

Ignashka still kept up his spirits; he kept constantly pulling at the reins, stamping and pounding his feet. The bell also sounded strange. The horses sometimes snorted, but plunged along more quietly, though they stumbled more and more often. Ignashka again sprang up, swung his mittens, and began to sing in his clear, strong voice. Not ceasing to sing, he stopped the troïka, tossed the reins on the dasher, and got out. The wind howled madly; the snow, as though shovelled down, was dashed upon the folds of my furs.

I looked around. The third troïka was nowhere to be seen (it had stopped somewhere). Next the second troïka, in a mist of snow, could be seen the little old man making his way with long strides. Ignashka went three steps from the sledge, sat down in the snow, took off his girdle, and began to remove his boots.

"What are you going to do?" I asked.

"Must change my boots: this leg is frozen solid," he replied, and went on with his work.

It was cold for me to keep my neck out of my collar to watch what he was doing. I sat straight, looking at the off-horse, which, with legs spread, stood feebly switching its snow-covered tail. The thump which Ignat gave the sledge as he clambered to his place startled me.

"Well, where are we now?" I asked. "Are we getting anywhere in the world?"

"Don't you worry. We shall get there," he replied. "Now my feet are thoroughly warm, since I changed them."

And he drove on; the bells jingled, the sledge again began to rock, and the wind whistled under the runners, and once more we struggled to swim through the limitless ocean of snow.

X.

I sunk into a sound sleep. When Alyoshka awoke me by punching me in the leg, and I opened my eyes, it was morning. It seemed even colder than it had been during the night. There was nothing to be seen but snow; but a strong dry wind still swept the powdery snow across the field, and especially under the hoofs of the horses, and the runners of the sledge. The sky on the right toward the east was of a deep purple color, but the bright reddish-orange rays of the sunrise kept growing more and more clearly defined in it; above our heads, between the hurrying white clouds, scarcely tinged as yet, gleamed the sickly blue of the sky; in the west the clouds were bright, light, and fluctuating. Everywhere around, as far as the eye could see, lay the snow, white and deep, in sharply defined strata. Everywhere could be seen gray hillocks where lay the fine, dry, powdery snow. Nothing was to be seen,—not even the shadow of a sledge, nor of a human being, nor of a beast. The outline and color of the driver's back, and of the horses, began to stand out clear and sharp against the white background. The rim of Ignashka's dark-blue cap, his collar, his hair, and even his boots, were white. The sledge was perfectly covered. The whole right side and the mane of the brown shaft-horse were plastered with snow. The legs of my off-horse were thick with it up to the knee, and the whole of the shaggy right flank had the same sticky covering. The tassel leaped up and down in some sort of rhythm, the structure of which it would not be easy to represent; and the off-horse also kept to it in her gait: only by the gaunt belly rising and sinking, and by the hanging ears, could it be seen how tired she was.

Only one new object attracted the attention: this was a verst-post, from which the snow had been blown away, leaving it clear to the ground, and making a perfect mountain on one side; while the wind was still sweeping it across, and drifting it from one side to the other.

It was odd to me to think that we had gone the whole night without change of horses, not knowing for twelve hours where we were, and not coming to our destination, and yet not really missing the road. Our bells seemed to sound more cheerful than ever. Ignat buttoned his coat up, and began to shout again. Behind us snorted the horses, and jingled the bells, of the troïka that carried the little old man and the mentor; but the one who was asleep had wandered away from us somewhere on the steppe.

After going half a verst farther, we came upon the fresh, and as yet unobliterated, traces of a sledge and troïka; and occasionally drops of blood, caused by the whip on the horses' side, could be seen.

"That was Filipp. See, he's got in ahead of us," said Ignashka.

And here appears a little house with a sign, alone by itself, near the road, standing in the midst of the snow which covers it almost to the roof. Near the inn stands a troïka of gray horses, their hair rough with sweat, with wide-spread legs and drooping heads. At the door, the snow is shovelled away, and the shovel is standing in it; but it still falls from the roof, and the roaring wind whirls the snow around.

Out from the door at the sound of our bells comes a big ruddy, red-headed driver, with a glass of wine in his hand, and shouts something. Ignashka turns to me, and asks permission to stop. Then for the first time I fairly see his face.

XI.

His features were not dark, dry, and regular, as I had reason to expect from his hair and build. His face was round, jolly, with a snub nose and a big mouth, and clear-shining eyes, blue and round. His cheeks and neck were like well-worn cloth. His eyebrows, his long eyelashes, and the beard which evenly covered the lower part of his face, were crusted thick with snow, and perfectly white.

The distance to the station was all of a half-verst, and we stopped.

"Only be quick about it," I said.

"Just a minute," replied Ignashka, springing down from his seat, and going up to Filipp.

"Let us have it, brother," said he, taking the glass in his right hand; and throwing his mitten and whip down on the snow, tipping back his head, he drank down at a gulp the glass of vodka.

The inn-keeper, who must have been a discharged Cossack, came, with a bottle in his hand, out of the door.

"Who have you got there?" he asked.

The tall Vasíli, a lean, blond muzhík with a goatee, and the fat mentor, with white eyebrows, and a thick white beard framing his ruddy face, came up and also drank a glass. The little old man joined the group of drinkers; but no one offered him any thing, and he went off again to his horses, fastened behind, and began to stroke one of them on the back and side.

The little old man was pretty much what I had imagined him to be; small, ugly, with wrinkled, strongly marked features, a thin little beard, a sharp nose, and worn yellow teeth. He wore a driver's cap, perfectly new; but his sheepskin jacket[20] was old, soiled with oil, and torn on the shoulders and flaps, and did not cover his knees or his hempen trousers tucked into his huge felt boots. He himself was bent, and frowned all the time, and, with trembling lips and limbs, tramped around his sledge in his efforts to keep warm.

"Well, Mitritch, you ought to have a drink; it would warm you up," said the mentor to him.

Mitritch gave a start. He arranged the horses' harness, straightened the bell-bow, and then came to me.

"Say, bárin," said he, taking his cap off from his white hair and bowing very low, "all night long we have been wandering together; we have found the road. We would seem to deserve a bit of a drink. Isn't that so, sir, your eminence?[21] just enough to get warmed," he added with an obsequious smile.

I gave him a quarter-ruble. The inn-keeper brought out a glass of vodka, and handed it to the old man. He laid aside his mitten and whip, and took the glass in his small, dark hand, bony and somewhat bluish; but strangely enough he could not control his thumb. Before he had lifted the glass to his lips, he dropped it in the snow, spilling the wine.

All the drivers burst out laughing.

"See, Mitritch-to is half-frozen like; he can't hold his wine."

But Mitritch was greatly vexed because he had spilt the wine.

They brought him, however, another glass, and poured it into his mouth. He immediately became jolly, went into the inn, lighted his pipe, began to show his yellow worn teeth, and to scold at every word. After they had taken their last drinks, the drivers came back to their troikas, and we set off.

The snow kept growing whiter and brighter, till it made one's eyes ache to look at it. The orange-colored reddish streaks stretched brighter and brighter, higher and higher, across the heavens; now the red circle of the sun appeared on the horizon through the bluish clouds; the blue sky came out in constantly increasing brilliancy and depth. On the road around the station the tracks were clear, distinct, and yellow; in some places were cradle-holes. In the frosty, bracing atmosphere, there was a pleasant exhilaration and freshness.

My troïka glided along very swiftly. The head of the shaft-horse, and the neck with the mane tossing up to the bell-bow, constantly made the same quick, swinging motions under the hunting-bell, the tongue of which no longer struck, but scraped around the rim. The good side-horses, in friendly rivalry tugging at the frozen twisted traces, energetically galloped on, the tassels striking against their ribs and necks. Occasionally the off-horse would plunge into some drift, and kick up the snow, filling the eyes with the fine powder. Ignashka kept shouting in his gay tenor. The runners creaked over the dry, frosty snow. Behind us, with a loud festival sound, rang the two sledge-chimes; and the voices of the drivers, made jolly by wine, could be heard.

I looked back: the gray shaggy side-horses arching their necks, regularly puffing out the breath, with their curved bits, galloped over the snow. Filipp was flourishing his whip and adjusting his cap. The little old man, with his legs hanging out, was reclining as before in the middle of his sledge.

At the end of two minutes the sledge scraped against the boards of the well-cleared entrance of the station-house; and Ignashka turned to me, his jolly face covered with snow, where his breath had turned to ice, and said,—

"Here we are, bárin!"

[20] polushúbchishka.

[21] bátiushka, váshe siátelstvo.

POLIKUSHKA.

A STORY.

I.

"As you may please to order, madame. But it would be too bad to send any of the Dutlofs. They are all, without exception, good boys; but if you don't take one of the house-servants[1] you will have to send one of them without fail," said the overseer; "and now all point to them. However, as you wish."

And he placed his right hand on his left, holding them both over his stomach, tipped his head on one side, sucked in his thin lips, almost smacking them, turned away his eyes, and held his peace, with the evident intention of holding it long, and of listening without reply to all the nonsense which the mistress might say to him in this regard.

The overseer had formerly been one of the household servants, and now, this autumn evening, he was holding conference with his mistress, and was standing before her, clean-shaven, in his long coat, the special dress of the overseer. The conference as the mistress understood it was to be devoted to reckoning the profits and losses of the past season, and in making arrangements for the one to come. As Yégor Mikhaïlovitch the overseer understood it, the conference consisted of the rite of standing in a corner firmly on his two feet, set wide apart, with his face turned to the sofa, listening to all the good lady's unending and aimless babble, and leading her by various expedients to the point of saying hastily and impatiently, "Very good, very good," to all his suggestions.

The point at issue just at present was the conscription. Three soldiers had to be sent from Pokrovskoé. Two were unquestionably named by Providence itself, with a due regard for family, moral, and economical conditions. Concerning them there could be neither hesitation nor quarrel on the part of the Commune,[2] or the lady of the manor, or the people in general.

The third was harder to decide upon. The overseer wanted to avoid sending any of the three Dutlofs, and proposed Polikushka, a servant who had a family and a very bad reputation, having more than once been convicted of stealing corn, reins, and hay; but the mistress, who had often caressed Polikushka's ragged children, and by means of evangelical teachings had improved his morals, did not wish to let him go. At the same time she had no ill-will against the Dutlofs, whom she did not know and had never seen. And so she could not come to any decision at all, and the overseer hadn't the courage to explain to her explicitly that if Polikushka did not go Dutlof would have to go.

"Well, I don't wish to cause the Dutlofs any unhappiness," she said with feeling.

"If you don't want them to go, then pay three hundred rubles for a substitute," was the reply that he should have made her; but his diplomacy was not equal to such an emergency.

And so Yégor Mikhaïlovitch straightened himself up calmly, even leaned slightly on the door-post, and with a certain obsequiousness in his face watched how his mistress moved her lips, and how the shadow of the ruching on her head-dress moved up and down on the wall under the picture. But he did not find it necessary to penetrate the meaning of her words. She spoke long and rapidly. His ears were moved by the convulsion of a yawn, but he adroitly changed it into a cough, which he hid with his hand, making a hypocritical noise.

Not long ago I saw Lord Palmerston sitting with his hat on at the time when he was a member of the opposition, and destroyed the ministry, and, suddenly rising, replied in a three-hours' speech to all the points of his opponent. I saw that, and was not filled with amazement, because something not unlike it I had seen a thousand times in the dealings of Yégor Mikhaïlovitch with his mistress. Either because he was afraid of going to sleep, or because it seemed to him that she had already gone to great lengths, he shifted the weight of his body from his left leg to his right, and began with the sacramental introduction as he always began:—

"As you please, my lady—only—only—the Commune is to meet at my office, and it must be decided. In the requisition it says that Pokrovskoé must send a recruit to the city. And out of all the serfs, they point to the Dutlofs, and to no one else. But the Commune doesn't care for your interests; it's all the same to them if we ruin the Dutlofs.... You see, I know how they have been struggling to get along. Since I have had charge, they have been in the depths of poverty. Now that the old man is just about to have his young nephew's help, we've got to ruin them. But I, you will please take notice, am working as much for your interest as my own. 'Tis too bad, my lady, that you should set your mind on it so. They are no kith or kin of mine, and I have had nothing from them." ...

"Oh, I didn't think, Yégor," interrupted the lady, and immediately she felt convinced that he had been bribed by the Dutlofs.

"And they've got the best farm in all Pokrovskoé; God-fearing, work-loving muzhíks. The old man has been an elder in the church[3] for thirty years. He doesn't drink wine, nor use bad language, and he's a church-goer. [The overseer knew how to be plausible.] And chief of all, I will tell you, he has only two sons, and the other one's a nephew. The Commune make the decree; but, according to the existing rule, it would be necessary for a man with two to have a special vote. Others who have had three sons have given them farms of their own, and come to wretchedness; but these people are acting right, and this is the way their virtue is rewarded."

The lady did not understand this at all,—did not understand what he meant by "special vote," and "virtue." She heard only sounds, and she looked at the nankeen buttons on the overseer's coat: the upper button he rarely fastened, so that it was on tight; but the strain had come upon the middle one, and it hung by a thread, so that it would soon need to be sewed on again. But, as everybody knows, it is absolutely unnecessary in a business conversation for you to understand what is said, but it is necessary only to bear in mind what you yourself wish to say. And the lady acted on this principle.

"Why aren't you willing to understand, Yégor Mikhailovïtch?" said she. "I am sure I don't wish any of the Dutlofs to go as a soldier. I should think, that, as well as you know me, you might feel assured that I would do every thing to help my people, and that I do not wish them to be unhappy. You know that I am ready to sacrifice every thing to avoid this wretched necessity, and keep both of the men from going. [I know not whether it came into the overseer's head, that the avoidance of the wretched necessity did not require the sacrifice of every thing, but merely three hundred rubles; but this thought might have easily occurred to him.] One thing I assure you, and that is, we will not let Polikéï go. When, after that affair of the clock, he confessed to me, and wept, and vowed that he would reform, I had a long talk with him; and I saw that he was touched, and that he really repented. ["Well, she's in for it," thought Yégor Mikhaïlovitch, and began to gaze at the jam which stood in a glass of water by her side. "Is it orange, or lemon? I think it must taste bitter," he said to himself.] Since that time seven months have passed, and he has not been once drunk, and he has behaved admirably. His wife told me that he had become another man. And now, why do you wish me to punish him, when he has reformed? Yes; and wouldn't it be inhumane, to send a man who has five children, and no one to help him? No, you had better not speak about that, Yégor."... And the lady took a sip from the glass.

Yégor Mikhaïlovitch watched the water disappearing down her throat, and consequently his answer was short and dry:—

"Then you order one of the Dutlofs to be sent?"

The lady clasped her hands.

"Why can't you understand me? Do I wish to make Dutlof unhappy? Have I any thing against him? God is my witness how ready I am to do every thing for them. [She glanced at the picture in the corner, but remembered that it was not a holy picture. "Well, it's all the same, that's not the point at all," she thought. Again it was strange that it did not occur to her to offer the three hundred rubles!] But what can I do about it? Do I know the ways and means? I have no way of knowing. Well, I depend upon you; you know my wishes. Do what you can to satisfy everybody; but have it legal. What's to be done? They are not the only ones. Troublous times come to all. Only, Polikéï must not be sent. You must know that that would be terrible for me."

She would have gone on speaking,—she was so excited,—but just then a chambermaid came into the room.

"Is that you, Duniasha?"

"A muzhík is here, and asks for Yégor Mikhaïluitch; they are waiting for him at the meeting," said Duniasha, and looked angrily at Yégor Mikhaïlovitch.

"What an overseer he is!" she said to herself, "stirring up my mistress. Now she won't get to sleep till two o'clock again."

"Now go, Yégor," said the lady. "Do the best you can."

"I obey. [He now said nothing at all about Dutlof.] But shall I send to the gardener for the money?"

"Hasn't Petrushka got back from town."

"Not yet."

"But can't Nikolaï go?"

"Papa has the lumbago," said Duniasha.

"Won't you have me go to-morrow?" asked the overseer.

"No, you are needed here, Yégor." The lady paused to consider. "How much money?"

"Four hundred and sixty-two rubles."

"Send Polikéï to me," said the lady, looking resolutely into Yégor's face.

The overseer not opening his teeth stretched his lips into a sort of smile, but did not alter his expression.

"Very well."

"Send him to me."

"Very well." And Yégor Mikhaïlovitch went to his office.

[1] Most of the serfs in Russia were attached to the land, and could

not be sold apart from It. Others, called dvoróvui, constituted the class of domestic servants, and plied various trades. Their owners gave them monthly rations or a small allowance for rations. Often they were allowed to go to the large cities on obrok, a sort of leave of absence, for which they paid their masters out of their earnings. The bárin or báruin'ya—that is, the lord or lady of the estate—had the right to excuse any one from the conscription; but unless a substitute were sent, a sum of money was required. Other things being equal, the draft was made first on families where there were three or more grown-up men besides the head of the house, the troïniki; next, on the dvoïniki, families where there were two grown-up sons or nephews; and last of all, where there was only one. Families where several generations, and even with collateral branches, lived under one roof, were apt to be more prosperous than when the sous scattered, and took separate farms.

[2] mir

[3] stárosta tserkovnui, a small office, giving the man the privilege of selling candles, etc.

II.

Polikéï, as a man of no consequence, and inclined to be disreputable, and moreover as being from another village, had no one to look out for his interests, neither the housekeeper nor the butler, neither the overseer nor the housemaid. And his corner, where he lived with his wife and five children, was as wretched as it could be. The corners had been arranged by the late lamented bárin as follows: The hut was about twenty feet long, and built of stone; in the middle stood the great Russian stove; around it ran a corridor, as the servants called it; and in each corner a room was partitioned off by boards. Of course there was not much room, especially in Polikéï's corner which was next the door. The nuptial couch, with quilted counterpane and chintz pillows; a cradle with a baby in it; a three-legged table which served for cooking, washing, piling up all the household utensils, and as a work-table for Polikéï, who was a horse-doctor; tubs, clothes, hens, a calf, and the seven members of the household,—occupied the corner; and there would mot have been room to move, had it not been that the common stove offered its share of room (though even this was covered with things and human beings), and that it was possible to get out upon the door-steps. It was not always possible, if you stop to think: in October it begins to grow cold, and there was only one warm sheep-skin garment for the whole family. And so the young children were obliged to get warm by running about, and the older ones by working and taking turns in climbing upon the big stove, where the temperature was as high as ninety degrees. It must have been terrible to live in such circumstances, but they did not find it so: they were able to get along.

Akulína did the washing and mending for her husband and children; she spun and wove and bleached her linen; she cooked and baked at the common stove, and scolded and quarrelled with her neighbors. The monthly rations sufficed not only for the children, but also for the feed of the cow. The firewood was plentiful, also fodder for the cattle; and hay from the stable fell to their share. They had an occasional bunch of vegetables. The cow would give them a calf; then they had their hens. Polikéï had charge of the stable: he took care of the young colts, and bled horses and cattle; he cleaned their hoofs, he tapped varicose veins, and made a salve of peculiar virtue, and this brought him in some money and provisions. Some of the oats belonging to the estate also made their way into his possession: in the village there was a man who regularly once a month, for two small measures, gave twenty pounds of mutton.

It would have been easy for them to get along, had there not been moral suffering. But this suffering was severe for the whole family. Polikéï had been from childhood in a stable, in another village. The groom who had charge of him was the worst thief in the neighborhood; the Commune banished him to Siberia. Polikéï soon began to follow this groom's example, and thus became from early youth accustomed to these little tricks, so that afterward, when he would have been glad to break loose from the habit, he could not.

He was young and weak; his father and mother were dead, and his education had been neglected. He liked to get drunk, but he did not like to see things lying round loose: whether it were ropes or saddle, lock or coupling-bolt, or any thing even more costly, no matter, it found its way into Polikéï's possession. Everywhere were men who would take these things, and pay for them in wine or money according to agreement. Money gained this way comes easy, the people say: no learning is needed, no hard work, nothing; and if you try it once, you won't like other work. One thing is, however, not good in such labors: however cheaply and easily things are acquired in this way, and however pleasant life becomes, still there is danger that disaffected people may suddenly object to your profession, and cause you tears, and make your life unhappy.

This was what happened in Polikéï's case. He got married, and God gave him great happiness: his wife, the daughter of a herder, proved to be a healthy, bright, industrious woman. Their children came in quick succession. Polikéï had not entirely abandoned his trade, and all went well. Suddenly temptation came to him, and he fell; and it was a mere trifle that caused his fall. He secreted a pair of leather reins that belonged to a muzhík. He was detected, thrashed, taken to the mistress, and afterwards watched. A second time, a third time, he fell. The people began to make complaints. The overseer threatened to send him to the army; the lady of the house expostulated; his wife wept, and began to pine away: in fact, every thing went entirely wrong. As a man, he was kindly, and not naturally bad, but weak; he loved to drink, and he had such a strong taste for it, that he could not resist. His wife would scold him and even beat him when he came in drunk, but he would weep. "Wretched man that I am," he would say, "what shall I do? Tear out my eyes. I will swear off, I won't do it again." But lo! in a month's time he goes out, gets drunk, and is not seen for two days.

"Where on earth does he get the money to go on sprees?" the people asked themselves. His latest escapade was in the matter of the office-clock. In the office there was an old clock hanging on the wall. It had not gone for years. Polikéï got into the office alone when it happened to be unlocked. He took a fancy to the clock, carried it off, and disposed of it in town. Not long afterward it happened that the shop-keeper, to whom he sold it, came out on some holiday to visit his daughter, who was married to one of the house-servants; and he happened to mention the clock. An investigation was made, though it was hardly necessary. The overseer especially disliked Polikéï. The theft was traced to him. They laid the matter before the lady of the house. The lady of the house summoned Polikéï. He fell at her feet, and, with touching contrition, confessed every thing as his wife had counselled him to do. He accomplished it admirably. The lady began to reason with him. She talked and she talked, she lectured and she lectured, about God and duty and the future life, and about his wife, and about his children; and she affected him to tears. The lady said,—

"I will forgive you, only promise me that you will never do it again."

"Never in the world. May the earth swallow me, may I be torn in pieces!" said Polikéï; and he wept in a touching manner.

Polikéï went home, and at home wept all day like a calf, and lay on the stove. From that time forth Polikéï had conducted himself in a way above reproach. But his life ceased to be happy. The people regarded him as a thief; and now that the hour of conscription had come, all felt that it was a good way to get rid of him.

Polikéï was a horse-doctor, as we have already said. How he so suddenly developed into a horse-doctor, was a mystery to every one, and to himself most of all. In the stable where he had been with the groom who had been exiled to Siberia, he had fulfilled no other duty than that of clearing manure out of the stalls, or occasionally currying the horses, and carrying water. It was not there that he could have learned it. Then he became a weaver; then he worked in a garden, cleared paths; then he got leave of absence, and became a porter[4] for a merchant. But he could not have got any practice there. But when he was last at home, somehow or other, little by little, his reputation began to spread for having an extraordinary, if not even supernatural, knowledge of the ailments of horses.

He let blood two or three times; then he tripped up a horse, and made an incision in its fetlock; then he asked to have the horse brought to a stall, and began to cut her with a needle until the blood came, although she kicked, and even squealed: and he said that this was meant "to let the blood out from under the hoof." Then he explained to a muzhík that it was necessary to bleed the veins in both frogs "for greater comfort," and he began to strike his wooden mallet upon the blunt lancet. Then under the side of the dvornik's horse he twisted a bandage made of a woman's kerchief. Finally he began to scatter oil of vitriol over the whole wound, wet it from a bottle, and to give occasionally something to take internally, as it occurred to him. And the more he tormented and killed the poor horses, the more people believed in him, and brought him their horses to cure.

I think that it is pot quite seemly of us gentlemen to make sport of Polikéï. The remedies which he employed to stimulate belief in him were the very same which were efficacious for our fathers, and will be efficacious for us and our children. The muzhík, as he held down the head of his one mare, which not only constituted his wealth, but was almost a part of his family, and watched, with both confidence and terror, Polikéï's face marked by a consequential frown, and his slender hands, with the sleeves rolled up, with which he managed always to pinch the very places that were most tender, and boldly to hack the living body with the secret thought, "Now here's to luck," and making believe that he knew where the blood was, and where the matter, where was the dry and where was the fluid vein, and holding the handkerchief of healing or the phial of sulphuric acid,—this muzhík could not imagine such a thing as Polikéï raising his hand to cut without the requisite knowledge. He himself could not have done such a thing. And, as soon as the incision was made, he did not reproach himself because he had hacked unnecessarily.

I don't know how it is with you; but I have had experience with a doctor who, at my own request, treated people who were very dear to my heart in almost exactly the same way. The veterinary lancet and the mysterious white phial with corrosive sublimate, and the words, "apoplexy, hemorrhoids, blood-letting, pus," and so forth, are they so different from "nerves, rheumatism, organism," and the others? Wage du zu irren und zu träumen,—"dare to be in error and to dream,"—was said not only to poets, but to doctors and veterinary surgeons.

[4] dvornik.

III.

On that very evening, while the elders had come together at the office to settle upon a recruit, and while their voices were heard amid the chill darkness of the October night, Polikéï was sitting upon the edge of his bed at the table, and was triturating in a bottle some veterinary medicament, the nature of which he himself knew not. It was a mixture of corrosive sublimate, sulphur, Glauber's salts, and grass, which he was compounding, under some impression that this grass was good for broken wind and other ailments.

The children were already abed; two on the stove, two on the couch, one in the cradle, beside which sat Akulína with her spinning. The candle-end, which remained from some of his mistress's that had not been properly put away, and Polikéï had taken care of, stood in a wooden candlestick on the window; and in order that her husband might not be disturbed in his important task, Akulína got up to snuff the candle with her fingers. There were conceited fellows who considered Polikéï as a worthless horse-doctor, and a worthless man. Others—and they were in the majority—considered him worthless as a man, but a great master of his calling. Akulína, notwithstanding the fact that she often berated and even beat her husband, considered him beyond a peradventure the first horse-doctor and the first man in the world.

Polikéï poured into the hollow of his hand some spice. (He did not use scales, and he spoke ironically of the Germans who used scales. "This," he would say, "is not an apothecary-shop.") Polikéï hefted the spice in his hand, and shook it up; but it seemed to him too little in quantity, and, for the tenth time, he added more. "I will put it all in, it will have a better effect," he said to himself. Akulína quickly looked up as she heard the voice of her lord and master, expecting orders; but seeing that it was nothing that concerned her, she shrugged her shoulders. "Ho! great chemist! Where did he learn it all?" she thought to herself, and again took up her work. The paper from which the spice was taken fell under the table. Akulína did not let this pass.

"Aniutka!"[5] she cried, "here, your father has dropped something: come and pick it up."

Aniutka stuck out her slender bare legs from under the dress that covered her, and, like a kitten, crept under the table, and picked up the paper.

"Here it is, papa," said she, and again plunged into the bed with her cold feet.

"Stop pushing me," whimpered her younger sister, in a sleepy voice, hissing her s's.

"I'll give it to you," said Akulína, and both heads disappeared under the wrapper.

"If he will pay three silver rubles," muttered Polikéï, shaking the bottle, "I will cure his horse. Cheap enough," he added. "I've racked my brains for it. Come now, Akulína, go and borrow some tobacco of Nikíta. We will pay it back to-morrow."

And Polikéï drew from his trousers a linden-wood pipe, that had once been painted, and that had sealing-wax for a mouthpiece, and began to put it in order.

Akulína pushed aside her flax-wheel, and went out without a word of reply, though it was a struggle for her. Polikéï opened the cupboard, put away his bottle, and applied to his mouth an empty jug. But the vodka was all gone. He scowled; but when his wife brought him the tobacco, and he had lighted his pipe, and began to smoke, sitting on the couch, his face gleamed with complacency and the pride that a man feels when he has ended his day's work.

He was even thinking how, on the morrow, he would seize the tongue of a horse, and pour into her mouth that marvellous mixture, or he was ruminating on the fact of how a man of importance met with no refusals, as was proved by Nikíta sending him the tobacco; and the thought was pleasant to him. Suddenly the door, which swung upon one hinge, was flung open; and into the room came a girl from the upper house,—not the second girl, but a small damsel employed to run of errands. (Everybody calls the manor-house upper, even though it may be built on a lower level.) Aksintka, as the damsel was called, always flew like lightning; and on this account her arms were not folded, but swung like pendulums, in proportion to the swiftness of her motions, not by her side, but in front of her body. Her cheeks were always redder than her pink dress; her tongue always ran as swiftly as her legs. She flew into the room, and holding by the stove, for some reason or other, she began to wave her arms; and as though she wished to utter not less than two or three words at once, and scarcely stopping to get breath, she suddenly broke out as follows, addressing Akulína:—

"Our lady bids Polikéï Ilyitch to come up to the house this minute,—she does. [Here she stopped, and drew a long breath.] Yégor Mikháltch was at the house, and talked with our lady about the necruits; and they've took Polikéï Ilyitch.... Avdót'ya Mikolávna bids you come up this very minute.... Avdót'ya Mikolávna bids you [again a long breath] come up this minute."

For thirty seconds Aksiutka stared at Polikéï, at Akulína, at the children, who were asleep under the wrapper; then she seized a hazel-nut shell that was rolling around on the stove, and threw it at Aniutka, and once more repeating, "Come up this minute," flew like a whirlwind out of the room; and the pendulums, with their wonted quickness, outstripped the course of her feet.

Akulína got up again, and fetched her husband his boots. The boots were soiled and ripped: they had been made for a soldier. She took down from the stove a kaftan, and handed it to him without looking at him.

"Ilyitch, are you going to change your shirt?"

"Nay," said Polikéï.

Akulína did not look into his face once while he silently put on his boots and coat, and she did well not to look at him. Polikéï's face was pale, his chin trembled, and in his eyes there came that expression of deep and submissive unhappiness, akin to tears, peculiar to weak and kindly men who have fallen into sin. He brushed his hair, and was about to go. His wife kept him back, and arranged his shirt-band, which hung below his cloak, and straightened his cap.

"Say, Polikéï Ilyitch, what does the mistress want of you?" said the voice of the joiner's wife on the other side of the partition.

The joiner's wife had, that very morning, been engaged in a warm dispute with Akulína, in regard to a pot of lye which Polikéï's children had spilt; and, at the first moment, she was glad to hear that Polikéï was summoned to the mistress. It could not be for any thing good. Moreover, she was a sharp, shrewd, and shrewish woman. No one understood better than she how to use her tongue; at least, so she herself thought.

"It must be that they are going to send you to the city to be a merchant," she continued. "I suppose they want to get a trusty man, and so will send you. You must sell me then some tea for a quarter, Polikéï Ilyitch."

Akulína restrained her tears, and her lips took on an expression of bitter anger, as though she would have wound her fingers in the untidy hair of that slattern, the joiner's wife; but when she glanced at her children, and thought that they might be left orphans, and she a soldier's widow, she forgot the shrewish joiner's wife, covered her face with her hands, sat down on the bed, and leaned her head on the pillow.

"Mámuska, you are squeesing me," cried the little girl who hissed her s's, and she pulled away her dress from under her mother's elbow.

"I wish you were all of you dead! You were born for misfortune," cried Akulína; and she began to walk up and down the corner, wailing, much to the delight of the joiner's wife, who had not yet forgotten about the lye.

[5] Peasant diminutive for Anna.

IV.

A half-hour passed by. The baby began to cry. Akulína took him, and gave him the breast. She was no longer weeping; but resting her thin, tear-stained face on her hand, she fixed her eyes on the flickering candle, and asked herself why she had got married, and why so many soldiers were needed, and, still more, how she might pay back the joiner's wife.

Her husband's steps were heard; she wiped away the traces of the tears, and got up to light his way. Polikéï came in with an air of triumph, threw his hat on the bed, drew a long breath, and began to take off his clothes.

"Well, what was it? why did she call you?"

"Hm! a good reason! Polikushka is the lowest of men; but, when there is something needed, who is called on? Polikushka!"

"What is it?"

Polikéï did not make haste to reply: he smoked his pipe, and kept spitting.

"She wants me to go to the merchant, and get her money."

"Get her money!" repeated Akulína.

Polikéï grinned and nodded.

"How well she knows how to talk! 'You had,' says she, 'the reputation of being untrustworthy, but I have more faith in you than in any one else. [Polikéï raised his voice so that his neighbors might hear.] 'You promised me to reform,' says she, 'and here is the first proof that I believe in you: go,' says she, 'to the merchant, get some money for me, and bring it back.' And says I, 'My lady,' says I, 'we be all your slaves, and it be our duty to serve you as faithfully as we serve God, and so I feel that I can do every thing for your well-being, because I owe it to you, and I could not refuse no service; so, whatever you order, that I will perform, because I be your slave.' [He again smiled with that peculiar smile of a man who is weak, but good-natured, and has been guilty of some sin.] 'And so,' says she, 'will you do this faithfully? Do you understand,' says she, 'that your fate depends upon this?'—'How can I help comprehending that I can do it? People may slander me, and any one may fall into sin; but it would be a moral impossibility for me do any thing contrary to your interest, nor even think of it.' So, you see, I talked to her till my lady was just as soft as wax. 'You will be,' says she, 'my principal man.' [He was quiet for a moment, and again the same smile played over his face.] I know very well how to talk with her. When I used to go on leave of absence, I got practice in talking. Only let me talk with 'em, I make 'em just like silk."

"Much money?" asked Akulína.

"Fifteen hundred rubles," replied Polikéï carelessly.

She shook her head.

"When do you go?"

"To-morrow, she said. 'Take a horse,' says she, 'any one you wish, come to the office, and God be with you.'"

"Glory to thee, O Lord!" exclaimed Akulína, getting up and crossing herself. "God be thy help, Ilyitch," she added in a whisper, so as not to be heard beyond the partition, and holding him by the sleeve of his shirt. "Ilyitch, heed what I say; I will pray Christ the Lord, that you go in safety. Kiss the cross, that you will not take a drop into your mouth."

"But of course I am not going to drink, when I have all that money with me!" he said with a snort. "Some one was playing there on the piano,—handsomely, my!" he added, after a silence breaking into a laugh. "It must have been the young lady. I was standing right before her, near the shiffonere—that is, before her ladyship; but the young lady was there behind the door, pounding away. She bangs and she bangs so harmoniously—like—She just makes it sing, I tell you! I should like to play a little, that's a fact. I'd have liked to gone in just for once. I am just right for such things. To-morrow give me a clean shirt."

And they went to bed happy.

V.

Meantime the office was buzzing with the voices of the muzhíks. It was no laughing matter. Almost all the muzhíks were in the meeting; and while Yégor Mikháïlovitch was conferring with her ladyship, the men put on their hats, more voices began to be heard above the general conversation, and the voices became louder.

The murmur of many voices, occasionally interrupted by some eager, heated discourse, filled the air; and this murmur, like the sound of the roaring sea, came to the ears of the lady of the house, who felt at hearing it a nervous unrest analogous to the feeling excited by a heavy thunder-shower. It was neither terrible nor yet unpleasant to her. It seemed to her that the voices kept growing louder and more turbulent, and then some one person would make himself heard. "Why should it be impossible to do every thing gently, peaceably, without quarrel, without noise?" she said, "according to the sweet law of Christianity and brotherly love?"

Many voices suddenly were heard together, but louder than all shouted

Feódor Rézun, the carpenter. He was a man who had two grown sons, and he attacked the Dutlofs. The old man Dutlof spoke in his own defence; he came out in front of the crowd, behind which he had been standing, and spreading his arms wide and lifting up his beard spoke so rapidly, in a choked voice, that it would have been hard for himself to know what he was saying. His children and nephews, fine young fellows, stood and pressed behind him; and the old man Dutlof reminded one of the one who is the old hen in the game of Korshun,[6] or "Hawk." Rézun was the hawk; and not Rézun alone, but all those who had two sons, and all the bachelors, almost all the meeting, in fact, united against Dutlof. The trouble lay in this: Dutlofs brother had been sent as a soldier thirty years before; and therefore he did not wish to be considered as one of those who had three men in the family, but he desired his brother's service to be taken into account, and that he should be reckoned as one who had two grown assistants, and that the third recruit should be taken from that set.

There were four families, besides Dutlofs, that had three able-bodied men. But one was the village elder's, and his mistress had freed him from service. From another family, a recruit had been taken at the last conscription. From the other two families, two men had been already nominated, and one of them had not come to the meeting; but his wife stood, heavy at heart, in the very rear, anxiously hoping that somehow the wheel would turn in favor of her happiness. The other of the two nominees, the red-haired Román, in a torn cloak (though he was not poor), stood leaning against the door-step, with downcast head; he said nothing all the while, but occasionally looked up attentively when any one spoke louder than usual, and then dropped his head again; and thus his unhappiness was expressed in his whole appearance. The old man, Sem'yón Dutlof, would have given the impression, even to these who knew him slightly, that he had laid up hundreds and thousands of rubles. He was dignified, God-fearing, substantial; he was, moreover, an elder of the Church. So much the more striking was the chance in which he found himself.

Rézun the carpenter was, on the contrary, a tall, dark, dissipated man, quick to quarrel, and fond of speaking in meetings and in the market-place, with workmen, merchants, muzhíks, or gentlemen. Now he was calm and sarcastic, and with all the advantage of his stature, all the force of his loud voice, and his oratorical talent, was nagging the elder of the church, who was such a slip-shod speaker, and had been driven far out of his path.

The others who took part in the discussion were as follows: The round-faced, young-looking Garaska Kopilof, stocky, with a four-square head, and curly beard; one of the speakers who imitated Rézun rather than the younger generation, always distinguished for his bitter speech, and already a man of weight in the meeting. Then Féodor Melnitchnui, a tall, yellow, gaunt, round-shouldered muzhík, also young, with thin hair and beard, and with small eyes; always prone to anger, sour-tempered, ready to see every one's bad side, and frequently embarrassing the meeting with his abrupt and unexpected questions and remarks. Both of these speakers were on Rézun's side. Moreover, two chatterers occasionally took part,—one who had a good-natured phiz, and a large and bushy red beard; his name was Khrapkof, and he was forever saying, "My dearly beloved friend:" and the other, Zhidkof, a small man, with a bird-like face, who was also in the habit of saying, "It follows, my brethren;" he kept turning to all sides, and his words were without rhyme or reason. One of these two took one side, the other the other; but no one heeded what they said. There were others like them; but these two kept moving in and out in the crowd, shouted more than anybody else, disturbing the mistress, were listened to less than anybody else, and, being confused by the racket and shouting, found full satisfaction in talking nonsense.

There were many different characters in this group of peasants: some were morose, some courteous, some indifferent, some disputatious; there were also a few women behind the muzhíks, with sticks. But about all these I will tell some other time, as God shall give. The throng consisted, for the most part, however, of muzhíks, who behaved during the meeting as though it were church, and standing in the rear talked in a whisper about their domestic affairs, exchanging views, for instance, about the best time for beginning to cut their wood, or quietly hoped that they soon adjourn the meeting. And then there were some well-to-do men, whose comfort the meeting could not benefit or curtail. To this number belonged Yermil, with his broad, shiny face, whom the muzhíks called "big-belly" because he was rich. To this number also belonged Starostin, on whose face a self-satisfied expression of power was habitual: "Say whatever you please among yourselves, but I am safe enough. I have four sons, but you won't take any of them." Occasionally, the opinionated young orators, like Kopilof or Rézun, would have a fling at them; and they would reply, but calmly and decidedly in the consciousness of their unassailable position.

However much Dutlof was like the old hen in the game of "Hawk," it could not be said that his lads were like the chickens. They did not hop about nor scream, but stood calmly behind him. The oldest, Ignat, was now thirty years old; the second, Vasíli, was already married, but was not old enough to come under the conscription; the third, Ilyushka, the nephew who had just been married, had a red and white complexion, and was dressed in an elegant sheepskin coat (he was a driver[7] by profession); he stood gazing at the people, occasionally scratching the back of his head under the cap, as though the affair did not concern him at all any more than if it were the game of "Hawk."

"Because my grandfather went as a soldier," Rézun was saying, "that's no reason why I should refuse the lot. Friends, it is no kind of a law at all. At the last conscription they took Mikhéichef, and his uncle is still in the service."

"Neither your father nor your uncle ever served the Tsar both at once," said Dutlof, "and you never served gentlemen nor the Commune; but you've always been a tippler, and your children take after you. It's impossible to live with you, and yet you point out other men. But for ten years I have been police-commissioner,[8] and I have been elder, and twice I have been burnt out, and no one ever helped me; and is it because we live peaceably at our place, ay and honorably, that I am to be ruined? Give me back my brother. He died there, didn't he? Judge right, judge according to God's law, O orthodox Commune! and do not listen to the lies of that drunkard."

At this instant Gerásim said to Dutlof,—

"You refer to your brother. But he was not sent by the Commune, but the master sent him because of his good-for-nothingness; so he's no excuse for you."

Gerásim had no chance to say another word, for the tall, yellow Feódor Melnitchnui leaning forward began to speak in a gloomy tone:—

"Well, masters send whomever they please; then let the Commune make the best of it. The Commune tells your son to go; and if you don't like it, ask the mistress: she has the right to command me or any of my children to wear the uniform. A fine law!" said he bitterly; and, again waving his hand, took his former place.

The red-haired Román, whose son had been drafted, lifted his head, and said, "That's so, that's so," and sat down morosely on the step.

But there were many other voices that also joined suddenly in the hubbub. Besides those who stood in the background and talked about their affairs, there were the babblers, who did not forget their duty.

"Certainly, O orthodox Commune," said the little Zhidkof, slightly varying Dutlofs words, "it is necessary to decide according to Christianity; according to Christianity, my brethren, it is necessary to decide."

"It is necessary to decide on our consciences, my dearly beloved friend," said the good-natured Khrapkof, slightly varying Kopilof's words, and taking hold of Dutlofs sheepskin coat; "it is according to the will of our lady, and not the decision of the Commune."

"Indeed, how is that?" exclaimed several.

"What's that drunken fellow barking about?" retorted Rézun. "Did you get me drunk, or was it your son whom they have found rolling round in the road, and does he dare to fling at me about drink? I tell you, brethren, we must act more wisely. If you want to let Dutlof off, though he is not of those who have two grown men, then name some one who has only one son; but he will laugh at us."

"Let Dutlof go. What's to be said?"

"Of course. We must cast lots for the men of large family[9] first," said several voices.

"Just as the mistress commands. Yégor Mikháiluitch said she wanted to send one of the household servants," said some one's voice.

This observation raised a great hubbub; but it quickly subsided, and single individuals again got the floor.

Ignat, who, according to Rerun's remark, had been found drunk in the street, began to accuse Rézun of having stolen a saw of some passing carpenter, and of having beaten his wife almost to death during a drunken spree.

Rézun replied that he beat his wife when he was sober as well as when he was drunk, and very little anyway; and this made every one laugh. Referring to the saw he suddenly lost his temper, and pressing nearer to Ignat began to question him:—

"Who was it stole the saw?"

"You did," replied the strong Ignat, boldly advancing still nearer to him.

"Who stole it? Wasn't it yourself?"

"No, you!" screamed Ignat.

After the saw, they disputed about the stealing of a horse, then of some bags of oats, then of some vegetables from the fields, then of some dead body. And such strange things both muzhíks said of each other, that if the hundredth part of their mutual charges had been true, it would have been incumbent on the authorities according to law to send both of them instanter to Siberia at the least.

Dutlof meantime sought another kind of protection. His son's outburst had not been pleasing to him; in order to restrain him he said, "It's a sin! it's no use, I tell you." And he himself went to work to show that the men whose sons lived under the same roof with their fathers were no more to be put in the category of those liable to the subscription than those whose sons lived on separate farms: and he referred to Stárostin.

Stárostin smiled slightly, gave a snort, and, stroking his beard after the manner of the well-to-do muzhík, he replied that it was as it seemed fit to her ladyship; his son would go, of course, if she ordered him to go.

As regarded divided families, Gerásim also demolished Dutlofs arguments, remarking that it was far better not to allow families to live apart, as it had been in the time of the old bárin; that "at the end of summer it isn't the time to get strawberries" (that is, it was too late to talk about it); that now it wasn't the time to send those who were the sole protection of their families.

"Do we set up separate establishments just for the fun of it? Why shouldn't we get some advantage for it?" asked some of those who had left their fathers' houses; and the babblers took the same side.

"Well, hire a substitute if you don't like it. You can afford it," said Rézun to Dutlof.

Dutlof in despair buttoned up his kaftan, and turned to the other muzhíks.

"You seem to know a good deal about my affairs," he replied viciously. "Here comes Yégor with word from the mistress."

[6] A game somewhat like "snap the whip."

[7] yamshchík.

[8] sotsky, centurion; an officer chosen by the Commune.

[9] troïniki: a peasant family with three able-bodied men.

VI.

In fact, Yégor Mikhaïlovitch at this moment came out of the house. The peasants one after another removed their hats, and, as the overseer advanced, there were exposed one after another heads in various stages of baldness, and shocks of white, gray, black, red, or blond hair; and little by little, little by little, the voices were hushed, and finally there was perfect silence. The overseer stood on the step, and made it evident that he had something to say.

Yégor Mikhaïlovitch, in his long frock coat, with his hands negligently thrust into his pockets, with his factory-made uniform cap pushed well forward, and standing firmly, with his legs set wide apart, on a height looking down upon all these faces lifted and turned to him, faces for the most part dignified with age, and for the most part handsome and full-bearded, had an entirely different mien from that which he wore in presence of his mistress. He was majestic.

"Well, boys, here's the mistress's message: she is not willing to let any of the household servants go, and whoever among you-you may see fit to send will have to go. This time three are required. At present accounts the matter is five-sixths settled; now there's only half a choice left. But it makes no difference: put it off till another time if you don't want to decide to-day."

"Now's the time! let's have it settled," cried several voices.

"In my opinion," continued Yégor Mikhaïlovitch, "if Khoriushkin and Mitiukhin's Vaska go, it will be in accordance with the will of God."

"That's a fact, true enough," cried a number of voices.

"For the third we shall have to send either Dutlof, or from one of the families where there are two grown sons."

"Dutlof, Dutlof," echoed the voices. "Dutlof has three."

And again, little by little, little by little, the din began, and again recriminations flew about in regard to vegetables taken from the fields, and things stolen from the manor-house. Yégor Mikhaïlovitch had been manager of the estate now for twenty years, and was a man of sense and experience. He stood in silence for fifteen minutes and listened; then he suddenly commanded all to be silent, and bade Dutlof cast lots as to which of his family should go. They cast the lots into a cap, and when it had been well shaken Khrapkof drew from it. The lot fell to Ilyushkin. All were silent.

"So it's mine, is it? Let me see," said the nephew in a broken voice.

All looked on in silence. Yégor Mikhaïlovitch commanded to bring on the next day the conscription money, seven kopeks for each peasant farm, and, explaining that all the business was now at an end, adjourned the meeting. The crowd moved away, putting on their caps, as they went around the house with a noise of voices and shuffling steps. The overseer stood on the doorstep, gazing after the departing people. When the young Dutlofs had gone out of sight, he called the old man who had remained behind, and the two went into the office.

"I am sorry for you, old man," said the overseer, sitting down in an arm-chair by the table. "It was your turn though. Will you hire a substitute for your nephew, or not?"

The old man without replying looked earnestly at the overseer.

"You won't let him go?" queried the overseer in reply to his look.

"We'd gladly buy him off, but haven't any thing, Yégor Mikhaïlovitch. Lost two horses this summer. I have just got my nephew married. You see, it's our luck, just because we've lived decently. Fine for him to talk as he did." (The old man referred to Rézun.)

The overseer rubbed his face with his hand, and yawned. It was getting tiresome to him, and besides it was tea-time.

"Well, old man, don't be blue," said he; "but just dig in your cellar, and perhaps you can find enough to make up four hundred silver rubles. I will hire you a substitute. A few days ago a man offered himself."

"What! in the government?" asked Dutlof, meaning by "government" the chief city.

"Well, will you hire him?"

"I'd be glad to, but, before God, I"—

The overseer looked at him sternly.

"Now, you just listen to me, old man: don't let Ilyushka do any harm to himself; when I send to-night or to-morrow, have him come immediately. You bring him, and you shall be answerable for him; and if any thing happens to him, God be my witness, I will take your oldest son. Do you hear?"

"But couldn't they have taken some one else, Yégor Mikháiluitch?" he said in an aggrieved tone after a short silence; "because my brother died in the army, must they take his son also? Why should such luck come to me?" he added, almost weeping, and ready to get on his knees.

"Now, hold on, hold on!" said the overseer. "There's no need of any trouble; it's my orders. You look out for your nephew; you're responsible for him."

Dutlof went home, carefully helping himself with his cane over the irregularities of the road.

VII.

On the next day, early in the morning, there was drawn up before the door of the wing a travelling carriage (the one which the overseer generally used), with a wide-tailed brown gelding called, for some inscrutable reason, Barabán, or the drum. At a safe distance from his head stood Aniutka, Polikéï's oldest daughter, barefoot, in spite of the rain and sleet, and the cold wind, holding the bridle in one hand with evident terror, and protecting her own head with a yellow-green jacket, which fulfilled in the family the manifold functions of dress, sheepskin, head-dress, carpet, overcoat for Polikéï, and many other uses besides.

In the corner a tumult was let loose. It was still dark. The morning light, ushering in a rainy day, fell through the window, the broken panes of which were in places mended with pieces of paper.

Akulína, who was up betimes to get ready for breakfast, and her children, the younger of whom were not yet up, were shivering with cold, as their covering had been taken from them for Aniutka's use, and they had only their mother's kerchief for protection. Akulína was busily engaged in getting her husband started on his journey. His shirt was clean. His boots, which, as they say, were asking for gruel, caused her the greatest labor. In the first place, she took off her own long woollen stockings, and gave them to her spouse; next, out of the saddle-cloth which had been lying round in the stable, and Ilyitch had brought into the hut a few days before, she managed to make some insoles and lining, so as to stop up the holes, and protect Ilyitch's feet from the dampness. Ilyitch himself, sitting with his feet on the bed, was busy in turning his belt so that it might not have the appearance of a dirty rope. The cross little girl who hissed her s's, wearing a sheepskin, which not only covered her head, but protected her legs, had been sent to Nikíta to borrow a cap.

The hubbub was increased by the household servants, who came to ask Ilyitch to do errands for them in the city: to buy a needle for one woman, tea for another, olive-oil for another; tobacco for this muzhík, and sugar for the joiner's wife, who had already made haste to set up her samovar, and in order to bribe Ilyitch had asked him to share in the concoction which she called tea.

Although Nikíta refused to loan his cap, and he was obliged to put his own in order, that is to say, to fasten on the shreds of wool that were falling off or hanging by a thread, and to sew up the holes with his veterinary needle; though he could not get on his boots with the felt insoles made out of the saddle-cloth; though Aniutka had got so chilled that she let Barabán go, and Mashka, in her sheepskin, went in her place; and then Mashka was obliged to give her father the sheepskin, and Akulína herself went to hold Barabán,—still at last Ilyitch managed to get dressed, making use of all the clothing that appertained to his family, and leaving only the one jacket and some dirty rags, and, now in spick and span order, took his seat in the telyéga, bundled himself up, arranged the hay, once more bundled himself up, picked up the reins, bundled himself up still more warmly, just as is done by very dignified people, and drove off.

His small boy Mishka rushing down the steps asked to be taken on. The sibilating Mashka began to ask for "a lide," and would be "warm enough, even if she hadn't any seepskin;"[10] and Polikéï reined in the horse, smiled his ineffectual smile, and Akulína helped the children to get in, and, bending close, whispered to him to remember his promise, and not drink any thing on the road. Polikéï carried the children as far as the blacksmith-shop, helped them out, again tucked himself in, again settled his cap, and drove off alone in a slow, dignified trot, his fat cheeks shaking, and his feet thumping on the floor of the wagon.

Mashka and Mishka, both barefooted, flew home down the little hill with such fleetness, and with such a noise, that a dog running from the village to the manor gazed after them, and, suddenly casting his tail between his legs, fled home with a yelp; so that the noise made by the Polikushka hopefuls was increased tenfold.

The weather was wretched, the wind was cutting; and something that was neither snow nor rain, nor yet sleet, began to lash Polikéï's face, and his bare hand with which he grasped the reins, protected as well as possible by the sleeve of his cloak; and it rattled on the leather cover of the horse-collar, and on the head of old Barabán, who lay back his ears, and blinked his eyes.

Then suddenly if stopped, and lighted up for an instant; the form of the dark purple snow-clouds became clearly visible; and the sun, as it were, prepared to glance forth, but irresolutely and gloomily, like Polikéï's own smile.

Nevertheless, the son of Ilya was absorbed in pleasant thoughts. He,—a man whom they thought of exiling, whom they threatened with the conscription, whom no one except the lazy spared either abuse or blows, whom they always saddled with the most unpleasant jobs,—he was now going to collect a sum o' money, and a big sum; and he had his mistress's confidence; and he was driving in the overseer's wagon with Barabán, his mistress's own horse; and he was driving like some rich householder, with leather tugs and reins. And Polikéï straightened himself up, smoothed the wool on his cap, and once more bundled him up.

However, if Polikéï thought that he was like a rich householder, he was greatly mistaken. Everybody knows that merchants who do a business of ten thousand rubles ride in carriages with leather trappings. Well, sometimes it's one way, and sometimes it's another. There comes a man with a beard, in a blue or it may be a black kaftan, sitting alone on the box behind a plump steed: as soon as you look at him and see whether his horse is plump, whether he himself is plump, how he sits, how his horse is harnessed, how the carriage shines, how he himself is girdled, you know instantly whether he is a muzhík, who makes a thousand or a hundred rubles' worth of sales. Every experienced man, as soon as he looked closely at Polikéï, at his hands, at his face, at his short neglected beard, at his girdle, at the hay spread carelessly over the box, at the lean Barabán, at the worn tire, would have known instantly that the rig belonged to a slave, and not a merchant, or a drover, or a householder with a thousand or a hundred or even ten rubles.

But Ilyitch did not realize this: he deceived himself, and deceived himself pleasantly. Fifteen hundred rubles he will carry in his bosom. It comes into his mind, that he might drive Barabán to Odesta instead of home, and then go where God might give. But he will not do that, but will certainly carry the money to his mistress, and it will be said that no amount of money tempted him.

As he came near a tavern, Barabán began to tug on the left rein, to slacken his pace, and to turn in; but Polikéï, in spite of the fact that he had money in his pocket given him for various commissions, cut Barabán with the knout, and drove by. The same thing took place at the next tavern; and at noon he dismounted from the telyéga, and opening the gate of the merchant's house, where the people from the estate always put up, drove the team in, unharnessed the horse, and gave him some hay, and ate his own dinner with the merchant's hired help, not failing to make the most of his important errand; and then, with his letter in his cap, betook himself to the gardener.

The gardener, who knew Polikéï, read the letter, and found it evidently difficult to believe that he was really to deliver the money to the bearer. Polikéï did his best to be offended, but was not able to accomplish it; he only smiled his peculiar smile. The gardener re-read the letter, and delivered the money. Polikéï placed the money in his bosom, and went back to his lodgings. Not a beer-saloon, not a tavern, nothing seduced him. He experienced a pleasant exhilaration in all his being; and not once did he loiter at the shops where all sorts of tempting wares were displayed,—boots, cloaks, caps. But as he walked along slowly, he had the pleasant consciousness: "I could buy all these things, but I'm not going to."

He went to the bazaar to execute his commissions, made them into a bundle, and then tried to beat down the price of a tanned sheepskin shuba, which was set at twenty-five rubles. The vender, looking critically at Polikéï, did not believe that he had the money to buy it with; but Polikéï pointed to his breast, saying that he had enough to buy out his whole establishment if he wanted. He asked to try it on, hesitated, pulled on it, crumpled it, blew the fur, kept it on long enough to smell of it, then took it off with a sigh. "Unconscionable price! If you would only let it go for fifteen rubles," he said. The dealer angrily pulled the garment over the counter, but Polikéï went out with a gay heart, and directed his steps to his lodgings. After eating his supper, and giving Barabán his water and oats, he climbed up on the stove, took out the envelope, and gazed at it long, and asked the lettered porter[11] to read the address to him, and the words, "with an enclosure of sixteen hundred and seventy paper rubles." The envelope was made of simple paper; the seals were of dark brown wax with the impression of an anchor; one large seal in the centre, four on the edge. On one side, a drop of wax had fallen. Ilyitch looked at all this, and fixed it in his memory, and even moved the sharp ends of the notes. He experienced a certain childish satisfaction in knowing that he held so much money in his hands. He put the envelope in the lining of his cap, made the cap into a pillow, and lay down; but several times during the night he woke up, and felt after the money. And every time, finding the envelope in its place, he experienced the same pleasurable feeling in the consciousness that he, the proscribed and ridiculed, was carrying so much money, and was going to deliver it faithfully,—as faithfully as the overseer himself.

[10] suba for shuba.

[11] dvornik.

VIII.

About midnight the merchant's people and Polikéï were aroused by a knocking at the gate and the shouting of muzhíks. It was the contingent of recruits, whom they were bringing in from Pokrovskoé. There were ten men in all: Khoriushkin, Mitiushkin, and Ilya, Dutlofs nephew, two substitutes, the stárosta or elder, the old man Dutlof, and three drivers. The night-lamp was burning in the house, and the cook was asleep on the bench under the holy images. She sprang up, and began to light the lamps. Polikéï also woke up, and bending down from the stove tried to see who the muzhíks were.

Some of them came in, crossed themselves, and sat down on the bench.

They were all extremely quiet, so that it was impossible to make out who belonged to the detachment. They greeted each other, jested, and asked for something to eat. To be sure, some were silent and glum; on the other hand, others were extraordinarily gay, and apparently the worse for liquor. In this number was Ilya, who had never been drunk before.

"Well, boys, are you going to have something to eat, or are you going to bed?" asked the village elder.

"Have something to eat," replied Ilya, throwing back his sheepskin, and sprawling out on the bench. "Send for some vodka."

"You've had enough vodka!" rejoined the elder shortly, and turned to the others.... "Better lunch on some bread, boys, and not keep the people sitting up."

"Give us some vodka," repeated Ilya, not looking at any one, and in a tone of voice that made it evident that he was not going to be put off.

The muzhíks listened to the elder's advice, brought from the cart a great loaf of bread, ate it up, asked for kvas,[12] and lay down to sleep; some on the floor, some on the stove.

Ilya kept saying occasionally, "Give me vodka, I say, give me vodka." Suddenly he caught sight of Polikéï. "Ilyitch—there's Ilyitch! you here, dear old fellow! Here I am going as a soldier; said good-by to mamma, and my wife,—how bad she felt! They made me a soldier.—Set up some vodka!"

"No money," said Polikéï. "However, it's as God gives: maybe they'll find you disqualified," he added in a comforting tone.

"No, brother, I have always been as sound as a birch: how could they find me disqualified? How many soldiers more does the Tsar need?"

Polikéï began to relate a story of how a muzhík gave a bribe to a dokhter, and so escaped.

Ilya came up to the stove, and continued the conversation.

"No, Ilyitch, now it's done, and I myself don't want to get off. My uncle didn't buy me off. Wouldn't they have bought themselves off? No, he didn't want to spare his son, and he didn't want to spare his money; and they sent me instead.... And now I don't want to get off. [He spoke quietly, confidentially, under the influence of deep dejection.] However, I'm sorry for mamma. And how the sweetheart took on! Yes, and my wife—that's the way they kill the women. Now it's all over; I am a soldier. Better not to have got married. Why did they make me marry? To-morrow we go."

"Why did they take you away with short notice?" asked Polikéï "Nothing had been said about it, and then suddenly" ...

"You see, they were afraid I should do something to myself," replied Ilyushka smiling. "I wouldn't have done any thing, of course. I sha'n't be ruined by going as a soldier; but I'm sorry for the old woman. Why did they make me marry?" he repeated in a soft and melancholy tone.

The door opened, squeaking loudly, and the old man Dutlof, shaking the wet from his hat, came into the room in his huge sabots, which fitted his feet almost like canoes.

"Afanási," said he, crossing himself and addressing the porter,[13] "isn't there some one to hold a lantern while I give the horses their oats?"

Dutlof did not look at his nephew, but quietly busied himself with making a candle-end burn. His glove and whip were thrust into his belt, and his cloak was closely buttoned; he had just come with the baggage. His ordinarily calm, peaceful, and thoughtful face was full of care.

Ilya, when he saw his uncle, stopped talking, again turned his eyes gloomily toward the bench, and then addressing the stárosta said,—

"Give me some vodka, Yermil; I want something to drink."

His voice was angry and stern.

"This is no time for wine now," replied the stárosta, sipping his cup of kvas.—"Don't you see the folks have gone to bed? What do you want to make a disturbance for?"

The words "make a disturbance" apparently suggested to him the idea of making a disturbance.

"Stárosta, I'll do myself some harm, if you don't give me some vodka."

"You'd better bring him to reason," said the stárosta to Dutlof, who had now lighted the lantern, but stood listening to what was coming, and looking askance with deep commiseration at his nephew, as though wondering at his childishness.

Ilya, in a tone of desperation, repeated his threat,—

"Give me wine, or I'll do myself some harm."

"Don't, Ilya," said the stárosta gently, "please don't. It's better not."

But these words had scarcely passed his lips ere Ilya leaped up, smashed the window-pane with his fist, and screamed with all his might.

"You won't listen, here's for you," and darted for the other window to smash that also.

Polikéï, in the twinkling of an eye, rolled over twice, and hid himself in an angle of the stove, raising a panic among all the cockroaches. The elder threw aside his cup, and hastened after Ilya. Dutlof slowly put down the lantern, took off his girdle, clucked with his tongue, shook his head, and went to Ilya, who was already struggling with the elder and the porter, who tried to keep him from the window. They had his hands behind his back, and held him tight apparently; but as soon as he saw his uncle with the belt in his hand, tenfold strength was given to him. He tore himself away, and, rolling his eyes in frenzy, flung himself upon Dutlof with doubled fist.

"I'll kill you, don't you dare—You have ruined me! Why did you make me marry? Don't you dare—I will kill you!"

Ilyushka was frantic. His face was purple, his eyes were wild, his whole healthy young body trembled as in an ague. It seemed as if he could and would kill all three of the muzhíks who were trying to subdue him.

"You will shed your kinsman's blood, you blood-hound!"

Something passed over Dutlofs ever-calm face. He made a step forward.

"You'd better not do it," he said; and then, however he got his energy, he threw himself with a quick motion on his nephew, rolled over with him on the floor, and with the help of the elder, began to bind his hands. Within five minutes they had him fast. At last Dutlof, with the aid of the muzhíks, got up, tearing Ilya's hands from his sheepskin, in which they were convulsively clutched, got up himself, and then carried the young man, with his hands behind his back, to a bench in one corner of the room.

"I said it would be worse," he remarked, getting his breath after the struggle, and adjusting his shirt-band. "Why should he sin? We must all die. Let him have a cloak for a pillow," he added, turning to the dvornik; "the blood will run to his head" and, after girding himself with a rope, he took his lantern, and went out to his horses.

Ilya with dishevelled locks, pale face, and disordered linen, glared about the room as though he were trying to remember where he was. The porter picked up the broken glass, and put a jacket in the window so as to keep out the cold. The elder again sat down with his cup of kvas.

"Ay, Ilyúkha, Ilyúkha, I'm sorry for you, indeed I am. What's to be done? Here's Khoriushkin, he's married too. No way of avoiding it."

"My uncle is my enemy, and he wants to kill me," reiterated Ilya with tearless wrath. "Much he pities his own!... Mátushka said the overseer told him to hire a substitute. He wouldn't do it. He says he wouldn't borrow. Did I and my brother bring nothing into the house?... He is our enemy."

Dutlof came into the house, said a prayer before the holy images, took off his coat and hat, and sat down by the elder. The maid brought him also a cup of kvas and a spoon. Ilya said nothing, shut his eyes, and lay still on the cloak. The stárosta silently pointed to him, and shook his head. Dutlof waved his hand.

"Am I not sorry to have him go? He's my own brother's son. And though I pity him so, they make it out that I'm his enemy. His wife[14] put it into his head; a crafty woman, but quite too young. The idea of her thinking that we had money enough to hire a substitute! And so she blamed me. And yet

I'm sorry for him."

"Akh, he's a fine young fellow," said the stárosta.

"With my little means I couldn't do any thing for him. To-morrow I am going to send Ignat in, and his wife will want to go."

"Send her along, first-rate," said the stárosta, and he got up and mounted the stove. "What's money? Money's dust."

"Who would begrudge money if he had it?" asked one of the merchant's people, lifting his head.

"Ekh! money, money! it causes many a sin," replied Dutlof. "Nothing in the world causes so much sin as money, and it says so in the Scriptures."

"It says every thing," said the porter. "A man told me the other day: there was a merchant, he had made a lot of money, and he did not want any of it to remain behind him. He loved his money so that he took it with him into his tomb. He came to die, and ordered every penny that he had to be put into a pillow in the grave with him. And so they did. By and by his sons began to seek for his money. None anywhere. One of them suspected that it was in the cushion. They go to the Tsar, and get permission to dig it up. And what do you think? They discovered that there was nothing there, but the grave was full of mould and worms; and then they dig again, and there they find the money."

"Truly, much sin!" said Dutlof, and, standing up, he began to say his prayers.

After he had prayed, he looked at his nephew. He was asleep. Dutlof went to him, took off his belt, and then lay down. Another muzhík went out to sleep with the horses.

[12] A sort of beer made of rye-bread soaked in water and fermented.

[13] dvornik.

[14] khozyáïka.

IX.

As soon as all was quiet, Polikéï, like one engaged in some guilty deed, quietly slipped down from the stove, and began to make ready to depart. It somehow seemed to him a trying task to spend the night here with the recruits. The cocks were already calling to each other.

Barabán had eaten all his oats, and was stretching after water. Ilyitch harnessed him, and led him out past the teams of the muzhíks. His cap with its precious contents was safe, and his carriage-wheels were soon rolling anew over the frosty Pokrovskí road. Polikéï began to breathe more easily as soon as he got out of the city. At first, somehow, it seemed to him that he heard some one right behind him, following him; it was as though they stopped him, and bound his hands behind him instead of Ilya, and to-morrow he would have to go to camp. It was neither from the cold nor from terror that a chill struck down his back, and he urged and urged Barabán to his utmost endeavor. The first man whom he met was a priest in a high winter cap, walking with a one-eyed workman. Polikéï grew even more troubled. But as he left the city behind, this terror gradually diminished. Barabán proceeded in a slow walk. It grew lighter, so that it was possible to see the road before him. Ilyitch took his cap, felt to see that the money was all right. "Shall I put it in my bosom?" he queried. "I should have to untie my girdle. Now I am coming to the hill. I'll get out of the telyéga when I get there. I'll be careful. My cap fits tight, and it can't slip out from under the lining, and I won't take off my cap till I get home."

When he came to the hill, Barabán, in his peculiar trot, dashed up the slope; and Polikéï, who, like the horse, felt a strong desire to get home, did not hinder him in his endeavor.

Every thing was in order, or, at least, seemed to him so; and he gave free course to his imagination in respect to his mistress's delight, and the five-silver-ruble piece which she would give him, and the joy of his family. He took off his cap, once more felt of the letter, crushed his cap down closer to his head, and smiled. The wool on his cap was rotten; and for the very reason that Akulína, the day before, had carefully sewed the torn place, he tore the other end; and the very motion that Polikéï made when he thought that he was pulling down the envelope with the money closer under the wool,—that same motion tore away the cap, and, gave the envelope a chance to escape from one corner under the pelt.

It began to grow light, and Polikéï, who had not slept all night, grew drowsy. Adjusting his cap again, and still more loosening the envelope, Polikéï leaned his head on the side of the wagon, and drowsed.

He woke up just as he reached home. His first impulse was to feel for his cap: it was firm on his head. He did not take it off, being convinced that the envelope was there. He whipped up Barabán, adjusted the hay, again assumed the dignity of a householder, and, looking around him with an air of importance, rattled up toward his home.

There was the cook-house, there the wing, there the joiner's wife hanging out her wash, there the office; there the manor-house, where, in a moment, Polikéï would give proof that he was a faithful and honest man, "for any man can be slandered," and the mistress would say, "Well, thank you, Polikéï, here's three—or maybe five, or maybe even ten—silver rubles for you;" and would have some tea brought to him, and perhaps some spirits besides. It would not come amiss after the chilly ride. "And with the ten rubles we'll have a holiday, and buy some boots, and pay back Nikíta the four rubles and a half, since he's begun to dun me for them."

Not driving the two hundred steps that remained, Polikéï straightened himself up, tightened his belt, adjusted his collar, took off his cap, smoothed his hair, and with confidence thrust his hand under the lining. His hand moved more and more nervously; he inserted the other also. His face grew paler and paler. One hand came out on the other side.... Polikéï fell on his knees, stopped the horse, and began to search all over the telyéga, the hay, the bundle of purchases, to feel in his bosom, in his overalls. The money was nowhere to be found.

"Mercy on me![15] What does this mean? What will be done to me?" he roared, tearing his hair.

But just then, remembering that he might be seen, he turned Barabán around, put on his cap, and drove the astonished and reluctant animal up the road again.

"I can't bear to have Polikéï drive me," Barabán must have said to himself. "Once in my life he has fed me and watered me in time, and just for the sake of deceiving me in the most unpleasant manner. How I put myself out to get home! He stopped me, and just as I smelled our hay, he drives me back again."

"You devilish good-for-nothing beast!" cried Polikéï through his tears, standing up in the telyéga, and sawing on Barabán's mouth, and plying the whip.

[15] bátiushki.

X.

That whole day no one at Pokrovskoé saw Polikéï. The mistress several times after dinner made inquiries, and Aksiutka flew down to Akulína: but Akulína said that he had not come; that the merchant must have detained him, or something had happened to the horse. "Can't he have gone lame?" she suggested. "The last time Maksim was gone four and twenty hours,—walked the whole way." And Aksiutka's pendulums brought back the message to the house; and Akulína thought over all the reasons for her husband's delay, and tried hard to calm her fears, but she did not succeed. Her heart was heavy, and her preparations for the next day's festival made little progress in her hands. She tormented herself all the more because the joiner's wife was convinced that she had seen him.

"A man just like Ilyitch had driven up the proshpect, and then turned back again."

The children also waited restlessly and impatiently for their papa; but for other reasons. Aniutka and Mashka were without any sheepskin or cloak; and so they were deprived of the possibility of taking turns in going into the street, and were therefore obliged to content themselves in their single garments, and to make circuits around the house with strenuous swiftness so as to be troubled as little as possible by the inhabitants of the wing coming and going. Once Mashka tripped over the feet of the joiner's wife, who was lugging water; and though she was crying lustily from the knock that she received on her knee, yet her hair was pulled violently, and she began to cry still more grievously. When she did not meet any one, she flew straight into the door, and mounted the stove by means of the tub.

The mistress and Akulína began to be really worried about Polikéï himself; the children, about what he wore. But Yégor Mikhailovitch, in reply to her ladyship's question, "Hasn't Polikéï come yet, and where can he be?" smiled, and said, "I cannot tell;" and it was evident that he was satisfied to have his pre-supposition confirmed. "He would have to come to dinner," he said significantly.

All that day no one at Pokrovskoé had any tidings of Polikéï: except it was noised abroad that some neighboring muzhíks had seen him without his cap, and asking every one "if they seen a letter."

Another man had seen him asleep by the side of the road, near a horse hitched into a telyéga. "I thought he was drunk," said this man, "and that the horse had not been fed or watered for a couple of days, his belly was so drawn up."

Akulína did not sleep all night, but sat up waiting for him; but not even in the night did he put in an appearance. If she had lived alone, and had a cook and second girl, she would have been still more unhappy; but as soon as the cocks began to crow for the third time, and the joiner's wife got up, Akulína was obliged to rise and betake herself to the stove. It was a holiday; so it was necessary before daylight to take out her bread, to make kvas, to bake cookies, to milk the cow, to iron the dresses and shirts, to wash the children, to bring water, and keep her neighbor from occupying the whole oven. Akulína ceased not to keep her ears open while she was fulfilling these duties. It was already broad daylight: already the bells had begun to peal, already the children were up, and still no Polikéï. Yesterday, winter had really set in; the fields, roads, and roofs were covered with patches of snow; but to-day, as though in honor of a festival, it was clear, sunny, and cool, so that one could see and hear a long distance. But Akulína standing by the oven, and with her head thrust into the door so as to watch the baking of her cookies, did not hear Polikéï as he came in, and only by the cries of the children did she know that her husband had come. Aniutka, as the eldest, had oiled her hair and dressed herself. She had on a new calico dress, somewhat rumpled, the gift of the gracious lady, and it fitted her like the bark on a tree, and dazzled the neighbors' eyes; her hair was shiny, having been rubbed with a candle-end; her shoos were not exactly new, but were elegant.

Mashka was still in jacket and rags, so Aniutka would not let her come near to her lest she should soil her clean things. Mashka was in the yard when her father came along with a bag.

"Papa's come!" she shouted, beginning to cry, and threw herself head-first into the door past Aniutka, leaving a great smutch on her dress. Aniutka, no longer afraid of getting soiled, immediately struck Mashka. Akulína could not leave her work, and had to shout to the children, "There now, stop! I'll give you both a good thrashing!" and she glanced toward the door. Ilyitch, with his sack in his hand, came through the entry, and instantly threw himself into his corner. Akulína noticed that he was pale, and that his face had an expression as though he had been neither weeping nor laughing: she could not understand it.

"Well, Ilyitch," she asked, not leaving the oven, "what luck?"

Ilyitch muttered something which she did not hear.

"How?" she screamed, "have you been to our lady's?"

Ilyitch sat down on the bed, looked wildly around, and smiled his guilty and deeply unhappy smile. For a long time he said nothing.

"Well, Ilyitch? why so long?" rang Akulína's voice.

"I, Akulína,—I gave the money to our lady; how thankful she was!" said he suddenly, and looked around even more restlessly than ever, still smiling. Two objects especially attracted his restless, feverishly-staring eyes,—the rope fastened to the cradle, and the baby. He went to the cradle, and with his slender fingers began rapidly to untie a knot in the rope. Then his eyes rested on the babe; but here Akulína, with the cookies on a platter, came into the corner. Ilyitch quickly hid the rope in his bosom, and sat down on the bed.

"What's the matter, Ilyitch? you don't seem like yourself," said Akulna.

"I haven't had any sleep," was his reply.

Suddenly something flashed by the window; and in an instant Aksiutka, the maid from the upper house, darted into the room.

"The gracious lady[16] commands Polikéï Ilyitch to come to her this minute," said she. "Avdót'ya Mikolávna commands you to come this minute,—this minute."

Polikéï gazed at Akulína, at the maid-servant.

"Right away! what more is wanted?" he asked so simply that Akulína's apprehensions were quieted: maybe he is going to be rewarded. "Say I will come right away."

He got up and went out. Akulína took a trough, placed it on the bench, poured in water from the buckets which stood by the door, filled it up with boiling water from the kettle, began to roll up her sleeves, and try the temperature of the water.

"Come, Mashka, I want to wash you."

The cross sibilating little girl began to cry.

"Come, you scabby wench! I want to put you on a clean shirt. Now, make up faces, will you? Come, I've got to wash your sister yet."

Polikéï meantime was going, not in the direction taken by the maid from the house, but exactly opposite. In the entry next the wall was a straight staircase leading to the loft. When Polikéï reached the entry he looked around, and, seeing no one, he bent down, and almost running climbed up this stairs quickly and with agility.

"What in the world does it mean that Polikéï doesn't come?" asked the lady impatiently, turning to Duniasha, who was combing her hair. "Where is

Polikéï? Why doesn't he come?"

Aksiutka again flew down to the servants' wing, and again flew into the entry, and summoned Ilyitch to the mistress. "But he went long ago," said Akulína, who, having washed Mashka, was at this time in the act of putting her contumacious little boy in the trough, and silently, in spite of his cries, was washing his red head. The boy screamed, wrinkled up his face, and tried to clutch something with his helpless hands. Akulína with one big hand supported his weak, soft little back, all dimples, and soaped it.

"See if he isn't asleep somewhere," she said, glancing around nervously.

The joiner's wife at this time with her hair unkempt, with her bosom open, and holding up her dress, was climbing up to the loft to get her clothes which were drying there. Suddenly a cry of horror was heard from the loft, and the joiner's wife, like one crazy, with wide-open eyes, came down on her hands and feet backwards, quicker than a cat, and fled from the stairs.

"Ilyitch," she cried.

Akulína dropped the child which she was holding.

"He has hung himself!" roared the joiner's wife.

Akulína—not noticing that the child, like a ball, rolled over and over on his face, and, kicking his little legs, fell head first into the water—ran to the entry.

"From the beam—he is hanging," repeated the joiner's wife, but stopped when she saw Akulína.

Akulína flew to the stairs, and before any one could prevent her climbed up, and with a terrible cry fell back like a dead body on the steps; and she would have killed herself if the people, coming from all parts, had not been in time to seize her.

[16] bárinya.

XI.

For some minutes it was impossible to bring any order out of the general chaos. The people ran about in crowds, all screaming, all talking; children and old people weeping. Akulína lay in a dead faint. At last some peasants, the joiner, and the overseer, who came running up, mounted the stairs; and the joiner's wife for the twentieth time related how she, without any thought of any thing, went after her clothes, looked in this way: "I see a man; I look more close: there's a cap lying on one side. I see his legs twitching. Then a cold chill ran down my back. At last I make out a man hanging there, and ... that I should have to see that! How ever I got down is more than I can tell. And it is a miracle that God saved me. Truly the Lord had mercy. It was so steep, and—such a height! I might have got my death."

The men who went into the loft told the same story. Ilyitch was hanging from the beam, in his shirt and stockings alone, with the very rope that he had taken off from the cradle. His cap which had fallen off lay beside him. He had taken off his jacket and sheepskin shuba, and folded them neatly. His feet just touched the floor, and there was not a sign of life. Akulína came to herself, and tried to climb to the loft again; but they would not let her.

"Mamma,[17] little brother has fallen into the water," suddenly screamed the sibilating girl from the corner. Akulína tore herself away, and darted back to the house. The babe, not stirring, lay head downwards in the tub, and his legs were motionless. Akulína seized him, but the child did not breathe, and gave no signs of life. Akulína threw him on the bed, put her arms akimbo, and burst into a fit of laughter so loud, discordant, and terrible, that Mashka, who at first began to laugh too, put her fingers in her ears, and ran weeping into the entry.

The people also poured into the corner, and filled it with their lamentations. They picked up the child, and tried to bring him to; but it was in vain. Akulína jumped about on the bed, and laughed and laughed so uncannily, that it threw a terror over those who heard it.

And now to see this heterogeneous throng of lusty peasants and women, of old men and children, pressing into the entry, one could get some idea of the number of people who lived in the servants' quarters.[18] All were running about this way and that, all talking at once; many were weeping, and no one did any thing useful. The joiner's wife kept finding new-comers who had not heard her story; and again and again she repeated how her deepest feelings had been stirred up by the unexpected sight, and how God had saved her from falling down the stairs. The old butler, in a woman's jacket, told how a woman in the time of the late bárin had drowned herself in the pond. The overseer sent messengers after the police inspector[19] and a priest, and stationed guards. The maid-servant Aksiutka, her eyes red with weeping, peeped through a hole in the loft; and though she could not see any thing there, yet she could not tear herself away and go to her mistress.

Agáfya Mikhaïlovna, who had been the dowager's lady's-maid, made some tea to calm her nerves, and wept. The experienced old grandmother, Anna, with her swollen hands smeared with olive-oil, was laying out upon the table the dead body of the little babe. The women stood around Akulína, and looked at her in silence. The children who lived in the corners looked at the mother, and began to cry, then choked down their sobs, and then again, looking at her, began to weep louder than ever. The boys and men collected around the steps, and with terror-stricken faces peered into the door and into the windows, unable to see any thing, and not understanding it all, and asking each other questions about what had happened. One said that the joiner had cut his wife's leg off with an axe. Another said that the laundress had had triplets. A third said that the cook's cat had had a fit, and bitten the people. But the truth gradually became generally known, and at last reached the mistress's ears. And it seems that they hadn't the wit to break the news gently to her: the rough Yégor told her point-blank, and so shattered her nerves that for a long time afterwards she could not get over it.

The crowd now began to grow calmer! The joiner's wife set up her samovar, and made some warm tea; and so those from outside, not receiving an invitation, took the hint that it was incumbent upon them to go home. The boys began to tear themselves away from the steps. Everybody now knew what the trouble was, and crossing themselves were beginning to scatter in different directions, when suddenly the cry was raised, "bárinya, bárinya."[20] and all came rushing back again, and crowding together so as to give her room to pass. Nevertheless, all wanted to see what the lady would do.

The bárinya, pale, and with tears in her eyes, passed through the entry, and crossed the threshold into Akulína's corner. A dozen heads crowded together and peered through the door. They pressed so violently against one woman who was heavy with child, that she screamed, but nevertheless, taking advantage of the situation, this same woman managed to get the foremost place. And how could they help wishing to see the mistress in Akulína's corner! For the domestics it was much the same as a Bengal fire at the end of an exhibition. Of course it's a fine thing to burn the Bengal fire; and of course it's a fine thing when the mistress, in her silk and laces, goes into Akulína's corner. The lady went up to Akulína, and took her by the hand. But Akulína snatched it away. The old domestics shook their heads disapprovingly.

"Akulína," said the lady, "for your children's sake calm yourself."

Akulína gave a loud laugh and drew herself up.

"My children are solid silver, solid silver! I don't deal in paper notes," she muttered rapidly. "I told Ilyitch, 'Don't keep the bank-notes,' and now they've smeared him with tar, smeared him—with tar and soap, lady. So if he's got the barn-itch, it'll cure him right away;" and again she went into a fit of laughter, louder than before.

The mistress turned around, and asked for the doctor's boy with some mustard. "Give me some cold water," and she herself began to look about for water. But when she saw the dead child, and the old grandmother Anna standing by him, the mistress turned away, and all saw that she covered her face with a handkerchief and wept. But the grandmother Anna (it was a pity that the mistress did not see it: she would have appreciated it, and it was all done for her too) covered the child with a piece of linen, folded the little arms with her soft, skilful hand, and arranged the little head, composed the lips, and feelingly closed the eyes, and sighed, so that every one could see what a beautiful heart she had. But the mistress did not see it, and she could not have seen it. She began to sob, and when the first attack of hysterics was over they led her out into the entry, and they led her home.

"That's all she could do," was what many thought, and they began to separate. Akulína was still laughing, and talking nonsense. They led her into another room, cupped her, put on mustard-plasters, applied ice to her forehead; but all the time she did not understand it in the least, did not weep, but laughed, and said and did such things that the kind people who were waiting on her could not restrain themselves, but even laughed.

[17] mámuska.

[18] fliger, peasant corruption of flügel, the wing; the collection of izbás occupied by the dvoróvui or domestic servants.

[19] stanovóï.

[20] "The mistress, the mistress," or, "the gracious lady." Bárin and báruinya or bárinya are the terms used by the domestics for the master and mistress.

XII.

The festival was not gay at Pokrovskoé. Notwithstanding the fact that the day was beautiful, the people did not go out to enjoy themselves: the girls did not collect to sing songs: the factory-boys who came out from the city did not play the harmonica or on the balaláïka;[21] they did not jest with the girls. All sat around in the corners; and if they talked, they talked quietly, as though some ill-disposed person were there, and might overhear them.

All day nothing happened. But in the evening, as it grew dusk, the dogs began to howl: and, as though signifying some misfortune, a wind sprang up and howled in the chimneys; and such fear fell upon all the inhabitants of the dvor, that those who had candles lighted them before, it was necessary; those who were alone in any corner went to ask their neighbors to give them a night's lodging where there were more people; and whoever had to go to the stables did not go, and did not hesitate to leave the cattle without fodder that night. And the holy water, which every one keeps in a vial, was all that night in constant requisition. Many were sure that they heard, during the night, some one walking up and down with a heavy tread over the loft; and the blacksmith saw how a serpent flew straight to the loft.

None of the family staid in Polikéï's corner. The children and the crazy woman had been carried to other quarters. The dead little baby lay there, however. And there were two old grandmothers and a pilgrim-woman[22] who diligently read the psalter, not for the sake of the child so much as for the solace of all this unhappiness. This was the mistress's desire. These old grandmothers and the pilgrim-woman themselves heard, while one portion of the psalter was read, how the beam above creaked, and some one groaned. When they read the words, "Let God rise up," the sounds ceased.

The joiner's wife asked in one of her cronies; and that night they did not sleep, but drank up enough tea to last her a week. They also heard how the beam creaked, and something sounded like the falling of heavy bags. The muzhíks on guard imparted some courage to the domestics, otherwise they would all have perished with fear. The muzhíks lay in the entry on the hay, and afterwards they also became convinced that they heard marvels in the loft; although that same night they calmly talked about the necruits, munched their bread, combed their hair, and, most of all, filled the entry with that odor peculiar to the muzhíks, so that the joiner's wife, passing by them, spat, and scolded them for foul peasants.

However it was, the suicide all the time was hanging in the loft; and it seemed as if the evil spirit himself that night overshadowed the premises with his monstrous pinions, showing his power, and coming nearer to all these people than ever before. At least, all of them had that impression.

I don't know whether they were right. I am inclined to think that they were entirely wrong. I think that if some man, that terrible night, had had courage enough to take a candle or a lantern, and blessing himself, or even not blessing himself, with the sign of the cross, had gone to the loft, slowly driving before him, by the flame of the candle, the terror of the night, and lighting up the beams, the sand, the cobweb-garlanded chimney, and the forgotten washing of the joiner's wife,—had gone straight up to Ilyitch, and if, not giving way to the feeling of fear, he had lifted the lantern to the level of his face, then he would have seen the familiar, emaciated body, with the legs touching the floor (the rope had stretched), lifelessly falling to one side, the unbuttoned shirt, under the opening of which his baptismal cross could not be seen, and with the head bent over on the breast, and the good-natured face, with the sightless eyes wide open, and the sweet, guilty smile, and a stern calmness, and silence over all.

Truly the joiner's wife, huddling up in the corner of her bed, with dishevelled hair and frightened eyes, telling how she heard what seemed like bags falling, was a far more terrible and fear-inspiring object than Ilyitch, though he had taken off his cross and laid it on a bench.

Above—that is, at the great house—there was the same fear that reigned in the wing. In the lady's room there was an odor of eau de cologne and medicine. Duniasha was melting beeswax, and making a cerate. Why a cerate especialty, is more than I can tell; but I know that a beeswax plaster was always made when the mistress was ill. And now she was so disturbed that she was really ill. Duniasha's aunt had come to spend the night with her, so as to keep her courage up. Four of them were sitting in the girls' sitting-room,—among them the little maid,—and were quietly conversing.

"Who is going after the oil?" asked Duniasha.

"I wouldn't go, not for any thing, Avdót'ya Mikolávna," said the second girl in atone of determination.

"Come now, go with Aksiutka."

"I will run alone. I ain't afraid of nothing," said Aksiutka, "but she's afraid of every thing."

"Well, then, go ahead, dear; borrow it of the old granny Anna, and don't spill it," said Duniasha.

Aksiutka lifted her skirt with one hand, and though on account of this she could not swing both arms, she swung one twice as violently across the line of her direction, and flew off. It was terrible to her; and she felt that if she should see or hear any thing whatsoever, even though it were her own mother, she should fall with fright. She flew, with her eyes shut, over the well-known path.

[21] A sort of primitive guitar, with long neck, and short three-cornered sounding-board, strung with two or three strings, and thrummed with the fingers.

[22] stránnitsa.

XIII.

"Is our lady asleep, or not?" asked a muzhík's hoarse voice suddenly near Aksiutka. She opened her eyes, which had been tightly shut, and saw a form which it seemed to her was higher than the wing. She wheeled round, and sped back so fast that her petticoat did not have time to catch up with her. With one bound she was on the steps, with another in the sitting-room, and giving a wild shriek flung herself on the lounge.

Duniasha, her aunt, and the second girl almost died of fright; but they had no time to open their eyes, ere heavy, deliberate, and irresolute steps were heard in the entry and at the door. Duniasha ran into her mistress's room, dropping the cerate. The second girl hid behind a skirt that was hanging on the wall. The aunt, who had more resolution, was about to hold the door; but the door opened, and a muzhík strode into the room.

It was Dutlof in his huge boots. Not paying any heed to the affrighted women, his eyes sought the ikons; and, not finding the small holy image that hung in a corner, he crossed himself toward the cupboard, laid his cap down on the window, and thrusting his thick hand into his sheepskin coat, as though he were trying to scratch himself under the arm, he drew out a letter with five brown seals, imprinted with an anchor. Duniasha's aunt put her hand to her breast; she was scarcely able to articulate,—

"How you frightened me, Naumuitch![23] I ca-n-n't sa-y a wo-r-d. I thought that the end ... had ... come."

"What do you want?" asked the second girl, emerging from behind the skirt.

"And they have stirred up our lady so," said Duniasha coming from the other room. "What made you come up to the sitting-room without knocking? You stupid muzhík!"

Dutlof, without making any excuse, said that he must see the mistress.

"She is ill," said Duniasha.

By this time Aksiutka was snorting with such unbecomingly loud laughter, that she was again obliged to hide her head under the pillows, from which, for a whole hour, notwithstanding Duniasha's and her aunt's threats, she was unable to lift it without falling into renewed fits of laughter, as though something were loose in her rosy bosom and red cheeks. It seemed to her so ridiculous that they were all so frightened—and she again would hide her head, and, as it were in convulsions, shuffle her shoes, and shake with her whole body.

Dutlof straightened himself up, looked at her attentively as though wishing to account for this peculiar manifestation; but, not finding any solution, he turned away and continued to explain his errand.

"Of course, as this is a very important business," he said, "just tell her that a muzhík has brought her the letter with the money."

"What money?"

Duniasha, before referring the matter to the mistress, read the address, and asked Dutlof when and how he had got this money which Ilyitch should have brought back from the city. Having learned all the particulars, and sent the errand-girl, who still continued to laugh, out into the entry, Duniasha went to the mistress; but to Dutlof's surprise the lady would not receive him at all, and sent no message to him through Duniasha.

"I know nothing about it, and wish to know nothing," said the mistress, "about any muzhík or any money. I can not and I will not see any one. Let him leave me in peace."

"But what shall I do?" asked Dutlof, turning the envelope around and around; "it's no small amount of money. It's written on there, isn't it?" he inquired of Duniasha, who again read to him the superscription.

It seemed hard for Dutlof to believe Duniasha. He seemed to hope that the money did not belong to the gracious lady, and that the address read otherwise. But Duniasha repeated it a second time. He sighed, placed the envelope in his breast, and prepared to go out.

"I must give it to the police inspector," he said.

"Simpleton, I will ask her again; I will tell her," said Duniasha, detaining him when she saw the envelope disappearing under his coat. "Give me the letter."

Dutlof took it out again, but did not immediately put it into Duniasha's outstretched hand.

"Tell her that Dutlof Sem'yón found it on the road."

"Well, give it here."

"I was thinking—well, take it. A soldier read the address for me—that it had money."

"Well, let me have it."

"I didn't dare to go home on account of this," said Dutlof again, not letting go the precious envelope. "Well, let her see it."

Duniasha took the envelope, and once more went to her ladyship.

"Duniasha,"[24] said the mistress in a reproachful tone, "don't speak to me about that money. I can't think of any thing else except that poor little babe."

"The muzhík, my lady,[25] knows not who you want him to give it to," insisted Duniasha.

The lady broke the seals, shuddered as soon as she saw the money, and pondered for a moment.

"Horrible money! it has brought nothing but woe," she mused.

"It is Dutlof, my lady. Do you wish him to go, or will you come and see him? Is all the money there?" asked Duniasha.

"I do not wish this money. This is horrible money. What harm it has done! Tell him that he may have it if he wants it," suddenly exclaimed the lady, seizing Duniasha's hand.

"Fifteen hundred rubles," remarked Duniasha, smiling gently as to a child.

"Let him have it all," repeated the lady impatiently. "Why, don't you understand me? This is misfortune's money: don't ever speak about it to me again. Let this muzhík have it, if he brought it. Go, go right away!"

Duniasha returned into the sitting-room.

"Was it all there?" asked Dutlof.

"Count for yourself," said Duniasha, handing him the envelope: "she told me to give it to you."

Dutlof stuffed his cap under his arm, and bending over tried to count.

"Haven't you got a counting-machine?"

Dutlof understood that it was a whim of the mistress's not to count, and that she had bidden him to do it.

"Take it home, and count it. It's yours,—your money," said Duniasha severely. "Says she, 'I don't want it; let the man have it who found it.'"

Dutlof, not straightening himself up, fixed his eyes on Duniasha.

Duniasha's aunt also clapped her hands. "Goodness gracious![26] God has given you such luck! Goodness gracious!"

The second girl could not believe it. "You're joking! Did really Avdót'ya Nikolóvna say that?"

"What do you mean—joking! She told me to give it to the muzhík. Now take your money, and be off," said Duniasha, not hiding her vexation. "One has sorrow, another joy."

"It must be a joke,—fifteen hundred rubles!" said the aunt.

"More than that," said Duniasha sharply. "Now you will place a great big candle for Mikola,"[27] she continued maliciously. "What! have you lost your wits? It would be good for some poor fellow. And you have so much of your own."

Dutlof finally arrived at a comprehension that it was meant in earnest; and he began to fold together and smooth down the envelope with the money, which in the counting he had burst open: but his hands trembled, and he kept looking at the women, to persuade himself that it was not a jest.

"You see you haven't come to your senses with joy," said Duniasha, making it evident that she despised both the muzhík and money. "Give it to me, I'll fix it for you."

And she offered to take it, but Dutlof did not trust it in her hands. He doubled the money up, thrust it in still farther, and took his cap.

"Glad?"

"I don't know; what's to be said? Here it's"—He did not finish his sentence, but waved his hand, grinned, almost burst into tears, and went out.

The bell tinkled in the mistress's room.

"Well, did you give it to him?"

"I did."

"Well, was he very glad?"

"He was like one gone crazy."

"Oh, bring him back! I want to ask him how he found it. Bring him in here. I can't go out to him."

Duniasha flew out, and overtook the muzhík in the hall. He had not put on his hat, but had taken out his purse, and bending over was opening it; but the money he held between his teeth. Maybe it seemed to him that it was not his until he had put it in his purse. When Duniasha called him back, he was startled.

"What ... Avdót'ya?... Avdót'ya Mikolavna? Is she going to take it away from me? If you would only take my part, I would bring you some honey,—before God I would."

"All right, bring it,'"

Again the door opened, and the muzhík was led into the mistress's presence. It was not a happy moment for him. "Akh! she's going to take it back!" he said to himself, as he went through the rooms, lifting his feet very high, as though walking through tall grass, so as not to make a noise with his big wooden shoes. He did not comprehend, and he scarcely noticed what was around him. He passed by the mirror; he saw some flowers, some muzhík or other lifting up his feet shod in sabots, the bárin painted with one eye and something that seemed to him like a green tub, and a white object.... Suddenly, from the white object issued a voice. It was the mistress. He could not distinguish any one clearly, but he rolled his eyes around. He knew not where he was, and every thing seemed to be in a mist.

"Is it you, Dutlof?"

"It's me, your ladyship.[28] It's just as it was. I didn't touch it," he said. "I wasn't glad,—before God, I wasn't. I almost killed my horse."

"It's your good luck," she said with a perfectly sweet smile. "Keep it, keep it. It's yours."

He only opened wide his eyes.

"I am glad that you have it. God grant that it prove useful to you. Are you glad to have it?"

"How could I help being glad? Glad as I can be, mátushka! I will always pray to God for you. I am as glad as I can be, that, glory to God, our mistress is alive. Only it was my fault."

"How did you find it?"

"You know that we can always work for our lady for honor's sake, and, if not that" ...

"He's getting all mixed up, my lady said," Duniasha.

"I carried my nephew, who's gone as a necruit, and on my way back I found it on the road. Polikéï must have dropped it accidentally."

"Well, now go, now go! I am glad."

"So am I glad, mátushka," said the muzhík.

Then he recollected that he had not thanked her, but he did not know how to go about it in the proper manner. The lady and Duniasha both smiled, as he again started to walk, as though through tall grass, and by main force conquered his impulse to break into a run. But all the time it seemed to him that they were going to hold him, and take it from him.

[23] The son of Nahum. It is customary among the peasantry to call each other by the patronymic. Thus Polikéï is generally called Ilyitch, son of Ilya, instead of the more formal Polikéï Ilyitch.

[24] Akh Bozhe moï.

[25] sudárinya.

[26] mátushki rodimuïa!

[27] St. Nicholas.

[28] Ya-s sudárinya.

XIV.

Making his way out into the fresh air, Dutlof turned off from the road to the lindens, unloosed his belt so the more conveniently to get at his purse, and then began to put away the money. He moved his lips, sucking them in and pushing them out again, though he made no sound. After he had stowed away the money, and buckled his girdle again, he crossed himself, and went roiling along the path as though he were drunk; so absorbed was he by the thoughts rushing through his brain. Suddenly he saw before him the form of a muzhík, coming to meet him. He screamed. It was Yefím, who with a club was acting as guard on the outside of the wing.

"Ah, uncle Sem'yón," said Yefímka joyfully as he came nearer. [It was rather gloomy for him to be all alone.] "Well, have you got the recruits off?"

"Yes. What are you doing?"

"They stationed me here to guard Ilyitch, who hung himself."

"But where is Ilyitch?"

"Here in the loft: they say he's hanging there," replied Yefímka, pointing with his stick through the darkness, to the roof of the wing.

Dutlof looked in the direction indicated; and though he saw nothing, he blinked his eyes and shook his head.

"The police inspector has come," said Yefímka. "The coachman told me. They are going to take him right down. Kind of a fearful night, uncle.[29] I wouldn't go in there to-night, not even if orders had come from the upper house. Not if Yégor Mikhaluitch beat me to death would I go in there."

"What a terrible misfortune!" said Dutlof, evidently from a sense of propriety; for in reality he was not thinking of what he was saying, and was anxious to go his way. But the overseer's voice chained him to the spot.

"Hey, guard, come here!" cried Yégor Mikháilovitch, from the steps.

Yefímka responded to the call.

"What muzhík was standing there with you?"

"Dutlof."

"You too, Sem'yón, come here."

As Dutlof drew near, he saw, by the light of the lantern carried by the coachman, not only the overseer, but a strange man in a uniform cap with a cockade, and wearing a cloak: this was the police inspector.

"Here is an old man will go with us," said the overseer, pointing to him.

The old man winced, but there was nothing to be done.

"And you, Yefímka, you're only a young man; just run on ahead to the loft where he's hanging, and clear away the stairs so that his honor can get up."

Yefímka, although he would not for any thing go into the wing, started off, tramping with his feet as though they were beams.

The police inspector struck a light, and began to smoke his pipe. He lived two versts away; and he had just been engaged in receiving from the captain of police[30] a sharp dressing for drunkenness, and was, consequently, still suffering from an attack of ill humor. The overseer asked Dutlof why he was there. Dutlof told him in a straightforward way about the finding of the money, and what the bárinya had done. Dutlof said that he was going to ask the overseer's permission. The overseer, to Dutlof's horror, asked for the envelope, and looked at it. The police inspector also took the envelope, and asked, in a few dry words, about the particulars.

"Now, good-by to my money," thought Dutlof, and began already to excuse himself. But the police inspector gave him the money.

"That's luck for the rascal!" he said.

"Comes in good time," said the overseer. "He's just taken his nephew to camp. Now he can buy him off."

"Ah!" said the police inspector, and started on.

"Are you going to get Ilyushka a substitute?" inquired the overseer.

"How get him a substitute? Is there money enough? And, besides, it's too late."

"You know best," said the overseer, and both followed the police inspector.

They went into the wing, at the entry of which the ill-smelling guards were waiting with a lantern. Dutlof followed them. The guards had a guilty look, which was to be attributed only to the odor arising from them, because they had been doing nothing wrong. All were silent.

"Where?" asked the police inspector.

"Here," whispered the overseer. "Yefímka," he added, "you're a fine young man, go ahead with the lantern."

Yefímka straightened his forelock; it seemed as if he had lost all his fear. Going up two or three steps, he kept turning round, with a glad countenance, and throwing the light on the police inspector's way. Behind the inspector followed the overseer. When they were out of sight, Dutlof, resting one foot on the step, sighed and stopped. In the course of two minutes, the sound of the steps ceased; evidently they were approaching the body.

"Uncle! you're wanted," cried Yefímka, in the skylight.

Dutlof went up. The police inspector and the overseer could be seen in the light of the lantern, but the beam partly hid them from sight. Near them stood some one with back toward them. It was Polikéï. Dutlof went beyond the beam, and, crossing himself, halted.

"Turn him round, boys," commanded the coroner. No one stirred.

"Yefímka, you're a fine young man," said the overseer.

The "fine young man" walked up to the beam, and turning Ilyitch's body round stood by him, looking with the same pleased expression, now at Ilyitch, now at the officer, just as a showman exhibiting an albino, or some monstrosity,[31] looks now at the public, now at the object of his exhibition, and is ready to fulfil all the desires of his spectators.

"Turn him round again."

The body turned around once more, waved its hands slightly, and the leg made a circle on the sanded floor.

"Come now, take him down."

"Do you order him cut down, Vasíli Borisovitch?" demanded the overseer. "Bring an axe, friends!"

Twice the order had to be given to Dutlof and the guards to lift him up. But the "fine young man" handled Ilyitch as he would the carcass of a sheep. Finally they cut the rope, took down the body, and threw a cloth over it. The police inspector said that the doctor would come on the next day, and sent the people away.

[29] d'yadiushka, diminutive of d'yád'ya.

[30] ispravnik.

[31] Tulia Pastrana: a girl like a monkey, with hairy arms and face, exhibited all over Europe, some years ago.

XV.

Dutlof, still moving his lips, went home. At first, it was hard for him; but in proportion as he drew near the village, this feeling passed away, and a feeling of pleasure more and more penetrated his heart. Songs and drunken voices were heard in the village. Dutlof never drank, and now he went straight home. It was already late when he reached his cottage.[32] His old woman was asleep. His oldest son and the grand-children were asleep on the oven, the other son in the closet. The nephew's wife[33] was the only person awake; and she, in a dirty, every-day shirt, with her hair unkempt, was sitting on the bench and weeping. She did not get up to open the door for the uncle, but began to weep more bitterly, and to reproach him, as soon as he came into the cottage. By the old woman's advice she talked very clearly and well, though, being still young, she could not have had any practice.

The old woman got up, and began to get her husband something to eat. Dutlof drove his nephew's wife away from the table. "That'll do! that'll do!" said he. Aksínya got up, and then throwing herself down on the bench still continued to weep. The old woman silently set the things on the table, and then put them in order. The old man also refrained from saying a single word. After performing his devotions, he belched once or twice, washed his hands, and, taking the abacus down from the nail, went to his closet. There he began to whisper with his old wife: then the old woman left him alone, and he began to rattle the abacus; finally he lifted the lid of a chest, and climbed down into a sort of cellar. He rummaged round long in the closet and in the cellar. When he came out, it was dark in the cottage; the pitch-pine knot had burnt out.

The old woman, who by day was ordinarily mild and quiet, had retired to her room, and was snoring so as to be heard all over the cottage. The noisy niece,[34] on the other hand, was also asleep, and her breathing could not be heard. She was asleep on the bench just as she was, not having undressed, and without any thing under her head. Dutlof said his prayers, then glanced at his niece, raised her head a little, slipped a stick under it, and, after belching again, climbed upon the oven, and lay down next his grandson. In the darkness he took off his shoes, and lay on his back, and tried to make out the objects on the stove, barely visible above his head; and listened to the cockroaches rustling over the wall, to the breathing, and the restless moving of feet, and to the noises of the cattle in the yard.

It was long before he went to sleep. The moon came up, and it grew lighter in the cottage. He could see Aksínya in the corner, and something which he could not make out. Was it a cloak that his son had forgotten? or had the women left a tub there? or was it some one standing? Whether he drowsed or not, who can say? but now he began to look again.... Evidently that dark spirit which led Ilyitch to commit the terrible deed, and which impressed the domestics that night with its presence,—evidently that spirit spread its pinions over the whole estate, and over Dutlof's cottage, where was concealed that money which he enjoyed at the cost of Ilyitch's ruin. At all events, Dutlof felt it there. And Dutlof was not in his usual spirits,—could not sleep, nor sit up. When he saw something that he could not explain, he remembered his nephew with his pinioned arms, he remembered Aksínya's face and her flowing discourse, he remembered Ilyitch with his dangling hands.

Suddenly it seemed to the old man that some one passed by the window. "What is that? Can it be the elder[35] has come to ask the news?" he said to himself. "How did he unlock the door?" the old man asked himself in surprise, hearing steps in the entry; "or did the old woman leave it open when she went to the door?" The dog howled in the back yard, but IT passed along the entry, and, as the old man afterwards related the story, seemed to hunt for the door, passed by, once more tried to feel along the wall, stumbled across the tub, and it rang. And once more IT tried to feel along the wall, actually found the latch-string. Then IT took hold of it. A chill ran over the old man's body. Here the latch was lifted, and the form of a man came in. Dutlof already knew that it was IT. He tried to get hold of his cross, but could not. IT came to the table, on which lay a cloth, threw it on the floor, and came to the oven. The old man knew that IT was in Ilyitch's form. He trembled; his hands shook. IT came to the oven, threw itself on the old man, and began to choke him.

"My money," said Ilyitch.

Sem'yón tried, but could not say, "Let me go, I will not."

Ilyitch pressed down upon him with all the weight of a mountain of stone resting upon his breast. Dutlof knew that if he could say a prayer, IT would leave him; and he knew what kind of a prayer he ought to say, but this prayer would not form itself on his lips.

His grandson was sleeping next him. The boy uttered a piercing scream, and began to weep. The grandfather had crowded him against the wall. The child's cry unsealed the old man's lips. "Let God arise up," he repeated. IT loosed its hold a little. "And scatter our enemies," whispered Dutlof. IT got down from the stove. Dutlof listened as IT touched both feet to the floor. Dutlof kept repeating all the prayers that he knew; said them all in order. IT went to the door, passed the table, and struck the door such a rap that the cottage trembled. Every one was asleep except the old man and his grandson. The grandfather repeated the prayers, and trembled all over: the grandson wept as he fell asleep, and cuddled up to his grandfather.

All became quiet again. The old man lay motionless. The cock crowed behind the wall at Dutlof's ear. He heard how the hens began to stir themselves; how the young cockerel endeavored to imitate the old cock, and did not succeed. Something moved on the old man's legs. It was the cat. She jumped down on her soft paws from the oven to the ground, and began to miaw at the door.

The grandfather got up, opened the window. In the street it was dark, muddy. The corpse stood there under the very window. He went in his stocking-feet to the yard,[36] crossing himself as he went. And here it was evident that the master[37] was coming. The mare, standing under the shed by the wall, with her leg caught in the bridle, was lying in the husks, and raised her head, waiting for the master. The foal was stretched out on the manure. The old man lifted him on his legs, freed the mare, gave her some fodder, and went back to the cottage. The old woman got up, and kindled the fire.

"Wake the boys; I am going to town."

And lighting one of the wax candles that stood before the sacred images, he took it, and went with it down into the cellar. When he came up, not only was his own fire burning, but those in the neighboring cottages were lighted. The children were up, and all ready. Women were coming and going with pails and tubs of milk. Ignat was harnessing a telyéga. The other son was oiling another. The niece[38] was not to be seen, but, dressed in her best, and with a shawl on, was sitting on the bench in the cottage, and waiting for the time to go to town and say good-by to her husband.

The old man had an appearance of peculiar sternness. He said not a word to any one: put on his new kaftan, girdled himself tightly, and with all of Polikéï's money under his coat, went to the overseer.

"You wait for me," he shouted to Ignat, who was whirling the wheel round on the raised axle, and oiling it. "I'll be back in a moment. Be all ready."

The overseer, who was just up, was drinking his tea, and had made his preparations to go to the city to deliver the recruits over to the authorities.

"What do you wish?" he asked.

"Yégor Mikháluitch, I want to buy the young fellow off. Be so good. You told me a day or two ago that you knew a substitute in the city. Tell me how. I am ignorant."

"What! have you reconsidered it?"

"I have, Yégor Mikháluitch. It's too bad,—my brother's son. Whatever he did, I'm sorry for him. Much sin comes from it, from this money. So please tell me," said he, making a low bow.

The overseer, as always in such circumstances, drew in his lips silently, and went into a brown study; then having made up his mind, wrote two letters, and told him what and how he must do in town.

When Dutlof reached home, the niece was just coming out with Ignat; and the gray, pot-bellied mare, completely harnessed, was standing at the gate. He broke off a switch from the hedge. Wrapping himself up, he took his seat on the box, and started up the horse.

Dutlof drove the mare so fast that her belly seemed to shrink away, and he did not dare to look at her lest he should feel compunction. He was tormented by the thought that he might be late in reaching camp, that Ilyúkha would have already gone as a soldier, and that the devilish money would still be in his hands.

I am not going to give a detailed description of all Dutlof's adventures that morning. I will only say that he was remarkably successful. At the house of the man to whom the overseer gave him a letter, there was a substitute ready and waiting, who had spent twenty-three silver rubles of his bounty-money, and had already passed muster. His master[39] wanted to get for him four hundred rubles; but another man,[40] who had already been after him for three weeks, was anxious to beat him down to three hundred.

Dutlof concluded the business with few words. "Will you take three hundred and twenty-five?" said he, offering his hand, but with an expression that made it evident that he was ready to give even more. The master held out his hand, and continued to demand four hundred.

"Won't you take three hundred and twenty-five?" repeated Dutlof, seizing the master's right hand with his left, and making the motion to clap it with the other. "You won't take it? Well, God be with you," he exclaimed, suddenly striking hands with the master, and, with the violence of the motion, swinging his whole body round from him. "Then, make it this way! Take three hundred and fifty. Make out the fitanets.[41] Bring the young man. And now for the earnest-money. Will two ten-ruble pieces do?"

And Dutlof unbuckled his belt, and drew out the money.

Though the master did not withdraw his hand, yet apparently he was not wholly satisfied, and before accepting the earnest-money, he demanded a fee, and entertainment money for the substitute.

"Don't commit a sin," said Dutlof, pressing the money upon him. "We must all die," he went on in such a short, didactic, and confident voice that the master said, "There's nothing to be done," once more shook hands, and began to say a prayer. "With God's blessing," he said.

They awoke the substitute, who was still sleeping off his yesterday's spree; they inspected him, and then all went to the authorities. The substitute was hilarious, asked to be refreshed with some rum, for which Dutlof gave him money, and began to feel scared only at the moment when they first entered the vestibule of the court-house. They stood long in the vestibule: the old master[42] in a blue overcoat, and the substitute in a short sheepskin, with lifted eyebrows and wide-staring eyes; long they stood there whispering together, asked questions of this man and that, were sent from pillar to post, took off their hats and bowed before every petty clerk, and solemnly listened to the speech made by a clerk whom the master knew. All hope of finishing the business that day was vanishing, and the substitute was already beginning to feel more cheerful and easy, when Dutlof caught sight of Yégor Mikhailovitch, immediately went to him, and began to beseech him, and make low bows. The overseer's influence was so powerful, that by three o'clock the substitute, much to his disgust and surprise, was conducted into the audience-chamber, enrolled on the army list, and to the satisfaction of every one, from door-tender to president, was stripped, shaved, dressed in uniform, and sent out to camp. And at the end of five minutes Dutlof had paid the money over, and taken his receipt; and after saying good-by to the recruit and his master, he went to the merchant's lodging-house where the recruits from Pokrovskoé were stopping.

His nephew and the wife were sitting in one corner of the merchant's kitchen; and when the old man came in, they ceased talking, and behaved toward him in a humble and yet hostile manner.

"Don't be vexed, Ilyúkha," he said, approaching his nephew. "Day before yesterday you said a harsh word to me. Am I not sorry for you? I remember how my brother commended you to my care. If it had been in my power, would I have let you go? God granted me a piece of good fortune: you see I have not been mean. Here is this paper," said he, laying the receipt on the table, and carefully smoothing it out with his crooked, stiffened fingers.

All of the Prokrovski muzhíks, and the merchant's people, and also some of the neighbors, came into the inn.[43] All watched inquisitively what was going on. No one interrupted the old man's triumphal words.

"Here's the paper. I paid nearly four hundred silver rubles for it. Don't blame your uncle!"

Ilyúkha stood up; but said nothing, not knowing what to say. His lips trembled with emotion. His old mother came to him sobbing, and wanted to throw herself on his neck; but the old man slowly and imperiously pushed her away with his hand, and proceeded to speak:—

"You said a harsh word to me," repeated the old man. "With that word you stabbed me to the heart, as with a knife. Your dying father commended you to my care. You have taken the place of my own son; but if I have done you any harm, I am sorry. We are all sinners. Is that not so, Orthodox believers?" he asked, turning to the muzhíks standing around. "Here is your own mother, and your young wife;[44] here is the fitanets for you. God bless it,—the money. But forgive me, for Christ's sake!"

And spreading his cloak out on the floor, he slowly got down upon his knees, and bent low before the feet of Ilyushka and his wife. The young people tried in vain to raise him: not until he had touched his head to the ground, did he rise, and shaking himself sit down upon the bench. Ilyushka's mother and the young wife wept for joy. In the crowd were heard voices expressing approbation.

"That's right, that's God's way," said one.

"What money? It must have taken a lot."

"What a joy!" said a third. "A righteous man, that's the word for it."

But the muzhíks, who had been named as recruits, said nothing, and went noiselessly out into the court-yard.

In two hours' time, the two Dutlofs' telyégas drove through the suburbs of the city. In the first, drawn by the pot-bellied gray mare with sweaty neck, sat the old man and Ignat. Behind rattled a number of pretzels and crackers. In the second telyéga, which no one drove, dignified and happy, sat the young wife and her mother-in-law wrapped up in shawls. The young woman held a jug under her apron. Ilyúshka, bending over with his back to the horse, with ruddy face, shaking on the dasher, was munching a cracker[45] and talking in a steady stream. And the voices, and the rumble of the wheels on the bridge, and the occasional snorting of the horses, all united into one merry sound. The horses, switching their tails, trotted along steadily, feeling that they were on the home stretch. Those whom they passed and those whom they met looked upon a happy family.

Just as they were leaving the city the Dutlofs overtook a detachment of recruits. A group of the soldiers stood in a circle in front of a drinking-saloon. One recruit, with that peculiarly unnatural expression which a shorn brow gives a man, with his gray uniform cap pushed on the back of his head, was skilfully picking on a three-stringed balaláïka; another, without any thing on his head, and holding a jug of vodka in one hand, was dancing in the midst of the circle. Ignat halted his horse, and got out to gather up the reins. All the Dutlofs looked on with curiosity, satisfaction, and joy, at the man who was dancing.

The recruit did not seem to notice any one, but had the consciousness that an admiring public was attracted by his antics, and this gave him strength and ability. He danced dexterously. His forehead was wrinkled, his ruddy face was motionless, his mouth was parted in a smile which had long lost all expression. It seemed as though all the energies of his soul were directed to making one leg follow the other with all possible swiftness, now on the heel and now on the toe. Sometimes he would suddenly stop, and signal to the accompanist, who would instantly begin to thrum on all the strings, and even to rap on the back of the instrument with his knuckles. The recruit stopped, but even when he stopped still, he seemed, as it were, to be all the time dancing. Suddenly he began to slacken his pace, shrugging his shoulders, and, leaping into the air, landed on his heels, and with a wild shriek set up the Russian national dance.

The lads laughed, the women shook their heads, the lusty peasants smiled with satisfaction. An old non-commissioned officer stood calmly near the dancer with a look that said, "To you this is wonderful, but to us it's an old story." The balaláïka-player stood up in plain sight, surveyed the crowd with a cool stare, struck a false chord, and suddenly rapped his fingers on the back, and the dance was done.

"Hey! Alyókha," cried the accompanist to the dancer, and pointed to Dutlof. "Isn't that your sponsor?"

"Where? O my dearly beloved friend!" screamed the recruit,—the same one whom Dutlof had bought,—and stumbling out on his weary feet, and lifting his jug of vodka above his head, he made for the team. "Mishka! waiter! a glass," he shouted. "Master! O my dear old friend! How glad I am! fact!" he went on, jerking his tipsy head towards the telyéga, and began to treat the muzhíks and the women to vodka. The muzhíks accepted, the women declined. "You are darlings, why shouldn't I treat you?" cried the recruit, throwing his arms around the old women.

A woman peddling eatables was standing in the throng. The recruit saw her, grabbed her tray, and flung its contents into the telyéga.

"D-don't worry, I'll p-pay—the d-deuce," he began to scream in a drunken voice; and here he drew out of his stocking a purse with money in it, and flung it to the waiter.

He stood leaning with his elbows on the wagon, and stared, with moist eyes, at those who sat in it.

"Which is my mátushka?" he asked. "Be you her? I've got something for her too."

He pondered a moment, and diving into his pocket brought out a new handkerchief folded, untied another which he had put on as a girdle under his coat, hastily took the red scarf from his neck, bundled them together, and thrust them into the old woman's lap.

"Na! I give 'em to you," he said, in a voice that grew weaker and weaker.

"Why? thank you, friend!—What a simple lad he is!" said she, addressing the old man Dutlof, who came up to their telyéga.

The recruit was now entirely quiet and dumb, and kept dropping his head lower and lower, as though he were going to sleep then and there.

"I'm going for you, I'm going to destruction for you," he repeated. "And so I make you a present."

"I s'pose he's really got a mother," cried some one in the crowd. "Fine young fellow! Too bad!"

The recruit lifted his head. "I've got a mother," he said. "I've got a father[46] too. They've all given me up, though. Listen, old woman!" he added, seizing Ilyushkin's mother by the hand. "I made you a present. Listen to me, for Christ's sake. Go to my village of Vodnoe, ask there for Nikonof's old woman,—she's my own mother, you understand,—and tell this same old woman, Nikonof's old woman—third hut at the end—new pump—tell her that Alyókha—your son—you know—Come! musician, strike up!" he screamed.

And once more he began to dance, talking all the time, and spilling the vodka that was left in the jug all over the ground.

Ignat climbed into his wagon, and started to drive on.

"Good-by, good luck to you," cried the old woman, as she wrapped herself up in her sheepskin.

The recruit suddenly stopped.

"Go to the devil!" he shouted, threatening the teams with his doubled fist.

"Oh, good Lord!"[47] ejaculated Ilyushkin's mother, crossing herself.

Ignat started up the mare, and the teams drove away. Alekséi the recruit still stood in the middle of the road, and doubling up his fists, with an expression of wrath on his face, berated the mushíks to the best of his ability.

"What are you standing here for? She's gone. The devil, cannibals!" he screamed. "You won't escape from me! You devils! You dotards!"

With these words his voice failed him; he fell at full length, just where he stood in the middle of the road.

Swiftly the Dutlofs drove across the country, and as they looked around, the crowd of recruits were already lost from sight. When they had gone five versts, and were slowing up a little, Ignat got out of his father's wagon, when the old man was drowsing, and got in with his cousin.

The two young men drank up the jug of vodka which they had brought from the city. Then after a little, Ilya struck up a song; the women joined in with him; Ignat gayly shouted in harmony. A jolly party, in a post-wagon, dashed swiftly by. The driver shouted to the horses harnessed to the two jolly telyégas. The postilion glanced at the handsome faces of the muzhíks and the women in the telyéga as they dashed by, singing their merry songs, and waved his hand.

[32] izbá.

[33] Ilyushkin's baba.

[34] Ilyushkina baba.

[35] stárosta.

[36] dvor.

[37] khozyáïn.

[38] molodáïka.

[39] khozhyáïn.

[40] a meshchánin.

[41] Mispronunciation of quittance.

[42] starik-khozhyáïn.

[43] izbá.

[44] khozyáïka.

[45] kalátch.

[46] bátiushka.

[47] okh Gospodi.

KHOLSTOMÍR.

THE HISTORY OF A HORSE.[1]

(1861.)

I.

Constantly higher and higher the sky lifted itself, wider and wider spread the dawn, whiter and whiter grew the unpolished silver of the dew, more and more lifeless the sickle of the moon, more vocal the forest. The men began to arise; and at the stables belonging to the bárin were heard with increasing frequency the whinnying of the horses, the stamping of hoofs on the straw, and also the angry, shrill neighing of the animals collecting together, and even disputing with each other over something.

"Noo! you got time enough; mighty hungry, ain't you?" said the old drover, quickly opening the creaking gates. "Where you going?" he shouted, waving his hands at a mare which tried to run through the gate.

Nester, the drover, was dressed in a Cossack coat,[2] with a decorated leather belt around his waist; his knout was slung over his shoulder, and a handkerchief, containing some bread, was tied into his belt. In his arms he carried a saddle and halter.

The horses were not in the least startled, nor did they show any resentment, at the drover's sarcastic tone: they made believe that it was all the same to them, and leisurely moved back from the gate,—all except one old dark-bay mare, with a long flowing mane, who laid back her ears and quickly turned around. At this opportunity a young mare, who was standing behind, and had nothing at all to do with this, whinnied, and began to kick at the first horse that she fell in with.

"No!" shouted the drover still more loudly and angrily, and turned to the corner of the yard.[3]

Out of all the horses,—there must have been nearly a hundred—that were moving off toward their breakfast, none manifested so little impatience as a piebald gelding, which stood alone in one corner under the shed, and gazed with half-shut eyes, and bit on the oaken lining of the shed.

It is hard to say what enjoyment the piebald gelding got from this, but his expression while doing so was solemn and thoughtful.

"Nonsense!" again cried the drover in the same tone, turning to him; and going up to him he laid the saddle and shiny blanket on a pile of manure near him.

The piebald gelding ceased biting, and looked long at Nester without moving. He did not manifest any sign of mirth or anger or sullenness, but only drew in his whole belly and sighed heavily, heavily, and then turned away. The drover took him by the neck, and gave him his breakfast.

"What are you sighing for?" asked Nester.

The horse switched his tail as though to say, "Well, it's nothing, Nester." Nester put on the blanket and saddle, whereupon the horse pricked up his ears, expressing as plainly as could be his disgust; but he received nothing but execrations for this "rot," and then the saddle-girth was pulled tight.

At this the gelding tried to swell out; but his mouth was thrust open, and a knee was pressed into his side, so that he was forced to let out his breath. Notwithstanding this, when they got the bit between his teeth, he still pricked back his ears, and even turned round. Though he knew that this was of no avail, yet he seemed to reckon it essential to express his displeasure, and always showed it. When he was saddled, he pawed with his swollen right leg, and began to champ the bit,—here also for some special reason, because it was full time for him to know that there could be no taste in bits.

Nester mounted the gelding by the short stirrups, unwound his knout, freed his Cossack coat from under his knee, settled down in the saddle in that position peculiar to coachmen, hunters, and drivers, and twitched on the reins. The gelding lifted his head, showing a disposition to go where he should be directed, but he stirred not from the spot. He knew that before he went there would be much shouting on the part of him who sat on his back, and many orders to be given to Vaska, the other drover, and to the horses. In fact Nester began to shout, "Vaska! ha, Vaska! have you let out any of the mares,—hey? Where are you, you old devil? No-o! Are you asleep? Open the gate. Let the mares go first," and so on.

The gates creaked. Vaska, morose, and still full of sleep, holding a horse by the bridle, stood at the gate-post and let the horses out. The horses, one after the other, gingerly stepping over the straw and sniffing it, began to pass out,—the young fillies, the yearlings, the little colts; while the mares with young stepped along needfully, one at a time, avoiding all contact. The young fillies sometimes crowded in two at once, three at once, throwing their heads across each other's backs, and hitting their hoofs against the gates, each time receiving a volley of abuse from the drovers. The colts sometimes kicked the mares whom they did not know, and whinnied loudly in answer to the short neighing of their mothers.

A young filly, full of wantonness, as soon as she got outside the gate, tossed her head up and around, began to back, and whinnied, but nevertheless did not venture to dash ahead of the old gray, grain-bestrewed Zhuldiba, who, with a gentle but solid step, swinging her belly from side to side, was always the dignified leader of the other horses.

After a few moments the lively yard was left in melancholy loneliness; the posts stood out in sadness under the empty sheds, and only the sodden straw, soiled with dung, was to be seen.

Familiar as this picture of emptiness was to the piebald gelding, it seemed to have a melancholy effect upon him. He slowly, as though making a bow, lowered and lifted his head, sighed as deeply as the tightly drawn girth permitted, and dragging his somewhat bent and decrepit legs, he started off after the herd, carrying the old Nester on his bony back.

"I know now. As soon as we get out on the road, he will go to work to make a light, and smoke his wooden pipe with its copper mounting and chain," thought the gelding. "I am glad of this, because it is early in the morning and the dew is on the grass, and this odor is agreeable to me, and brings up many pleasant recollections. I am sorry only that when the old man has his pipe in his mouth he always becomes excited, gets to imagining things, and sits on one side, far over on one side, and on that side it always hurts. However, God be with him. It's no new thing for me to suffer for the sake of others. I have even come to find some equine satisfaction in this. Let him play that he's cock of the walk, poor fellow; but it's for his own pleasure that he looks so big, since no one sees him at all. Let him ride sidewise," said the horse to himself; and, stepping gingerly on his crooked legs, he walked along the middle of the road.

[1] Dedicated to the memory of M. A. Stakhovitch, the originator of the subject, which was given by his brother to Count Tolstoi.

[2] kasakín.

[3] dvor.

II.

After driving the herd down to the river, near which the horses were to graze, Nester dismounted and took off the saddle. Meantime the herd began slowly to scatter over the as yet untrodden field, covered with dew and with vapor rising alike from the damp meadow and the river that encircled it.

Taking off the blanket from the piebald gelding, Nester scratched him on his neck; and the horse in reply expressed his happiness and satisfaction by shutting his eyes.

"The old dog likes it," said Nester.

The gelding really did not like this scratching very much, and only out of delicacy intimated that it was agreeable to him. He shook his head as a sign of assent. But suddenly, unexpectedly, and without any reason, Nester, imagining perhaps that too great familiarity might give the horse false ideas about what he meant,—Nester, without any warning, pushed away his head, and, lifting up the bridle, struck the horse very severely with the buckle on his bare leg, and, without saying any thing, went up the hillock to a stump, near which he sat down as though nothing had happened.

Though this proceeding incensed the gelding, he did not manifest it;

and leisurely switching his thin tail, and sniffing at something, and merely for recreation cropping at the grass, he wandered down toward the river.

Not paying any heed to the antics played around him by the young fillies, the colts, and the yearlings, and knowing that the health of everybody, and especially one who had attained his years, was subserved by getting a good drink of water on an empty stomach, and then eating, he turned his steps to where the bank was less steep and slippery; and wetting his hoofs and gambrels, he thrust his snout into the river, and began to suck the water through his lips drawn back, to puff with his distending sides, and out of pure satisfaction to switch his thin, piebald tail with its leathery stump.

A chestnut filly, always mischievous, always nagging the old horse, and causing him manifold unpleasantnesses, came down to the water as though for her own necessities, but really merely for the sake of roiling the water in front of his nose.

But the gelding had already drunk enough, and apparently giving no thought to the impudent mare, calmly put one miry leg before the other, shook his head, and, turning aside from the wanton youngster, began to eat. Dragging his legs in a peculiar manner, and not tramping down the abundant grass, the horse grazed for nearly three hours, scarcely stirring from the spot. Having eaten so much that his belly hung down like a bag from his thin, sharp ribs, he stood solidly on his four weak legs, so that as little strain as possible might come on any one of them,—at least on the right foreleg, which was weaker than all,—and went to sleep.

There is an honorable old age, there is a miserable old age, there is a pitiable old age; there is also an old age that is both honorable and miserable. The old age which the piebald gelding had reached was of this latter sort.

The old horse was of a great size,—more than seventeen hands high.[4] His color was white, spotted with black; at least, it used to be so, but now the black spots had changed to a dirty brown. The regions of black spots were three in number: one on the head, including the mane, and side of the nose, the star on the forehead, and half of the neck; the long mane, tangled with burrs, was striped white and brownish; the second spotted place ran along the right side, and covered half the belly; the third was on the flank, including the upper part of the tail and half of the loins; the rest of the tail was whitish, variegated.

The huge, corrugated head, with deep hollows under the eyes, and with pendent black lips, somewhat lacerated, sat heavily and draggingly on the neck, which bent under its leanness, and seemed to be made of wood. From under the pendent lip could be seen the dark-red tongue protruding on one side, and the yellow, worn tusks of his lower teeth. His ears, one of which was slit, fell over sidewise, and only occasionally he twitched them a little to scare away the sticky flies. One long tuft still remaining of the forelock hung behind the ears; the broad forehead was hollowed and rough; the skin hung loose on the big cheek-bones. On the neck and head the veins stood out in knots, trembling and twitching whenever a fly touched them. The expression of his face was sternly patient, deeply thoughtful, and expressive of pain.

His forelegs were crooked at the knees. On both hoofs were swellings; and on the one which was half covered by the marking, there was near the knee at the back a sore boil. The hind legs were in better condition, but there had been severe bruises long before on the haunches, and the hair did not grow on those places. His legs seemed disproportionately long, because his body was so emaciated. His ribs, though also thick, were so exposed and drawn that the hide seemed dried in the hollows between them.

The back and withers were variated with old scars, and behind was still a freshly galled and purulent slough. The black stump of the tail, where the vertebræ could be counted, stood out long and almost bare. On the brown flank near the tail, where it was overgrown with white hairs, was a scar as big as one's hand, that must have been from a bite. Another cicatrice was to be seen on the off shoulder. The houghs of the hind legs and the tail were foul with excrement. The hair all over the body, though short, stood out straight.

But in spite of the filthy old age to which this horse had come, any one looking at him would have involuntarily thought, and a connoisseur would have said immediately, that he must have been in his day a remarkably fine horse. The connoisseur would have said also that there was only one breed in Russia[5] that could give such broad bones, such huge joints, such hoofs, such slender leg-bones, such an arched neck, and, most of all, such a skull,— eyes large, black, and brilliant, and such a thoroughbred network of nerves over his head and neck, and such delicate skin and hair.

In reality there was something noble in the form of this horse, and in the terrible union in him of the repulsive signs of decrepitude, the increased variegatedness of his hide, and his actions, and the expression of self-dependence, and the calm consciousness of beauty and strength.

Like a living ruin he stood in the middle of the dewy field, alone; while not far away from him were heard the galloping, the neighing, the lively whinnying, the snorting, of the scattered herd.

[4] Two arshin, three vershoks,= 6.65 feet.

III.

The sun was now risen above the forest, and shone brightly on the grass and the winding river. The dew dried away and fell off in drops. Like smoke the last of the morning mist rolled up. Curly clouds made their appearance, but as yet there was no wind. On the other side of the gleaming river stood the rye, bending on its stalks, and the air was fragrant with bright verdure and the flowers. The cuckoo cooed from the forest with echoing voice; and Nester, lying flat on his back, was reckoning up how many years of life lay before him. The larks arose from the rye and the field. The belated hare stood up among the horses and leaped without restraint, and sat down by the copse and pricked up his ears to listen.

Vaska went to sleep, burying his head in the grass; the mares, making wide circuits around him, scattered themselves on the field below. The older ones, neighing, picked out a shining track across the dewy grass, and constantly tried to find some place where they might be undisturbed. They no longer grazed, but only nibbled on the sweet grass-blades. The whole herd was imperceptibly moving in one direction.

And again the old Zhuldiba, stately stepping before the others, showed how far it was possible to go. The young Mushka, who had cast her first foal, constantly hinnying, and lifting her tail, was scolding her violet-colored colt. The young Atlásnaya, with smooth and shining skin, dropping her head so that her black and silken forelock hid her forehead and eyes, was gambolling in the grass, nipping and tossing and stamping her leg, with its hairy fetlock. One of the older little colts,—he must have been imagining, some kind of game,—lifting, for the twenty-sixth time, his rather short and tangled tail, like a plume, gambolled around his dam, who calmly picked at the herbage, having evidently had time to sum up her son's character, and only occasionally stopping to look askance at him out of her big black eye.

One of these same young colts,—black as a coal, with a large head with a marvellous top-knot rising above his ears, and his tail still inclining to the side on which he had laid in his mother's belly—pricking up his ears, and opening his stupid eyes, as he stood motionless in his place, looked steadily at the colt jumping and dancing, not at all understanding why he did it, whether out of jealousy or indignation.

Some suckle, butting with their noses; others, for some unknown reason, notwithstanding their mothers' invitation, move along in a short, awkward trot, in a diametrically opposite direction, as though seeking something, and then, no one knows why, stop short and hinny in a desperately penetrating voice. Some lie on their sides in a row; some take lessons in grazing; some try to scratch themselves with their hind legs behind the ear.

Two mares, still with young, go off by themselves, and slowly moving their legs continue to graze. Evidently their condition is respected by the others, and none of the young colts ventures to go near or disturb them. If any saucy young steed takes it into his head to approach too near to them, then merely a motion of an ear or tail is sufficient to show him all the impropriety of his behavior.

The yearlings and the young fillies pretend to be full-grown and dignified, and rarely indulge in pranks, or join their gay companions. They ceremoniously nibble at the blades of grass, bending their swan-like, short-shorn necks, and, as though they also were blessed with tails, switch their little brushes. Just like the big horses, some of them lie down, roll over, and scratch each others' backs.

A very jolly band consists of the two-year-old and the three-year-old mares who have never foaled. They almost all wander off by themselves, and make a specially jolly virgin throng. Among them is heard a great tramping and stamping, hinnying and whinnying. They gather together, lay their heads over each others' shoulders, snuff the air, leap; and sometimes, lifting the tail like an oriflamme, proudly and coquettishly, in a half-trot, half-gallop, caracole in front of their companions.

Conspicuous for beauty and sprightly dashing ways, among all this young throng, was the wanton bay mare. Whatever she set on foot, the others also did; wherever she went, there in her track followed also the whole throng of beauties.

The wanton was in a specially playful frame of mind this morning. The spirit of mischief was in her, just as it sometimes comes upon men. Even at the river-side, playing her pranks upon the old gelding, she had galloped along in the water, pretending that something had scared her, snorting, and then dashed off at full speed across the field; so that Vaska was constrained to gallop after her, and after the others who were at her heels. Then, after grazing a little while, she began to roll, then to tease the old mares, by dashing in front of them. Then she separated a suckling colt from its dam, and began to chase after it, pretending that she wanted to bite it. The mother was frightened, and ceased to graze; the little colt squealed in piteous tones. But the wanton young mare did not touch it, but only scared it, and made a spectacle for her comrades, who looked with sympathy on her antics.

Then she set out to turn the head of the roan horse, which a muzhík, far away on the other side of the river, was driving with a plough in the rye-field. She stood proudly, somewhat on one side, lifting her head high, shook herself, and neighed in a sweet, significant, and alluring voice.

'Tis the time when the rail-bird, running from place to place among the thick reeds, passionately calls his mate; when also the cuckoo and the quail sing of love; and the flowers send to each other, on the breeze, their aromatic dust.

"And I am young and kind and strong," said the jolly wanton's neighing, "and till now it has not been given to me to experience the sweetness of this feeling, never yet to feel it; and no lover, no, not one, has yet come to woo me."

And the significant neighing rang with youthful melancholy over lowland and field, and it came to the ears of the roan horse far away. He pricked up his ears, and stopped. The muzhík kicked him with his wooden shoe; but the roan was bewitched by the silver sound of the distant neighing, and whinnied in reply. The muzhík grew angry, twitched him with the reins, and again kicked him in the belly with his bast shoe, so that he did not have a chance to complete all that he had to say in his neighing, but was forced to go on his way. And the roan horse felt a sweet sadness in his heart; and the sounds from the far-off rye-field, of that unfinished and passionate neigh, and the angry voice of the muzhík, long echoed in the ears of the herd.

If through one sound of her voice the roan horse could become so captivated as to forget his duty, what would have become of him if he had had full view of the beautiful wanton, as she stood pricking up her ears, inflating her nostrils, breathing in the air, and filled with longing, while her young and beauteous body trembled as she called to him?

But the wanton did not long ponder over her novel sensations. When the voice of the roan was still, she whinnied scornfully, and, sinking her head, began to paw the ground; and then she trotted off to wake up and tease the piebald gelding. The piebald gelding was a long-suffering butt for the amusement of this happy young wanton. She made him suffer more than men did. But in neither case did he give way to wrath. He was indispensable to men, but why should these young horses torment him?

IV.

He was old, they were young; he was lean, they were fat; he was sad, they were happy. So he was thoroughly strange, alien, an absolutely different creature; and it was impossible for them to have compassion on him. Horses have pity only on themselves, and rarely on those whose places they may easily come themselves to fill. But, indeed, was not the piebald gelding himself to blame, that he was old and gaunt and crippled?...

One would think that he was not to blame. But in equine ethics he was, and only those were right who were strong, young, and happy; those who had all life before them; those whose every muscle was tense with superfluous energy, and curled their tails into a wheel.

Maybe the piebald gelding himself understood this, and in tranquil moments was agreed that he was to blame because he had lived out all his life, that he must pay for his life; but he was after all only a horse, and he could not restrain himself often from feeling hurt, melancholy, and discontented, when he looked on all these young horses who tormented him for the very thing to which they would be subjected when they came to the end of their lives.

The reason for the heartlessness of these horses was a peculiarly aristocratic feeling. Every one of them was related, either on the side of father or mother, to the celebrated Smetanka; but it was not known from what stock the piebald gelding sprang. The gelding was a chance comer, bought at market three years before for eighty paper rubles.

The young chestnut mare, as though accidentally wandering about, came up to the piebald gelding's very nose, and brushed against him. He knew before-hand what it meant, and did not open his eyes, but laid back his ears and showed his teeth. The mare wheeled around, and made believe that she was going to let fly at him with her heels. He opened his eyes, and wandered off to another part. He had no desire to sleep, and began to crop the grass. Again the wanton young mare, accompanied by her confederates, went to the gelding. A two-year-old mare with a star on her forehead, very stupid, always in mischief, and always ready to imitate the chestnut mare, trotted along with her, and, as imitators always do, began to: play the same trick that the instigator had done.

The brown mare marched along at an ordinary gait, as though bent on her own affairs, and passed by the gelding's very nose, not looking at him, so that he really did not know whether to be angry or not; and this was the very fun of the thing.

This was what she did; but the starred mare following in her steps, and feeling very gay, hit the gelding on the chest. He showed his teeth once more, whinnied, and, with a quickness of motion unexpected on his part, sprang at the mare, and bit her on the flank. The young mare with the star flew out with her bind legs, and kicked the old horse heavily on his thin bare ribs. The old horse uttered a hoarse noise, and was about to make another lunge, but thought better of it, and sighing deeply turned away.

It must have been that all the young horses of the drove regarded as a personal insult the boldness which the piebald gelding permitted himself to show toward the starred mare; for all the rest of the day they gave him no chance to graze, and left him not a moment of peace, so that the drover several times rebuked them, and could not comprehend what they were doing.

The gelding was so abused that he himself walked up to Nester when it was time for the old man to drive back the drove, and he showed greater happiness and content when Nester saddled him and mounted him.

God knows what the old gelding's thoughts were as he bore on his back the old man Nester. Did he think with bitterness of these importunate and merciless youngsters? or, with a scornful and silent pride peculiar to old age, did he pardon his persecutors? At all events, he did not make manifest any of his thoughts till he reached home.

That evening some cronies had come to see Nester; and as the horses were driven by the huts of the domestics, he noticed a horse and telyéga standing at his doorstep. After he had driven in the horses, he was in such a hurry that he did not take the saddle off: he left the gelding at the yard,[5] and shouted to Vaska to unsaddle the animal, then shut the gate, and hurried to his friends.

Perhaps owing to the affront put upon the starred mare, the descendant of Smetanka, by that "low trash" bought for a horse, and not knowing father or mother, and therefore offending the aristocratic sentiment of the whole community; or because the gelding with the high saddle without a rider presented a strangely fantastic spectacle for the horses,—at all events, that night something extraordinary took place in the paddock. All the horses, young and old, showing their teeth, tagged after the gelding, and drove him from one part of the yard to the other; the trampling of their hoofs echoed around him as he sighed and drew in his thin sides.

The gelding could not longer endure this, could not longer avoid their kicks. He halted in the middle of the field: his face expressed the repulsive, weak anger of helpless old age, and despair besides. He laid back his ears, and suddenly[6] something happened that caused all the horses suddenly to become quiet. A very old mare, Viazopúrikha, came up and sniffed the gelding, and sighed. The gelding also sighed.

. . . .

[5] dvor.

[6] So in the original.

V.

In the middle of the yard, flooded with the moonlight, stood the tall, gaunt figure of the gelding, still wearing the high saddle with its prominent pommel. The horses, motionless and in deep silence, stood around him, as though they were learning something new and extraordinary from him. And, indeed, something new and extraordinary they learned from him.

This is what they learned from him:—

. . . .

. . . .

FIRST NIGHT.

"Yes, I was sired by Liubeznuï I. Baba was my dam. According to the genealogy my name is Muzhík I. Muzhík I., I am according to my pedigree; but generally I am known as Kholstomír, on account of a long and glorious gallop, the like of which never took place in Russia. In lineage no horse in the world stands higher than I, for good blood. I would never have told you this. Why should I? You would never have known me as Viazopúrikha knew me when we used to be together at Khrénova, and who only just now recognized me. You would not have believed me had it not been for Viazopúrikha's witness, and I would never have told you this. I do not need the pity of my kind. But you insisted upon it. Well, I am that Kholstomír whom the amateurs are seeking for and cannot find, that Kholstomír whom the count himself named, and whom he let go from his stud because I outran his favorite 'Lebedi.'

. . . .

. . . .

"When I was born I did not know what they meant when they called me a piebald;[7] I thought that I was a horse. The first remark made about my hide, I remember, deeply surprised me and my dam.

"I must have been foaled in the night. In the morning, licked clean by my dam's tongue, I stood on my legs. I remember all my sensations, and that every thing seemed to me perfectly wonderful, and, at the same time, perfectly simple. Our stalls were in a long, warm corridor, with latticed gates, through which nothing could be seen.

"My dam tempted me to suckle; but I was so innocent as yet that I bunted her with my nose, now under her fore-legs, now in other places. Suddenly my dam gazed at the latticed gate, and, throwing her leg over me, stepped to one side. One of the grooms was looking in at us through the lattice.

"'See, Baba has foaled!' he exclaimed, and began to draw the bolt. He came in over the straw bed, and took me up in his arms. 'Come and look, Taras!' he cried; 'see what a piebald colt, a perfect magpie!'

"I tore myself away from him, and fell on my knees.

"'See, a perfect little devil!' he said.

"My dam became disquieted; but she did not take my part, and merely drew a long, long breath, and stepped to one side. The grooms came, and began to look at me. One ran to tell the equerry.

"All laughed as they looked at my spotting, and gave me various odd names. I did not understand these names, nor did my dam either. Up to that time in all my family there had never been a single piebald known. We had no idea that there was any thing disgraceful in it. And then all examined my structure and strength.

"See what a lively one!" said the hostler. 'You can't hold him.'

"In a little while came the equerry, and began to marvel at my coloring. He also seemed disgusted.

"'What a nasty beast!' he cried. 'The general will not keep him in the stud. Ekh! Baba, you have caused me much trouble,' he said, turning to my dam. 'You ought to have foaled a colt with a star, but this is completely piebald.'

"My dam vouchsafed no answer, and, as always in such circumstances, merely sighed again.

"'What kind of a devil was his sire? A regular muzhík!' he went on to say. 'It is impossible to keep him in the stud; it's a shame! But we'll see, we'll see,' said he; and all said the same as they looked at me.

"After a few days the general himself came. He took a look at me, and again all seemed horror-struck, and scolded me and my mother also on account of my hide. 'But we'll see, we'll see,' said every one, as soon as they caught sight of me.

"Until spring we young colts lived in separate cells with our dams; only occasionally, when the snow on the roof of the sheds began to melt in the sun, they would let us out into the wide yard, spread with fresh straw. There for the first time I became acquainted with all my kin, near and remote. There I saw how from different doors issued all the famous mares of that time with their colts. There was the old Holland mare, Mushka, sired by Smetankin, Krasnukha, the saddle-horse Dobrokhotíkha, all celebrities at that time. All gathered together there with their colts, walked up and down in the sunshine, rolled over on the fresh straw, and sniffed of each other like ordinary horses.

"I cannot even now forget the sight of that paddock, full of the beauties of that day. It may seem strange to you to think of me as ever having been young and frisky, but I used to be. This very same Viazopúrikha was there then, a yearling, whose mane had just been cut,[8]—a kind, jolly, frolicsome little horse. But let it not be taken as unkindly meant when I say, that, though she is now considered a rarity among you on account of her pedigree, then she was only one of the meanest horses of that stud. She herself will corroborate this.

"Though my coat of many colors had been displeasing to the men, it was exceedingly attractive to all the horses. They all stood round me, expressing their delight, and frisking with me. I even began to forget the words of the men about my hide, and felt happy. But I soon experienced the first sorrow of my life, and the cause of it was my dam. As soon as it began to thaw, and the swallows chirped on the roof, and the spring made itself felt more and more in the air, my dam began to change in her behavior toward me.

"Her whole character was transformed. Suddenly, without any reason, she began to frisk, galloping around the yard, which certainly did not accord with her dignified growth; then she would pause and consider, and begin to whinny; then she would bite and kick her sister mares; then she began to smell of me, and neigh with dissatisfaction; then trotting out into the sun she would lay her head across the shoulder of my two-year-old sister Kúpchika, and long and earnestly scratch her back, and push me away from nursing her. One time the equerry came, commanded the halter to be put on her, and they led her out of the paddock. She whinnied; I replied to her, and darted after her, but she would not even look at me. The groom Taras seized me in both arms, just as they shut the door on my mother's retreating form.

"I struggled, threw the groom on the straw; but the door was closed, and I only heard my mother's whinnying growing fainter and fainter. And in this whinnying I perceived that she called not for me, but I perceived a very different expression. In reply to her voice, there was heard in the distance a mighty voice.

"I don't remember how Taras got out of my stall; it was too grievous for me. I felt that I had forever lost my mother's love; and wholly because I was a piebald, I said to myself, remembering what the people said of my hide; and such passionate anger came over me, that I began to pound the sides of the stall with my head and feet, and I pounded them until the sweat poured from me, and I could not stand up from exhaustion.

"After some time my dam returned to me. I heard her as she came along the corridor in a prancing trot, wholly unusual to her, and entered our stall. The door was opened for her. I did not recognize her, so much younger and handsomer had she grown. She snuffed at me, neighed, and began to snort. But in her whole expression I could see that she did not love me.

"Soon they led us to pasture. I now began to experience new pleasures which consoled me for the loss of my mother's love. I had friends and companions. We learned together to eat grass, to neigh like the old horses, and to lift our tails and gallop in wide circles around our dams. This was a happy time. Every thing was forgiven to me; all loved me, and were loved by me, and looked indulgently on all that I did. This did not last long.

"Here something terrible happened to me."

The gelding sighed deeply, deeply, and moved aside from the horses.

The dawn was already far advanced. The gates creaked. Nester came. The horses scattered. The drover straightened the saddle on the gelding's back, and drove away the horses.

[7] pyégi.

[8] All expressed in the word strigúnchik.

VI.

SECOND NIGHT.

As soon as the horses were driven in, they once more gathered around the piebald.

"In the month of August," continued the horse, u I was separated from my mother, and I did not experience any unusual grief. I saw that she was already suckling a small brother,—the famous Usan,—and I was not what I had been before. I was not jealous, but I felt that I had become more than ever cool toward her. Besides, I knew that in leaving my mother I should be transferred to the general division of young horses, where we were stalled in twos and threes, and every day all went out to exercise.

I was in one stall with Milui. Milui was a saddle-horse, and afterwards belonged to the emperor himself, and was put into pictures and statuary. At that time he was a mere colt, with a shiny soft coat, a swan-like neck, and slender straight legs. He was always lively, good-natured, and lovable; was always ready to frisk, and be caressed, and sport with either horse or man. He and I could not help being good friends, living together as we did; and our friendship lasted till we grew up. He was gay, and inclined to be wanton. Even then he began to feel the tender passion to disport with the fillies, and he used to make sport of my guilelessness. To my unhappiness I myself, out of egotism, tried to follow his example, and very soon was in love. And this early inclination of mine was the cause, in great measure, of my fate.

"But I am not going to relate all the story of my unhappy first love; she herself remembers my stupid passion, which ended for me in the most important change in my life.

"The drovers came along, drove her away, and pounded me. In the evening they led me into a special stall. I whinnied the whole night long, as though with a presentiment of what was coming on the morrow.

"In the morning the general, the equerry, the under grooms, and the hostlers came into the corridor where my stall was, and set up a terrible screaming. The general screamed to the head groom; the groom justified himself, saying that he had not given orders to send me away, but that the under grooms had done it of their own free will. The general said that it had spoiled every thing, but that it was impossible to keep young stallions. The head groom replied that he would have it attended to. They calmed down and went out, I did not understand it at all,—except that something concerning me was under consideration.

. . . .

. . . .

"On the next day I had ceased forever to whinny; I became what I am now. All the light of my eyes was quenched. Nothing seemed sweet to me; I became self-absorbed, and began to be pensive. At first I felt indifferent to every thing. I ceased even to eat, to drink, and to run; and all thought of sprightly sport was gone. Then it nevermore came into my mind to kick up my heels, to roll over, to whinny, without bringing up the terrible question,—Why? for what purpose?' And my vigor died away.

"Once they led me out at eventide, at the time when they were driving the stud home from the field. From afar I saw already the cloud of dust in which could be barely distinguished the familiar lineaments of all of our mothers. I heard the cheerful snorting, and the trampling of hoofs. I stopped short, though the halter-rope by which the groom held me cut my neck; and I gazed at the approaching drove as one gazes at happiness that is lost forever and will ne'er return again. They drew near, and my eyes fell upon forms so well known to me,—beautiful, grand, plump, full of life every one. Who among them all deigned to glance at me? I did not feel the pain that the groom in pulling the rope inflicted. I forgot myself, and involuntarily tried to whinny as of yore, and to gallop off; but my whinnying sounded melancholy, ridiculous, and unbecoming. There was no ribaldry among the stud, but I noticed that many of them from politeness turned away from me.

"It was evident that in their eyes I was despicable and pitiable, and worst of all ridiculous. My slender, weakly neck, my big head (I had become thin), my long, thick legs, and the awkward gait that I struck up, in my old fashion, around the groom, all must have seemed absurd to them. No one heeded my whinnying, all turned away from me.

"Suddenly I comprehended it all, comprehended how I was forever sundered from them, every one; and I know not how I stumbled home behind the groom.

"I had already shown a tendency toward gravity and thoughtfulness; but now a decided change came over me. My variegated coat, which occasioned such a strange prejudice in men, my terrible and unexpected unhappiness, and, moreover, my peculiarly isolated position in the stud—which I felt, but could never explain to myself—compelled me to turn my thoughts inward upon myself. I pondered on the disgust that people showed when they berated me for being a piebald; I pondered on the inconstancy of maternal and especially of female affection, and its dependence upon physical conditions; and, above all, I pondered on the characteristics of that strange race of mortals with whom we are so closely bound, and whom we call men,—those characteristics which were the source of the peculiarity of my position in the stud, felt by me but incomprehensible.

"The significance of this, peculiarity, and of the human characteristics on which it was based, was discovered to me by the following incident:—

"It was winter, at Christmas-tide. All day long no fodder had been given to me, nor had I been led out to water. I afterwards learned that this arose from our groom being drunk. On this day the equerry came to me, saw that I had no food, and began to use hard language about the missing groom, and went %way.

"On the next day, the groom with his mates came out to our stalls to give us some hay. I noticed that he was especially pale and glum, and in the expression of his long back there was a something significant and demanding sympathy.

"He austerely flung the hay behind the grating. I laid my head over his shoulder; but he struck me such a hard blow with his fist on the nose, that I started back. Then he kicked me in the belly with his boot.

"'If it hadn't been for this scurvy beast,' said he, 'there wouldn't have been any trouble.'

"'Why?' asked another groom.

"'He doesn't come to inquire about the count's you bet! But twice a day he comes out to look after his own.'

"'Have they given him the piebald?' inquired another.

"'Whether they've given it to him or sold it to him, the dog only knows! The count's might die o' starvation—it wouldn't make any difference; but see how it upset him when I didn't give his horse his fodder! 'Go to bed,' says he, 'and then you'll get a basting.' No Christianity in it. More pity on the cattle than on a man. I don't believe he's ever been christened, he himself counted the blows, the barbarian! The general did not use the whip so. He made my back all welts. There's no soul of a Christian in him!'

"Now, what they said about whips and Christianity, I understood well enough; but it was perfectly dark to me as to the meaning of the words, my horse, his horse, by which I perceived that men understood some sort of bond between me and the groom. Wherein consisted this bond, I could not then understand at all. Only long after, when I was separated from the other horses, I came to learn what it meant. At that time I could not understand at all that it meant that they considered me the property of a man. To say my horse in reference to me, a live horse, seemed to me as strange as to say, my earth, my atmosphere, my water.

"But these words had a monstrous influence upon me. I pondered upon them ceaselessly; and only after long and varied relations with men did I come at last to comprehend the meaning that men find in these strange words.

"The meaning is this: Men rule in life, not by deeds, but by words. They love not so much the possibility of doing or not doing any thing, as the possibility of talking about different objects in words agreed upon between them. Such words, considered very important among them, are the words, my, mine, ours, which they employ for various things, beings, and objects; even for the earth, people, and horses. In regard to any particular thing, they agree that only one person shall say 'It is mine.' And he who in this play, which they engage in, can say mine in regard to the greatest number of things, is considered the most fortunate among them. Why this is so, I know not; but it is so. Long before, I had tried to explain this to my satisfaction, by some direct advantage; but it seemed that I was wrong.

"Many of the men who, for instance, called me their horse, did not ride on me, but entirely different men rode on me. They themselves did not feed me, but entirely different people fed me. Again, it was not those who called me their horse who treated me kindly, but the coachman, the veterinary, and, as a general thing, outside men.

"Afterwards, as I widened the sphere of my experiences, I became convinced that the concept my, as applied not only to us horses, but to other things, has no other foundation than a low and animal, a human instinct, which they call the sentiment or right of property. Man says, my house, and never lives in it, but is only cumbered with the building and maintenance of it. The merchant says, my shop,—my clothing-shop, for example,—and he does not even wear clothes made of the best cloth in the shop.

"There are people who call land theirs, and have never seen their land, and have never been on it. There are men who call other people theirs, but have never seen these people; and the whole relationship of these owners, to these people, consists in doing them harm.

"There are men who call women theirs,—their wives or mistresses; but these women live with other men. And men struggle in life not to do what they consider good, but to be possessors of what they call their own.

"I am convinced now that herein lies the substantial difference between men and us. And, therefore, not speaking of other things, where we are superior to men, we are able boldly to say that in this one respect at least, we stand, in the scale of living beings, higher than men. The activity of men—at all events, of those with whom I have had to do—is guided by words; ours, by deeds.

"And here the head groom obtained this right to say about me, my horse; and hence he lashed the hostler. This discovery deeply disturbed me; and those thoughts and opinions which my variegated coat aroused in men, and the thoughtfulness aroused in me by the change in my mother, together subserved to make me into that solemn and contemplative gelding that I am.

"I was threefold unhappy: I was piebald; I was a gelding; and men imagined that I did not belong to God and myself, as is the prerogative of every living thing, but that I belonged to the equerry.

"The consequences of their imagining this about me were many. The first was, that they kept me apart from the others, fed me better, led me more often, and harnessed me up earlier. They harnessed me first when I was in my third year. I remember the first time, the equerry himself, who imagined that I was his, began, with a crowd of grooms, to harness me, expecting from me some ebullition of temper or contrariness. They put leather straps on me, and conducted me into the stalls. They laid on my back a wide leather cross, and attached it to the thills, so that I should not kick; but I was only waiting an opportunity to show my gait, and my love for work.

"They marvelled because I went like an old horse. They began to drive me, and I began to practise trotting. Every day I made greater and greater improvement, so that in three months the general himself, and many others, praised my gait. But this was a strange thing: for the very reason that they imagined that I was the equerry's, and not theirs, my gait had for them an entirely different significance.

"The stallions, my brothers, were put through their paces; their time was reckoned; people came to see them; they were driven in gilded drozhkies. Costly saddles were put upon them. But I was driven in the equerry's simple drozhkies, when he had business at Chesmenka and other manor-houses. All this resulted from the fact that I was piebald, but more than all from the fact that I was, according to their idea, not the property of the count, but of the equerry.

"To-morrow, if we are alive, I will tell you what a serious influence upon me was exercised by this right of proprietorship which the equerry arrogated to himself."

All that day the horses treated Kholstomír with great consideration; but Nester, from old custom, rode him into the field. But Nester's ways were so rough! The muzhík's gray stallion, coming toward the drove, whinnied: and again the chestnut filly coquettishly replied to him.

VII.

THIRD NIGHT.

The moon had quartered; and her narrow band poured a mild light on Kholstomír, standing in the middle of the yard, with the horses clustered around him.

"The principal and most surprising consequence to me of the fact that I was not the property of the count nor of God, but of the equerry," continued the piebald, "was that what constitutes our chief activity—the eager race—was made the cause of my banishment. They were driving Lebedi around the ring; and a jockey from Chesmenka was riding me, and entered the course. Lebedi dashed past us. He trotted well, but he seemed to want to show off. He had not that skill which I had cultivated in myself; that is, of compelling one leg instantly to follow on the motion of the other, and not to waste the least degree of energy, but use it all in pressing forward. Lebedi dashed by us. I entered the ring: the jockey did not hold me back.

"'Say, will you time my piebald?' he cried; and when Lebedi came abreast of us a second time, he let me out. He had the advantage of his momentum, and so I was left behind in the first heat; but in the second I began to gain on him; came up to him in the drozhsky, caught up with him, passed beyond him, and won the race. They tried it a second time—the same thing. I was the swifter. And this filled them all with dismay. The general begged them to send me away as soon as possible, so that I might not be heard of again. 'Otherwise the count will know about it, and there will be trouble,' said he. And they sent me to the horse-dealer. I did not remain there long. A hussar, who came along to get a remount, bought me. All this had been so disagreeable, so cruel, that I was glad when they took me from Khrénova, and forever separated me from all that had been near and dear to me. It was too hard for me among them. Before them stood love, honor, freedom; before me labor, humiliation,—humiliation, labor, to the end of my days. Why? Because I was piebald, and because I was compelled to be somebody's horse."

VIII.

FOURTH NIGHT.

The next evening when the gates were closed, and all was still, the piebald continued thus:—

"I had many experiences, both among men and among my own kind, while changing about from hand to hand. I staid with two masters the longest: with the prince, the officer of the hussars, and then with an old man who lived at Nikola Yavleonoï Church.

"I spent the happiest days of my life with the hussar.

"Though he was the cause of my destruction, though he loved nothing and nobody, yet I loved him, and still love him, for this very reason.

"He pleased me precisely, because he was handsome, fortunate, rich, and therefore loved no one.

"You are familiar with this lofty equine sentiment of ours. His coldness, and my dependence upon him, added greatly to the strength of my affection for him. Because he beat me, and drove me to death, I used to think in those happy days, for that very reason I was all the happier.

"He bought me of the horse-dealer to whom the equerry had sold me, for eight hundred rubles. He bought me because there was no demand for piebald horses. Those were my happiest days.

"He had a mistress. I knew it because every day I took him to her; and I took her out driving, and sometimes took them together.

"His mistress was a handsome woman, and he was handsome, and his coachman was handsome; and I loved them all because they were. And life was worth living then.

"This is the way that my life was spent: In the morning the man came to groom me,—not the coachman, but the groom. The groom was a young lad, taken from among the muzhíks. He would open the door, let the wind drive out the steam from the horses, shovel out the manure, take off the blanket, begin to flourish the brush over my body, and with the curry-comb to brush out the scruff on the floor of the stall, marked by the stamping of hoofs. I would make believe bite his sleeves, would push him with my leg.

"Then we were led out, one after the other, to drink from a tub of cold water; and the youngster admired my sleek spotted coat, my legs straight as an arrow, my broad hoofs, my polished flank, and back wide enough to sleep on. Then he would throw the hay behind the broad rack, and pour the oats into the oaken cribs. Then Feofán and the old coachman would come.

"The master and the coachman were alike. Neither the one nor the other feared any one or loved any one except themselves, and therefore everybody loved them. Feofán came in a red shirt, plush breeches, and coat. I used to like to hear him when, all pomaded for a holiday, he would come to the stable in his coat, and cry,—

"'Well, cattle, are you asleep?' and poke me in the loin with the handle of his fork; but never so as to hurt, only in fun. I could instantly take a joke, and I would lay back my ears and show my teeth.

"We had a chestnut stallion that belonged to a pair. Sometimes they would harness us together. This Polkan could not understand a joke, and was simply ugly as the devil. I used to stand in the next stall to him, and feel seriously pained. Feofán was not afraid of him. He used to go straight up to him, shout to him,—it seemed as though he were going to kick him,—but no, straight by, and put on the halter.

"Once we ran away together, in a pair, over the Kuznetskoë. Neither the master nor the coachman was frightened; they laughed, they shouted to the people, and they sawed on the reins and pulled up, and so I did not run over anybody.

"In their service I expended my best qualities, and half of my life. Then I was given too much water to drink, and my legs gave out.... But in spite of every thing, that was the best part of my life. At twelve they would come, harness us, oil my hoofs, moisten my forelock and mane, and put us between the thills.

"The sledge was of cane, plaited, upholstered in velvet. The harness had little silver buckles, the reins of silk, and once I wore a fly-net. The whole harness was such, that, when all the straps and belts were put on and drawn, it was impossible to make out where the harness ended and the horse began. They would finish harnessing in the shed. Feofán would come out, his middle wider than his shoulders, with his red girdle under his arms. He would inspect the harness, take his seat, straighten his kaftan, put his foot in the stirrup, get off some joke, always crack his whip, though he scarcely ever touched me with it,—merely for form's sake,—and cry, 'Now off with you!'[9] And frisking at every step, I would prance out of the gate; and the cook, coming out to empty her slops, would pause in the road; and the muzhík, bringing in his firewood, would open his eyes. We would drive up and down, occasionally stopping. The lackeys come out, the coachmen drive up. There is constant conversation. Always kept waiting. Sometimes for three hours we were kept at the door; occasionally we take a turn around, and talk a while, and again we halt.

"At last there would be a tumult in the hallway; the gray-haired Tikhon, fat in paunch, comes out in his dress-coat. 'Drive on;' then there was none of that use of superfluous words that obtains now. Feofán clucks as if I did not know what 'forward' meant; comes up to the door, and drives away quickly, unconcernedly, as though there was nothing wonderful either in the sledge or the horses, or Feofán himself, as he bends his back and holds out his hands in such a way that it would seem impossible to keep it up long.

"The prince comes out in his shako and cloak, with a gray beaver collar concealing his handsome, ruddy, black-browed face, which ought never to be covered. He would come out with clanking sabre, jingling spurs, and copper-heeled boots; stepping over the carpet as though in a hurry, and not paying any heed to me or to Feofán, whom everybody except himself looked at and admired.

"Feofán clucks. I pull at the reins, and with a respectable rapid trot we are off and away. I glance round at the prince, and toss my aristocratic head and delicate topknot. The prince is in good spirits; he sometimes jests with Feofán. Feofán replies, half turning round to the prince his handsome face, and, not dropping his hands, makes some ridiculous motion with the reins which I understand; and on, on, on, with ever wider and wider strides, straining every muscle, and sending the muddy snow over the dasher, off I go! Then there was none of the absurd way that obtains to-day of crying, O! as though the coachman were in pain, and couldn't speak. 'G'long! Look out there![10] G'long! Look out there,' shouts Feofán; and the people clear the way, and stand craning their necks to see the handsome gelding, the handsome coachman, and the handsome harm....

"I loved especially to outstrip some racer. When Feofán and I would see in the distance some team worthy of our mettle, flying like a whirlwind, we would gradually come nearer and nearer to him. And soon tossing the mud over the dasher, I would be even with the passenger, and would snort over his head, then even with the saddle, with the bell-bow;[11] then I would already see him and hear him behind me, gradually getting farther and farther away. But the prince and Feofán and I, we all kept silent, and made believe that we were merely out for a drive, and by our actions that we did not notice those with slow horses whom we overtook on our way. I loved to race, but I loved also to meet a good racer. One wink, sound, glance, and we would be off, and would fly along, each on his own side of the road." ...

Here the gates creaked, and the voices of Nester and Vaska were heard.

[9] pushchaï.

[10] podi! belegis.

[11] dugá.

IX.

FIFTH NIGHT.

The weather began to change. The sky was over-cast; and in the morning there was no dew, but it was warm, and the flies were sticky. As soon as the herd was driven in, the horses gathered around the piebald, and thus he finished his story:—

"The happy days of my life were soon over. I lived so only two years. At the end of the second winter, there happened an event which was most delightful to me, and immediately after came my deepest sorrow. It was at Shrove-tide. I took the prince to the races. Atlásnui and Buichók also ran in the race.

"I don't know what they were doing in the summer-house; but I know that he came, and ordered Feofán to enter the ring. I remember they drove me into the ring, stationed me and stationed Atlásnui. Atlásnui was in racing gear, but I was harnessed in a city sleigh. At the turning stake I left him behind. A laugh and a cry of victory greeted my achievement. When they began to lead me round, a crowd followed after, and a man offered the prince five thousand. He only laughed, showing his white teeth.

"'No,' said he, 'this isn't a horse, it's a friend. I wouldn't sell him for a mountain of gold. Good-day, gentlemen!'[12]

"He threw open the fur robes, and got in.

"'To Ostozhenka.'

"That was where his mistress lived. And we flew....

"It was our last happy day. We reached her home. He called her his. But she loved some one else, and had gone off with him. The prince ascertained this at her room. It was five o'clock; and, not letting me be unharnessed, he started in pursuit of her, though she had never really been his. They applied the knout to me, and made me gallop. For the first time, I began to flag, and I am ashamed to say, I wanted to rest.

"But suddenly I heard the prince himself shouting in an unnatural voice, 'Hurry up!'[13] and the knout whistled and cut me; and I dashed ahead again, my leg hitting against the iron of the dasher. We overtook her, after going twenty-five versts. I got him there; but I trembled all night, and could not eat any thing. In the morning they gave me water. I drank it, and forever ceased to be the horse that I was. I was sick. They tortured me and maimed me,—treated me as men are accustomed to do. My hoofs came off. I had abscesses, and my legs grew bent. I had no strength in my chest. Laziness and weakness were everywhere apparent. I was sent to the horse-dealer. He fed me on carrots and other things, and made me something quite unlike my old self, but yet capable of deceiving one who did not know. But there was no strength and no swiftness in me.

"Moreover, the horse-dealer tormented me, by coming to my stall when customers were on hand, and beginning to stir me up, and torture me with the knout, so that it drove me to madness. Then he would wipe the bloody foam off the whip, and lead me out.

"An old lady bought me of the dealer. She used to keep coming to Nikola Yavlennoï, and she used to whip the coachman. The coachman would come and weep in my stall. And I knew that his tears had an agreeable salt taste. Then the old woman chid her overseer,[14] took me into the country, and sold me to a peddler; then I was fed on wheat, and grew sicker still. I was sold to a muzhík. There I had to plough, had almost nothing to eat, and I cut my leg with a ploughshare. I became sick again. A gypsy got possession of me. He tortured me horribly, and at last I was sold to the overseer here. And here I am." ... All were silent. The rain began to fall.

[12] do svidánya = au revoir.

[13] valyaï.

[14] priskashchik.

X.

As the herd returned home the following evening, they met the master[15] and a guest. Zhulduiba, leading the way, cast her eyes on two men's figures: one was the young master in a straw hat; the other, a tall, stout, military man, with wrinkled face. The old mare gazed at the man, and swerving went near to him; the rest, the younger ones, were thrown into some confusion, huddled together, especially when the master and his guest came directly into the midst of the horses, making gestures to each other, and talking.

"Here's this one. I bought it of Voyéïkof,—the dapple-gray horse," said the master.

"And that young black mare, with the white legs,—where did you get her? Fine one," said the guest. They examined many of the horses as they walked around, or stood on the field. They remarked also the chestnut mare.

"That's one of the saddle-horses,—the breed of Khrenovsky."

They quietly gazed at all the horses as they went by. The master shouted to Nester; and the old man, hastily digging his heels into the sides of the piebald, trotted out. The piebald horse hobbled along, limping on one leg;

but his gait was such that it was evident that in other circumstances he would not have complained, even if he had been compelled to go in this way, as long as his strength held out, to the world's end. He was ready even to go at full gallop, and at first even broke into one.

"I have no hesitation in saying that there isn't a better horse in Russia than that one," said the master, pointing to one of the mares. The guest corroborated this praise. The master, full of satisfaction, walked up and down, made observations, and told the story and pedigree of each of the horses.

It was apparently somewhat of a bore to the guest to listen to the master; but he devised questions, to make it seem as if he were interested in it.

"Yes, yes," said he in some confusion.

"Look," said the host, not replying to the questions, "look at those legs, look at the ... She cost me dear, but I shall have a three-year-old from her that'll go!"

"Does she trot well?" asked the guest.

Thus they scrutinized almost all the horses, and there was nothing more to show. And they were silent.

"Well, shall we go?"

"Yes, let us go."

They went out through the gate. The guest was glad that the exhibition was over, and that he was going home where he would eat, drink, smoke, and have a good time. As they went by Nester, who was sitting on the piebald and waiting for further orders, the guest struck his big fat hand on the horse's side.

"Here's good blood," said he. "He's like the piebald horse, if you remember, that I told you about."

The master perceived that it was not of his horses that the guest was speaking; and he did not listen, but, looking around, continued to gaze at his stud.

Suddenly, at his very ear, was heard a dull, weak, senile neigh. It was the piebald horse that began to neigh, but could not finish it. Becoming, as it were, confused, he broke short off.

Neither the guest nor the master paid any attention to this neigh, but went home. Kholstomír had recognized in the wrinkled old man his beloved former master, the once brilliant, handsome, and wealthy Sierpukhovskoï.

[15] khozhyáïn.

XI.

The rain continued to fall. In the paddock it was gloomy, but at the manor-house[16] it was quite the reverse. The luxurious evening meal was spread in the luxurious dining-room. At the table sat master, mistress, and the guest who had just arrived.

The master held in his hand a box of specially fine ten-year-old cigars, such as no one else had, according to his story, and proceeded to offer them to the guest. The master was a handsome young man of twenty-five, fresh, neatly dressed, smoothly brushed. He was dressed in a fresh, loosely-fitting suit of clothes, made in London. On his watch-chain were big expensive charms. His cuff-buttons were of gold, large, even massive, set with turquoises. His beard was à la Napoleon III.; and his moustaches were waxed, and stood out as though he had got them nowhere else than in Paris.

The lady wore a silk-muslin dress, brocaded with large variegated flowers; on her head, large gold hair-pins in her thick auburn hair, which was beautiful, though not entirely her own. Her hands were adorned with bracelets and rings, all expensive.

The samovar was silver, the service exquisite. The lackey, magnificent in his dress-coat and white vest and necktie, stood like a statue at the door, awaiting orders. The furniture was of bent wood, and bright; the wall-papers dark, with large flowers. Around the table tinkled a cunning little dog, with a silver collar bearing an extremely hard English name, which neither of them could pronounce because they knew not English.

In the corner, among the flowers, stood the pianoforte, inlaid with mother-of-pearl.[17] Every thing breathed of newness, luxury, and rareness.

Every thing was extremely good; but it all bore a peculiar impress of profusion, wealth, and an absence of intellectual interests.

The master was a great lover of racing, strong and hot-headed; one of those whom one meets everywhere, who drive out in sable furs, send costly bouquets to actresses, drink the most expensive wine, of the very latest brand, at the most expensive restaurant, offer prizes in their own names, and entertain the most expensive....

The new-comer, Nikíta Sierpukhovskoï, was a man of forty years, tall, stout, bald, with huge mustaches and side-whiskers. He ought to have been very handsome; but it was evident that he had wasted his forces—physical and moral and pecuniary.

He was so deeply in debt that he was obliged to go into the service so as to escape the sponging-house. He had now come to the government city as chief of the imperial stud. His influential relations had obtained this for him.

He was dressed in an army kittel and blue trousers. His kittel and trousers were such as only those who are rich can afford to wear; so with his linen also. His watch was English. His boots had peculiar soles, as thick as a finger.

Nikíta Sierpukhovskoï had squandered a fortune of two millions, and was still in debt to the amount of one hundred and twenty thousand rubles. From such a course there always remains a certain momentum of life, giving credit, and the possibility of living almost luxuriously for another ten years.

The ten years had already passed, and the momentum was finished; and it had become hard for him to live. He had already begun to drink too much; that is, to get fuddled with wine, which had never been the case with him before. Properly speaking, he had never begun and never finished drinking.

More noticeable in him than all else was the restlessness of his eyes (they had begun to wander), and the uncertainty of his intonations and motions. This restlessness was surprising, from the fact that it was evidently a new thing in him, because it could be seen that he had been accustomed, all his life long, to fear nothing and nobody, and that now he endured severe sufferings from some dread that was thoroughly alien to his nature.

The host and hostess[18] remarked this, exchanged glances, showing that they understood each other, postponed until they should get to bed the consideration of this subject; and, evidently, merely endured poor Sierpukhovskoï.

The sight of the young master's happiness humiliated Nikíta, and compelled him to painful envy, as he remembered his own irrevocable past.

"You don't object to cigars, Marie?" he asked, addressing the lady in that peculiar tone, acquired only by practice, full of urbanity and friendliness, but not wholly satisfactory,—such as men use who are familiar with the society of women not enjoying the dignity of wifehood. Not that he could have wished to insult her: on the contrary, he was much more anxious to gain her good-will and that of the host, though he would not for any thing have acknowledged it to himself. But he was already used to talking thus with such women. He knew that she would have been astonished, even affronted, if he had behaved to her as toward a lady. Moreover, it was necessary for him to preserve that peculiar shade of deference for the acknowledged wife of his friend. He treated such women always with consideration, not because he shared those so-called convictions that are promulgated in newspapers (he never read such trash), about esteem as the prerogative of every man, about the absurdity of marriage, etc., because all well-bred men act thus, and he was a well-bred man, though inclined to drink.

He took a cigar. But his host awkwardly seized a handful of cigars, and placed them before the guest.

"No, just see how good these are! try them."

Nikíta pushed away the cigars with his hand, and in his eyes flashed something like injury and shame.

"Thanks,"—he took out his cigar-case,—"try mine."

The lady was on the watch. She perceived how it affected him. She began hastily to talk with him.

"I am very fond of cigars. I should smoke myself if everybody about did not smoke."

And she gave him one of her bright, kindly smiles. He half-smiled in reply. Two of his teeth were gone.

"No, take this," continued the host, not heeding. "Those others are not so strong. Fritz, bringen Sie noch eine Kasten," he said, "dort zwei."

The German lackey brought another box.

"Do you like these larger ones? They are stronger. This is a very good kind. Take them all," he added, continuing to force them upon his guest.

He was evidently glad that there was some one on whom he could lavish his rarities, and he saw nothing out of the way in it. Sierpukhovskoï began to smoke, and hastened to take up the subject that had been dropped.

"How much did you have to go on Atlásnui?" he asked.

"He cost me dear,—not less than five thousand, but at all events I am secured. Plenty of colts, I tell you!"

"Do they trot?" inquired Sierpukhovskoï.

"First-rate. To-day Atlásnui's colt took three prizes: one at Tula, one at Moscow, and one at Petersburg. He raced with Voyéïkof's Vorónui. The rascally jockey made four abatements, and almost put him out of the race."

"He was rather raw; too much Dutch stock in him, I should say," said Sierpukhovskoï.

"Well, but the mares are finer ones. I will show you to-morrow. I paid three thousand for Dobruina, two thousand for Laskovaya."

And again the host began to enumerate his wealth. The mistress saw that this was hard for Sierpukhovskoï, and that he only pretended to listen.

"Won't you have some more tea?" asked the hostess.

"I don't care for any more," said the host, and he went on with his story.

She got up; the host detained her, took her in his arms, and kissed her.

Sierpukhovskoï smiled at first, as he looked at them; but his smile seemed to them unnatural. When his host got up, and took her in his arms, and went out with her as far as the portière, his face suddenly changed; he sighed deeply, and an expression of despair took possession of his wrinkled face. There was also wrath in it.

"Yes, you said that you bought him of Voyéïkof," said Sierpukhovskoï, with assumed indifference.

[16] barski dom.

[17] incrusté.

[18] khozyáïn and khozyáïka.

XII.

The host returned, and smiled as he sat down opposite his guest. Neither of them spoke.

"Oh, yes! I was speaking of Atlásnui. I had a great mind to buy the mares of Dubovitsky. Nothing but rubbish was left."

"He was burned out," said Sierpukhovskoï, and suddenly stood up and looked around. He remembered that he owed this ruined man twenty thousand rubles; and that, if burned out were said of any one, it might by good rights be said about himself. He began to laugh.

Both kept silence long. The master was revolving in his mind how he might boast a little before his guest. Sierpukhovskoï was cogitating how he might show that he did not consider himself burned out. But the thoughts of both moved with difficulty, in spite of the fact that they tried to enliven themselves with cigars.

"Well, when shall we have something to drink?" asked the guest of himself.

"At all events, we must have something to drink, else we shall die of the blues," said the host to himself.

"How is it? are you going to stay here long?" asked Sierpukhovskoï.

"About a month yet. Shall we have a little lunch? What say you? Fritz, is every thing ready?"

They went back to the dining-room. There, under a hanging lamp, stood the table loaded with candles and very extraordinary things: siphons, and bottles with fancy stoppers, extraordinary wine in decanters, extraordinary liqueurs and vodka. They drank, sat down, drank again, sat down, and tried to talk. Sierpukhovskoï grew flushed, and began to speak unreservedly.

They talked about women: who kept such and such an one; the gypsy, the ballet-girl, the soubrette.[19]

"Why, you left Mathieu, didn't you?" asked the host.

This was the mistress who had caused Sierpukhovskoï such pain.

"No, she left me. O my friend,[20] how one remembers what one has squandered in life! Now I am glad, fact, when I get a thousand rubles; glad, fact, when I get out of everybody's way. I cannot in Moscow. Ah! what's to be said!"

The host was bored to listen to Sierpukhovskoï. He wanted to talk about himself,—to brag. But Sierpukhovskoï also wanted to talk about himself,—about his glittering past. The host poured out some more wine, and waited till he had finished, so as to tell him about his affairs,—how he was going to arrange his stud as no one ever had before; and how Marie loved him, not for his money, but for himself.

"I was going to tell you that in my stud" ... he began. But Sierpukhovskoï interrupted him.

"There was a time, I may say," he began, "when I loved, and knew how to live. You were talking just now about racing; please tell me what is your best racer."

The host was glad of the chance to tell some more about his stud, but Sierpukhovskoï again interrupted him.

"Yes, yes," said he. "But the trouble with you breeders is, that you do it only for ostentation, and not for pleasure, for life. It wasn't so with me. I was telling you this very day that I used to have a piebald racer, with just such spots as I saw among your colts. Okh! what a horse he was! You can't imagine it: this was in '42. I had just come to Moscow. I went to a dealer, and saw a piebald gelding. All in best form. He pleased me. Price? Thousand rubles. He pleased me. I took him, and began to ride him. I never had, and you never had and never will have, such a horse. I never knew a better horse, either for gait, or strength, or beauty. You were a lad then. You could not have known, but you may have heard, I suppose. All Moscow knew him."

"Yes, I heard about him," said the host reluctantly; "but I was going to tell you about my" ...

So you heard about him. I bought him just as he was, without pedigree, without proof; but then I knew Voyéïkof, and I traced him. He was sired by Liubeznuï I. He was called Kholstomír.[21] He'd measure linen for you! On account of his spotting, he was given to the equerry at the Khrenovski stud; and he had him gelded, and sold him to the dealer. Aren't any horses like him anymore, friend! Akh! "What a time that was! Akh! vanished youth!" he said, quoting the words of a gypsy song. He began to get wild. "Ekh! that was a golden time! I was twenty-five. I had eighty thousand a year income; then I hadn't a gray hair; all my teeth like pearls.... Whatever I undertook prospered. And yet all came to an end." ...

"Well, you didn't have such lively times then," said the host, taking advantage of the interruption. "I tell you that my first horses began to run without" ...

"Your horses! Horses were more mettlesome then" ...

"How more mettlesome?"

"Yes, more mettlesome. I remember how one time I was at Moscow at the races. None of my horses were in it. I did not care for racing; but I had blooded horses, General Chaulet, Mahomet. I had my piebald with me. My coachman was a splendid young fellow. I liked him. But he was rather given to drink, so I drove.—'Sierpukhovskoï,' said they, 'when are you going to get some trotters?'—'I don't care for your low-bred beasts,[22] the devil take 'em! I have a hackdriver's piebald that's worth all of yours.'—Yes, but he doesn't race.'—'Bet you a thousand rubles.' They took me up. He went round in five seconds, won the wager of a thousand rubles. But that was nothing. With my blooded horses I went in a troïka a hundred versts in three hours. All Moscow knew about it."

And Sierpukhovskoï began to brag so fluently and steadily that the host could not get in a word, and sat facing him with dejected countenance. Only, by way of diversion, he would fill up his glass and that of his companion.

It began already to grow light, but still they sat there. It became painfully tiresome to the host. He got up.

"Sleep,—let's go to sleep, then," said Sierpukhovskoï, as he got up, and went staggering and puffing to the room that had been assigned to him.

. . . .

. . . .

. . . .

The master of the house rejoined his mistress.

"Oh, he's unendurable. He got drunk, and lied faster than he could talk."

"And he made love to me too."

"I fear that he's going to borrow of me."

Sierpukhovskoï threw himself on the bed without undressing, and drew a long breath.

"I must have talked a good deal of nonsense," he thought. "Well, it's all the same. Good wine, but he's a big hog. Something cheap about him.[23] And I am a hog myself," he remarked, and laughed aloud. "Well, I used to support others: now it's my turn. I guess the Winkler girl will help me. I'll borrow some money of her. He may come to it. Suppose I've got to undress. Can't get my boot off. Hey, hey!" he cried; but the man who had been ordered to wait on him had long before gone to bed.

He sat up, took off his kittel and his vest, and somehow managed to crawl out of his trousers; but it was long before his boots would stir: with his stout belly it was hard work to stoop over. He got one off; he struggled and struggled with the other, got out of breath, and gave it up. And so with one leg in the boot he threw himself down, and began to snore, filling the whole room with the odor of wine, tobacco, and vile old age.

[19] Frantsuzhenka.

[20] akh, brat brother.

[21] Kholstomír means a cloth measurer: suggesting the greatest distance from linger to linger of the outstretched arms, and rapidity in accomplishing the motion.

[22] literally, muzhíks.

[23] kupésheskoe, merchant-like.

XIII.

If Kholstomír remembered any thing that night, it was the frolic that Vaska gave him. He threw over him a blanket, and galloped off. He was left till morning at the door of a tavern, with a muzhík's horse. They licked each other. When it became light he went back to the herd, and itched all over.

"Something makes me itch fearfully," he thought.

Five days passed. They brought a veterinary. He said cheerfully,—

"The mange. You'll have to dispose of him to the gypsies."

"Better have his throat cut; only have it done to-day."

The morning was calm and clear. The herd had gone to pasture. Kholstomír remained behind. A strange man came along; thin, dark, dirty, in a kaftan spotted with something black. This was the scavenger. He took

Kholstomír by the halter, and without looking at him started off. The horse followed quietly, not looking round, and, as always, dragging his legs and kicking up the straw with his hind-legs.

As he went out of the gate, he turned his head toward the well; but the scavenger twitched the halter, and said,—

"It's not worth while."

The scavenger, and Vaska who followed, proceeded to a depression behind the brick barn, and stopped, as though there were something peculiar in this most ordinary place; and the scavenger, handing the halter to Vaska, took off his kaftan, rolled up his sleeves, and produced a knife and whetstone from his boot-leg.

The piebald pulled at the halter, and out of sheer ennui tried to bite it, but it was too far off. He sighed, and closed his eyes. He hung down his lip, showing his worn yellow teeth, and began to drowse, lulled by the sound of the knife on the stone. Only his sick and swollen leg trembled a little.

Suddenly he perceived that he was grasped by the lower jaw, and that his head was lifted up. He opened his eyes. Two dogs were in front of him. One was snuffing in the direction of the scavenger, the other sat looking at the gelding as though expecting something especially from him. The gelding looked at them, and began to rub his jaw against the hand that held him.

"Of course they want to cure me," he said: "let it come!"

And the thought had hardly passed through his mind, before they did something to his throat. It hurt him; he started back, stamped his foot, but restrained himself, and waited for what was to follow.... What followed, was some liquid pouring in a stream down his neck and breast. He drew a deep breath, lifting his sides. And it seemed easier, much easier, to him.

The whole burden of his life was taken from him.

He closed his eyes, and began to droop his head,—no one held it. Then his legs quivered, his whole body swayed. He was not so much terrified as he was astonished....

Every thing was so new. He was astonished; he tried to run ahead, up the hill, ... but instead of this, his legs, moving where he stood, interfered. He began to roll over on his side, and while expecting to make a step he fell forward, and on his left side.

The scavenger waited till the death-struggle was over, drove away the dogs that were creeping nearer, and then seized the horse by the legs, turned him over on the back, and, telling Vaska to hold his leg, began to take off the hide.

"That was a horse indeed!" said Vaska.

"If he'd been fatter, it would have been a fine hide," said the scavenger.

That evening the herd passed by the hill; and those who were on the left wing saw a red object below them, and around it some dogs busily romping, and crows and hawks flying over it. One dog, with his paws on the carcass, and shaking his head, was growling over what he was tearing with his teeth. The brown filly stopped, lifted her head and neck, and long sniffed the air. It took force to drive her away.

At sunrise, in a ravine of the ancient forest, in the bottom of an overgrown glade, some wolf-whelps were beside themselves with joy. There were five of them,—four about of a size, and one little one with a head bigger than his body. A lean, hairless she-wolf, her belly with hanging dugs almost touching the ground, crept out of the bushes, and sat down in front of the wolves. The wolves sat in a semi-circle in front of her. She went to the smallest, and lowering her stumpy tail, and bending her nose to the ground, made a few convulsive motions, and opening her jaws filled with teeth she struggled, and disgorged a great piece of horse-flesh.

The larger whelps made a movement to seize it; but she restrained them with a threatening growl, and let the little one have it all. The little one, as though in anger, seized the morsel, hiding it under him, and began to devour it. Then the she-wolf disgorged for the second, and the third, and in the same way for all five, and finally lay down in front of them to rest.

At the end of a week there lay behind the brick barn only the great skull, and two shoulder-blades; all the rest had disappeared. In the summer a muzhík who gathered up the bones carried off also the skull and shoulder-blades, and put them to use.

The dead body of Sierpukhovskoï who had been about in the world, and had eaten and drunken, was buried long after. Neither his skin nor his flesh nor his bones were of any use.

And just as his dead body, which had been about in the world, had been a great burden to others for twenty years, so the disposal of this body became only an additional charge upon men. Long it had been useless to every one, long it had been only a burden. But still the dead who bury their dead found it expedient to dress this soon-to-be-decaying, swollen body, in a fine uniform, in fine boots; to place it in a fine new coffin, with new tassels on the four corners; then to place this new coffin in another, made of lead, and carry it to Moscow; and there to dig up the bones of people long buried, and then to lay away this mal-odorous body devoured by worms, in its new uniform and polished boots, and to cover the whole with earth.

About Author

In the 1870s Tolstoy experienced a profound moral crisis, followed by what he regarded as an equally profound spiritual awakening, as outlined in his non-fiction work A Confession (1882). His literal interpretation of the ethical teachings of Jesus, centering on the Sermon on the Mount, caused him to become a fervent Christian anarchist and pacifist. Tolstoy's ideas on nonviolent resistance, expressed in such works as The Kingdom of God Is Within You (1894), were to have a profound impact on such pivotal 20th-century figures as Mahatma Gandhi and Martin Luther King Jr. Tolstoy also became a dedicated advocate of Georgism, the economic philosophy of Henry George, which he incorporated into his writing, particularly Resurrection (1899).

Origins

The Tolstoys were a well-known family of old Russian nobility who traced their ancestry to a mythical nobleman named Indris described by Pyotr Tolstoy as arriving "from Nemec, from the lands of Caesar" to Chernigov in 1353 along with his two sons Litvinos (or Litvonis) and Zimonten (or Zigmont) and a druzhina of 3000 people. While the word "Nemec" has been long used to describe Germans only, at that time it was applied to any foreigner who didn't speak Russian (from the word nemoy meaning mute). Indris was then converted to Eastern Orthodoxy under the name of Leonty and his sons – as Konstantin and Feodor, respectively. Konstantin's grandson Andrei Kharitonovich was nicknamed Tolstiy (translated as fat) by Vasily II of Moscow after he moved from Chernigov to Moscow.

Because of the pagan names and the fact that Chernigov at the time was ruled by Demetrius I Starshy some researches concluded that they were Lithuanians who arrived from the Grand Duchy of Lithuania, then part of the State of the Teutonic Order. At the same time, no mention of Indris was ever found in the 14th – 16th-century documents, while the Chernigov Chronicles used by Pyotr Tolstoy as a reference were lost. The first documented members of the Tolstoy family also lived during the 17th century, thus Pyotr

Tolstoy himself is generally considered the founder of the noble house, being granted the title of count by Peter the Great.

Life and career

Tolstoy was born at Yasnaya Polyana, a family estate 12 kilometres (7.5 mi) southwest of Tula, Russia, and 200 kilometers (120 mi) south of Moscow. He was the fourth of five children of Count Nikolai Ilyich Tolstoy (1794–1837), a veteran of the Patriotic War of 1812, and Countess Mariya Tolstaya (née Volkonskaya; 1790–1830). After his mother died when he was two and his father when he was nine, Tolstoy and his siblings were brought up by relatives. In 1844, he began studying law and oriental languages at Kazan University, where teachers described him as "both unable and unwilling to learn." Tolstoy left the university in the middle of his studies, returned to Yasnaya Polyana and then spent much of his time in Moscow, Tula and Saint Petersburg, leading a lax and leisurely lifestyle. He began writing during this period, including his first novel Childhood, a fictitious account of his own youth, which was published in 1852. In 1851, after running up heavy gambling debts, he went with his older brother to the Caucasus and joined the army. Tolstoy served as a young artillery officer during the Crimean War and was in Sevastopol during the 11-month-long siege of Sevastopol in 1854–55, including the Battle of the Chernaya. During the war he was recognised for his bravery and courage and promoted to lieutenant. He was appalled by the number of deaths involved in warfare, and left the army after the end of the Crimean War.

His conversion from a dissolute and privileged society author to the non-violent and spiritual anarchist of his latter days was brought about by his experience in the army as well as two trips around Europe in 1857 and 1860–61. Others who followed the same path were Alexander Herzen, Mikhail Bakunin and Peter Kropotkin. During his 1857 visit, Tolstoy witnessed a public execution in Paris, a traumatic experience that would mark the rest of his life. Writing in a letter to his friend Vasily Botkin: "The truth is that the State is a conspiracy designed not only to exploit, but above all to corrupt its citizens ... Henceforth, I shall never serve any government anywhere." Tolstoy's concept of non-violence or Ahimsa was bolstered when he read a

German version of the Tirukkural. He later instilled the concept in Mahatma Gandhi through his A Letter to a Hindu when young Gandhi corresponded with him seeking his advice.

His European trip in 1860–61 shaped both his political and literary development when he met Victor Hugo, whose literary talents Tolstoy praised after reading Hugo's newly finished Les Misérables. The similar evocation of battle scenes in Hugo's novel and Tolstoy's War and Peace indicates this influence. Tolstoy's political philosophy was also influenced by a March 1861 visit to French anarchist Pierre-Joseph Proudhon, then living in exile under an assumed name in Brussels. Apart from reviewing Proudhon's forthcoming publication, La Guerre et la Paix (War and Peace in French), whose title Tolstoy would borrow for his masterpiece, the two men discussed education, as Tolstoy wrote in his educational notebooks: "If I recount this conversation with Proudhon, it is to show that, in my personal experience, he was the only man who understood the significance of education and of the printing press in our time."

Fired by enthusiasm, Tolstoy returned to Yasnaya Polyana and founded 13 schools for the children of Russia's peasants, who had just been emancipated from serfdom in 1861. Tolstoy described the school's principles in his 1862 essay "The School at Yasnaya Polyana". Tolstoy's educational experiments were short-lived, partly due to harassment by the Tsarist secret police. However, as a direct forerunner to A.S. Neill's Summerhill School, the school at Yasnaya Polyana can justifiably be claimed the first example of a coherent theory of democratic education.

Towards the end of his career, Tolstoy was selected to receive the first Nobel Prize in Literature in 1901, but turned down the honor in October of the same year, worrying that the prize money would bring unwanted complications to his life.

Personal life

The death of his brother Nikolay in 1860 had an impact on Tolstoy, and led him to a desire to marry. On 23 September 1862, Tolstoy married Sophia Andreevna Behrs, who was 16 years his junior and the daughter of a court physician. She was called Sonya, the Russian diminutive of Sofia, by her family and friends. They had 13 children, eight of whom survived childhood:

Count Sergei Lvovich Tolstoy (1863–1947), composer and ethnomusicologist

Countess Tatyana Lvovna Tolstaya (1864–1950), wife of Mikhail Sergeevich Sukhotin

Count Ilya Lvovich Tolstoy (1866–1933), writer

Count Lev Lvovich Tolstoy (1869–1945), writer and sculptor

Countess Maria Lvovna Tolstaya (1871–1906), wife of Nikolai Leonidovich Obolensky

Count Peter Lvovich Tolstoy (1872–1873), died in infancy

Count Nikolai Lvovich Tolstoy (1874–1875), died in infancy

Countess Varvara Lvovna Tolstaya (1875–1875), died in infancy

Count Andrei Lvovich Tolstoy (1877–1916), served in the Russo-Japanese War

Count Michael Lvovich Tolstoy (1879–1944)

Count Alexei Lvovich Tolstoy (1881–1886)

Countess Alexandra Lvovna Tolstaya (1884–1979)

Count Ivan Lvovich Tolstoy (1888–1895)

The marriage was marked from the outset by sexual passion and emotional insensitivity when Tolstoy, on the eve of their marriage, gave her his diaries detailing his extensive sexual past and the fact that one of the serfs on his estate had borne him a son. Even so, their early married life was happy and allowed Tolstoy much freedom and the support system to compose War and Peace and Anna Karenina with Sonya acting as his secretary, editor, and financial manager. Sonya was copying and handwriting his epic works time after time. Tolstoy would continue editing War and Peace and had to have clean final drafts to be delivered to the publisher.

However, their later life together has been described by A.N. Wilson as one of the unhappiest in literary history. Tolstoy's relationship with his wife deteriorated as his beliefs became increasingly radical. This saw him seeking to reject his inherited and earned wealth, including the renunciation of the copyrights on his earlier works.

Some of the members of the Tolstoy family left Russia in the aftermath of the 1905 Russian Revolution and the subsequent establishment of the Soviet Union, and many of Leo Tolstoy's relatives and descendants today live in Sweden, Germany, the United Kingdom, France and the United States. Among them are Swedish jazz singer Viktoria Tolstoy and the Swedish landowner Christopher Paus, whose family owns the major estate Herresta outside Stockholm.

One of his great-great-grandsons, Vladimir Tolstoy (born 1962), is a director of the Yasnaya Polyana museum since 1994 and an adviser to the President of Russia on cultural affairs since 2012. Ilya Tolstoy's great-grandson, Pyotr Tolstoy, is a well-known Russian journalist and TV presenter as well as a State Duma deputy since 2016. His cousin Fyokla Tolstaya (born Anna Tolstaya in 1971), daughter of the acclaimed Soviet Slavist Nikita Tolstoy (ru) (1923–1996), is also a Russian journalist, TV and radio host.

Novels and fictional works

Tolstoy is considered one of the giants of Russian literature; his works include the novels War and Peace and Anna Karenina and novellas such as Hadji Murad and The Death of Ivan Ilyich.

Tolstoy's earliest works, the autobiographical novels Childhood, Boyhood, and Youth (1852–1856), tell of a rich landowner's son and his slow realization of the chasm between himself and his peasants. Though he later rejected them as sentimental, a great deal of Tolstoy's own life is revealed. They retain their relevance as accounts of the universal story of growing up.

Tolstoy served as a second lieutenant in an artillery regiment during the Crimean War, recounted in his Sevastopol Sketches. His experiences in battle helped stir his subsequent pacifism and gave him material for realistic depiction of the horrors of war in his later work.

His fiction consistently attempts to convey realistically the Russian society in which he lived. The Cossacks (1863) describes the Cossack life and people through a story of a Russian aristocrat in love with a Cossack girl. Anna Karenina (1877) tells parallel stories of an adulterous woman trapped by the conventions and falsities of society and of a philosophical landowner (much like Tolstoy), who works alongside the peasants in the fields and seeks to reform their lives. Tolstoy not only drew from his own life experiences but also created characters in his own image, such as Pierre Bezukhov and Prince Andrei in War and Peace, Levin in Anna Karenina and to some extent, Prince Nekhlyudov in Resurrection.

War and Peace is generally thought to be one of the greatest novels ever written, remarkable for its dramatic breadth and unity. Its vast canvas includes 580 characters, many historical with others fictional. The story moves from family life to the headquarters of Napoleon, from the court of Alexander I of Russia to the battlefields of Austerlitz and Borodino. Tolstoy's original idea for the novel was to investigate the causes of the Decembrist revolt, to which it refers only in the last chapters, from which can be deduced that Andrei Bolkonsky's son will become one of the Decembrists. The novel explores Tolstoy's theory of history, and in particular the insignificance of individuals such as Napoleon and Alexander. Somewhat surprisingly, Tolstoy did not consider War and Peace to be a novel (nor did he consider many of the great Russian fictions written at that time to be novels). This view becomes less surprising if one considers that Tolstoy was a novelist of the realist school who considered the novel to be a framework for the examination of social and political issues in nineteenth-century life. War and Peace (which is to Tolstoy really an epic in prose) therefore did not qualify. Tolstoy thought that Anna Karenina was his first true novel.

After Anna Karenina, Tolstoy concentrated on Christian themes, and his later novels such as The Death of Ivan Ilyich (1886) and What Is to Be Done? develop a radical anarcho-pacifist Christian philosophy which led to his excommunication from the Russian Orthodox Church in 1901. For all the praise showered on Anna Karenina and War and Peace, Tolstoy rejected the two works later in his life as something not as true of reality.

In his novel Resurrection, Tolstoy attempts to expose the injustice of man-made laws and the hypocrisy of institutionalized church. Tolstoy also explores and explains the economic philosophy of Georgism, of which he had become a very strong advocate towards the end of his life.

Tolstoy also tried himself in poetry with several soldier songs written during his military service and fairy tales in verse such as Volga-bogatyr and Oaf stylized as national folk songs. They were written between 1871 and 1874 for his Russian Book for Reading, a collection of short stories in four volumes (total of 629 stories in various genres) published along with the New Azbuka textbook and addressed to schoolchildren. Nevertheless, he was skeptical about poetry as a genre. As he famously said, "Writing poetry is like ploughing and dancing at the same time". According to Valentin Bulgakov, he criticised poets, including Alexander Pushkin, for their "false" epithets used "simply to make it rhyme".

Critical appraisal by other authors

Tolstoy's contemporaries paid him lofty tributes. Fyodor Dostoyevsky, who died thirty years before Tolstoy's death, thought him the greatest of all living novelists. Gustave Flaubert, on reading a translation of War and Peace, exclaimed, "What an artist and what a psychologist!" Anton Chekhov, who often visited Tolstoy at his country estate, wrote, "When literature possesses a Tolstoy, it is easy and pleasant to be a writer; even when you know you have achieved nothing yourself and are still achieving nothing, this is not as terrible as it might otherwise be, because Tolstoy achieves for everyone. What he does serves to justify all the hopes and aspirations invested in literature." The 19th-century British poet and critic Matthew Arnold opined that "A novel by Tolstoy is not a work of art but a piece of life."

Later novelists continued to appreciate Tolstoy's art, but sometimes also expressed criticism. Arthur Conan Doyle wrote "I am attracted by his earnestness and by his power of detail, but I am repelled by his looseness of construction and by his unreasonable and impracticable mysticism." Virginia

Woolf declared him "the greatest of all novelists." James Joyce noted that "He is never dull, never stupid, never tired, never pedantic, never theatrical!" Thomas Mann wrote of Tolstoy's seemingly guileless artistry: "Seldom did art work so much like nature." Vladimir Nabokov heaped superlatives upon The Death of Ivan Ilyich and Anna Karenina; he questioned, however, the reputation of War and Peace, and sharply criticized Resurrection and The Kreutzer Sonata.

Religious and political beliefs

After reading Schopenhauer's The World as Will and Representation, Tolstoy gradually became converted to the ascetic morality upheld in that work as the proper spiritual path for the upper classes: "Do you know what this summer has meant for me? Constant raptures over Schopenhauer and a whole series of spiritual delights which I've never experienced before. ... no student has ever studied so much on his course, and learned so much, as I have this summer"

In Chapter VI of A Confession, Tolstoy quoted the final paragraph of Schopenhauer's work. It explained how the nothingness that results from complete denial of self is only a relative nothingness, and is not to be feared. The novelist was struck by the description of Christian, Buddhist, and Hindu ascetic renunciation as being the path to holiness. After reading passages such as the following, which abound in Schopenhauer's ethical chapters, the Russian nobleman chose poverty and formal denial of the will:

But this very necessity of involuntary suffering (by poor people) for eternal salvation is also expressed by that utterance of the Savior (Matthew 19:24): "It is easier for a camel to go through the eye of a needle, than for a rich man to enter into the kingdom of God." Therefore, those who were greatly in earnest about their eternal salvation, chose voluntary poverty when fate had denied this to them and they had been born in wealth. Thus Buddha Sakyamuni was born a prince, but voluntarily took to the mendicant's staff; and Francis of Assisi, the founder of the mendicant orders who, as a youngster at a ball, where the daughters of all the notabilities were sitting together, was asked: "Now Francis, will you not soon make your choice from these beauties?"

and who replied: "I have made a far more beautiful choice!" "Whom?" "La povertà (poverty)": whereupon he abandoned every thing shortly afterwards and wandered through the land as a mendicant.

In 1884, Tolstoy wrote a book called What I Believe, in which he openly confessed his Christian beliefs. He affirmed his belief in Jesus Christ's teachings and was particularly influenced by the Sermon on the Mount, and the injunction to turn the other cheek, which he understood as a "commandment of non-resistance to evil by force" and a doctrine of pacifism and nonviolence. In his work The Kingdom of God Is Within You, he explains that he considered mistaken the Church's doctrine because they had made a "perversion" of Christ's teachings. Tolstoy also received letters from American Quakers who introduced him to the non-violence writings of Quaker Christians such as George Fox, William Penn and Jonathan Dymond. Tolstoy believed being a Christian required him to be a pacifist; the consequences of being a pacifist, and the apparently inevitable waging of war by government, are the reason why he is considered a philosophical anarchist.

Later, various versions of "Tolstoy's Bible" would be published, indicating the passages Tolstoy most relied on, specifically, the reported words of Jesus himself.

Tolstoy believed that a true Christian could find lasting happiness by striving for inner self-perfection through following the Great Commandment of loving one's neighbor and God rather than looking outward to the Church or state for guidance. His belief in nonresistance when faced by conflict is another distinct attribute of his philosophy based on Christ's teachings. By directly influencing Mahatma Gandhi with this idea through his work The Kingdom of God Is Within You (full text of English translation available on Wikisource), Tolstoy's profound influence on the nonviolent resistance movement reverberates to this day. He believed that the aristocracy were a burden on the poor, and that the only solution to how we live together is through anarchism.

He also opposed private property in land ownership and the institution of marriage and valued the ideals of chastity and sexual abstinence (discussed in Father Sergius and his preface to The Kreutzer Sonata), ideals also held by the young Gandhi. Tolstoy's later work derives a passion and verve from the depth of his austere moral views. The sequence of the temptation of Sergius in Father Sergius, for example, is among his later triumphs. Gorky relates how Tolstoy once read this passage before himself and Chekhov and that Tolstoy was moved to tears by the end of the reading. Other later passages of rare power include the personal crises that were faced by the protagonists of The Death of Ivan Ilyich, and of Master and Man, where the main character in the former or the reader in the latter are made aware of the foolishness of the protagonists' lives.

Tolstoy had a profound influence on the development of Christian anarchist thought. The Tolstoyans were a small Christian anarchist group formed by Tolstoy's companion, Vladimir Chertkov (1854–1936), to spread Tolstoy's religious teachings. Philosopher Peter Kropotkin wrote of Tolstoy in the article on anarchism in the 1911 Encyclopædia Britannica:

Without naming himself an anarchist, Leo Tolstoy, like his predecessors in the popular religious movements of the 15th and 16th centuries, Chojecki, Denk and many others, took the anarchist position as regards the state and property rights, deducing his conclusions from the general spirit of the teachings of Jesus and from the necessary dictates of reason. With all the might of his talent, Tolstoy made (especially in The Kingdom of God Is Within You) a powerful criticism of the church, the state and law altogether, and especially of the present property laws. He describes the state as the domination of the wicked ones, supported by brutal force. Robbers, he says, are far less dangerous than a well-organized government. He makes a searching criticism of the prejudices which are current now concerning the benefits conferred upon men by the church, the state, and the existing distribution of property, and from the teachings of Jesus he deduces the rule of non-resistance and the absolute condemnation of all wars. His religious arguments are, however, so well combined with arguments borrowed from a dispassionate observation of the present evils, that the anarchist portions of his works appeal to the religious and the non-religious reader alike.

During the Boxer Rebellion in China, Tolstoy praised the Boxers. He was harshly critical of the atrocities committed by the Russians, Germans, Americans, Japanese, and other western troops. He accused them of engaging in slaughter when he heard about the lootings, rapes, and murders, in what he saw as Christian brutality. Tolstoy also named the two monarchs most responsible for the atrocities; Nicholas II of Russia and Wilhelm II of Germany. Tolstoy, a famous sinophile, also read the works of Chinese thinker and philosopher, Confucius. Tolstoy corresponded with the Chinese intellectual Gu Hongming and recommended that China remain an agrarian nation and warned against reform like what Japan implemented.

The Eight-Nation Alliance intervention in the Boxer Rebellion was denounced by Tolstoy as were the Philippine–American War and the Second Boer War between the British Empire and the two independent Boer republics. The words "terrible for its injustice and cruelty" were used to describe the Czarist intervention in China by Tolstoy. Confucius's works were studied by Tolstoy. The attack on China in the Boxer Rebellion was railed against by Tolstoy. The war against China was criticized by Leonid Andreev and Gorkey. To the Chinese people, an epistle, was written by Tolstoy as part of the criticism of the war by intellectuals in Russia. The activities of Russia in China by Nicholas II were described in an open letter where they were slammed and denounced by Leo Tolstoy in 1902. Tolstoy corresponded with Gu Hongming and they both opposed the Hundred Day's Reform by Kang Youwei and agreed that the reform movement was perilous. Tolstoys' ideology on non violence shaped the anarchist thought of the Society for the Study of Socialism in China. Lao Zi and Confucius's teachings were studied by Tolstoy. Chinese Wisdom was a text written by Tolstoy. The Boxer Rebellion stirred Tolstoy's interest in Chinese philosophy. The Boxer and Boxer wars were denounced by Tolstoy.

In hundreds of essays over the last 20 years of his life, Tolstoy reiterated the anarchist critique of the state and recommended books by Kropotkin and Proudhon to his readers, whilst rejecting anarchism's espousal of violent revolutionary means. In the 1900 essay, "On Anarchy", he wrote; "The Anarchists are right in everything; in the negation of the existing order, and in the assertion that, without Authority, there could not be worse violence than that of Authority under existing conditions. They are mistaken only in thinking that Anarchy can be instituted by a revolution. But it will be instituted only by there being more and more people who do not require the protection of governmental power ... There can be only one permanent revolution—a moral one: the regeneration of the inner man." Despite his misgivings about anarchist violence, Tolstoy took risks to circulate the prohibited publications of anarchist thinkers in Russia, and corrected the proofs of Kropotkin's "Words of a Rebel", illegally published in St Petersburg in 1906.

Tolstoy was enthused by the economic thinking of Henry George, incorporating it approvingly into later works such as Resurrection (1899), the book that played a major factor in his excommunication.

In 1908, Tolstoy wrote A Letter to a Hindu outlining his belief in non-violence as a means for India to gain independence from British colonial rule. In 1909, a copy of the letter was read by Gandhi, who was working as a lawyer in South Africa at the time and just becoming an activist. Tolstoy's letter was significant for Gandhi, who wrote Tolstoy seeking proof that he was the real author, leading to further correspondence between them.

Reading Tolstoy's The Kingdom of God Is Within You also convinced Gandhi to avoid violence and espouse nonviolent resistance, a debt Gandhi acknowledged in his autobiography, calling Tolstoy "the greatest apostle of non-violence that the present age has produced". The correspondence between Tolstoy and Gandhi would only last a year, from October 1909 until Tolstoy's death in November 1910, but led Gandhi to give the name Tolstoy Colony to his second ashram in South Africa. Besides nonviolent resistance, the two men shared a common belief in the merits of vegetarianism, the subject of several of Tolstoy's essays.

Tolstoy also became a major supporter of the Esperanto movement. Tolstoy was impressed by the pacifist beliefs of the Doukhobors and brought their persecution to the attention of the international community, after they burned their weapons in peaceful protest in 1895. He aided the Doukhobors in migrating to Canada. In 1904, during the Russo-Japanese War, Tolstoy condemned the war and wrote to the Japanese Buddhist priest Soyen Shaku in a failed attempt to make a joint pacifist statement.

Towards the end of his life, Tolstoy become more and more occupied with the economic theory and social philosophy of Georgism. He spoke of great admiration of Henry George, stating once that "People do not argue with the teaching of George; they simply do not know it. And it is impossible to do otherwise with his teaching, for he who becomes acquainted with it cannot but agree." He also wrote a preface to George's Social Problems. Tolstoy and George both rejected private property in land (the most important source of income of the passive Russian aristocracy that Tolstoy so heavily criticized) whilst simultaneously both rejecting a centrally planned socialist economy. Some assume that this development in Tolstoy's thinking was a move away from his anarchist views, since Georgism requires a central administration to collect land rent and spend it on infrastructure. However, anarchist versions of Georgism have also been proposed since. Tolstoy's 1899 novel Resurrection explores his thoughts on Georgism in more detail and hints that Tolstoy indeed had such a view. It suggests the possibility of small communities with some form of local governance to manage the collective land rents for common goods; whilst still heavily criticising institutions of the state such as the justice system.

Death

Tolstoy died in 1910, at the age of 82. Just prior to his death, his health had been a concern of his family, who were actively engaged in his care on a daily basis. During his last few days, he had spoken and written about dying. Renouncing his aristocratic lifestyle, he had finally gathered the nerve to separate from his wife, and left home in the middle of winter, in the dead of night. His secretive departure was an apparent attempt to escape unannounced from Sophia's jealous tirades. She was outspokenly opposed to many of his teachings, and in recent years had grown envious of the attention which it seemed to her Tolstoy lavished upon his Tolstoyan "disciples".

Tolstoy died of pneumonia at Astapovo train station, after a day's rail journey south. The station master took Tolstoy to his apartment, and his personal doctors were called to the scene. He was given injections of morphine and camphor.

The police tried to limit access to his funeral procession, but thousands of peasants lined the streets. Still, some were heard to say that, other than knowing that "some nobleman had died", they knew little else about Tolstoy.

According to some sources, Tolstoy spent the last hours of his life preaching love, nonviolence, and Georgism to his fellow passengers on the train. (Source: Wikipedia)

CPSIA information can be obtained
at www.ICGtesting.com
Printed in the USA
LVHW041729130420
653275LV00001B/115

9 789390 026463